Baptizing the Cat

a novel

by

Roberta George

For Jane, Who always makes me smile! Roberta George 2011

Published by
Snake~Nation~Press
Valdosta, Georgia 31601

Published by Snake Nation Press
Valdosta, Georgia 31601

Printed and bound in the United States of America.

ISBN: 978-0-9825430-8-5

Design by Force Street Media
Cover art by Ann Johnston

110 West Force Street, Valdosta, Georgia   31601
www.snakenationpress.org

Baptizing the Cat

a novel

by

Roberta George

Published by
Snake~Nation~Press
Valdosta, Georgia 31601
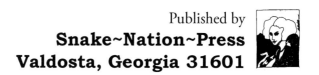

Dedication

For my husband, Noel George, for his love and support all these years, and my children, Mary Catherine, Robin, Jody, Victoria, Noel Jr., Robert, and Nashlee, and all their husbands, children, and friends.

For Jean Arambula for her encouragement and especially for keeping Snake Nation Press, The Snake, alive.

For the Snake Handlers Writers Group: Barbara Passmore, Morris Smith, Vicki Pennington, Mario Bartoletti, Jack Pruden, and A.J. Brantley.

For all my beloved friends down through the years, in the yoga classes, the Taboli Club, and at the Turner Center for the Arts, too many to mention.

Chapter 1

For the first time in twelve years, it dawns on me that the condo here in St. Pete, even with three bedrooms, is not as large as Grandpa Emile's home in Cleveland, Ohio. I grew up in that rambling, multi-roomed farm house on two acres of land with only two other people, my mother and grandfather. But here, in this condo in south Florida, there are five, five bodies: Susan my wife, Nursey the maid, my daughters—April and May—and me, all crammed in together. A $500,000 condo, and not enough room to swing a cat. Not enough room to breathe. An artist needs breathing room. Susan, even right now, is taking up all the air.

I place imaginary hands around my wife's fat neck and squeeze, but the rolls of flesh get in the way of closing off her thorax completely. It's a fantasy I often indulge in: the resistance of tissue and finally making it through to the breakage of cartilage ridges under my fingers. But, of course, the daydream does nothing to curtail Susan's wheezing comments.

"Phillip, you'll never believe who I thought I saw at the pool today," she says. "Father Clive, and with the most interesting-looking woman. Of course, I was mistaken. The man had a beard like Father Clive and a towel over his head, and I wasn't wearing my glasses, so I couldn't tell at first. But she was very pleasant. A real smile. Not one of those phony, pretend things you get from the Yankees down here in St. Pete. She spoke to May, too, said, 'Little girl, you're going to be a great swimmer.' Really, quite nice."

I sit on the couch, drink my first Rob Roy of the day, and Susan sets the table. She wears a flowered muumuu, orange and yellow, one she's slipped over her naked body after a quick shower. It's not a becoming color for her monochromatic complexion. Her pale hair, frizzed out by sea water and wind, is a brownish-red halo around her face. Her skin is freckled and red from the sun, and her breasts hang in two longish folds from the middle of her chest toward her underarms. I close my eyes against the sight. Regretfully, I cannot close my ears. She speaks in a clotted rasp, as though she needs to blow her nose. My wife is one of the few people on earth who suffers from allergies at the beach.

But Susan's observant—I'll say that for her—sees things I would otherwise miss. Still, she can be fooled by a smile or a congenial wave. Of course, she was totally different when we first met, which, I imagine, is what most husbands say about most wives after twelve years of marriage. Still it's true of Susan. She went from bold spirit, a hippie of long yellow hair and bra-less wonder, into a thick-waisted, cautious matron in what seemed like over night. I felt her change, saw the transformation from the beginning, yet never anticipated the end product: Susan turned into her own mother, Miz Mildred—short, seventy-five pounds overweight, rim-less glasses, mousey hair permed into reddish corkscrews—the whole little-old-lady package.

The proof stands before me now, a carbon copy of my mother-in-law, setting stiff aqua place mats out for dinner on our all-purpose, Florida-condo table. Susan's careful to protect the glass surface. That's my wife these days, careful, watchful, dull. Next, she'll put down the big solid-colored dinner plates, chargers, then smaller ones with a fish pattern, and then cloth napkins. I know this table-setting routine by heart. Long ago, I gave up on the argument about extra plates under plates, for no other reason except they looked better, right to Susan. "We have the china; why not use it?" was always her answer. Her mother arranges her own dinner table that way, and Susan will do no differently.

She prepares the settings while Nursey cooks our evening meal. Surely the old black woman has a real name, but I don't remember it, that is, if I ever knew. She's been Susan's nanny from birth, and she's in there now, "fixing"—that all-purpose southern word—a seafood concoction in our minuscule condo kitchen. The spicy aromas of shellfish drift in and soothe me somewhat. April, Susan's thirteen-year-old daughter from her "wild days" and my adopted child, and six-year-old May, ours together, sit outside in the swing on the narrow patio, drying from the swimming pool in the last bit of daylight.

It's another one of my wife's rituals, the cocktail hour, incorporated into our lives because her parents honor that activity. The girls know to stay outdoors and be quiet as their mother sets the table, and I have my first drink, and supposedly we "talk." Which means my wife speaks at me. She doesn't expect answers. Under her words is the muffled screech, back and forth, of the porch glider, marking the minutes before our daughters can come inside and set me free. Metal grates on metal: screech, screech. I promise myself to oil that damn rusty mechanism tomorrow, that is, if I don't forget, again.

My first Rob Roy, cold and sweetly tart, the best part of the day, is some consolation. I try, without being too obvious, to scan the room and locate my folded-up newspaper containing the crossword puzzle I started this morning.

"The man wasn't too bearded, just a five-o'clock shadow as Daddy calls it. I'll find out the number of their condo tomorrow, so we can get together. It'll break up the week if we have another couple to spend some time with. I know you'll like her. She's your type, blonde, very attractive."

There is a sticky quality to these words; it's Susan's way of criticizing my previous marital record without coming right out and saying what she means. I was a two-time loser when we met in the artists' colony at Taos, sort of at the tag end of the free-love and communal-living era. But Susan said those unions didn't count, said they were not real marriages because they were not "blessed by the Catholic Church."

I'd never had any kind of religious training, never been baptized, so I took to all the rituals and rules set down by Catholic tradition. It was different, almost comforting. The Church had an answer to every question, gave boundaries and meaning to Susan's and my disjointed lives, and pulled things together, especially for me. It was a way of starting over; confession gave me a clean slate. My conversion from nothing, the big white-dress wedding for Susan, topped off with my adoption of one-year-old April, won my place into the Bower family, and without any plotting or planning on my part into the Bower fortune. "The Bower Bankroll," I secretly call it, started from an ancient grandmother's candy recipe.

Susan prattles on: first she thought the man with the towel over his head was Father Clive, but that couldn't be because he hadn't been a pastor at Sacred Heart Church for years. Talk about confused. She's sure, now, she was mistaken, but she wants to find out where the couple lives, so we can all be jolly good friends on the basis of a smile and a word to May. How like Susan, carried along with what comes along.

I finish my drink, glance up at my wife with a look I hope she mistakes for interest, and then contemplate my hairy white leg stretched out on a hassock. I'm only forty-five years old, but lately I've grown disgustingly flabby and old mannish. My brown runner's legs of college days vanished completely. The blue-green of the veins branch down my ankle and into my sandled foot and match the blue-green upholstery of this condo, an aqua print of fish and drifting plants.

All the furniture in the apartment: couches, cushions, and drapes are all that same wearisome hue. It's irksome that this entire three-bedroom condo, down to the dishes and glasses, is furnished in that peculiar shade, a sort of a powdery verdigris that apparently decorators think is a requirement for the Florida Gulf Coast. I've spied into several of the condos at this complex, called—what else?—Sandhills, and they're all decked out in pretty much the same hues, aqua with a sprinkling of coral. You'd think with these people's money, the interior designers they hire could come up with a few more original combinations, some more interesting color schemes.

But, what harm. It's just that I've had too much time, months actually, to study upholstery, rattan arms and legs of furniture, metal mirror frames, and even the plates and glasses of this condo. I usually sketch and paint landscapes, but lately it's been the interior of this all-purpose living room, and the blues and greens in my watercolor case are continually running out.

To rid my eye of these disgusting hues, I concentrate on the Baccarat martini glass in my hand. The late afternoon sunlight slides through the patio door, strikes the amber of the scotch, the pink-red maraschino cherry to the side, the clear wide slope of the glass' rim arching down to a diamond circle at the bottom. This composition of polish, sunshine, glass, and liquid would be hard to render on paper. I'm always painting pictures in my head, all of them perfect, that is if I never pick up a brush.

I finish my drink, eat the sweet fruit, twirl the stem between my fingers, and rise. In the kitchen I squeeze past Nursey who's stirring a pan of garlicky shrimp. Her dark bulk, the fishy smell, Susan's wheezy chatter in the next room suddenly becomes a lethal combination meant to drive me crazy. I lean my forehead on the cool door of the refrigerator. "Get a grip, man," I whisper to the white surface. "This routine can't go on forever." Or maybe it can, and one day you'll die here, like this, with an empty martini glass in your hand. Quickly, I pour myself another large pale drink from the shaker and squeeze back past Nursey.

It used to bother me that the old black woman came along on these six-month beach trips—another family tradition—from South Carolina to the St. Pete condo, especially since there are only three bedrooms and one average-sized living room and a dining room, but she is really quite unobtrusive. And it was always Nursey who got up in the middle of the night to take care of May, when she was a baby, and who now grocery shops and cooks, and watches the girls if Susan and I want to go to a movie. A built-in baby sitter.

Funny how my wife cannot see any connection between herself and the "spoiled Southern women" she so often criticizes back in Spartanburg. But a black woman living out her entire life, day and night, with a white family, even though she's paid $300 a week from the Bower Bankroll, and has Social Security, retirement, and a week's vacation every year to visit relatives, still seems mighty close to slavery to me.

"You Yankees will never understand, Phillip," Susan says. "Nursey was fifteen when I was born, when she first came to work for Momma and Daddy. I was her one and only baby. We're her family and she's ours." Susan switch-hits on this southern and northern stuff, feels free to criticize both the South and the North in one breath.

"Ready for a freshener, darling?" I call out, even though I know Susan's already taken her one obligatory sip, and now her glass sits forgotten on an end table. I've marked the spot, for later. If I'm quick enough, I can down Susan's drink before Nursey's Kamikaze cleaning can whisk the glass away and dump the contents. If I didn't know better I'd swear that old black woman tries to keep me from getting my full quota of alcohol in an evening.

Drink in hand and having spent my required time in "private adult conversation," I slide the glass door open and step out onto the patio. The Florida heat closes in. Thick, bathroom air, hot and heavy, enfolds me. I force a breath. Sweat starts a teasing trickle from under my arms, down my sides, which will soon glue my shirt to my body. I take out a handkerchief and pat my forehead, ward off the drops that will fall, stinging into my eyes. Too much time inside this air-conditioned condo or in my Tampa studio hasn't acclimated me to these steam-room conditions. I suppose Susan's right about being outside, that it gets one used to the heat, but my method of survival these days, existing with her, Nursey, and the girls in this limited space, is to keep my distance, set up perimeters.

"Are you two warmed up enough?" I ask my daughters and immediately hate the syrupy, condescending tone I always take on when I first speak to children. It's the same sing-songy voice Susan uses all the time, and I've picked it up, too. I promise myself to return to normal speech with the next question. The girls nod but don't look in my direction. Both hold a small computer toy in their hands, rapidly punching with their thumbs and pushing in unison at the floor with their feet to keep the glider moving. The infernal grind of metal on metal, screech, screech, fractures what should be a tranquil evening sunset.

I step out onto the grass and start backing as far away as possible.

From a distance, my daughters, April and May, are adorable youngsters, both blonde and tanned from days in the sun. It's Susan's choice of names, something about the months they were born in— another southern thing. April's 13-year-old nipples peek through the thin fabric of her suit, and she looks so much like Susan once did that my heart squeezes with regret. May still has the roundness of a baby about her, a fine drift of shiny down on her cheeks and arms that gleams in the slanting light.

"Why don't you ever come to the beach with us, Daddy?" May calls out without looking up from her game or stopping the motion of her thin feet. At six, she's the more insightful of the two girls.

"I don't know, honey," I answer truthfully in my now-adult voice, which I imagine they appreciate after a full day of Susan's baby talk.

"What beach did you go to today?" I ask, walking out as far as I can to the edge of lawn where the grass ends and the land falls away to the shore some twenty or twenty-five feet below.

May murmurs something about the pool, but I barely hear, for the couple Susan's been yapping about are suddenly there at the water's edge, walking toward the staircase that leads up to Sandhills: it's Towelhead and the blonde.

She's wearing a brown racing-style bathing suit with gold trim, and he's in baggy, striped swim trunks and a white T-shirt. Coming up from the far end of the beach, I have plenty of time to observe the "interesting couple" of my wife's enthusiasm. They stroll, not touching, but still close enough to inhabit each other's circle of privacy, a linking that indicates intimacy to anyone watching. They are separate and yet totally together, and seem to my artist's eyes united by gossamer shining threads. A few fortunate couples, new lovers especially, possess that connection even if they're a room apart. It's an ESP kind of thing I have, I can read people. It would have made me a good CIA agent—what I pretend to be—or spy, or something along that line, if I'd had the chance.

When Susan and I first met, I foolishly hinted, that along with being a full-time painter, that I was some kind of CIA "operative." How in the hell I came up with that word, I'll never know. Over our first weeks together, the story grew like a balloon filling with helium, mainly because it made such an impression on this new girlfriend. Susan's slightly bulging blue eyes opened wider whenever I mentioned my Ranger training and my not-to-be-talked-about CIA connections. In the service of my country, I could be vague, secretive about the particulars. The truth, which I sometimes don't even remember, is that I went through basic training at Fort Benning and started Ranger school but broke my ankle the first day my outfit practiced parachute jumping. I still can't believe I landed wrong on the second leap, in spite of years of running track in high school and safely clearing hurdles.

Still, the CIA story comes in handy, more so as the years pass. It gives me leeway. I can walk out of the house in Spartanburg or the condo here in Tampa anytime, morning, noon, or night, and not have to come up with a detailed explanation. I can say, "Have to check in" and be gone for an hour or an evening; it doesn't matter. Now, I have a vibrating beeper and supposedly it jiggles my leg and no one can tell. I pretend I've been summoned and simply leave, sometimes just to walk out onto the beach in the dark, to look back at the lighted rooms of the condo, to see Susan and the girls' shadows moving against the blinds. It's a strange game, but I need it.

And right now, I yearn more than ever to be Super Spy, to have a zoom camera with a long-range lens so I can focus on the faces of those two people down there on the beach. I want close-ups: eyelashes and freckles, the view that camera men take of ball players on the mound and of their sweethearts in the stands, registering every blink, every swallow. I want to examine this couple's expressions, hear what they say. What do they find in each other that is so wonderfully engrossing? Particularly I want to see the woman's face.

Do today's private investigators have devices that relay voices from a distance? Maybe. Saw something in a movie once: a detective sits in a car, points a gadget towards an upstairs window, and he can hear every word said inside and snap a picture when the quarry comes out. Amazing.

But all I can do now from this distance is interpret gestures, the inward tilt of bodies and heads, one covered by a towel, the other possessing an abundance of unruly sandy-blonde hair. They stop walking. She listens intently, judging by her posture. His hands move as though to explain something of great fascination. He reaches out, yet constrains himself, not touching. At one point, the man—I've dubbed him Towel Head—slides his long, loose fingers down through the air, two inches from the woman's breasts. She steps a fraction closer. I imagine her perfume, that is if she wears any or, if that artificial scent has been washed away by the ocean air, her own natural female aroma. I imagine it to be a subtle combination of skin and hair, overlaid with the iodine taste of the sea, an essence like the first sweet sip of a margarita and the gritty aftertaste of rock salt lining the edge of the glass.

Their preoccupation with one another—they are walking again—their steps in sync, is a dance they've choreographed, and the depth of their concentration can be seen even from the distance and height of this cliff. Are they in that first stage of affection or perhaps already in love?

Suddenly, an invisible projectile, too sharp and painful to believe or identify at first, flies upward from their bodies toward me. I see the barb coming but cannot move out of the way. It's the poison-tipped dart of envy—spiny and piercing—and it finds its mark in my heart with an intensity that is physical. I have never looked at or had a woman look back at me with such complete absorption. The sensation of loss is tangible, and it is all I can do to keep from bringing my palm to my chest in that ancient, melodramatic gesture. I feel an involuntary "Uh" somewhere deep in my gut as if I've been hit, and I find myself mouthing Susan's words for consolation and explanation: "Yes, they are attractive and interesting." And I add, with the sourness of indigestion, as if I've known those two people all my life, "And welcome to each other."

In a fog of half anger, I turn back to find that my daughters have gone inside. Susan stands with her dimpled arms folded under her breasts, her inflated blue eyes wide, accusing. She bleats, sarcastic, and not for the first time, I'm sure, "Do come in for supper, Phillip."

Chapter 2

In the mornings I usually stay in bed with the door closed, read newspapers, do the crossword, and watch television until everyone but Nursey has left for the beach or the pool. Then I rise, have a bagel and coffee, and sketch. Nursey cleans, washes clothes, but I'm used to her quiet bustling. At lunch time, to avoid the noon sun, the girls and Susan return to the condo, and my wife takes a stab at home-schooling. I escape to my studio in Tampa, to paint, to collect the mail, and while away the hottest hours, checking on ocean and sand conditions farther up the coast road. In the last few months, the water in front of Sandhills has become frothy with brown scum, and huge slabs of peat or something like that are exposed. The condo manager says the city officials are debating whether or not to leave the ugly things where they are, depending upon what purpose they serve, like keeping down erosion.

I grumble, "Only makes the water filthier than it already is."

This current manager, a leathery refugee from some unnamed country and whose accent I cannot place, is a hireling of the condo association. He spends his days fielding much noisier complaints than mine, so he pretends not to hear. In the evenings, over dinner, I report back to Susan the best spot along the coast for her and the girls to go swimming the next day.

But today, as soon as the condo's door closes on Susan and the girls' noisy departure for the beach, I rise, dress, grab a cup of coffee from the counter, and leave. "Going to take pictures," I half explain to Nursey's uninterested, bowed head. Her plaits, a complicated weave, run from a center part into a pattern of greased coils. She doesn't look up from the newspaper.

I sometimes take candid shots of dunes and sea gulls, catamarans on the water's edge, waves, and sail boats. Watercolors of these prosaic scenes sell well down here in St. Pete. People can't seem to get enough of what they could see just by looking out their windows. In the reverse, pictures of pines and lakes retail equally well back in Spartanburg, South Carolina. I used to think just the opposite, but it's not so. I admit I'm no great shakes as a sketcher or watercolorist. I'm adequate, nothing more, nothing less. At my best, a two or three-hour afternoon of painting is all I can muster. And in the last year or so, the wild enthusiasm I once felt for a blank sheet of cold-pressed watercolor paper has ebbed to an all-time low. Now, it's an ordeal to face the easel in the store-front studio I've set up in a strip mall in Tampa, and I've wasted the last two months in the condo painting odd light patterns on furniture.

Still, I'm haunted by the little drama on the beach with Towel Head and, who is she? his wife? his girlfriend?—does a wife ever hold such fascination? This vision has convinced me to upgrade my Cannon 200 to a Leica with a telephoto lens. I can take clearer slides for paintings, and better yet I'm planning to have the new camera fitted with the long-distance listening device that I imagined. Surely, my buddy, good ole Harry at the pawn shop can get me one. He'll know right where to go.

Harry Rigger's Pawn & Gun Shop sits across the street from my Tampa studio, and he assures me that a Leica is a better camera all the way around and that such a listening device comes in a variety of models for every need.

Harry is a pudgy, bowling-pin-shaped man with a smooth bullet-round head to match, and no matter how early or late I drive over from St. Pete, there he is, anchored behind his show cases of guns and jewelry. I like this character. His single mindedness and plain mercenary view of the world appeals to me. With Harry there's no homey facade about good will toward the customer. I feel he likes me for the same reason. We share a common thread, an appreciation of cause and effect. I always spend more than I intend and yet come away from his crammed counters and shelves feeling as though I've struck a good bargain. Just recently I purchased a rare over-and-under shotgun with silver scrolling on the stock for only $1,750.

"Harry," I say, "I'm looking for a good camera and a long-distance bug. You know what I mean. I saw one on TV, I think."

Harry bubbles, rubs his grimy, conical hands together in financial delight. "Sure do, Mr. Craine, a great 'catch-um-with-their-pants-down' surveillance miracle. Wolf Ears, a parabolic microphone. You can buy them almost anywhere now. Maybe I can scare one up for you."

Whether this means Harry will contact other pawn brokers in the area or that he will utilize more nefarious ways, I don't ask. Harry has made it clear in the past that he has "contacts." It was vague back then, whether he had drugs or guns in mind. But now, I intimate that I know what he means, that I have contacts, too. We both smile knowingly and then are silent, giving the macho bullshit a rest. My goal is to own this "pants-down" mechanism, as Harry has so aptly described it. I can already imagine the slick black case it will come in, the protective foam padding inside, the pamphlet explaining its many uses, and the crystal clear sound of whispering voices in the dark. The blonde's voice coming in through ear phones.

Buoyed by this vision of my new toy, I leave Harry's at noon and take up the other part of my daily schedule, which is a couple of beers and lunch at a little Tampa bistro three or four streets down. The place, called Bayside—can you believe the originality of these people?—is full of seashore kitsch. Lobster traps and fishing gear hang from the ceiling, while a bunch of grizzled retirees lean on an acrylic bar embedded with shells, sand dollars, and starfish. Bayside's two redeeming features are a remarkable fish sandwich, a thick slab of fried sea-perch, and mugs so cold the beer forms a cloud of frost in the middle. The old guys at the bar and I exchange "Hello" and "How's it going?" but I neither prolong the greetings nor encourage them. I sit in my customary place in a booth by the window. To show the old codgers that I've more important things to do, I keep a notebook open by my plate, sketch ideas for paintings, and make it clear that I'm not open for chit-chat.

After lunch, I head toward the finale of my daily agenda, a stop at a diminutive shop, part gallery, part art supplies, called The Paint

Box, another name that also irks my need for originality. Belle, the owner, a fleshy, weathered redhead in her early fifties and I have a mild flirtation going, so I can excuse the title of her establishment. I sometimes think she really likes me and I could turn the full-body embrace she greets me with into an on-the-side fling. Either because of nerves or laziness, I haven't followed through, haven't made that quick grab that would erase or draw a line between us. I've been faithful to Susan, to our vows in the Catholic Church for twelve years—a record of sorts, I guess, for any man. Hard to remember, now, why I wanted such fidelity, a "till death us do part" arrangement. Plus if Belle took an advance the wrong way . . . well, where would I go for art supplies, and who would display my one or two better paintings and talk them up into sales each month?

I open the shop door and Belle, from her customary spot at the display window, where she can see everything going on in the street, waves me in. Though not fat, the woman is abundant, from her dense purple-red hair to full rounded hips. She wears long colorful skirts or white pants cinched in at the waist with silver or gold metal belts, a hippie chic that appeals to me. The low necklines of her gathered blouses fall into folds over her substantial breasts. Still, I can't quite imagine her naked. Is she one of those females whose tits drop to their waists when they take off their brassieres? The straps and snaps that show through the back of her blouse don't look too supportive, so I'm encouraged. And she's so amiable, always right there to greet me as soon as I walk into her shop. Sometimes I feel she must be watching my studio—diagonally across the way—to be so Johnny-on-the-spot every time I visit. But since I have entrances at both front and back, she couldn't be that intuitive.

After our semi-lascivious hello hug, she motions me to sit on one of the stools in front of her high counter. I ease up onto the flimsy piece of furniture and think how a small arts gallery like this is not a bad way for a woman her age to pass the time. It's certainly something Susan could handle if I were not around, especially since she wouldn't need the income. Yet I suspect earnings are important to Belle. Maybe her sweety-pie manner to me is nothing more than smart salesmanship.

"Phil, honey, it's been a week since I've seen you," Belle says in a slightly petulant but teasing tone.

She rests the tips of her fingers on the crook of my bare forearm. Her hands are large for a woman, and the nails polished a bright pink and filed into points. Her caresses would scratch. Little needles of electricity fan up into my shoulder. It's an almost come-on. She knows it; I know it. Her wide white face on its strong neck is within inches of mine. Her complexion is pearl-like with make-up, and her hennaed hair spirals in damp-looking ringlets from under a tortoise-shell clasp placed squarely above her forehead. I think about painting her with a sinister shine, as though she has a secret she will hint at but never tell. The scent of citrus and sandalwood wafts toward me in waves. I breathe deeply.

"You ever been married, Belle?" I ask, for no better reason than it's something to say, to pass over the moment, to pretend my arm isn't tingling. After all, it's a standard question, isn't it? A preliminary to a closer friendship or something more?

"Sure," Belle replies, "hasn't everybody been spliced at one time or another?" Before I can answer, she slides off the stool. "Want coffee?" she asks, and then brushes past me to get the hot drink we always share during these visits. In spite of her size, there's the springiness of youth in her movements, and the word "splice" makes me feel loose around the edges.

I nod yes both to the notion that everyone's been married at least once and to the drink. Coffee wouldn't be my first choice, but since I had three beers with lunch, I figure I can hold out until Susan's cocktail hour. No need to tell Belle that I would prefer a good single-malt scotch or that Susan is my third wife, although thoughts of those previous two marriages are distant, nebulous memories pierced by great drunken holes.

Does a six-month alliance, right out of high school really count? I've asked myself, too often. My single clear recollection of Emily, my first wife, is high school graduation night on the dock of her parents' lake house. Completely naked, she stretched out on a webbed chaise lounge, her arms above her head. In the flood of moonlight, she was an Incan virgin ready for sacrifice, the dark vee between her legs the center of mystery, the center of the world.

Baptizing the Cat

Our plan, to atone for the elopement and a justice of the peace marriage the next day, was for Emily to stay in Cleveland with her mortified family until I finished the first year of college. As it turned out, Ohio State was only a more elaborate version of high school, more papers, and professors instead of teachers to please. But also no varsity track coach to cajole a make-up test or add a few extra points to eke out a passing grade. It was tough going. My infrequent visits to the flat Ohio farm where I'd spent the first nineteen years of life, the pleas of my opaque yet sly mother to "make something" of myself, coupled with the menacing silence of my grandfather, sent me running back to the bars rather than to the books. My one and only meal with Emily's parents climaxed in too much scotch and my telling them what I thought about their insulated, country-club existence. That first semester, I lost my track scholarship, so I really wasn't surprised when divorce papers arrived six months to the day to celebrate an end of Emily's and my half-year union. Still, it hurt.

Jenny, wife number two, was an airline attendant for Delta. After Fort Benning and my wash-out at Ranger training, I went back to school—still Ohio State—and in a beginner's art class found I had some facility, a flash now and then, an intuition, a linking between hand and eye that worked. The professor was complimentary, probably too much so, considering the job market for art graduates, but at the time I needed to be told I was good at something, that I had "talent." For tuition and living money I bartended, sold a little pot on the side, anything to get by. On a few low-key weed runs from Ohio to El Paso, Texas, and back, Jenny was a diversion, or so I thought, only to wake up married in Las Vegas. No memory of a ceremony but there was the license on the night stand and a thin gold ring on her finger. That marriage lasted three years, though I wouldn't call it a union, just a series of couplings since our meetings on her days off were spent in motels or friends' apartments. That final year we hardly saw each other, mostly we talked on the phone. I grew to like her as a sounding board, a disembodied, non-judgmental voice on the other end of the line. Eventually she found another airline passenger, someone more accessible, and surely with more money.

The sound of running water brings me back to the present, back to Belle, half hidden by a drapery of stringed spangles, moving around in the small kitchen. I smell fresh coffee and swivel on the stool to look out through the large plate-glass window toward the other stores across the street, a plaza arrangement around a tiled fountain. Directly in front of Belle's Paint Box is an alteration shop, Violet's, its front painted a pale lilac; and beyond that, a clothing boutique, Second Chance, painted a Chinese red, and in between, my studio, painted white—my one good acquisition bought with the Bower Bankroll. In contrast to those two bright shops, my place has an un-named, sealed-up appearance, the chalky horizontal blinds closed, the Windsor-blue door shut tight. I squint my eyes, turn the out-side scene into a color montage of squares and rectangles. This odd combination of pigments and shapes and even the signs themselves might be the makings of a good abstract. But who would buy it?

I turn back to Belle's familiar white-gray walls, which are hung with prints and originals—three of them mine. Whatnots and well-crafted statuary rest on tables and pedestals, and two curved gray-leather love seats face each other on a black and red Bokhara car-pet, a slate coffee table in between. The Paint Box is done in what decorators, I'm sure, would call good taste: gray walls, taupe fur-nishings, and points of dark color, reds and blacks in the carpet and pillows, to offset the monotones. The paintings on the walls are sea-scapes, sand dunes, oceans, sunsets. In its own way the trappings of this store irritate me as much as the blue-greens back at the condo. Everything is so calculated, so expensive, exactly what one would expect from a high-class art shop in a beach-side city.

Before I can further analyze why I'm so critical of the decor, Belle returns, balancing an artsy tray of mugs, cream pitcher, and sugar bowl, which she sets down on the counter between us. She pushes a stoneware cup toward me with a napkin under it.

"What's got you so interested in my marital status, sweety? So all of a sudden?" she asks, and lifts her drawn-on ginger eyebrows, creating two new lines, wrinkles, above them.

"You know I'm married," I say, and immediately feel asinine, for the thick platinum band, set with one round ruby and two diamond baguettes on either side, is prominent on my left hand.

"Sure," Belle says. "Never met anybody in Tampa who wasn't married, tied down, or so old and unhealthy that no one will touch them. Of course, you're married, angel. Good-looking, tall guy like you."

Baptizing the Cat

I feel an unpleasant constriction in my brain, a grainy annoy-ance that comes from some internal repugnance. What she says is so predictable, just like this room. She's flirting, what she thinks I expect. I mix cream in my coffee, try to keep my expression unread-able—my CIA face. Is this what she thinks I want: compliments, a lead-in to my saying something equally pleasant in return? I take a swallow of the hot liquid and turn my kisser, composed again, I hope, in a disguise of interest.

"So you're married?" I say, repeating her word.

Belle chuckles, "Well, not right now, no, but . . . ." She rounds her shoulders in a shrug, which tightens her blouse over her breasts. "I might take the plunge again if the right guy comes along."

I hallucinate my hand inside her bra, cupping the large brown-pink nipple, the prickling of flesh under my fingers.

"You're divorced?" I ask and silently answer, of course, what else? And then, regrettably, I project the inevitable conversations between us, an exchanges of notes on which spouse was to blame, who said what to whom.

Belle shakes her head, no, says, "No, widowed—twice."

Surprise! Somehow I'd imagined this middle-aged dame to be a two or three-time loser like myself. Why else the big friendly to a married man unless she's unhappy, disgruntled? Does she see me as a future husband? Hardly. Belle knows my whole set up, knew the Bower family, sold art stuff to Ed and Miz Mildred long before I came on the scene.

"Widowed? Twice?" I repeat, and can't keep amazement out of my voice.

And here is where that odd bit of ESP I have comes into focus. Belle nods her head once and so slightly that I'm not sure if she's responding "yes" or nothing. It's instinct, but I know Belle doesn't want to talk about her lost husbands. After all, they're dead aren't they? Yet, I want to ask, How? But across from me, I can tell Belle's holding herself implacably still until some strong memory passes.

Her lack of emotion reminds me of my own mother's weird way of lying, especially to my Grandfather, by giving a reply so soft it couldn't be heard or by complete silence. "Is that a new dress, Liza-beth?" he'd ask. My mother would stand completely silent at the stove, stirring one of her arthritis concoctions, the stench of menthol

23

and whatever weed some other old lady had recommended flooding the kitchen. Or she'd mumble a monosyllabic, unintelligible reply.

"Is it new, I'm asking?" Grandpa Emile would growl again. He'd be in his habitual place, a straight chair beside the plank table, the ladder back against the un-plastered wall. Another murmur from my mother, as faint as breath. He would ask his question again and again, rephrase it in different ways, and each time receive less of an answer. Eventually he would give up, cave in to her silence.

Belle drinks from her mug, some Indian design in the clay, her fingers obscuring most of it. Her eyes are downcast, concentrating on the tan surface of the coffee as though she can see past events, tragedies there. I wait for her to look up, to confirm that she was widowed twice in some ordinary way: two husbands whose fates were heart attacks or car accidents would be explanation enough. An old joke comes back to me. "You lost two husbands?" I want to say. "How careless of you." But all I can see in her large face is the exterior, the mask of make-up. Dark eyeliner and mascaraed lashes—thick as the kohl Arab women use—around her lowered eyes. The heavy blue shadow cakes the lids up to the drawn-on eyebrows; the pink-red rouge starts at the nostrils, darkens as it rolls up her cheeks and fans into her hairline. Her lip liner is an odd mauve color, not matching the rest of her lipstick shade, and it extends beyond the natural contours, in an effort I suppose, to make her lips appear larger. Who in the hell tells women to wear this ugly camouflage?

Still keeping her made-up eyes averted, Belle takes her coffee mug, slides off the stool, and stands apart from me to gaze up at her own walls as if she's never seen them before. She indicates one of my pictures and lies, "I think I have that water and boat scene sold." Her wide back turns. She points, arm extended, a person in a play. " . . .to Mrs. Martin . . . that old lady who lives over in St. Pete, right near Island's End."

"Great," I say, play-acting my part in the charade. "Give her an extra fifty bucks off if you think you can move it."

"Well, it's slow right now, but it'll pick up in November." Belle is completely distracted, her mind so far away that she slurs her words.

Then, as improbable as it seems, a red mist swirls up, a barely perceptible, incredibly thin bloody vapor hangs in the air between us. It's my artist's imagination, I'm sure, but still an instinct tells me she's done something wrong where her husbands are concerned, something associated with blood, and the image in her mind has taken a plasmic form between us. I hold my breath, not wanting to pull into my lungs the pinkish veil that hangs, a drapery between us, smelling faintly of copper.

The whole business jangles my nerves. Whatever she's done, I don't want to know. "Well, I really should head out," I say to Belle's profile. I stand to leave, to move away from this woman. But my words—like a chain on a dog who's run out too far—bring her back with a jolt.

"No way!" She turns, waves her hand in protest; her many silver bracelets tinkle, and her smile returns. Back is the old crowd-pleaser, the agreeable, loveable Belle. "I made a whole pot of coffee for you, sir, and you have to drink another cup."

Chapter 3

I expect this response from Belle and move toward the shop door, muttering something about having some other appointment. If it's back to the condo, so be it.

The quick-change artist in Belle has unnerved me. One moment she's off in a bloody reverie, and the next she's back in disguise, her good cheer repugnant. That wide-smiling mouth with its bad lipstick job, the large perfect teeth, the eyes squinted into good-natured slits are suddenly more than I can stand. It's all too calculated, like her shop, a made-up happy personality that goes along with her upscale, everything's fine and dandy facade. For the first time, I understand my younger daughter's overwhelming fear of circus clowns. There's something diabolic under Belle's good-old-girl, painted exterior.

Belle makes a perfunctory objection, "Okay, if you have to, Phillip," but I can tell her heart isn't in it. Death has taken the edge off our coffee-time *tête-à-tête*, and we both know it. Belle's revelation of the loss of not one but two husbands has caught her off guard somehow, revealed her.

But where can I go on a hot October afternoon? What else can I do? Walk back to my studio and try to paint? The thought of that half-finished canvas on the easel, a view of the palm outside of Sandhills' patio, is totally depressing. My black Lexus is parked beside Violet's shop, just where Belle can see if I don't drive away. I could return to the Bayside cafe and drink more beer, until six, time to go home. The retired guys would think me lonely, want to talk. Worse yet, I could head back to the condo early. Susan and the girls will be playing Monopoly. The game was left out from the day before and is Susan's half-baked idea of home-schooling. They'd be right in the middle of the distribution of property and money, April whining, "You never let me win," and Susan explaining in her best teacher's voice that the purpose of the game is to learn how to handle money and "winning is not important."

"Then why keep track of who owns Boardwalk or what the rent is?" I ask, and upset my wife's careful discourse on good sportsmanship.

I walk across the hot pavement toward my car, analyzing what it was in Belle's manner, in her silence, that made me see for an instant through a reddish haze into mystery. I reject my intuition and argue that first I must consider the physical. Was there a speck of blood in my eye, a little hemorrhage that fogged my vision? No, immediately I know this explanation is not the answer. Whatever took Belle back into the past came upon her in a rush; that somehow in answering me, "Widowed, twice," she'd brought unexpected memories into focus right before her eyes. She saw something so strong that for a minute I saw it, too, a floating bloody cloud all around her.

I open the car door, let the heat escape since it's hot as hell for October, sit in the driver's seat, and wait for my perception to clear. I've known since I began painting that people, places, things, all carry auras of colors around them. It's a good artist's technique, one everybody picks up on sooner or later, that when you first select a subject, you decide which hue will be predominant. Even when it's only a simple indoors arrangement of furniture, you catch one over-riding shade and go with it. Like thinking in a foreign language, I guess, I think in terms of color, people and their palettes. I don't even have to be planning to paint and still I see color themes. My wife Susan takes on the blue-green and coral qualities of the St. Pete condo whenever she's in it, wears those horrible tent muumuus, made it seems, out of flowered table cloths. In our home in Spartanburg, it's mainly a change in dress, but her skin picks up the colors there, too. She switches to sweaters and pants in tan and dark green combinations that go with the paneled walls, the hunter's green of the wallpaper, and the woodsy view from the rear windows that looks out onto a forest preserve. In contrast, my two daughters are easy; I've painted them more than fifty times, separately and together, mostly from photographs since they won't sit still for a real portrait. April is all pale ocher and a pink wash, with just a hint of taupe underneath, while May is a watery lilac, blending into a royal blue at the center. So Belle, who in my mind has always been smeared in bright garish oils across a large canvas, purple-red hair and white skin, is now obscured by this vermilion vapor that came up around her from . . . from her thoughts.

I start the Lexus and take the long route over the old Gandy Bridge Road, back to St. Pete, then on impulse I decide to go to Pass-A-Grille, to see my bud, Archie. I don't turn on the radio, and I don't roll down the window. I think: Belle was once married to a man who died, and then she remarried, and that man died, too. So? So what's so weird about that? Nothing, I answer my own question. Then why didn't she just give me the one or two-sentence explanation that would have kept us on an even keel, kept the conversation perking? "My husbands took the easy way out," she could have said, meaning anything: they died of natural causes or accidents or they committed suicide. Any response, other than that awkward silence, would have sufficed. Anyone who's had any kind of life at all comes up with these little scripts to fend people off, to tell them everything and nothing, all at the same time.

In high school, nosy teachers and bone-headed friends would ask, "What does your dad do for a living?"

"Anything he wants to," was always my response.

Since the place for a father's name was always changed to my grandfather's name, Emile Craine, on any application that I or my mother filled out, and since the only man living in our house was my grandfather, obviously I didn't know much about my father.

Another question that comes up far too often for my taste is, "You've been married three times?"

"Yeah, three's the charm, or maybe the curse," I answer, whenever Susan feels compelled to inform someone of my marital history, which she does surprisingly often. My rejoinder usually catches people off guard, warns them to back off. Most take the hint, maybe from my tone of voice, maybe from the dead-pan scowl on my face. If they press, I've got a few zingers stored up to shut them down. Susan's mother, Miz Mildred, was one who kept fishing.

Baptizing the Cat

"I guess you were terribly young when you first married?" she asked once, expecting that I would start at the beginning and spill my guts. Well, I'd already done that bit for Susan and for Father Clive, too, and I wasn't going to do it again for this nosy, fat old lady, who thought she owned me just because I was marrying into the family.

"I guess you were lucky to drag one guy up to the altar," I answered.

If I had it to do over again, I'd give Miz Mildred a simple, "Yes, I was very young," and let it go at that, but my mother-in-law is the snoopy type, who wouldn't have stopped with one question or one answer. She's a vampire, has no real life of her own, interior or exterior, that I can see, so she's always sucking people out of theirs, sucking them dry.

Susan gets the third-degree every time her mother comes over: "What did you have for lunch? May looks thin. Did you give them their vitamins today? Why did you buy these expensive paper towels?" God almighty; it's great to get a break from her down here in St. Pete. In Spartanburg, it's an unspoken agreement between my father-in-law and me that we find an excuse to leave the house five minutes after he and Miz Mildred arrive. I always drum up some household chore: a new washer for a bathroom faucet, some duct tape or oil that's on sale—believe it or not, those two old people still care about saving pennies—so Ed and I can head out. We stop at the hardware store for about thirty minutes and then spend the next two hours hanging out in a pool hall, cheap beer and hot dogs. Ed's delighted with the freedom, acts like he's broken out of prison. Maybe that's part of the reason he's so glad I married Susan.

My father-in-law sees me as some kind of savior of his daughter and her illegitimate child, and maybe I am. Until our marriage, she was their prodigal, their only daughter, running off to New Mexico, buying into the whole counter-culture package, at least the no work and sleep with whomever you please parts.

"Phillip, you're the son I never had," Ed says, and grapples me around the shoulders at least once every time he and Miz Mildred, the truculent whale, come to visit. Though I don't believe for one minute that my mother-in-law thinks of me as a son or a savior. At every encounter, she regards me with a narrow-eyed squint, lets

29

me know she doesn't buy into my hero status, the image I've more or less created. I guess my sarcastic reply about marriage set the framework, an air of brittleness between us for the rest of our lives. Maybe I hit the nail on the head when I said she was only able to drag one man to the altar, poor old easy-going Ed. Now the bitch hardly speaks to me unless she has to. No one seems to notice, so I lay low and pretend I'm the quiet type.

I set the cruise drive on fifty and head down the Pinellas four-lane, switch to Gulfport, and pay the toll to get out to Pass-A-Grille beach, not that anyone can see any sand or water for all the buildings.

The word Pass-A-Grille comes from some pirates passing by and stopping to grill fish. Believe it! A bronze plaque beside the Hurricane Bar states this hackneyed information. Historians or whoever it is that pays good money to put up those totems would have been better off inventing a lie to go with the Portuguese words, rather than those common-places: they passed by so we'll call it Pass-a, and they grilled fish, so we'll call it Grille. Still, the scenery is good; the pink and white Don CeSar Hotel stands four-stories high, towering over all the other low buildings and thick green shrubs and trees that grow in the lush tropical weather. The Don is an unusual structure, an unbalanced arrangement of turrets and cupolas, like a huge ungainly wedding cake. I've painted it more than ten times and sold the work, too. I drive under the hotel's white-railed overpass and slow down to better see the old Florida houses that line the bay-side street down to Island's End. I know all the peeling clapboards, the weathered stuccos, the little squatty bricks by heart.

It's my favorite drive, and I've been over practically every road between here and Tarpon Springs in the last twelve years. Somehow this three-mile bent-finger of land has escaped the neon motels and fast-food joints that clutter the streets of every other piece of real estate on the Bay or the Gulf of Mexico. There's an old-Florida feel to this crook of beach that I haven't found anywhere else.

At the very tip end of the peninsula is Archie's place, a group of gray, weathered-board cottages, one and two bedroom rentals around a small gazebo, ocean on three sides, that the owner, Archie Whitehall, has named Island's End. In my mind, this arrangement, unplanned and off-beat, is what the whole state must have looked like before it became so popular wiyh the snow-birds. I've painted Island's End, too, in watercolors, almost as often as I've painted the Don, and they've been good sellers. Archie lets me roam the grounds, set my easel up anywhere. Says in his off-handed way, "Live here, for all I care," which I know means that my presence adds to the refinement of the place, to have a working artist on the premises makes the tenants feel they have experienced something authentic.

I've taken Archie up on his offer, took a cabin a time or two, for a few nights when Susan's allergies, all the coughing and sniffling, got on my nerves so bad that I thought I'd explode. One night at the Hurricane, a ramshackle bar about a block up from Island's End, I even picked up a girl, a tiny eager brunette. We strolled the beach in the moonlight, which was great and made me feel like a kid. But when we closed the door to the cottage, it was a no-go. I was so drunk nothing worked, and finally we both fell asleep. After that, I tried hanging out at the bars again, figuring I might get lucky twice in a row, but when you're over forty, everyone doing the bar scene seems too young, too crazy, and they sure aren't interested in you. I started envying other guys my age, those who came in with a babe already on their arms, wondering how they managed, or worse yet watching couples who were about the same vintage as Susan and I but still acted like they enjoyed each other's company. I even stayed a full week once, calling the condo every other day when I knew Susan and the girls would be out on the beach. I'd leave a message, saying cryptically, "I'm all right" as if I were in some great danger. The First Gulf War was hot right then, so I watched CNN and came back with some good stories for Ed. "Nothing classified," I told him, "but it was hell watching those young guys on both sides getting blown apart."

I drive past the Hurricane, stop for a six-pack at the lone grocery store on Pass-A-Grille, then drive another two miles to park in front of the wooden fence that guards Archie's domain. The trees, called sea grapes, hang over the sun-bleached boards and cabins. Their fan-shaped leathery leaves are a dull autumn green, and their trunks are curved snakes the same gray color as the lumber of the cottages.

I walk into the enclosure and look for Archie or one of the German girls he imports to clean rooms and work the desk, but no one's in sight, so I settle into a plastic chair beside a free-standing hammock and open a beer.

The whole place is divided into sections. In the middle is a twenty-foot deck, a miniature pond, and a shingled gazebo full of white wicker furniture. The area is ringed by cabins, each with a tiny yard and a single tree surrounded by bleached sea shells. Every part is linked by wooden walk-ways, all of which lead out onto the dock and the perfect white beach that juts into the perfect blue-green water. Pelicans and gray herons pose like carvings on the thick-pillared piers.

I'm drinking a good cold beer, I can hear and smell the ocean . . . but. . . but today is different, I'm off center. I can't get the red mist of Belle's lie or lack of a lie out of my head. I don't really believe in ESP or any of that hoo-doo stuff, but I've had an insight or two in my day that proved correct, and this intimation of murder seems as clear to me as if Belle had described the details: She killed husband number one for the insurance money, married husband number two, and then killed him, also. I mull through the possibilities: She ran over husband number one with a car or she poisoned him or she had him killed by a boyfriend, who became husband number two, and then she killed him. Subtract ten or fifteen years from Belle's face and figure, and she'd have been a beaut, and probably a rodeo in the sack. The kind of woman who could convince a man that murder was the way to go. Throw in some insurance money and a movie-of-the-week unfolds.

I open another beer and from my plastic deck chair watch the tiny speckled lizards, a shade darker than the wood, run across the boards. A snowy egret, with an "S" of silky white feathers for a neck, takes high cautious steps down from the beach towards the deck and me. A white egret, too predictable to paint. White paper left bare is how I handle white in watercolors. White is the color for death in some eastern religions. According to Susan, in earlier times, Catholic priests wore black for funerals, but now they wear white because it means joy, supposed to make everyone feel better.

The egret turns its narrow head to the side, eyes me, then scans the sand for bits of food. It pecks and quickly raises its head again at that odd angle to keep me in view. I'm larger than it is, my arm moves up and down, I'm clearly a threat. Even this simple animal recognizes the food chain on some basic level. I could kill this bird for nourishment if I had to, or for the fun of it, or for no reason at all except that I'm bored and here it is walking toward me.

But how does a woman like Belle justify killing a husband, if that's what she did? I take too large a swig of beer, strangle and cough, snort some out through my nose. The egret startles, spreads its great white wings for an instant, but then immediately settles back only an inch or two away from its original spot. It takes a step closer. Is the animal losing its fear of me or simply trying to get a better look at this large creature who's invaded its turf?

If Belle killed two husbands, so what? It's none of my damn business. She's safe now, all tucked away in a neat little shop in Tampa, with nothing to do except pitch a few paintings to the locals and flirt with any attractive man who comes along. Before that brief flash of clairvoyance I had back there in The Paint Box, I would have said Belle was content, maybe even happy. And who's to say she's not? Are murderers happy? Do they get what they want at the cost of a human life? Even in the service, even in those few weeks of Ranger training, I never knew anyone who'd killed another human being. Well, maybe the drill sergeant had knocked off some Vietcong—"gooks" he called them.

"You pussies would never have made it out of Nam," he'd shout; "the gooks would have eaten you alive."

Wonder how many gooks he killed?

Through my musing thoughts, I hear Archie move behind me, making his way out onto the deck. My friend is a man full of pain, and I don't have to turn to visualize his slow, crippled progress across the walkways. He played college football and some pro ball back in the fifties and served a tour in Vietnam before he settled down here at Islands' End. He's what I'd paint if I ever wanted to show worn-out strength: bowed legs with aching knees, thick shoulders, and a huge belly gone to flab. I've never really understood how Archie came up with the money for this small ring of cottages on such choice real estate, but from what he's said from time to time, I gather he came back from Vietnam with a drug habit that led him to connect with all the right people. Sometimes I regret not connecting myself, not developing that little pot sideline I had going, when I was back in college. I might have hit on that one big deal that would have netted me my own thousands, but then I'd never have gone the starving-artist route, been in Taos, and met Susan. With no planning, no danger, no risk, my marriage into the Bower Bankroll turned into my big check in the mail. Go figure.

"Have a beer?" I ask Archie, not turning around, already pulling one from the plastic rings of the sweating six-pack and handing it to him. In ten years I've never known the man to refuse a drink.

"How long you been here?" Archie asks, lowering himself with great care onto the other plastic chair. He grimaces as his knees bend. Settled, he pops the tab and takes a long guzzle from the silver can. His knobby Adam's apple bobs up and down three or four times before he stops for air.

"Not long," I answer and take a prolonged swallow, too, trying to drain the can.

Archie breathes heavily through his mouth. A glistening line of wetness stays on his mixed dark and gray mustache, and moisture gleams on his protruding lower lip. As usual his grizzled face is about five days overdue for a shave, and his wrinkled khaki clothes and smudged hands say that a bath wouldn't hurt either. I've always wondered, looking at this unkempt, overweight man, and at myself, too, in the long bathroom mirror, at my dangling, unimpressive genitalia and hairy protruding stomach, how women find anything attractive about men. But Archie consistently has one of the young blonde immigrant girls keeping him company in the main two-storied house, just inside the compound. These imports, Spanish guys for gardeners and Slavic girls for cleaning and running the office, work at Island's End for five or six months before they move on to other jobs, and probably to better wages.

"Avoids all the green card problems and the romance stuff, too," Archie says, whenever I ask about a particular girl. I gave up years ago questioning the man on his arrangements.

I never ask Archie anything directly, just let him talk if he wants to. I've never been inside his two-storied house that has a calligraphy sign on its gate: "NO ADMITTANCE (no one! no how!)." There are other signs, too, placed along the walkways: "PLEASE

DO NOT FEED THE CATS (they're too fat already)," and "PLEASE DO NOT TAKE A SEA SHELL (if everyone did, there'd be none left to enjoy)." I like these white signs with dripping black letters: a rule with an explanation in parenthesis underneath. I do not go into Archie's house, I do not feed the cats, and I do not take sea shells. Archie and I normally sit outside on the deck if the weather is agreeable or inside the gazebo if it's not. We stare out at the sea, kill a six-pack, then I head off for a walk or to paint. Archie goes back to whatever it is that he does. If it's stormy, I don't make the drive over to Island's End.

"You ever know anyone who's killed somebody?" I ask Archie between swallows of beer that's starting to warm.

It's not as strange a question as it might seem on the surface. Over the ten years I've been coming to Island's End to paint and chew the fat with this man, we've touched on just about every subject imaginable. He reads everything from newspapers to Nietzsche, and even seems to have gleaned some bits of education from his four years at Alabama State. When the football scholarship ran out, he hadn't earned a degree, and the New Orleans Saints used him up in two years, but he never says a bitter word. He joined the Marines in '65 and landed in the medic corp. So when Archie gives an opinion, I listen.

"Everyone killed somebody in Vietnam," he answers. "You shot the shit out of anything that moved back then." Archie never says Nam or gooks when talking about the war. "And I guess I met up with a killer or two in TCI; although, you understand, no one was ever guilty up there." He chuckles, his ragged profile a study in remembering.

TCI, I process the initials whenever they drop into Archie's conversation: T for Tallahassee, C for Correctional, and I for Institute. It's always a surprise to me that Archie spent three years in prison and that he can speak so easily about the experience. Little by little, the story's come out. Archie refused to turn state's evidence on some pals, did "dead time" for not ratting anyone out.

"You thinking about killing somebody, Bubba?" Archie asks.

My friend, originally from Alabama, calls me Bubba from time to time. He calls all his blonde Germanic girlfriends "Hun."

"No, of course not. It's just a strange thing happened over at The Paint Box. You know the woman who owns it——Belle?"

"Yeah, the one that's always hitting on you, and you, such a good little boy, not jumping into the sack for—how long you two been playing patty-fingers—six, seven years?"

"Well, I'm glad I didn't. I asked her was she divorced, and it, like, triggered a fit in her, like an epileptic seizure where the person phases out for a few minutes. She said yes, she was widowed twice, and then she went into some kind of trance—I don't know what— but I could tell she was remembering how her husbands died."

I don't tell Archie about the bloody mist rising up around Belle. He'd think I was frigging crazy.

"She could hardly talk, but I knew she was recalling something horrible, and when she finally came back into herself, it was like a costume she put on, a mask slipped on for her act."

Archie turns and gives me a full-in-the-face look, something we don't often do, with a thoughtful narrowing of his dark eyes. "I know what you mean," he says, and bounces his head in small nods of agreement. "It's like you can read their minds."

Then it's my turn to nod. "She gave me the willies. One minute there's this strange evil woman and in the next she's back to her old bag of tricks, pretending she's the babe with the heart of gold." I take a last swig of tepid beer and equivocate, "Then there's the possibility that I was imagining it all. I'm an artist, you know. And we're given to such things, imaginings, even hallucinations." I laugh and add this last part to lighten things up, to let Archie know that I'm not taking myself too seriously, that I could be mistaken. Then without intending to, I blurt out what I've been hiding. "But I swear to God I was so spooked I could see a faint smear of blood rising up all around her."

"Pay attention to your clues, Bubba," Archie says, not looking at me now but down at the weathered boards. "You gotta follow your gut. I learned that a long time ago, even before I went into the joint. And it sure kept me out of trouble—lots of times. Watch out for those grinning kind. What does Shakespeare say, a man can smile and smile and still be a villain?"

Trying not to smile, I stare out at the tropical trees, the sea grapes that surround each cottage. The limbs and trunks curve like so many snakes, with over-lapping, coined-shaped lines on the bark that look like scales—"snake trees" I call them when I'm painting.

Archie drinks and continues, "Women go about killing a lot different from men. A female is more into poisons or getting some poor sap to do the dirty work. One guy at TCI was convinced that his wife tried to off him by cooking all his favorite foods—fried chicken, doughnuts, deep-dish pies—to clog his arteries, but then I think he deep-sixed her, so who's to know? You gotta watch out for the antifreeze in the wine bottle, Bubba. You better watch out for your Belle."

Archie and I knock off the last beers, he goes off to the Island End's office, and I drive back through Pass-A-Grille, turn under the Don's archway, and set the cruise on an easy fifty, going back toward Sandhills.

"My Belle?" Archie's warning makes me want to laugh. He agrees that Belle is, in all probability, exactly what I think she is, a husband killer. But why he should think I have something to fear from her is beyond me. I'm not planning on marrying the woman or even having an affair. Still, what clings in my mind is that if Belle knocked off two husbands, apparently she got away with it. Is it possible to kill and not get caught? Sure, I tell myself, if you're smart enough, think the deed through from beginning to end, and plan every detail. There's something reassuring, even consoling about the idea.

I whistle along with a song on the radio, an oldie, "Gonna Take a Sentimental Journey." The sun slides down the white-blue sky, sending long bands of light across the water and across the glossy black hood of the Lexus. It's a beautiful car, inside and out, with the sleekness of a mortar shell, a dash board like the cockpit of an airplane, and soft raven-wing seats. The new leather, new-car smell is still strong although the vehicle is already ten months old. It's spent a lot of time parked in the garage in Spartanburg, probably because I don't get as claustrophobic up there as I do down here on the beach. No half-naked women parading across the sand or lying beside the pool to remind me of what I'm doing without.

The Spartanburg house is my one good accomplishment, completely my conception, with the help of an architect my father-in-law recommended, two stories of purplish brick abutting a wild-life sanctuary, so no one can ever buy or build behind it. Some easy berth, huh? Susan was so proud that I took an interest in its design, even down to the arrangement of rooms, to the cold-resistant roses, and the Zoysia grass for the landscaping. "Phillip has impeccable taste. He's an artist, you know," my wife told the ladies in her bridge club at every opportunity. Yes, I was the prize husband back then. Even now, whenever there's a decision to be made about our walls or plantings—except for the Sandhills' condo, decorated and held inviolate long before Susan and I married—I'm the resident expert. My wife raises her blue cow-eyes from whatever book she's reading and says, "You're better at choosing color schemes than I'll ever be, Phillip, and you're more interested in that kind of stuff. You have such excellent taste. If I didn't know better I'd say you were gay." It's a joke between us; sometimes funny, sometimes not.

And what else is there to do with money and time, but make your surroundings as beautiful and comfortable as possible, and definitely different from what I grew up with. In Spartanburg, all the greens from pale Nile to dark emerald and the selections of cherry, oak, and mahogany were my choices, even in the kitchen; although I did ask Nursey what colors she preferred. White marble counters with stainless steel restaurant-grade appliances were her picks.

One reason I'm more content in the Spartanburg house is my studio, my lair—north light, of course—and a full bath at one end, while Susan, the girls, and Nursey are in a suite of rooms on the other side. The kitchen, living room, and guest bedrooms are a buffer between us, though we have few over-nighters, mostly friends of the girls.

Susan's bedroom is supposedly ours, but in the last year it's been mainly hers. I start the evening out lying on top of the spread on our king-sized bed, flipping the channels till I find a movie. Susan reads, waiting for the Benadryl, the aspirin, and the Tylenol PM to kick in. When she rolls her back to me and twists up the covers around her neck, then I move to my studio to fall asleep on the couch. Funny how I can't close my eyes and rest beside her anymore. Her allergies and medications are her excuse for not staying awake and my excuse for sleeping elsewhere. "What time did you get to bed last night?" she asks every morning, and I say, "You were snoring so I moved," or "I painted a couple of hours."

Still, I rarely leave the house at night in Spartanburg. Where would I go? Everyone knows me in the little village of shops closest to the Trubeck farm, the five acres we built on. The only night-time activity is a bunch of teenagers clustered around a video arcade until nine o'clock; and after that, the sidewalks roll up and the streets are deserted. What I can't figure is why this celibate distance doesn't bug Susan. The first five years of our marriage were pretty hot, but the next five were like the tide going out, the passion seeping away; the love a tall wave, but the next wave lower, not as intense, and lately nothing at all. After May was born, Susan never lost that overfed bovine contentment that drives me up the wall, makes me believe—like that book she's always quoting—that men and women do come from different planets. Thursday nights we eat with her parents at the Smithbrier, the Spartanburg Country Club, and any parties are with the same crowd she grew up with. My wife's favorite evenings consist of television and a book, and nothing more. Thank God for Dewar's scotch. It's during the six winter months in St. Pete, by this sugar-white beach and under this endless blue-bowl of sky that I get so antsy.

"Funny how you're called on to do more for them down here than you are at home," my wife accuses.

Susan never says CIA, always calls them "them" as if it were their special code name.

"Winter's always the working months," I lie. "And I'm only a consultant; someone called in for an opinion, that's all."

You'd think with all her reading my wife would be a little more savvy. But apparently mysteries and romances are full of ordinary men being spies and princes.

And now I ask, What about murderers?

Suddenly, in the mellowness of the music and autumn's tempered sky, I decide it might look more favorable if I were a better husband to Susan, and a better father to April and May. It wouldn't even hurt to go to the beach with them once in a while, even if the sun does bring out every freckle I possess. I could sit under an umbrella. And why not play Monopoly? The game would be nothing like the destructive marathon games I played with my mother and grandfather.

Back then the bare light bulb hanging over the kitchen table hopped and swayed whenever Emile rose in anger at landing on an expensive rental square, or when he was sent to jail and missed his $200. My mother consistently won but never said an overt word of self-congratulation. But she might just as well have screamed, "I'm number one" over and over, for her head-down victorious posture spoke louder and more eloquently than all of my grandfather's prancing about with his arms stretched wide, his fingers in the vee symbol of conquest.

Still, my odd, good mood hangs with me throughout dinner, throughout Nursey's clearing away food and dishes, throughout tucking the girls into bed—with stories, drinks of water, and bathroom trips. These are my delegated chores since Susan has the so-called onerous job of home schooling—and then I absolutely must get out of the apartment. No more domesticity for me, please, I beg silently. Three Rob Roys have caused a restless itch in my psyche, and it sends me rushing outside.

As usual, I drive the car to the other side of the Sandhills' complex, park it behind the shrubs that hide the tennis courts, climb the stairs to the second-level walkways, then come back down to my own section. I've pulled this trick a hundred times. Then I stand in the dark, judging the amount of time that must elapse, the hour or so that has to pass as if I had driven up the beach road to a pay phone and made a call to my own personal Deep Throat. Sixty minutes, I remind myself, fifteen minutes to drive to the Quicky Mart, another thirty or so for "debriefing," as I call it, and then another fifteen for the drive back. God, what a crock! In the dark I lean against the pink stucco wall of the building; it's fairly smooth. Sometimes I almost doze, hidden from anyone's line of vision, waiting for the dragging allotment of minutes to slide by. I breathe in the wet salt air and look back at the lighted lancet windows and dark shapes of Sandhills. I survey the territory, the shadowy domain I know too well.

In the dim condo lights, the three buildings sit high on an eroded edge of craggy shoreline, an over-sized rosy group on five acres or more of carpet grass. The three structures loom above and the waves break below. I can climb down the two landings of gray wooden stairs and walk the beach for the appropriate time or I can glide from one darkened alcove—created by the corners of the buildings—to another, perhaps catch a peek of what the other residents of the apartments are up to.

In truth, there's not much to snoop on. Most of the condos are empty of all human habitation, the blinds and curtains closed. And from prowling around on other nights, I know that seventy-five percent of the apartments are vacant, abandoned in all their turquoise and coral splendor, even at the height of the winter season. A few lights show down the south row, a few more in the other direction, but most of the sliding glass doors and windows are dark and vacuous.

Tonight, I cross behind my own condo, pass beyond the patio near the drop-off that goes down to the beach, and avoid the light that spills from mine and Susan's sliding glass doors and bedroom windows. Then spy-like I edge backwards, my shoulders and hands pressed against the wall. I stop, squat, take a deep breath, and look in through the slender one-inch space between blind and window sill. Some would call it daring and perverse to peek in on one's own residence, on one's own wife, but my overwhelming emotion is simply boredom, of having nothing better to do. Still there's always the possibility that I might catch her in an intimate act, inspecting her privates, masturbating, things I do myself when I'm alone.

No such luck. Through the narrow slot, I see Susan's body, a sloping, breathing mound of serenity underneath the matching bedclothes. Even though I can't have been out of the condo more than ten minutes, she's already in bed, already completely oblivious to the television noise that fills the room, and definitely oblivious to any footstep outside her window.

A rush of what feels like ground glass grates through my nerves. A bit of Susan's wormy red-brown hair stands up at the edge of the neatly-folded sheet, her gnawed finger tips hold on to the edge of the fabric as if for protection, and the smooth stretch of coverlet next to her, folded back, indicates my expected arrival. All these elements feel like a long hateful tether, an umbilical cord between us stretched now to the breaking point. I shudder with a chill of loathing even though the air around me is warm. The slow-motion rise and fall of my wife's great wheezing body under the covers repels me. It's the same feeling I get when seeing a dying jelly fish stranded on the beach sand, heaving for oxygen. I wish my wife gone, out of my life, vanished forever. But Susan rests unaware, unconscious. The great wave of revulsion that sweeps out of me apparently has no strength to penetrate walls or even cause a minute ripple in the so-called psychic link between husband and wife. Susan does not flail out, does not gasp for air—which she should have done at such a surge of hatred—does not even grunt or turn over.

"The sleep of the just," I mutter half out loud and, snorting my pronouncement, I move away from the wall and the distasteful view.

This time, on the way back through my own property, I don't try to avoid the squares of light on the concrete walk or the well-trimmed lawn. I obviously don't need all these fancy precautions or the elaborate lies. CIA agent *extraordinaire*. What bullshit! To leave the house, all I have to do is wait, wait until the girls are in bed, wait until Susan has settled, which usually occurs well before ten o'clock, and then I could be gone for hours, even an entire night. Who's awake to know or to care? Who's keeping tabs? No one.

I charge away; panting heavily in the salt-filled air and dripping with perspiration, I sprint across my own patio and turn down the narrow service alley. A sullen temper pounds inside my head to the tempo of my feet flapping on the concrete. I want to run as fast and as far away as I can, run as I did in my high-school years when my mother's stinking cabbage cooking on the stove and my grandfather's weekly lawn-mowing schedule drove me to this same kind of despair. A malevolent, dark emotion possessed me then and possesses me now, a need to strike out, to maim, to demolish.

I veer sharply to my left, run farther and faster through the service alley, and arrive, without planning, next to the patio of apartment, 3-D. I stop abruptly, utterly winded from that short race down the alley. Feeling like I might vomit, partly from the exertion but more from loathing, I pull back into the blackness of the wall.

On any other night of past years, the long sliding glass doors to this complex were always completely dark, with no lights from the bedrooms either. But tonight, the vertical blinds are diffused with light, creating a grid of patterns across a small round table flanked by two ice-cream parlor chairs that sit outside on the concrete. I vaguely recall, a couple of weeks ago, seeing a moving van pulled up to the side port of condo 3-D and Susan on tiptoes, stretching, her belly hanging over the kitchen sink, her hand holding the slats open, commenting on the furnishings that were being hauled in.

"One very fine Bentwood rocker," I remember her saying.

My wife is full of bits of random information: name brand furniture and clothes—although she never puts that knowledge to any use, except to compare with her friends and her mother: who bought what and where.

To allay the bile in my throat, I force my attention to the lighted scene off to my left. In the unlit dimness of this nook, I am invisible.

The television in apartment 3-D is tuned to a travel show, some drivel about food at a backwoods bed-and-breakfast. "The host of Bridgeport Inn uses greens from his very own kitchen garden for a refreshing fall salad."

I can hear clearly through one of the decorative cross-shaped holes cut through the stucco wall, which juts out to give a boundary line to each patio. I can see, too, for the horizontal panels are pulled back and the sliding glass door is open a good five inches. Also, I can feel the air-conditioning turned up high, for a flood of refrigerated air pours past the door and through the two openings in the stucco, bracing me somewhat, taking my nausea away. I rest my shoulder against the wall, pull the chilly air into my lungs, and feel some relief from my fit of distemper.

I hear a woman's low chuckle and see a female hand reach to turn the television volume down.

Muffled and pleasant, she says, "There are still several problems with the Big Bang theory, not that I'll ever be able to explain them the way that physics professor did at the lecture. Let me see: There's the smoothness of all the radio waves throughout the universe, and the way our sun, really a yellow star, keeps giving off steady heat, holding a balance between its pull of gravity and the nuclear reaction that tries to pull it apart. I can't remember the third objection he brought up. But it seems to me that something or someone is in charge, keeping everything in balance—like on the edge of a knife."

A man's deeper, raspier voice answers with no comprehension, "I can't make heads or tails of it. And there's nothing we can do about it, anyway."

I squat next to the bottom cross-shaped hole, hold on to the wall for balance, and refute this woman's ridiculous assertion. It's too simple, an explanation that one would give to a child. "Something or someone holds a balance." Those words are so easy, I want to say, and sneer. If this were a thoughtful discussion, such as Susan and I used to have, one should substitute "Universal Force" or "Mind" or "God" for the "something or someone." But apparently this is not talk to be taken seriously, for the woman laughs again, a melodic, agreeable response.

"You don't even want to think about it, do you?"

"Naah, how'd you guess?"

I ease down and lean closer toward the lower opening in the wall. The view into the sanctum of these two people is perfect, although the grass prickles sharply against the backs of my legs. The lawn is cut too often by the nephews of the building manager—probably because they're paid by the hour—so it's stubbly, but still thick and comfortable. Now, with my body more at ease and my eyes completely adjusted to the dark, I peer through the breach placed in the wall for no other reason, it seems, than to give me a convenient access to another set of lives. I see into a slice of the all-purpose room of apartment 3-D, furnished differently from Susan's and mine, but essentially the same rattan and seashore mind at work, the same colors, turquoise and coral. Yet in contrast to those conventional hues, impressive paintings line the walls and eclectic carved objects sit on the tables. African masks are visible in the hall and twisted black sculptures sit on the glass-topped coffee and end tables. A large, bone-white conch shell lies on a black base. Avidly, I note each article. Secret glimpses, even as simple as these, the ordinary objects of daily life, arouse excitement in me. One of the few pleasures of long-distance running through the downtown streets of Cleveland was that as I passed over the uneven sidewalks, I could glance into the living rooms of strangers, obtain a view of unsuspecting people in their daily existence. My heart and head thrum with delight when the woman I've been hearing crosses my line of vision.

I'll be damned! It's her, the same female from the long walk on the beach with Towelhead. Is that him now, answering? I see her from the rear, my favorite view of the female anatomy: a neat, round derriere, a small erect head, thick sandy-blonde hair twisted back and held by a wooden clasp, narrow shoulders and slightly wider hips, very appealing. She sets two glasses of pale wine on the coffee table and turns to reveal a longish nose, angled cheekbones and chin, all matched in symmetry. She wears white shorts and a sleeveless lavender blouse tucked in at the waist. Her arms and legs though not muscular have a healthy leanness, and they taper into small flexing wrists and ankles. Her body is younger than her face, and her skin is only slightly browned by the sun, not what one would expect from mile-long treks on the sea shore. I learn her name.

"Catherine, I don't see why you're even interested," the man says. It's Towelhead. Who else?

"I think the answer is God," she replies. "God is in, and behind, up and under everything, and no amount of investigating will ferret him out, with physics or telescopes or whatever. 'As high as the sky is above the earth; so high are the ways of God above the ways of man.' That's from scripture, somewhere, isn't it? There's a plan—I guess—well—maybe . . . ." Her voice trails off.

I'm glad she doesn't continue with this mindless twaddle. Soundlessly, I sigh and wish her to be more insightful, more worldly. She reminds me of Susan when we were first going to Father Clive for instruction.

"You have to make a leap of faith, Phillip, darling," she'd interrupt, whenever I would address a query to the priest.

He, a strangely bent and aged Italian, with some kind of arthritic condition that left his body and hands curved into question marks, remained silent, his attention turned toward my fiancée, letting her take over. "Some doubts just can't be answered."

Her round but still firm face, studded by two fervent marble-blue eyes, compelled me then into some sort of mindless belief, a comfortable acceptance of a benign father figure guarding the world. Faith, it was a package deal that went along with the house in South Carolina and the condo here in St. Pete and money in the bank. I signed papers that declared my desire for baptism and marriage into the Catholic Church in the same way one might buy a fine car that came with good terms. The God thing was okay, too, put me on the side of right and legal for a change.

Now, in the darkness behind the wall, and in contrariness toward Susan's mindless acceptance and this Catherine's flat statement of bland faith, I refute Father Clive and my wife and that effortless belief I myself accepted twelve years ago. Whatever God might be, he'd not fit into this pat little scenario that this woman has just described. I align myself with Towelhead's disinterest. Also, I align myself against the Big Bang Theory, all this coming from a point smaller than an atom, that is, if that's what she's proposing. Even more, I align myself against a God who will not take responsibility for all the killing and cruelty going on in the world.

But arguing doesn't seem to be on this couple's agenda.

Catherine sits beside Towelhead on the couch. He adjusts his arm over the rounded edge of the cushions, clasping her shoulder with one hand, accommodating her nearness. I can see them in their entirety. I can also hear his gravelly voice and observe a bare, unattractive foot on the coffee table, a muscular arm around Catherine, and curved spatulate fingers, stroking unblemished skin. And in one of those bits of unasked-for clairvoyance, like knowing who is calling on the telephone in the instant before one picks it up, I discern that these two occupy that happy atmosphere that surrounds people who are setting out upon an evening that ends in love making.

I project my insight into that future, into anticipation, that is if only Towelhead will stop his aggravating fingering of the skin at the rim of the sleeveless blouse. For although Catherine seems to be enjoying his touch, leaning back against his arm, her head is held at an odd, concentrating angle and her light eyes are alert, looking toward the patio door. Yet, I figure that soon something must happen, soon Towelhead must unbutton the mother of pearl buttons at the neckline of the blouse and slip the garment half way down her shoulder, exposing the brassiere strap and her smallish breast encased in . . .?

Here, I pause and my imagination puts her breasts into what? A black bra? No, that would show through the lavender material. No, I put her breasts—I can almost feeling their slight, buoyant weight in the palms of my hands—into a pale lilac satin undergarment.

Baptizing the Cat

But, of course, my insightful moment passes, and Towelhead does nothing of the kind. Catherine reaches forward to retrieve her glass and toasts him. "Saluda," she says, and he responds, "Cheers." I catch a glimpse of thick dark hair atop Towelhead's crown as he bends to set the half empty glass back on the table. The two are silent for what seems an extremely long interval, but what is probably not more than a minute in real time or two seconds to them. Do they enjoy each other's silences as much as their conversations?

It comes to me then, in the stiffness of my legs pulled into a cross-legged position and by the glow of my wristwatch, which says 10:45, that I have been here behind this bit of wall, peeking through the slot placed so conveniently, for at least forty-five minutes. The hour wait I earlier imposed upon myself outside my own condo window has flown. I've been gone from my apartment almost double that amount of time, but as I thought before, Who's to care? Perhaps this opportunity to watch and hear will never come again. After all, how many people, with the air-conditioning on full blast, leave their patio doors open? And it is only because of the flow of cool air that seems vented in my direction, pulled through the cut in the stucco, that I can sit here on the grass half-way comfortably and observe and listen. Invited to eavesdrop, invited it almost seems, perhaps by Catherine's God.

Chapter 4

Determined to stay at this station as long as possible, I glance around to make sure no one is observing my curious loitering. The noisome beach is just beyond the drop-off, and the angular edges of the pink buildings, clothed in alternating lines of yellow light and black swathes, lead off to my right. It's a Dali painting of a midnight castle on a Spanish coastline. I lean my tense shoulders against the wall and await the next word from Catherine, although now all I can hear over the surf are the vague murmurings about weather from the travel-show host.

Still, these weird and yet amazing circumstances reassure me of the serendipity of life. Here's Susan's interesting couple that I probably would have ignored after one glance if she hadn't marked them out so well. First, they were there, down on the beach, their involvement plain from a hundred yards away, and now they are here, all snug, except for the patio door cracked open five inches and the horizontal blinds only half way drawn. Atop all these layers of happenstance, the best is still to come, that later, maybe even tomorrow, I'll be the owner of a device that will enable me to watch and listen, and to take pictures if I want. Even if these two little sweethearts decide to move to a side bedroom and pull the blinds shut, after tomorrow I'll be able to hear them.

I glance down the side of the building to see how the rooms are placed. Yes, the glass door and window is exactly like Susan's and mine, one high small square in the stucco shows where the bathroom is and two long rectangles delineate the largest bedroom. The two smaller rooms, the ones in our apartment that belong to Nursey and the girls, are on the front side of the condo with another bathroom in between. As from a height, I see the arrangement, a carbon copy of my own quarters: a wide entrance hall leading to a small kitchen and ending at a combined dining and living area, where the couple now sits.

Some progression in the lovemaking has occurred while I was looking about, for now, Catherine says, "Here, dear, first unbutton the back."

She stands and turns with sloping shoulders to show Towelhead the pearl-like buttons that hold the opening of her blouse. She chuckles a single "ha" in a throaty voice that has dropped an octave into a more sultry range. Towelhead also has risen and, and fumble-fingered, he undoes the buttons slowly, pausing to kiss the nape of her neck. In one smooth motion, Catherine slips her arms out, folds the blouse in half, and places the neat rectangle over the end of the couch. Delight rises within me. In bending forward, the indention of her spine under the spotless flesh lengthened sinuously. Her brassiere and the straps are of a white flexible lace. She twists to face Towelhead; the front of the undergarment is white lace also, inset with satin panels. Her breasts look larger than I thought, filling the bottoms of the bra cups. Again, I can almost feel the floating heft of them in my hands, and a whir of excitement sings in my brain. A sexual shift follows in my shorts, a growing tautness. This woman, in bed, I'm convinced— knowledgeable spy that I am—will do anything. The feather-weight of her frame, the charming supple humor that sounds in her language, in her movements, and in her avid acceptance of all of Towelhead's prosaic foreplay, tells me this. Anything.

Catherine says, "Take your shirt off, B.J. Why do women always wind up naked while men still have all their clothes on?"

Towelhead, aka "B.J.", pulls the dark knit shirt up over his head and drops the garment to the floor, revealing a thick upper torso, fringed from front to back and across the shoulders with coarse black hair. The towel he wore on the beach hid not only his head but a corded neck. His arms, though average sized, show he must lift weights, for the lines over his biceps and triceps are clearly defined. All the old anatomy names from nude drawing classes come back to me.

Towelhead must have worn a t-shirt on the beach, too, for my memory—unreliable computer that it is—has made him older and given him a rangy, nondescript body, more like my own. I begrudge the ten or so years he's dropped just by taking off his shirt. His unguessed-at girth and youth disturbs my desire, for my wish would be to watch Catherine take off her clothes slowly, and alone.

Now, Towelhead, abruptly more masterful, turns her around to unsnap the bra. From the side I see his sloping flattened pectoral and both of Catherine's exposed breasts. Her pinkish-brown nipples, crinkled with desire or the air conditioning, sit atop firm flesh that lifts when she raises her arms to clasp B.J.'s shaggy crown. I recall from one of those sexual-science television shows that women's breasts enlarge by one-fourth during arousal.

Towelhead nuzzles the side of her neck. Again comes a single gurgle from Catherine.

He bends, trying unsuccessfully to undo the button at her waist to release her shorts.

"Sometimes I think women buy clothes just because they're so hard to get off," Towelhead grumbles.

Dumb-ass! I want to hiss.

Catherine turns and starts to release the catch at her waist but then hesitates, holds her hands up to cover her breasts. "Wait," she says, and glances toward the patio door, toward the space made by the open blinds, toward the cross-cut aperture in the stucco. Yet I know she can't see me; dark's on my side, light is on hers. Still, it's exactly the same look she had while Towelhead and she sat on the couch—something distant, disturbing in her eyes. "I need to think this through one more time."

What's going on here? I question. Why would she say that?

Towel Head grumbles some response that I don't manage to catch, and then says, "Come on, baby, don't be a tease."

"You don't understand. This isn't easy for me." For a second longer, Catherine keeps her hands over her chest.

"Let's get it on, baby," Towelhead half sings, off key and suggestive. He puts his hands to the beltline of his shorts.

I force myself to look down into the darkness at my feet, for I have no desire to see this young man in boxers or briefs. The first stages in this miniature strip-tease dance promised the woman's total nudity, and I was looking forward to that display, but the thought of Towelhead in the buff is totally appalling. I can already imagine the bulky shaft of his penis, promised by his general color and body type. Too often I've seen those show-off jocks, proud of their equipment, in live-drawing classes. Their penises, the thick purple veins around the shaft and the smaller blue ones under the skin, the mushroom-shaped head, the *meatus urinarius*, other anatomy words, are already too disgustingly vivid in my imagination

I command myself to stand, to brace against the wall. What am I? A peeping tom, a voyeur, a poor soul who has to depend on other people's exposed lives to get his rocks off? I order myself to move, to get the hell out of there.

Just as before, when the sight of my unconscious wife in our bed forced me to run down the corridors of Sandhills, now I force myself to silently step the ten feet or so back into the service alley, and then I force myself to run. Run.

Good. I'm off, back down the alley as fast as I can put one foot in front of the other. Once out of hearing range of those two oblivious lovers, I continue a loping trot across the grass that circles the gated fence around the deserted pool. I move quickly past the uncomfortable Adirondack chairs that squat in a line, four lonely blue-green sentinels, overlooking the cliff. I head toward the decrepit staircase that leads down to the beach. Without looking, and yet aware of how dangerous it is to race down the weathered steps, I pitch myself forward. The thought of that splendid woman embracing that young simpleton, squandering herself on his muscled body, fills me with revulsion and with envy. I plunge down the stairs and arrive, surprised that I've not fallen—the landings are tricky—at the bottom on the cupped-out spot of sand made by many feet.

The empty beach, full of water and wind, stretches off to my right and to my left. Go either way, I think, just go. During the day the sand is blindingly white as new snow, and now, even at night, it retains some of that fluorescent brightness. I run across a shell-embedded span, hundreds of sea creatures smashed under my feet, and arrive at the flatter, firmer strip at the edge of the scudding water. At a canter, I start down the shore, though my walking shoes bog down wetly with each step. The ocean is dotted with the lights of fishing boats, and the sky is full of stars, so it's difficult to make out the horizon, where the inky water stops and the sky begins. The darkness, a great curving spangled curtain, billows out above me, and the worn cliffs, veined with water stains, are my edge of earth.

I plod, determined to keep up a steady pace, determined by exertion to erase the scene I've just left. But within a mile, the strain of running reaches fingers of pain up into the tendons of my calves and from there into the bony gristle of my knees. I pant in rhythm to my splashing footfalls, cursing Towelhead for his dumb luck and myself for lost lung and muscle strength. Whatever track prowess I once possessed in college has ebbed away in the dull inactive life I lead alongside Susan, my stationary hill of a wife. I force myself to keep running, thinking of our sedentary existence.

Susan moves only in great heaving lurches from one reading place to another: from the apartment to the beach, from the beach to the apartment. That routine comprises her daily exercise, her entire existence—that, and don't forget, she sets table. My own itinerary is no better: I drive from the condo to the studio in Tampa, from Tampa back to the condo. I sit at counters, at bars, at the easel, but do no real physical activity. Now, if I found a half-way attractive woman, someone better looking and more refined than Belle, someone more like Catherine, would she find me appealing or even interesting? I run and list my corporeal flaws in pounding bursts of blood in my temples: pale freckled skin, thin ashen hair, scrawny arms and legs sprouting out of a drooping pot belly like a bloated spider.

At last, completely winded, I throw myself face down on the beach and let the surf roll me from side to side on the abrasive sand. I turn on my back, yet hardly feel the small cool breakers pulling my head in one direction and my legs in another. The sky above is an immeasurable darkness, frosted through with stars. The vertigo of all that space overhead pulls at me, makes me feel I could fall up, up into the void. I perceive that I am on the skin of this planet, this round ball, and all the water and sand and my meager self could be easily detached and drawn up into the abyss. I see myself as if I were God looking down at a puny four-armed starfish of no consequence. Then I remember: there is no deity. Didn't I just side with Towelhead against Catherine's argument for a beneficent supreme being holding everything, especially this dot of world in its place?

Baptizing the Cat

"There is no one, over or under, you poor deluded bitch!" I shout as loud as I can up into the sky, hoping that Towelhead back in the apartment, probably already in bed with Catherine, will hear the sound and be distracted, interrupted.

"No one cares about this puny bit of a world," I continue, grumbling. "We're all just specks amid specks."

But now I'm not even speaking loud enough to be heard above the sliding water. Maybe if I just lie here unresisting, the tide will draw me out into the higher whitecaps, miles from shore, and finally the undertow will pull me below the surface. I wonder, could I hold on to courage and not fight the waves until I'm so far gone that there would be no swimming back to safety? I see myself drowned, the long spiraling drift of my body down through the unlit water, down to the ocean floor. How does one go about it? Take in great gulps of water on the descent until the stomach is full, until the weight of fluid overcomes the natural buoyancy of the body, and then start breathing in liquid? Uncomfortable, for sure, but then this empty existence would be over.

My corpse, bloated and gnawed by fish, would wash ashore in a day or two. Or maybe not. Maybe a shark would hit at my swollen hull, bite off a foot. Maybe one of my black tennis shoes would turn up in a shark's maw when it was caught out in the Gulf. A good painting. I can see it: a small cluster of Mexican peons in white pants, multi-colored shirts, and large sombreros standing around a shark's split carcass on the beach. The sodden tragic shoe held up high in a brown hand, my severed foot still inside, a dark red circle in the neck of the Sketcher. Put some snow-capped blue mountains in the background, some frondy green palm trees leading down to a white beach, a few fishing shacks with cone-shaped roofs that would echo the form of the sombreros. The tragic focal point would be off to the right, the shoe made unshapely by days in the sea and the shark's belly, and the circle of burgundy blood and flesh, with maybe a bit of white bone showing.

Good. I would be gone. Another tragic drowning. Susan would be free. I would be free of Susan. She could continue her life exactly as she does now but probably even better since there would be no drinking, kibitzing Phillip hanging around, no silent, discontented Phillip to put up with. Her father and mother would help raise the girls, and there would be no bad-influence Phillip to carry Ed off for afternoons of beer in the pool halls of Spartanburg. Susan could wear solid black dresses for years, since there's no doubt she'd be heartbroken. A change in her wardrobe would be good since black is so slimming. She might even find another husband. Where did I read that it was always easier to get married the second time? Look at my record. She might hook up with that Jewish guy, Spielman, whom she had those college weekends with. He still has hot memories of their dates—I can tell—doesn't seem to mind that she's gotten so fleshy, calf-eyes her at the country club whenever he thinks no one's paying attention. Susan's admitted that she let him feel her up, but I'm sure there was more to it than that. She was really the hot number when I first met her: short, bubbly, brave, keeping a child by someone she barely knew and yet eager to go to bed with me. So much fun. Where did all that sexual energy go? Can she truly be enjoying her present life?

The incoming tide is deeper now, and I turn and dunk my face into the frothy water and pull in a snoot full. Damn! I blow out the stinging brine. Drowning won't be easy. And maybe the sharks would come before I lost complete consciousness. Wouldn't that be just my luck? Eaten-alive!

I rise from the surf, which has risen, knee deep, and wade back to shore. I give up the foolish idea of a death by drowning; only a nut like Virginia Woolf could pull off that scenario. The air feels chilly at first, but then my clothes start to dry in the warm billows coming off the ocean. The sky's darker and the sliver of moon, a silver fingernail, has risen higher. I sit on a little shelf of sand washed up by the incoming tide.

If anyone should go, it should be Susan, not me. She doesn't want any more out of life; she's accomplished all her desires. She's told me so a thousand times: when we were first married, when May was born, when our house was built. "I have everything I've ever wanted, Phillip," she's said over and over, with that self-satisfied expression that means it's all downhill from now on; she doesn't have to put out any more effort. I'm tired of hearing how pleased she is with everything. What kind of existence is that? Just like her mother, Miz Mildred, all those wasted hours watching TV, reading romances and mysteries, and shopping for ever bigger dress sizes.

Baptizing the Cat

April and May would certainly be better off without Susan's pattern
to follow: her hovering, her spoiling, that ridiculous home-schooling crap.

The girls need to be in a good private school—we can afford the
fees—or even public school. Give them a few competitive friends
to go up against. Then they wouldn't go crazy like Susan did when
she finally got a bit of freedom. All things considered, Susan's a bad
example of what it is to be a woman. If anyone should vanish, she's
the one. If I'm not on the scene, the girls are going to grow up just
like she did, too protected, too inexperienced, too easy. A few brief
years of rebellion and then they'll settle down into the Bower Bankroll, the well-feathered nest of do-it-just like momma and grandma.
God, how boring.

In fact, we'd all be better off without Susan. What if she were
killed in a traffic accident? That happens. I'd put the girls in a good
Catholic boarding school in South Carolina; they could come home
for Christmas and vacations. We could still summer in St. Pete like
normal people, instead of like these retired snowbirds, migrating in
the fall and winter. Of course, I wouldn't enroll them right away.
I would let everybody get over the shock of losing their mother,
their daughter, "poor Susan, gone before her time." Afterwards, I'd
spend another three months here at the beach and then decide that I
just can't do home-schooling. I'd give in, let Miz Mildred help me
find a good academy. Even she doesn't think Susan's teaching is so
all-fired great, fusses that the children need outside experiences, and
for once the old girl's right. A few hours a day of Susan's slapdash
tutoring is not a full day of school work in anyone's book. Soon,
they'll need chemistry labs, foreign languages, advanced algebra,
tennis maybe—courses like that. Although April and May have
passed all those standardized tests, so they must be learning something, but not nearly enough.

Then it hits me. Ed would take Susan's death poorly, in that
keep-it-inside silent way of his that's so hard to get past. He lost a
dog, an ancient cocker spaniel, ten years ago, and to this day can't
bring himself to talk about the stupid animal. Gets up and leaves the
room if Miz Mildred forgets and mentions the dog's name, Precious.
How would he bear up under the death of his only daughter? Have
a heart attack and die? The idea of the poor bastard coping with

Susan's demise pulls a dull blanket over the whole pleasant idea of my wife's extinction. But it seemed so good there at first: Susan just gone, poof, out of this world. Although God knows allergies, if they could, should have knocked her off years ago. All that eye watering, nose running, head-snorting congestion, always settling into her big fleshy chest, always turning into bronchitis. How do you kill a person and prove she died of allergies? Could a bad cold move to the lungs and turn into pneumonia? Not much possibility of that ever happening, thanks to antibiotics.

What did Archie say about women going about murder differently than men? They use poison or get some poor sap to do the dirty deed. Could I get Belle to blab how she did it? Pour some B&B or good Kahlua into her coffee and find out how she murdered her husbands? That is, if she did? Maybe she's just remembering the unhappiness, like Ed with his dog. Maybe Belle just couldn't bear to think about the deaths and the funerals. Did she change her *modus operandi*? Did she do the second murder like the first? Surely it would be easier, like getting married, the second time around.

I look up at the sky thick with stars and that bottom curve of moon moving over the water, and vow that I will speak no more of killing, not to anyone. I shouldn't have even mentioned it to Archie today, about Belle. If it came to testifying under oath, he would remember. Years of drinking beer and watching the sun go down together doesn't mean he'd lie for me. "Yes, your honor, he asked if I'd ever killed anybody, then brought up some suspicion that a shop owner in Tampa had murdered her husbands, but I'm sure he was just jawing. Doesn't mean he'd do away with his wife." That would be Archie, sticking up for me but still telling the truth.

I figure some period of time has to elapse, six months maybe, maybe even a year, before I can put any kind of plan into action, and who knows what can happen in that span of time. It will have to be something no one can detect, a crime a woman would commit, not a man. Poison. I'll need time to work out each detail, investigate all the options. I remember there's a bag of tobacco poison in the barn on Trubek Farm up in Spartanburg—been there for years.

Right after we bought the place from a Mr. Fizell, I spent a few hours with an ancient tawny black man, trim and dapper with sur-

Baptizing the Cat

prisingly pale-green eyes. He had a double first name—another southern thing—Ben-William and a last name of Williams, who'd been a share cropper on the farm his entire life. Glad for an audience, he proudly showed me around, explaining the cut-out tunnel under the road where cattle ran through to move them from pasture to pasture. "Took um three months to dig out and set the concrete blocks and cost $4,000, cash money. That was when a dollar meant somthin', Mr. Craine."

Of the dark abundant woods at the edge of the field behind our house, he lamented: "Hunnerd thousand dollars of hard timber stole from Mr. Fizell by the gov'ment, Mr. Craine. Pure-d flat-out stole."

And in the narrow barn with two slanting sheds on either side, he motioned to a small innocent-looking white paper sack sitting on one of the short shelves made by the wall supports.

"'Bacca poison in there, Mr. Craine," the man said, pointing with a knobby arthritic forefinger. "Might oughta get shet of it." Then he turned and favored me with a conspirator's grin, revealing even dentures under a whisper-thin gray mustache. "You ain't gonna grow 'bacca, now are you, Mr. Craine?" he grinned.

"No, I reckon not, Mr. Williams," I admitted, going along with the joke. "Shade 'bacca's not my vocation."

"It's arsenic," Ben-William said, still smiling as if revealing a family secret. "But we called it 'bacca poison back then, till that gal down the road up and swallered a spoonful to spite her folks. Didn't die but came down with a powerful bellyache, and then her momma sent her off to the state hospital. Af'terds, the county agent came round and told everybody that 'bacca poison was arsenic, that field hands oughta be careful putting it out on the bud-worms."

"Bud-worms?" I asked, mildly interested. I'd learned more than I wanted about the cultivation of shade tobacco during his tours, looking at those abandoned fields that had once raised the large-leaf Durham that wrapped cigars. "No, that's not my vocation," I'd say, every time he started in on some aspect of farming.

"It's a worm what gets down in the flower top of the 'bacca stalk, eats the heart out, and the plant don't grow, puts out little crooked leaves." Ben-William accompanied this explanation with a motion of his worn-out fingers, showing how to put the poison into the flower and forming the size of the misshaped leaves. "Course, I ain't got no vacation growing 'bacca either, not no more.'

The old tiger might have been putting me on, but the play on words made a funny story to tell Susan, and later her parents.

"Colored people are smarter than you might think," Miz Mildred said, her puckered mouth set in a straight line, although Ed and I were still chuckling about Ben-William's 'vacation.'

A dammed sight smarter than you are lady, I thought, you old bigot.

The architect had suggested tearing down the barn, but its slanting weathered shape, the narrow doors and lean-to sheds confirmed the Trubek Farm name to me and completed some image in my mind of what the place used to be. The old buildings were part of the landscape seen from my studio windows, and I painted them: scenes of morning mist, small herds of deer stepping timidly out from the tree line, a buck with a full rack of antlers leading the way.

Actually a stag never goes first. It's always the doe that ventures out of cover, but an artist can't put that bit of male cowardice on display. I painted one canvas with Ben-William's tan face lost in the boards of the barn, making his intelligent laughing eyes and wrinkles seem like just two more knot holes among the grain markings in the wood, hardly noticeable until one looked closely. But after the painting sat three months on an easel in the local Art Center's storefront window, I took the portrait back and gave it to the old man as a going-away gift. Eighty-four years old, he went to live with his daughter in Charleston.

The trash in the barn, old farm equipment, broken baskets, webbing from the stands that shaded the young tobacco plants, so much that there was no way to get back to the wall and take the sack of 'bacca poison, the arsenic, down from its perch on the shelf. The first year or two in our newly-built house, Susan and I, and even Nursey at times threatened to clean out the barn, to make it a real storage area. In the end we only added our own outdated paraphernalia, covering the oddments of farm life with old rugs, broken lamps, discarded papers, and such. Still, I never glanced down from either one of my studio's four-foot wide windows without thinking of that little white sack with its killing potential, and the young black girl who had tried to take her life and failed.

Baptizing the Cat

Now, sitting on the beach, I discard the notion of giving Susan arsenic. First, because the powder—in my imagination it's a white talcumy dust—is probably so old that it's lost all its strength, and second because I also recall from some forgotten source that poisoning by arsenic means a slow, painful death, a death that can be confirmed by autopsy, even years later when the body is exhumed or even from ash if the body is cremated. Also, I have no relish for the idea of my wife complaining of bellyache and then dying a horrible, contorted death in front of her daughters, or worse yet not dying after all but finding out she was poisoned. Miz Mildred would see me in jail and "be proud of it" as she says of so many things.

And apparently it's not so easy to poison a person. In one of Susan's *True Crime* stories, she read aloud an account of a man who worked in a laboratory and yet was unable to kill off his rich father-in-law, in spite of feeding him all sorts of nauseating substances: rat feces, fungi, bacteria from typhus and cholera. The old man ate his meals, complained in the mornings of mild indigestion, and lived to a happy old age.

Susan laughed, "No worry about you wanting to get rid of Ed, is there, Phillip? You enjoy Daddy's company better than mine." I agreed, no need to worry, can't kill the goose that lays the Bower Bankroll.

Now, I wonder where you can purchase those little pills that kill in an instant, the capsules spies and CIA agents are supposed to carry on their persons and bite into in case of emergency, a way to avoid a fate worse than death? Movies and books always speak of the quick, easy exit from this life, but I've never once heard or read of where to buy them or what's in those ampoules. Cyanide?

I look at my watch. It's five after two in the morning, and I'm exhausted from my run, from the ocean, and from the excitement of spying on the couple in apartment 3-D. The day reels back like a weird movie. After months leaden with inactivity, it's too much to absorb in one 24 hour period. Still, I resolve to do several things at once. First, I'll start running again. It's the type of exercise I prefer; it clears my mind, my perceptions. I'll get back into shape, so that if I do meet someone, someone like Catherine, she'll find me a fit forty-five-year old man and not this inert pile of crap I've become. Today was my wake-up call, and I'm going to take it, return to some of the vigor I felt in college, get back some enjoyment of life. Second, I'll become an exemplary husband to Susan and a concerned father to April and May.

I'll allow myself to dream, to plan a single life again. Some of the pleasurable mood of that afternoon driving back from Island's End returns, for now my direction is clear. Susan is the problem. I must lull her, her family, and everyone we know into the belief that I am the ideal husband. These past two years my image has slipped. I've been drinking too much, been sullen and distant. I'll remedy all my bad habits. Of course, this stratagem will take time. But I can wait, be patient; after all it's what I've been doing up until now. In six months, Archie will forget all about our conversation concerning Belle and murders. And I will never again discuss killing or deaths with anyone. It's so funny, on police shows, to see spouses trying to get rid of a husband or wife, going to undercover agents. Seems like the only ones in the business of murder-for-hire are the police officers themselves. I'll be alert, look for a woman's way, the perfect way. I'll depend on planning or "God talking to us," as Susan calls every little coincidence that comes along.

Like yesterday, with a new kitchen clock. After she plugged it in, she found that the minute and hour hands were already aligned, exactly, to the correct time. Coming through the doorway, her face glowed with affirmation. "See," she said, pointing to the yellow sunflower burst that I had advised her to purchase. "Get something pale yellow," were my exact words, "something to offset all this vomit blue-green around here." The skin on her underarm dangled in a wing-like flap. "See, I didn't have to reset a thing, not even the minute hand." She was thrilled with this coincidence as though proving some profound metaphysical theory that had been in debate between us.

"A miracle," I said, looking up and then back down to my crossword puzzle. The answer to the clue "aggravation" was "pest."

"It proves there are forces outside ourselves, Phillip, showing that we, the entire universe, is in tune on some level that no one understands." She eased herself down on the couch, settled on her haunches, and reached for a paperback. The television was on. Nursey was in the kitchen preparing a lunch of homemade pimento cheese sandwiches, Susan's favorite. April and May were taking showers. Hubby would soon be off on his daily rounds, whatever they were. After the women of the household had eaten, there would be a couple of desultory hours of school work and maybe naps. All was right in Susan's world.

"We shall see, my comfortable, complacent wife." I mouth the words out into the gusting wind off the ocean. The moon is higher, but still a shiny rim hung in the night sky. "We shall put this divine providential belief of yours, and Catherine's, too, to the test." I stand, crusted with sand from lying in the surf, and brush off, as well as I can, all the dried bits caught in the hair on my arms and legs.

"An intellectual experiment," I quietly address the landscape of frothy sea, spangled sky, and solitary moon. "If you want to kill someone and don't have a clue how do you go about it, what do you do? Prove to me, oh Invisible One or Anyone Out There, for that matter, that there is some force in the world who can answer questions, even the ones not voiced out loud, even the ones that are sinful and forbidden."

I turn and jog back up the rickety Sandhills' stairs to the condo. I breathe easier, finding a fuller capacity in the bottoms of my lungs, generated no doubt by those short emotional sprints through the condos and here on the beach. Even if there is no answer to my question, at least I'll be running again.

I leave the solution of my problem to the cosmos.

Chapter 5

So my new life begins.

I awake early the next morning, a Sunday, with a sense of purpose I haven't possessed in years. Susan sleeps beside me, and for the first time in a decade I don't resent her animal breathing, her labored snorts. In fact, a tenderness rises in my thoughts that I haven't experienced since we were first married. Poor girl, she does suffer; although up until now, I've really been quite unsympathetic with all the sniffles and coughs. The amount of mucous that woman can produce from her sinus cavities and lungs is truly amazing. She must have extruded a gallon of clear runny fluid in just the last month, from her nose, her eyes, her chest. Lately, she's had a tendency toward nose bleeds, waking in the morning with a mahogany splotch on the pillow case, a rim of dried blood crusted around the edge of a nostril. Does this mean her condition is worsening? Dr. Tamtino, a female allergy doctor, whom Susan sees here in St. Pete, seems to think so.

"Just more of the same, but now I have asthma," Susan said, after her last appointment. "She put me on another drug, Theophylline, to open up my lungs, and she wants to see me twice a week, to monitor the medication in my blood."

My wife accepts this horrific verdict of asthma—which would be god-awful news to me—with equanimity. She doesn't seem to mind all the trouble and inconvenience of allergy symptoms, the shots, the medications. She carries a box of tissues everywhere: to the couch, to the dining table, to the night stand beside our bed, and a handful of tissues bulges in her muumuu pockets as she heads out to the beach. The trash baskets in our living room and bedroom are always half-full of soggy wads of flimsy pastel papers. Somehow Nursey keeps up with Susan's drippings and does a good job of emptying the trash cans before they overflow.

"You pitiful child," Nursey said, just last week when Susan was having a particularly difficult spell. Her blood-shot eyes streamed water, and her inflamed nose drained in long slimy threads, too much mucous to completely catch with a tissue. The maid brought my wife a hot washcloth to bathe her face.

Surprising me, Susan answered, "It could be worse, Nursey, you know; I could have something serious like cancer. Allergies are a mild cross. A lot of people suffer far more painful diseases. Why, I could be in Bosnia with bombs dropping and still have allergies, but with no antihistamines and no doctors to give me pills or shots."

Now, Susan rolls toward me and sighs a soft push of air through lips so pale that they are hardly distinguishable from the skin around them. Maybe she's sicker than anyone knows. In a bright slant of light from one of the blinds turned the wrong way, she looks practically dead already. Her splotchy cheeks and nose are overlaid with reddish freckles that seem more like leprosy, than natural pigmentation. Could she be getting skin cancer? Melanoma? The most lethal form? All those days on the beach, even covered up by muumuus and broad-brimmed hats, might be exacting a penalty. Susan has always slathered sun-screen on the girls and herself, but now the so-called health experts are saying that sun screen has ingredients that might also cause cancer. I wouldn't know these facts except that my wife reads magazine snippets of medical information aloud, lamenting that here she's always been so cautious, using sun protection for years, and now her safeguards might be causing the very thing she's sought to avoid. Poor Susan, you can't win.

Then, apparently feeling my gaze, the fixed look of the predator on her face—as all creatures are said to do—Susan opens her sleep-mattered eyes. "Phillip, you're awake. What's wrong?"

"Nothing, my love. Just lying here waiting for you to wake up."

I slide my hand along Susan's arm, which lies outside the bed clothes. It's flabby and mottled like her face, yet the texture of the skin is satiny, encased in a fine, light covering of hair. If I close my eyes and don't look, the touch itself might be enjoyable.

Susan shivers slightly and goose flesh rises under my fingers. She giggles two syllables, "Hee, hee," suddenly nervous and uncomfortable beside me. Does she think I'm stroking her arm as a preliminary to sex? I remove my hand and roll over onto my back, fix my concentration on the narrow bars of light that stripe the ceiling. I could paint a picture of two people in a bed, lots of blacks, whites, and grays, the Leonardo shadows of draped covers and sheets, and under them a slender man beside a large woman. After the basic painting dried, I'd overlay it all with bands of dark lines from the blinds that resemble the bars of a prison.

No, dear wife, lust has nothing to do with what I am feeling right now.

Susan rises from the bed, a production that must be accomplished in three distinct operations: hunching up onto her elbows, then onto her hands, and finally swinging her legs out over the edge of the mattress. Her movements are slow and considered, yet her efforts tug the sheets from my legs and slide them unpleasantly across the tops of my toes. Irksome how she cannot move from the bed or the couch without effort.

"Going to Mass?" I call out the question just to put some other sounds into the room. I want noise to cover Susan's lumbering walk into the bathroom and then the thick sound of her morning urination. Separate lavatories would accomplish a lot to keep marriages together.

"Of course, Phillip. How silly. It's Sunday, isn't it. The girls and I always go to Mass."

"Of course, how silly," I whisper. Must follow the rules: Mass on Sunday, brunch afterwards at the trough buffet at the Marriott, back to the condo for rest, then down to the beach, back for another nap, and then a PG movie suitable for children to pass the evening. A predictable life; I'll say that for it. Nursey is gone the entire day to the black Baptist Church across the Bay in Tampa.

"I feel like Mass," I call out and struggle from the bed. Might as well get this good-husband show on the road.

Susan comes to the bathroom door in a thin hospital-green nightgown that does nothing to conceal her large stomach and drooping breasts; the brown nipples, two eyes, stare at me through the cloth.

Baptizing the Cat

Her toothbrush, still in her mouth, she speaks around it. "That's good," she says, her pale eyebrows arched in puzzlement.

We head out to St. Vincent's Church. The girls are equally baffled by my presence since I haven't accompanied them to Mass in over six months, not since last Easter in Spartanburg. I drive. Susan rides in the front passenger's seat, so April has to sit in back with May.

"I'm always up front with Mama," she complains, but then seems to fall into an appreciation of my being there in the car with them. "I'm glad you're coming, Daddy. You'll think Father O'Keefe is so funny. He's always making little jokes that don't make any sense. Like last Sunday, he said, 'No one can baptize a cat'." Leaning between the seats, April repeats the punch line, trying to figure out the meaning. "No matter how bad you want to, you can't baptize a cat."

This nonsensical truth strikes me as wonderfully amusing, and I chuckle, glance at my oldest daughter in the rear-view mirror. Her 13-year-old face is round, still in the soft planes of pre-adolescence.

"He's right, you know, baby, 'You can't baptize a cat.' Imagine holding one of those feral cats, or even the tamer barn cats back in Spartanburg, pouring water and trying to say the words all in the same instant. You'd be scratched to pieces."

May says nothing, except that after getting into the car, she looked out from the back seat, and with her incredible lavender-blue eyes— a shade darker than her mother's—asked, "What's up?" without a word.

St. Vincent's hasn't changed since last fall, the outside yellow brick with Parthenon white columns, and inside every inch of wall decorated with an icon, a statue, a scripture, giving it an overall feeling of Eastern Orthodox rather than Roman Catholic. A faint bouquet of incense, a combination of musk and mint, has permeated the stones and pews. "All smells and bells," is how my Lutheran-in-name-only grandfather would have described the over-decorated edifice that my wife and her family have attended here in St. Pete for the last forty years. Susan stakes out the same pew every Sunday and gets upset if someone beats her to it. She pulls up her five feet, two inches, rigid, until the stranger slides over, out of what she claims was once the Bower and is now the Craine pew. It's the same in Spartanburg.

"I'm not comfortable attending Mass if I can't sit two rows back and to the left of the altar," my wife declares.

"Then you should join a church that has place cards," I've said more than once.

I actually enjoy St. Vincent's as architecture, like to squint my eyes and compose abstract paintings out of the red carpet that ascends three steps to the marble altar and the wide expanse of white brick walls on either side of a huge dark-wood cross with an ivory corpus. But the music is always atrocious: one egomaniacal tenor leading a trailing congregation of voices. Still the light streaming in through the multi-colored side windows in prismatic rays is diverting, and the scene dramatic and ritualistic, like most things Catholic.

To keep from making mind paintings—they never sell, so why give them the time of day?—I close my eyes and take in the "smells and bells." Restful, and it's a good way of seeming to participate without the bother. I can appear pious, profoundly religious, and still be almost asleep. I drift, and before I realize it, Father O'Keefe is starting his homily with a joke, just as April predicted. He presents the three questions of life, which to him are: "Why are we here? Where are we going?" and "Where are the cookies?" April giggles, truly pleased; this is humor she can appreciate. Susan, beside me, and May on the other side of her mother might be smiling but that's all. I don't hear a peep from either of them. Myself, I'm disappointed. I expected the joke to be something more along the line of baptizing a cat. Within a few minutes, behind closed lids, again I drift, not hearing, and feel as if I've been lifted out of my body and lie upon the slanting red-tiled roof of St. Vincent's, taking in the sun on this glorious morning. "Where are we going?" beats a refrain in my head, and, without any intention on my part, changes into "Where am I going?" I whisper back, "Nowhere," just to shut the question down.

One hour—the unofficial time limit and the main thing I like about the Catholic Mass—passes swiftly. I have no idea what the rest of O'Keefe's sermon is about; he seemed to be paraphrasing

66

what was just read in the gospel, and not a very good paraphrase at that. Sort of like saying Romeo and Juliet were teenaged lovers who killed themselves. To repeat good writing in simple language just doesn't work. The standing and kneeling parts of the service passed as blurry interruptions in my almost snooze. This eyes-closed business makes the time pass so quickly that I resolve to make it be part of my weekly good-husband, church-going act. A form of meditation, no thoughts whatsoever, except for that intrusive "Where am I going?" chorus, which faded quickly.

Right after Susan and I married, I used to come home from church all fired up. I wanted to make sense of the epistles and gospels, discuss them, and dissect every passage. But my dense wife was never too interested in deciphering the meaning of her own theology. "Why on earth do you think God made you, Susan?" I'd ask. "Don't you want to understand?"

"God made me to know Him, to love Him, and to serve Him, Phillip, and to be happy with Him in this life and the next—like we learned in religion class. Remember, the prayer book says we're celebrating a mystery. That's the part I like best. 'We celebrate the mystery.' You don't need to cut up the liturgy into little pieces before you can believe it."

Still, I especially like some sections of the gospel, the readings that say, "There will be no giving or taking in marriage in heaven." Good, that frees me from my first and second wives, and even from Susan. But there are other readings that directly contradict each other from week to week: David kills Captain Uriah in his army one Sunday, yet is still beloved by God on the next. As Susan and I became more and more married, I attended Mass less and less. Strange, for all of her pressure on me to become a Catholic, she isn't too upset at my absences, and after a few hazy complaints, "You really shouldn't miss, Phillip," doesn't seem to mind. Her own father, Ed, only goes once in a while, when he feels "moved by the spirit" as he says. Generally, men don't seem to take their Catholic religion as seriously as their women, and there are always more females then males at Mass.

Before I realize it, the hour is up, the last hymn, "On Eagle's Wings," is being sung or at least screeched, and Susan gently nudges me to stand, and we file out with our little family unit intact.

The next stop is the Marriott's Sunday brunch where we gorge, or at least Susan does, on a combination breakfast and lunch. The steam tables carry two distinct meals with Eggs Benedict, creamed spinach, croissants, and even an ice sculpture beside the huge hunk of roast beef that looks like it was taken from a bison instead of beef cattle. There's even champagne, but it's not my choice. I figure that management at last figured out that no one can eat 12 bucks worth of food, and they're right. April and May dish up little-girl portions, spherical dabs of eggs and grits and a single slice of French toast on their plates. The food, like paint on a palette, is separated by an inch of white space all round. I take reasonable servings of the same, but Susan comes back to our booth, the one she prefers every Sunday, with a heaping arrangement of eggs, sausage, bacon, pancakes, and fruit. When she's cleaned that plate, she'll go back to the counter and have servings of roast beef, mashed potatoes, green beans, and fried chicken, with a plate of mixed salad on the side. She always half-way apologizes, says, "Well, it's breakfast and dinner, you know, and I'm not going to eat anything for the rest of the day." She lies. But the food is so artfully arranged, contrasting colorful fruit beside the darker pancakes, and the brown meats with the green and yellow vegetables, that it all does look delicious. Years ago, I used to take second helpings myself, since everything she piled on her platter appeared so appetizing, but the mixture never tasted as good as it looked, and I'd end up leaving half. And I put on weight.

Susan drinks sweet iced tea—the Southern addiction—taking a full neat sip between every bite of food. I've tried in the past, hinting that if she'd just give up tea or a few snacks she might shed a few pounds. I know she wants to lose weight. Every once in a while she throws all hers and the girls' treats into the trash and announces to Nursey, "This family is going to start eating healthy." For a few days, she directs the old black woman to prepare broiled fish or chicken and steamed vegetables. Nursey is the soul of cooperation, agrees to cook the low-fat recipes Susan snips out of magazines. But after three or, at the most, four days, we're all exhausted with the blandness.

"Make country-fried steak tonight, Nursey," I find myself suggesting. "We can eat it without gravy." But, of course, the old girl, hungry as the rest of us, serves up the crisp browned meat with a small bowl of onion gravy on the side, and the diet is shot to hell. And a Sunday cannot roll around without us back at the Marriott buffet here in St. Pete or at the Smithbrier country club up in Spartanburg, eating as much and as harmfully as we ever did. What's that old saying? "Nothing is as sincere as the love of food."

I cannot bear to watch Susan eat. She does keep her lips daintily compressed, but her mouth twists to the side as she chews, and the folds of her chins jiggle. Often there is a sheen of grease left on her lower lip, which protrudes slightly. To avoid the horror, I fix my attention on my own plate, its neat alignment of bright yellow—are they dyed?—scrambled eggs, not touching the hash-browned potatoes or the French toast, and the crossword puzzle beside the plate.

The *Tampa Tribune* is delivered every morning, and its crossword grid and the clues can be easily handled when the leisure section is folded in fourths. Sunday's puzzle is twice as large, and even though it creases awkwardly, I look forward to the two or more hours it will take for me to work out all the answers. I don't know why filling in each little square with a letter is so satisfying when they intersect correctly, but it is. I've read that solving a crossword puzzle is similar to gambling, a turn of a card sets up conditions, like the letters setting up probable words, and the following cards or words resolve the problem, the numbers or letters falling into place. Every stipulation met, every question answered.

Today's first clue in the across section is "Lady Macbeth's solution," and the answer is: "Murder most foul."

I'm not in the least surprised at this concise connection between an inanimate publication and my own reality. The crossword often mimics my thoughts, relates back to what is happening in my life. I can be listening to a news cast, and the announcer will say "Washington," just as I am putting the "ing" into the empty boxes between the "Wash" and "ton." Or a stupid tune will go round in my head for a day. I'll know some of the words but can't think of the title, yet the next morning the answer to a crossword clue will be the name of that very melody. I've even imagined for a while that if I were diligent enough, I could take the puzzle, circle out whichever words I thought appropriate and determine my horoscope regardless of my sign.

"Lucky Sagittarius," my airline attendant ex-wife used to say, reading the always overly optimistic predictions. I figured if I worked out my own horoscope, it might be a real forecast that could lead me in some true direction, not something written up by some so-called astrologer. Who on earth believes in that crap? It's still a possibility, but I gave up when for days on end every word I circled came up on the negative side: "More of the same," "Dull as dishwater," "Gray." How's that for prophesy? Not exactly what I needed to plot my course.

At least the answer "Murder most foul" has some zing in it, something to speak, no matter how darkly, to my current interests. Without pause or real comprehension, almost as if there were a sentient being on the inside of the folded newspaper, I write, "How?" in the margin above the puzzle.

There! That's the impulse I came up with last night. Ask the universe to provide an answer. Ask the question directly. So I rush to fill in the rest of the blocks, hoping that I'll be able to finish before breakfast is over and I'll find my direction. Perhaps I'll be told to wait, bide my time and an accident will befall my wife. "Befall" is another one of the puzzle's answers.

Still the crossword doesn't give up its answers readily. I rate the *Tribune* puzzle's difficulty above the *St. Pete Daily,* whose crossword is a joke that could be accomplished by any half-way savvy third grader. The *New York Times'* puzzle, that my mother did with apparent ease, is a such killer that I don't even attempt it anymore. Too much of an ego hit to find out how ignorant one is. I buy the *Daily* every now and then for May to practice on. I tried to interest April in crosswords, but she's too much like her mother; if something's not immediately gratifying, it doesn't stand a chance. May, however, is more patient and now asks for the *Daily's* puzzle, always specifying, "the easy one, Daddy."

After an hour and Susan's two plates of food, we leave the restaurant. The crossword is mostly complete, a few blank squares remain like missed stitches in a piece of knitting.

Besides working crosswords, my mother knitted, always misshapen, odd-colored—cheap yarn—sweaters and too-long scarves, and always with a hole or two displaying where she'd carelessly let the knit or the purl loop drop. I grew adept at using a pencil to pull the neglected strand of wool up the ladder through the stitches, filling in the small running gap in a garment. This practice had the added benefit of tightening up the entire structure, sometimes making it fit better.

"Don't try for perfection, Phillip," Mother would say, catching me at the improvement of her sloppy efforts; "it's a big waste of time."

"Well, how about just trying to be okay," I'd reply.

I claimed to have lost, but actually threw away, one particularly gruesome olive-drab sweater, a Christmas gift. What a pleasure it was to watch that article of clothing as it flopped, unequal green arms extended, down into the brown water of the Cuyahoga River, to see several long running lines in its surface, and to know that I would not have to "waste" my time pulling the stitches into a semblance of order .

Poor Mother, looking back, I can see that she tried. Just to feed a child growing so rapidly into a six-foot teenager and covering his gangly ever-increasing body was a challenge. I knew, early on, perhaps by osmosis, that my Mother's and Grandpa Emile's arrangement was based on mutual need that had nothing to do with affection. Emile was my father's father, and Philip, my father, absent from our lives and conversations, had left mother and me in his tender care. Grandpa Emile's way was to wheedle and tease, to play tricks, to recall long bitter stories that seemed to have no meaning and definitely no end. He would hide whatever project—they were innumerable—my mother was working on, hiss and kick at her cats, and deliver when least expected his *coup de grâce*: the electricity turned off in the middle of a television show or the water heater set to the lowest temperature.

Mother's defense, I guess, although it might just have been her nature, was to clutter, to save everything imaginable: containers, books, magazines, worn-out clothes, stacks of discounted fabric, broken lots of knitting worsted, odd disjointed pieces of furniture, painting paraphernalia, bags of home remedies, and on and on. There was always that perfect little box to mail something in, or that large pickle jar exactly right for enormous leftovers, or that story or recipe or advice in a two-year-old periodical that put her in a mind to write such a story herself or to cook Chinese or to pass on sage words to one of her lady friends. Three-fourths of our dining-room table was taken up with her writing, hills of writers' magazines and a cast-off portable typewriter that had an unworkable "z".

"We can always ink in a 'z' she assured me whenever I had to write a term paper; "Thank your lucky stars it's not the "e" that's missing."

Sliding piles of writer's guidelines, pencils and pens, and yellowing manuscripts often competed for space with our dishes and glasses on the table's surface. Grandpa Emile would gather his full plate and silverware and retreat to the kitchen, saying, "Where I can eat in peace without a damn jumble falling into my food."

"And peace for us, too," my Mother would whisper, her faded hazel eyes shining with mischief as if she had planned Emile's departure.

If by peace my Grandfather meant quiet, no back talk, he had it, for my mother had a capacity for not responding, a preoccupied silence that could almost be excused by her absorbed interest in whatever "project" she was working on. Those were her words: "my activities, my enterprises, my projects," her weapons. To my grandfather they all looked like one and the same thing, a mess. From the beginning of our front drive-way where the mailbox sported a conceptual daisy bouquet, a third of its brilliant petals and leaves shining and the rest only traced in, to the back of the toilet where unfinished crossword puzzles piled up, my mother was a lady-in-waiting. Waiting, I guess, for the inspiration that started her "project" to return so she could finish it. She was always taking up the new and leaving the old behind in an accumulated mound of debris. Half-completed dreams lay throughout our house in very substantial piles of the materials that it might take to process them into reality. Her writing was on the dining-room table, her sewing in the laundry room, her knitting on the couch in the den, her quilting on another couch in the living room, her painting on the enclosed back porch, and in the kitchen a chaos that could only belong to a combination witch-doctor and experimental cook. Magazines, books, boxes of papers cluttered every counter and made walking lanes of the floor space. She was a voracious reader, just like Susan, but unlike my wife, who cuts out recipes for Nursey to try one time and then discard, my mother kept every scrap of paper that came by intent or accident into our home. In contrast, the outside, around the house was immaculate. The pine trees stood, tall soldiers, over their carpet of brown straw and the garden lay in neat rows. Mother's disorder drove my tidy Grandfather, if not to violence, at least to the rage that precedes it. He tended his surrounding acres meticulously, always throwing away any article that had no obvious purpose or could not be used immediately. He never struck Mother, but sometimes in pure frustration, he would raise his hand and she would cower in genuine fear. With his full head of gray hair and matching beard, he made me think of some ancient god whose only desire was for order and quiet.

On occasion I have felt that same impulse, a lifting of my arm that seems to come from outside myself, my anger directed at Susan when she turns her bland uncomprehending face up and asks, "Whatever do you mean, Phillip?" Her question is usually in reference to some ironic statement I've made, some subtle sarcastic joke, for my wife has no jump-shift facility of mind.

The phrase, "jump shift," comes from the card game, bridge, where one changes the bidding from one suit to another and raises it a level. That's something Susan is able to do in playing cards but not in thinking, especially in the area of humor.

Actually my wife is a credible bridge player, a member of two different clubs in Spartanburg, one that meets once a week and the other once a month. Thank God, that gets her out of the house and away from me. The groups play at the Country Club and sometimes at different homes. Susan's turn at being hostess used to please her. She could show off her gracious and well-appointed home and yard, her beautiful and courteous daughters, her devoted and efficient maid, and her artistic and half-way handsome husband—her magazine life. Now the bridge games are more of a chore and a cause for warnings, "If you must come downstairs, Phillip, please just get what you need and leave."

I confess, in the past couple of years I've appeared on the scene, still attractive I hope, but conspicuously high, with more than my share of the frosted strawberry daiquiris that Nursey whipped up for the ladies. Once, I obviously flirted with Mrs. Inez Kimbell, a slender fluffy-headed blonde with pouty red lips. Whether these two lapses from grace were intentional, I'm not sure, but at least now I'm no longer included in the tour of the house that Susan periodically conducts, no longer am I included with the comment, "And here, in his studio, is my darling husband, Phillip."

The drive back to Sandhills from the Marriott is under a cerulean sky and beside the white sand and aquamarine gulf promised by St. Pete's tourist brochures. Families are out of church, returning to their cars, with bobbing gray and white heads and some of that odd purple-blue that old ladies rinse their hair with. Bent figures using walkers and canes feel their way down the steps and sidewalks, with fewer scurrying children than in Spartanburg.

I roll down all the windows of the Range Rover, in spite of Susan's protests that we'll be blown away by the wind, and hot and sweaty to boot, before we get home, The Sunday afternoon air, somehow cleaner and thinner than during the rest of the week, flows across my arm on the window's edge. The girls in the back seat giggle. I'm not sure if it's with pleasure at the fresh breeze whipping their faces or at my having the nerve to disobey their mother.

"Aren't we going to the beach this afternoon, Susan?" I ask. "Won't we be blown about plenty, and hot and sweaty then, too?" I put the questions in a pleasant tone, not turning my head to look at her as I sometimes do with a set, hard feeling behind my eyes. I'm trying to be kind, still into my good-husband act. Yet I can feel Susan's questioning glance against the side of my face. Is he really coming to the beach? she's asking.

"Yah! Daddy's going swimming!" May calls from the backseat.

But I doubt it myself. Am I actually prepared to spend an entire Sunday afternoon with wifey and daughters? The weather, though magnificent viewed from the inside of an air-conditioned car or condo, will be an inferno on that white sand. Even under an umbrella and with plenty of sun screen, I'll still get a burn. The rays apparently bounce off the silicon facets of the sand grains and fan up and out in every direction. I always miss covering some area of my body with lotion, the tops of my feet, a tender line under my arms, or the tops of my ears. And my hands get sticky and gritty. The sand mixes in with the sunscreen, forming an abrasive, unpleasant combination that I still have to rub someplace. And it's difficult to keep the newspaper from flapping in the currents that come off the ocean, and when the girls run up to show me a shell or a starfish, they drip on the crossword and make it hard to read and impossible to write on. And I know they'll insist that I swim.

Stop, immediately! I silently order. If I keep compiling a list of all the bother, comparing an afternoon alone in the condo to one on the beach with Susan and the girls, I'll persuade myself to remain behind in lovely solitude, without even Nursey's unobtrusive presence. It's "quality time" with your family, I instruct my self-indulgent ego. Stick with your long-range plan to again be the model husband that no one will ever suspect. And doesn't that plan include a few outings on the beach? Certainly, because other than Sunday Mass, Marriott brunch, and the movies, the family goes nowhere else together. I draw the line at shopping with Susan, which, besides food and reading, is her only other occupation.

I give in. I'll make the sacrifice, no matter how tiresome, and spend the afternoon on the beach. Just as Susan does, I'll pack a bag with provisions that will see me through. On the way into the condo, I outline my strategy. The number one requirement is a large thermos of cold Rob Roys with maraschino cherries in a separate jar, and a decent glass, a short thick one—not plastic—that won't break easily. Number two: jogging shoes, the old ones that I ran in last night are ruined already, so I'll wear them. Number three will be my personal umbrella, larger and more opaque than the one Susan and the girls use. I'll stake out a separate location, far back from my wife and daughters' encampment, perhaps even up on the grass by the stairs. That site will give me the perfect opportunity to catch the manager and give him my complaints for the twentieth time: the running toilet in the girls' bathroom, his nephews mowing before six in the morning, the shabby state of the wooden stairs down to the beach, and the increase in condo fees with fewer services, especially the twice-a-week garbage pick-up.

Forget the manager, I order again, and pull my thoughts back to my survival kit. Number four will be my smallest sketch book to trace a few lines of the girls coming in and out of the surf, playing on the sand. I haven't drawn them in over a year, which makes a big difference with children. Maybe I'll even sketch Susan building those drip castles she loves so much. Fat women look amazingly good in watercolors, all those fleshy curves and slopes to shade with tint. My wife is the perfect model, sits absolutely still, her only motion is to grab up a handful of wet sand and let it dribble from her finger tips to form drop-sized sand-pancakes. Those tiny ovals land one on top of another to form pillars and colonnades that resemble the melting moss-covered turrets and towers of ancient feudal castles. She aligns those oddly-structured buildings, some as tall as a foot, into circles with a pool of sea water in the middle. Of course, the first wave that comes in from a rising tide destroys those constructions, but Susan doesn't mind. She rolls walrus-like a few feet up the shore and starts to dig and drip wet sand all over again.

"Why don't you move farther up on the beach so that waves won't wash all your work away?" I suggested during our first days of married life on what was then to me the miraculously snowy stretches below Sandhills. Her logical explanation was that if she moved, there wouldn't be enough water in the sand to make the "drip castles."

"Do you ever imagine people inside those towers?" I asked.

"No, not really," was my wife's response.

How many hours in the course of a year has Susan wasted, letting watery sand slide off the ends of her fingers? At least two hours every time she and the girls go to the beach, almost every day for the six months we spend in St. Pete. To that, add the time she sleeps, ten hours at night and one or two more during the day for naps, and the two or sometimes three hours she spends after dinner, flipping through television stations, trying to find something "suitable" to watch. Even then she doesn't give whatever program she's chosen her full attention but picks up a book or magazine and leafs through it, halfway reading, the scissors close at hand to cut out a recipe or some bit of female lore. Seventeen squandered hours a day, hardly a life worth living.

At the condo, Susan orders everyone to take off their Sunday clothes and lie down and rest, so "We'll miss the heat of the day."

Fine by me, I agree with my wife, who has already disappeared into the bedroom to shed her stiff, ice-blue Sunday dress for one of those tents she wears to the shore. With an hour to squander, I'll fortify myself with a few pre-preambles. A cocktail shaker of Rob Roys drunk in air-conditioning will take the edge off, and I can still take another full one down in my bag. Without Nursey around to give me the fish-eye, I can stir up as many drinks as I want. I head toward the kitchen, plan to put two short manhattan glasses into the freezer and make up two shakers of my favorite, stiff "fortifiers."

But in the narrow alcove, April and May have stopped, ask if I'm still part of the plan to hit the waves later on. I assure them I am, say, "What! And miss all that lovely sand and sunburn! I wouldn't think of it!"

April, so like Susan, happily accepts this declaration and sets off down the hallway to obey her mother's directions. May, more like me, remains just inside the front door, her small smooth hand raised in a gesture of half belief, her barely visible eyebrows are drawn together and register suspicion. I pick my child up in my arms. She is longer and heavier than when I last lifted her, and in her tiny body I feel muscles' growth and impunity. How small she is, yet how completely autonomous. Close, face to face, May looks straight into my eyes, her petite features unsmiling, her mother's pupils, streaked with gold lines, appraise me. She is tense in my arms.

"You don't want me to go?" I ask, and in an effort to escape the child's focused scrutiny, I press my lips to her full velvety cheek. She leans against me and whispers, "Yes, I want you to come." I can smell strawberry shampoo and, under that fruity odor, another soft clean smell of youthful health. For an instant I perceive the complex genetic equation that has made up this small human being. More often than not, since they are female, I view May and April as little copies of Susan, but in May's serious expression, her spindly length dangling against me, I feel the combination of her mother's and my heredity. I ease the child to the floor and lie, "I want to spend this afternoon with you, honey. I should have been doing it all along."

Without another question, May seems to accept my explanation. She turns and follows her sister. Her awkward, already feminine trot causes a melancholy pressure in my chest. She will grow up and marry. Marry what manner of man? Someone only capable of loving for a short duration, and after that brief flare, will love turn to hate? It's yet another reason to get Susan out of the picture. April and May need to be more independent, more discerning.

By the time my wife, my daughters, and I have made our preparations for the beach and taken our siesta—Susan and the girls in the bedrooms and me on the couch—it's almost three o'clock. I am two drinks into the first shaker and have the other one, with glasses, stashed away in the freezer—like money in the bank. My sketch book is in the canvas tote beside an insulated bag to hold the liquor and iced tumblers. My bathing suit is on under my shorts, but I seriously doubt I will go into the water. I watch from the couch as my wife loads up. Susan's packing of supplies is definitely more complicated than mine. She brings enough food and drink for four people, although I insist I'll not be hungry until we come back.

"You think that now, Phillip, but when you've been in the water and the sun for awhile you'll be starving—and thirsty," she assures me. "And you'll want something besides alcohol."

She says "alcohol" with a smirk—ah, the virtue of identifying someone else's weakness—and stuffs two boxes, snack crackers and cookies, into what can best be described as a satchel, then cheese, apples, bananas, and two liter bottles of Coke. Ice goes into a separate Styrofoam cooler, and Nursey's inevitable pimento cheese sandwiches in sealed plastic bags go on top of the ice. So much for my wife's promise not to eat for the rest of the day. Then magazines, writing paraphernalia—although Susan never writes anything but a once-a-week post card to her parents—are placed in another bag alongside a first-aid kit. "You never know; last week April stepped on a starfish." I give up, close my eyes and, bliss, feel my brain start that wonderful fall off into welcome sleep.

"Time to wake up, darling." Through a haze, I hear Susan's cheerful soprano. "We're all ready to head down."

Still in that somnolent state brought on by deep and sudden sleep, I view the three women of my family from under half-raised eyelids. It's the comic version of the preparations for a D-Day landing. The bright colors of the rainbow surround and encase my females. Through bleary eyes, I see them as a painting, a multi-faceted arrangement of kaleidoscopic hues. A broad-brimmed tangerine and yellow straw hat hides most of Susan's face and matches the muumuu that comes down to the edges of her dimpled, globular knees.

Baptizing the Cat

One would think my wife bought these togs at an outlet-mall or discount store. But no, these garish combinations are from the expensive boutiques found in clusters on every boardwalk throughout Tampa and St. Pete. Thonged flip-flops, towels, sun glasses, in addition to the carry-all and the chest on wheels that Susan has on either side, and each girl holds her own bag. Like mother, like daughters, I accuse silently, and add that to my inventory of grievances. I do not want the girls to grow up with their mother's sense of taste, her satisfaction with the common, the banal, just because it costs a lot of money.

Chapter 6

The thought of Susan's failures as a mother reminds me to play "Father of the Year" and propels me up from the comfortable spot I've pressed into the cushions. "Of course," I chirp in my wife's exact note of mindless cheer. I retrieve the frosted shaker and glasses from the freezer and deposit them in their separate plastic pouches. Thank the gods for modern technology that gives us icy drinks on the beach. I grab my umbrella from the stand by the door, aware that in my multi-flowered shirt, baggy shorts, and safari hat, I'm as ridiculous as my women.

I bring up the rear of our small parade: out the condo, down the paved paths of Sandhills, then across the grass, and around the pool. May declares her allegiance to me and drops back, tries to match my strides with her thin knobby legs. "We're the Swiss Family Craines," I call out and hear an appreciative laugh from April. Not a sound from Susan, who doesn't seem to get the reference.

Might as well make the best of this domestic performance, I decide, while trying to come up with an appropriate method of wife disposal. A cooperative husband, one who trails five steps behind on the way to the shore, will keep Susan pacified and probably absolutely gleeful. She's so easy to please; a simple acceptance of the goodness in everyone that I guess was instilled by her Catholic upbringing. Although, now that I think of it, Father Clive, in those long-ago pre-nuptial classes, said that everyone possessed original sin—Adam and Eve and the apple and all that shit—and therefore is inherently flawed. Well, I guess that sin applies to me, but not to my simple Susan.

During the first months of our marriage, she'd often kneel by our bedside and pray out loud, "Thank you for my most cherished soul mate, Phillip."

I would add from my prone position, never quite able to force myself down on my knees beside her, "And thank you for my little helpmeet, Susan," but my words were always directed toward her beatific face surrounded by bleached curls, and even more so to her slender and, what I didn't know then, so transitory body. At times, it came to me that Susan's prayers went straight up to that convenient God she believed in, while my words swirled like cigarette smoke around us and never made it past the ceiling. My overriding enjoyment in those first years was Susan's blowjobs, which I thought she liked as much as I did. She'd started off in our lovemaking, a cooperative and energetic partner, but within a year or two, oral sex became my forbidden pleasure.

"Don't wave that thing in my face, Phillip," she protests now, always with some excuse not to enter into what for me was the very first course in lovemaking. "It's too messy, all sticky and gross." Susan squirms away. And after May's birth, well just forget anything but missionary. Her ample surfaces became stationary and resisting in ways I couldn't quite figure out. From then on, she developed a streak that reminds me of my own mother, compliantly silent, yet with a stiffness in her back that won't completely relax. Now in the sweaty, hard-breathing aftermath of love making, there is never any of that languorous sweet analyzing of what went on before. Susan either drops off to sleep instantly—what men are accused of—or she calmly, as if we'd stopped right in the middle of a conversation to perform a few sets of calisthenics, picks up the thread of our talk again. "What do you want for lunch tomorrow, Phillip? You said yesterday you'd never eat another pimento cheese sandwich again as long as you live."

Notwithstanding, my wife still says her nightly prayers on her knees, albeit now silently, and now I have to endure her lumberous getting down and up, compressing the edge of the mattress, jiggling me uncomfortably even though I am as far over on my side as possible and facing in the other direction. She stays especially long on her haunches if I've been curt or unpleasant with her, Nursey, or the girls.

Well, nothing untoward today, I promise, and grasp May about the waist and let her feet skim above the pavement and then the grass. I quicken my steps to catch up to my wife and older daughter. "We look like we're making a major move here, ladies," I joke; "all these supplies for just a few hours on the beach. I should have brought a sleeping tent and then we could have spent the night."

They giggle. Dad's made a joke. We walk in unison past the condo's pool enclosure, which holds five or six sunbathers.

With a complex of over 50 apartments, I'm always surprised at the emptiness around the pool. A few professional sunbathers sit or lie on the white plastic furniture, and at the edge of the water, one old man, equally brown, leans forward over his silver-haired belly, a most amazing feature, like some hairy melon left out in the sun. Throughout the winter months, he is the one constant: every morning and late afternoon, he takes his place on the steps in the shallow end, half in and half out of the water. He tries to make contact with me, throwing out introductory lines, like a lonely fisherman fly-casting for company. Over a half-dozen times, obviously having seen Susan's and my license plates on our two cars in the parking lot, he's called out, "You from South Carolina, son?" I nod but don't answer, let him know this shop is not open for business, and once or twice, even more rudely, I've ignored him altogether.

But today, in my role as paragon husband, I'm glad to catch the old fellow's gaze as witness to my good behavior. I raise my hand in salutation. "How's it going?" I shout out, realizing even as I pronounce these inane words how ridiculous everyday exchanges are. How's what going? How do you think it's going for a guy, at least eighty, who spends his last days sitting in tepid water between splashing children and dedicated sun worshipers?

"It's going like shit" is how he should answer.

Instead, the old guy lights up like a Roman candle. "Going great guns, son, couldn't be better," he trills in undiluted pleasure and waves a withered splotchy arm in salute.

The girls run ahead. I pick up my pace so that now I'm directly behind Susan as we start down the stairs, two flights leading to the hot white sand. She, cautious as always, slows—flop, flop in those thongs—so that I almost rear-end her. We juggle our cumbersome gear, and I feel an impulse to call out, "Watch your step" and also an impatient one to holler, "Get the hell out of my way," so that I won't catch her heel. Last night, the splintered gray framework of this staircase had seemed fragile and dangerous under me, and now the whole structure shudders beneath the weight of four people carrying too much stuff. Twenty uneven steps down and then a sharp right turn to descend another fifteen steps. I've counted them a hundred times . . . .

Abruptly, Susan's heavy bag jams against the railing, and the weight rips the wooden boards away from their rusty nails. The bag slips off her shoulder and falls, and my wife, with a stifled cry, pitches sideways. Instinctively, I grab. My hand, of its own volition, stretches out and catches her elbow. Her heaviness almost pulls me over, too, for she's completely lost her footing. In slow motion, I see one of her legs slide between my feet to lie on top of the uneven planks while the other leg slips beneath the landing. Grotesquely, she straddles the two-by-fours, up to her crotch. I hang on, squat and grab at the terry cloth muumuu. She reaches up with one hand and grips my shirt. With all my strength, I haul her up. We sprawl backwards in a tangle of spilled ice and squashed sandwiches. The girls squeal, run up the stairs, and throw themselves across us as if I need their added weight to keep their mother from plunging down the 25 foot drop.

"God damn it, get off me," I bellow.

Whimpering, my daughters back away. "You saved her, Daddy, you saved Mama from falling all the way down," April says. Reverence shines in her voice and in her teary eyes. May has reverted to three-year-old behavior, her fingers in her mouth, nervously laughing and crying, all at the same time.

Susan makes no sound. Her features are translucent, blanched of all color. The tail of my shirt is still clenched in her fist, and I can hear that some of the people by the pool have been drawn away from their tanning by the noise of my wife's tumble.

"Are you hurt?" I ask, and realize even as the question comes that Susan is wounded. She turns her body, revealing the inside of a thigh below the bunched-up fabric of the muumuu. A five-inch gray streak lies just under the skin; a knife-like splinter of half-rotten wood has jammed into her flesh. The bluish surface over the point-ed sliver is puckered, and a thin line of bright crimson blood trickles from the entryway.

"It burns," she says, and presses her face into my shoulder. A quiver threads her words and passes through her body.

Susan is just before all-out squalling or maybe just before passing out. Her eyes roll up.

"It's okay, it's okay, it's nothing, baby," I intone and pat her back, the same way I speak to May when she's fallen and skinned her knees. "We'll call the ambulance and get you to a doctor right away. Hang on."

"No, no, I want to go home first," Susan says. "I have to go home."

But the wound is something, I know, even as I stand and partly pull, partly hoist Susan to an upright position. The old man and three other gawkers, a young boy and two middle-aged women, press around the landing. The ladies, all hats, sunglasses, and oily tanned arms and legs, have come forward with outstretched arms as though to take my injured wife from me.

"No, no, it's all right," I say, and wave them off. "She's okay. It's this god-dammed staircase. I've been telling them it's a fucking death trap for months now, and this proves it."

There's a murmur of agreement from the watchers, which causes moral indignation to rise in my chest. It's the truth: that dark little manager is to blame and, behind him, all the inept money-grubbing relatives he conspires to employ. I resist an urge to vent my inven-tory of grievances against the condo association, starting with that ridiculous lawn mower cranking up at daylight. Well, now I have a case against them. But Susan whimpers and leans even more pon-derously against my side.

"If you'll help with these bags," I suggest.

A hint is all that's needed to cause the two women and the boy to grab up our unwieldy equipment. The old man, I note, slumps away to retake his place on the pool steps. Apparently all he wants is conversation.

Then slowly, because Susan limps and moans with each step, the rest follow. Back along the grass and concrete paths, our group re-traces the route we've just traveled, and then all of us, in a snarly muddle of people and baggage, enter into the cold stagnant air of our condo.

The coolness and the momentary thought that at least I don't have to waste an entire afternoon on the beach brings me into focus. I shoo the good Samaritans away. "Yes, yes, I'm taking her to the emergency room right away," I assure them. "Yes, I'll call if anything's needed. Yes, I'll let you know my wife's condition as soon as I know it myself." The clichés soothe them, and inch by inch I loom, advance toward them until they're out the door.

Susan refuses to go in an ambulance, so after that, it's the usual drill. I caution the girls not to answer the doorbell for any reason, and then I drive Susan to the urgent-care center three miles down the main beach road. I've rushed her to that sterile haven twice before when she had an acute asthma attack. At the time, I had no designs on her health, so oblivious I sat behind draperies, listening to other patients' complaints, leafing through two-year-old magazines, and waiting for the one beleaguered doctor to give her an adrenalin shot to ease her breathing. If those night runs were to do over, I'd take mental notes on what the physician said. I'd ask questions: What brought on that particular asthma episode? What foods or medications should she avoid? Could the closing-up of her bronchial tubes really be life threatening?

But today there is just the ordinary first-aid aspect of a long sharp piece of wood lodged where it shouldn't be. The doctor, a bespectacled youngster, who could have passed for fifteen—not the elderly one who cared for Susan previously—comes in with a folder. The stethoscope around the collar of his blue shirt and an ID badge clipped to his front pocket does nothing to keep me from thinking that here's a kid playing the role of doctor in a high-school play.

Dr. Youngblood—not his real name, but I don't catch it—goes over Susan's medical history. "Theophylline?" he questions. "Are you being monitored?"

Susan answers yes, once a week by her allergist.

"Good," Youngblood pronounces; "that's a tricky drug, gotta watch it."

Susan winces as the doctor, who I've come to believe is merely a physician's assistant, unfolds the towel I wrapped around her leg before leaving the condo. No need getting blood on the car seat.

"That must hurt," he sympathizes and pats her knee with childish fingers, the nails as gnawed as any first graders. My wife squeezes my hand tightly, shudders under this youngster's touch, but is still amazingly controlled. Seeing the injury anew, I realize the full degree of her stumble and fall. The grotesque purple-blue wound has swollen—blood that cannot escape—and all up and down the injury and on the inside of the other thigh are fresh-forming bruises, along with bloody scratches where the edges of the boards scraped both limbs. I control my own shiver of empathy and wish that this young medical pup would send me out into the waiting room.

No such luck. I must stay and see my wife's flesh numbed with several slow injections from a small caliber needle. She lies back, unable to see the procedure, but I'm left standing, wide awake, to witness the shots and the "manipulation of the epidermis." That's what Doc Youngblood says as he runs a scalpel down the distinct line where the large prong of wood lies just beneath the surface. "Just a little manipulation of the epidermis here," he informs, and dark blood spurts and then flows in tiny rivulets down the inside of Susan's thigh. He uses those words, figuring, I guess, that my wife will not be able to understand that he's actually going to cut the wooden sliver out.

I want to say, "She's not some ignorant beach tourist, kiddie." But given Susan's orange and yellow get-up and my Hawaiian shirt and flip-flops, who's to blame him for thinking we might not know what "epidermis" means.

Dizzy, I hold Susan's cool damp palm, and, to keep from passing out, I focus my attention on a point beyond this boyscout's shoulder to the wall of shelves filled with medical supplies. Bottles of cotton balls, swabs in glass jars, flat white boxes with different sizes of gauze, and faintly-yellow latex gloves hang out like so many colorless tongues or amputated fingers. It's a white-on-white composition that could bear the name "Hospital" or maybe "Surgery." Of course, there's no way to convey the overpowering smell of bleach, or the layering of that stink with the odor of alcohol and butadiene, and under it all I catch a whiff of . . . . I try not to breathe in because what comes to my nostrils is the stench of Susan's own blood, an odor of copper and salt.

Something inside me heaves, and a golden halo starts at the edges of my vision, slides inward, obscuring the chalky tableau before my eyes. Involuntarily, I step backwards to feel the hardness of the tiled floor under my heel. I grab at the edge of the gurney for balance. Then a stool is against the backs of my knees and I sit. Apparently Doctor Kiddie saw I was going down.

"You're not going to faint on me now, are you?" I hear him ask from what sounds like a long way off. Then in an aside to the nurse, he whispers, "It's why we used to not let family members stay with patients,"

"Oh, Phillip, I'm so sorry." Susan's voice is groggy from a pain shot but close, since now I'm sitting on a low stool, her face next to mine. My eyesight clears, and I yield to a rare impulse and lean in to kiss her. Astonished, she takes a little gasp, and I feel her teeth, and then her mouth softens just as I draw away.

"Daddy, you're back! Is Mama okay?" The girls let us into the condo foyer with all the fanfare given to returning war heroes. Their utterances go from respectful whispers—Susan is on a crutch and her leg is wrapped in a bulky elastic bandage—to joyful yelps when she explains and comforts them. "I'm really, really fine—now that the splinter is out."

"A splinter the size of a sword," I declare.

Nursey, returned from her Sunday outing, looks washed-out with worry under her dusky skin. Arms wide, she waddles toward my wife. "God bless you, Mr. Phillip, is all I got to say." She repeats this benediction, not looking at me but keeping her eyes fastened on Susan. "God almighty bless you, Mr. Phillip, for saving my baby." Both women snivel and hold each other tight. Nursey apologizes for not being on the scene, although she never accompanies Susan and the girls to the beach.

My wife always extends a perfunctory invitation. "You want to go with us, Nursey?" to the maid's reply, "No ma'am, not today." And after the door closes, my standard line to her is, "You sure don't need a suntan, now do you, Nursey?" She never answers.

But now, in this moment of thanksgiving, in their embrace—quite a feat for two 200 pound women; their arms seem too short—and lamenting that she was not there to catch my wife herself, she helps Susan off toward the bedroom. The girls follow, and I head for my beach bag, still heaped where the do-gooders dropped our bundles earlier, which now seems like a night's dream long past. The shaker in the insulated bag is frosty, the glass cold, and the first swallow of Rob Roy glides down my throat, an icy blessing.

Within moments, my daughters return, plop down beside me on the couch, and proclaiming my hero status for all time, wonder if my marvelous act will be written up in the newspapers, like articles about dogs that wake sleeping masters when the house is on fire.

I speculate, too, but silently: What if Susan had fallen all the way down? What if Susan had died with witnesses? But I also see a positive slant the rescue puts on my situation. "Fast-Thinking Husband Saves Wife From Fatal Fall" the headline could read, for surely a 25-foot drop to the packed sand below would be fatal. Not bad press to establish a loving-spouse reputation. But what if the fall didn't kill her? What about a partially broken neck from just another accident? After all, sand is not concrete; it gives a little. What about a Susan rendered a complete invalid—that happens too—a para or quadriplegic? Christ! Every inch of the Sandhills' condo and the house up in Spartanburg would have to be remodeled to accommodate a handicapped person with wheelchairs, ramps, lifts, and pulleys. Susan would be unable to take the girls to the beach, to their dance and music lessons, unable to shop with them for clothes or with Nursey for groceries. Not exactly my plan.

Yet, perhaps a year later, the same headline, surrounded by a black band would be, "Hero Husband Loses Wife To Mysterious Causes." Still, I would come under even more suspicion if Susan were disabled and then died. Hardly a month passes here in St. Pete without some ancient husband or wife trying to dispose of an equally antique spouse—for their own good, of course. Last month's news' story: thirty Valium in a Sprite.

Well, Susan's not a paraplegic, my second Rob Roy reassures me, and she's not dead. There will be plenty of opportunities to come up with the perfect crime. This certainty settles in just as April informs me that she's called her grandparents in Spartanburg and they're on their way down.

"Why'd you do that?" I ask, unable to hide the irritation in my voice.

"I told them they didn't have to come because Mama wasn't hurt bad, because you caught her before she could fall off the stairs. Grandmama said she couldn't believe it."

I can't believe it either.

Baptizing the Cat

Later, after a science fiction movie that Susan would never have let us watch, the girls go off to bed, and I check in to see Nursey fast asleep, sitting upright in a chair beside my wife, who is also soundly unconscious. The television set is going full blast. Except for the old maid in the bedroom, it could be any other evening in our household, everyone down for the night, everyone except me. I mix another shaker of Rob Roys, long on Dewar's scotch and short on vermouth, and go back over every inch of the day, analyze the what and the wherefores of my reaction.

Susan was ahead, the striped canvas tote bag slid down her arm, pushing against the railing; the wood crackled away from the rusty nails, and she, pulled by its weight, almost went with it. I keep coming to that exact point, see my right hand, as if belonging to another person, reach out, and with iron-strong fingers, I latch and hold on to Susan's elbow. My appendage, obeying some instinct I didn't know it possessed, has made me the champion.

I rerun the entire scene, but this time give it a different ending: the railing breaks, Susan is pulled over, and where no one can see, I give a tiny push with my toe to her heel. She plunges, screams, falls end over end. Her body lands below on the shadowy side of the staircase, where the rocks are, her head at an odd angle, which tells me her neck is broken—I can almost hear the crack and then, the only sound, waves washing back and forth.

Another morning, same shit all over again, except this time with in-laws.

I really don't know which is harder to take, people's hatred and disdain or their excessive praise and respect. It's like that card game, High-Low: ace, you're the hero, deuce, you're the goat. To either, my response is always the same; I come away feeling shabby and inarticulate.

After my in-laws and I go through the accident step by step, I say, "No big deal."

Susan, her leg now in a smaller bandage, counters with, "He snatched me right out of the air." The girls add their version as they saw it from farther down the stairs. May says, "Mama would have landed on her head." April nods in agreement. Where can you go with this conversation? Nursey plays the part of the Greek chorus, chiming in every few minutes from the kitchen with a reverential, "He saved my baby's life." Everyone talks at once, and then we all fall into stifling silence.

Some relief comes, from the adoring words and empty pauses, when I leave the dining room to get a drink in the kitchen, but even there Nursey hugs me before I can escape. With no qualms, I gulp down one quick straight scotch and pour an orange juice and vodka to take back to the table. Ha, today I can get away with all the liquor I want. Right now, I could come into the room buck naked, and they would clap. Sir Phillip Craine can do no wrong! "Jesus, Mary, and Joseph—and the little donkey"—as Susan says.

Finally, we sit down to breakfast. Miz Mildred is to my left, but I avoid her glance, a tortured-animal appeal from water-blue eyes magnified by unshed tears and metal-rimmed bifocals. This humble adoration coming from my mother-in-law is really too much. I'd prefer the hard-eyed squint she's always leveled at me before, for now I can almost read her thoughts. She regrets all the miserable criticisms she's heaped on me over the years. And although Susan's never relayed any of her mother's exact words, it was plain from the beginning that Miz Mildred was not completely taken in by my ex-Ranger, CIA-operative-artist pose. Did Susan, in spite of my many warnings against it, divulge my secret CIA consultant status to her mother? For sure. As for my drinking and off-color remarks, they always caused Miz Mildred to crimp her lips as if agreeing with some foregone opinion: "It's exactly what I expect from him." Now, every bit of that all-knowing censure in my mother-in-law's crinkled, freckled face has been replaced by this disgusting puppy-dog expression.

Congratulations, I tell myself. By bringing Miz Mildred and Ed down from Spartanburg, you've managed to make the dull routine in St. Pete even worse than before. If I wanted to endure the Bower milieu—three stocky, talky people filling every square inch of space and remarking on everything as if their opinions mattered—I could have stayed in South Carolina. At least the house up there has enough rooms for me to hide in, to avoid in-laws, and there's Susan's bridge and girlfriends to keep her busy. In this condo's one all-purpose room—a gross architectural mistake—we're on top of one another, and if I leave, Ed will want to tag along.

Baptizing the Cat

At the table, something of the family's southern thickness, a gluey syrup, flows over everything, even into the food itself. Nursey has prepared—or "fixed" as Susan would say—a sausage, egg, and bread casserole that she'd never have dared place on the table if it were only for me and the girls. The dish sits steaming amid the plates, glasses, and flatware, a soupy mixture with the look of yellow and gray congealed vomit. I cannot stand casseroles, foods all mixed together, with the muddy qualities of different colors blended on an amateur's palette.

Standing to the side to serve, Nursey scoops up a heaping portion of this mess, gesturing with her free hand for me to surrender my plate. Instantly I am returned to my mother's long-ago kitchen and the so-called healthy mixtures she inflicted on my grandfather and me. One Thanksgiving—I kid not—a tofu turkey; "tofu-erky" she called it: pounds of molded soy curd, glazed with some translucent brown stuff that had the consistency and smell of glue.

"No thank-you, Nursey," I say as softly as I can and look to Susan.

We, twelve-years-married, know each other's signals only too well. She catches the chilly metal in my response and glances up in that wounded-creature way I despise. What did I just read somewhere in the newspaper: "Bigamy is one wife too many. Monogamy is the same." An irrepressible temper builds behind my eyeballs. Both Susan and Nursey know my feelings about amalgamated food, and the only reason they dare place this insult in front of me now is that they think the in-laws' presence will tame my reaction. The last casserole dish that appeared before me like this committed suicide, an unfortunate slide over the edge of the table, assisted by my knife during the meal-time prayer. Squash, I remember, a blend of cheese, bread crumbs, eggs—the usual—I could make out all the mashed-up ingredients amid the shattered crockery on the tile beside my chair.

"It's a celebration, Phillip," Susan says, imitating my civil rejection of the dish to a tee. My wife is not without a certain amount of grit, especially in front of her parents. "Because you saved me."

Much to my regret, I swear silently, and it won't happen again. Aloud, I reply, "No food right now, Susan, I'm kind of sick to my stomach." I could add, at the sight of that ghastly combination dish.

I turn away from her disappointed gaze to catch my father-in-law's face. Full of the glow of existence, he extends his plate to the maid and with a grateful smile nods to me. "Give me Phillip's share, Nursey; a hero's got a right to a bit of nerves."

Somehow this statement manages to twist my rejection into something complimentary. I am in awe of this man, not so much of what he says as of his graciousness. The light of trust and good will glows through the drooping folds of Ed's jowls, the pallor of his forehead, the bushy, bull-horned eyebrows; all his features vibrate with a mysterious inward pleasure, beyond my comprehension. This old man is totally alive, at the top of his form. The daily reality of a fat, boring wife with no change in sight is no hardship for him. Why? I feel squashed beneath his grinning, lip-smacking acceptance. They all, even my daughters, receive a serving and start to wolf down their eggy breakfast. I close my eyes and take another long swallow of the screw-driver clenched in my hand.

Mentally, I clothe myself in a khaki army coat and from beneath its folds, I pull out a snub-nosed oil-gray Uzi. The look of surprise and then terror on all their ample, complacent faces is more than satisfying. "See," I bellow, in my imagination, to their startled eyes, "See, it's not so comfortable and predictable as you might believe. Even here in these gated confines, at your oh-so-safe morning table, with your mouths full of slop, even here you can be astonished, alarmed, betrayed."

I try for an instant to omit my daughters from this imaginary scene; they seem hardly wisps of flesh beside their corpulent mother and grandparents. But then I leave them in the scenario. Let them have their eyes opened, stop them from just biding time at meals until they can return to those damn computer games. Let them see how quickly their nonchalant acceptance of the way things are can be disrupted, destroyed in an instant. An asteroid could crash down through a roof. A tidal wave, a tsunami, could flood a shoreline and wash people out of ten-storied buildings, and here we all are, on the first floor. A beloved father, a staple in their lives, a pillar who holds up the walls, might also be a monster, a killer in his heart. And isn't that where it counts, inside? He who lusts in his heart, and all that? He's not what he appears to be, a good man, a wife saver, a . . . .

I stand, none too steadily, and announce, "You must excuse me, dear family. All this commotion has apparently taken more of a toll than I realized." I can hear the liquor slur in my voice, but they probably think it's only nerves, as Ed claimed.

"Oh, Phillip," Susan says, all contrition now.

"No, no." I wave her off, take my nearly empty glass, and with only one slight misstep—the toe of my slipper catching at the fringe of carpet—I head for the bedroom.

"God please, get me the fuck out of here," I whisper and throw myself across the bed. Of course, it's already made up—Nursey's housekeeping—made up so neatly that no one would ever guess that my wife's great body had slept in it overnight. I squeeze my eyes shut against the perfection of the room and the brilliant morning sun streaming in through the blinds. "Get me out of here, pleeease," I wetly mouth against the pebbles of thread that Susan has told me are candle-wicking, a fifty-year-old ecru counterpane that she rescued from her mother's attic. These people, who buy everything, throw nothing away. "If you don't give me some relief, God, I swear I'll have to kill her today," I confide into the old-fashioned coverlet.

Something in my brain goes "ping." That's it! I'm going crazy. How else does a sane human being decide to kill another? Yes! Susan is driving me insane—a short trip—with her screwed-up, apathetic life, her allergies, her compulsive eating, her addiction to reading. And, now, with her hoggish family added to the brew, I swear I'm over the edge.

I feel exactly as I did lying in the surf, night before last, resolving to murder Susan as soon as an opportunity presented itself. Of course, I missed my big chance yesterday when she fell, but so what? That accident and my part in saving her will only keep me from being a suspect later on. I try to recapture the surety I felt then. What were my plans? To be an ideal husband, and . . . the idea comes back . . . to start running again.

I roll over and rise from the bed. That's the answer. If I run, or even say I'm running, Ed won't follow.

Avoiding my slack, middle-aged image in the mirror, I change into the thin jersey shorts that I wore years ago when I ran every day. Why did I stop? Susan's fault. "I don't see how you can stand the heat," or "the rain" or "the cold, Phillip," were always her parting words as I went out the door. Why didn't I respond to her habits with equal criticism? "I don't see how you can eat another cracker, another piece of hard candy, a pimento cheese sandwich an hour after dinner. I don't see how you can sit in that one spot on the couch for three hours straight."

Chapter 7

At first, getting out of the condo seems like it's going to be easy, like leaving on all those fictitious CIA assignments. I announce that I've recovered from my nausea and that I'm off for a run, that fresh air will do me good. The family, all five of them, still anchored at the table, nod in approval. It's perfectly acceptable behavior for a husband and father to want to run; in fact, running is praiseworthy conduct: Phillip is allowed to run.

But before I can escape, Ed stands and grabs me by the shoulders. "Wait up, dear boy," he says, swallowing a mouthful of food and wiping his shining lips with a cloth napkin the size of a small tent. "I have an announcement to spring on you. We were going to hold off for a more formal occasion, after all the legalities were taken care of. That'll come later, maybe at the country club. But Mother and I made a decision last night on the way down." Ed pauses a second to let silence give his pronouncement more weight. "We talked it over thoroughly," he says, and hesitates again, almost as if rethinking his declaration. "We've decided, Mother and I, to make you a full partner in Bower Enterprises."

Admittedly my thinking processes are clouded by alcohol and the lack of any breakfast, so I nearly blurt: "I thought I was a full partner." Wasn't I getting exactly the same amount of money as Susan, deposited in my bank account every month? But some discretion, if not in my brain, still reigns in my mouth, and I keep it closed. I nod dumbly as if completely understanding Ed's and Miz Mildred's settlement upon me. What happens now? I wonder. Do I kneel and let Ed dub me with his breakfast knife, still covered with butter and orange marmalade?

My father-in-law snorts, backs up a foot, and formally extends his hand for a shake. "Welcome aboard, partner . . . and son," he intones, and his voice, full of emotion, sinks into a ceremonial timbre. "Our company now has four full-fledged leaders. You'll be at all the board and stockholders' meetings, share equally in all end-of-the-year profits, and . . . and get whatever else it is that we take out of our little candy company."

The mystery of this change eludes me, but I know in every synapse of my mind that Ed and Miz Mildred have spent the long dark hours between Spartanburg and St. Pete—they have a driver—going over every detail of this arrangement. Apparently, my heroic act has awakened the great *deus ex machine* that resides in the Bowers's chain of restaurants, truck stops, and motels—awakened it to my true worth. I scan the table. The adults' dishes are scraped almost clean, although the girls have barely touched their portions of that god-awful casserole. I'm hoping for a clue as to my award; does this change in my status mean more money? But Miz Mildred and Susan only give me twin beatific smiles out of their pale-moon faces, the female saints of the Bower lineage.

A thin trickle of gratitude runs through my chest. After all, what besides money do these people have to exchange for their daughter's happiness and life? They have no aesthetic appreciation, no artistic gifts, not even the curiosity or energy to find out if they have a talent. God damn, what a sorry lot we are.

I shake Ed's hand, giving him back the manly grip he expects, and then move around the table kissing each girl on the cheek. Forced to say something, I utter, "Your daddy's an important man, now." For her parents' sake, I kiss Susan on the mouth, a real pressing of lips for a change. They're one of her best features, exceptionally plush and softly wet, so I don't mind. I come to Miz Mildred, and here, God help me, for I cannot help myself, I murmur against her forehead, "Thank you, Mother Bower."

"Off, off, on your run now, Phillip," she chimes, and her freckled hands simultaneously pat and push me away. "You've deserved this all along; we just didn't know it."

My need to bolt gets me out the door, but what I really want to do now is to sit back down with Ed and Miz Mildred, push the break-

96

fast dishes aside, and say, "Bring on the papers; explain this partnership thing. What does it mean in actual cash?"

Patience, I counsel, and set off at a lope that soon turns into a steady jog down the grassy strip next to the highway. Just as I had to wait two months when Susan and I first married to verify that the $3,000, showing up in my bank account every first of the month, was an automatic deposit out of the Bower trust fund, so now I'll have to wait to find out what a partnership means. Ed said, "four full-fledged leaders." That means Susan has always been a partner, though she's never said a word. Did she know? "End of the year profits" certainly has a ring. Has she been getting those, too, tucked away somewhere in a secret account? I balance my check book every month, an onerous chore, and sock any surplus away in CDs in my name only. Who knows when the money might stop? With Susan everything financial is handled by the accountants in South Carolina, who might as well be the angels in the heaven. She signs credit card slips without a thought, never questioning the amount. Still, I've never really understood rich people. They act like they could care less about ordinary money concerns but always catch a ten-cent error in a restaurant tab, and all along they're as interested and curious as the next guy as to who owns what, who receives what—maybe more so. Ed knows to a figure the net worth of his golf-playing buddies. "Rounded off," he always says.

The fresh morning sky is a blue bowl overhead and thin curdled clouds keep the sun from being too hot. Even the sparse grass under my feet, strewn with the litter of passing cars, cannot spoil my lifted spirits. I just have to be careful not to step in a hole or on a bottle or can and turn my ankle. The energetic trot I started off with soon deteriorates into an acceptable brisk walk. There are no sidewalks next to these expensive seaside accommodations, and the space between condos and asphalt is apparently a no-man's land, belonging to neither city nor county, neglected except for mowing. It's still too early for the usual stream of cars to be whizzing by, and even though my head feels soggy from the drinks on an empty stomach, the green gleam of money has put a different slant on my disposition, an underpinning of good humor like the Veronicas I paint under the nature scenes I turn out so regularly.

The process, which I started with that old guy, Williams, on the Trubek Farm, is called a Veronica, putting one picture on top of another, named for St. Veronica, the woman who wiped Christ's face on his way to be crucified, leaving his countenance on the cloth. Before I dab the first bit of color from my palette, I always sketch an idealized woman's form onto the canvas; then I make the trees or shoreline or water conform, blend into those features. Sometimes I go back and highlight her eyes or lips, maybe an ear, the curve of a breast, just a touch to remind me she's there, though I might be the only one who can see her. It's a stunt to half-way fool the people who look at my oh-so commercial output, and the subterfuge keeps me entertained. Then, whenever I glance at one of my paintings, no matter how parochial, I can see the face, the breast, the curve of a thigh. It's a gimmick, too, that often makes a sale, if I choose to tell a potential buyer about the Veronica, trace out where the face or body is hidden. Usually it's a guy, who appreciates that sort of thing, that he can see a woman's lips resting along the edge of a stag's belly.

After two miles, even though I'm just walking, I'm relieved to reach Emily's Diner, a breakfast and lunch place. I'm totally spent, my calf muscles noodley, like the mayonnaisey macaroni salad Nursey serves up with Susan's beloved pimento cheese. I open the varnished front door set with frosted glass panels and step out of the brightness of the day into a dimmer radiance from the wide windows. My eyes take a minute to adjust, to see the chrome tables, the padded booths, and, not believing it, to see Towelhead hunched over breakfast at the bar. At first I'm not sure. Maybe all dark, bulky, thick-haired young men resemble each other from the back, especially if they're wearing jeans and plaid shirts. But he lifts his head and calls for more coffee, raising his cup and nodding to the waitress. It's the bastard himself!

I choose the booth directly behind this apparition, wanting to hear whatever comes out of his mouth, wanting to know why in the hell he's here without Catherine, and why in the hell is he dressed like all the other working slobs, eking by on day wages, who inhabit these seaside towns?

Baptizing the Cat

Well, it doesn't happen, talk that is. The gorilla shovels his food—his fork scrapes the glass plate—slurps his coffee, and leaves a five dollar bill on the counter. The breakfast special on the menu costs $4.25, plus tax; so what's the girl's tip, a quarter? The ape hikes his balls through his baggy jeans and slouches out of the diner to get into a beat-up, faded-green truck, with a sign, Wilson's Electric Company, on the door. Metal ladders, rusted boxes, and oily tools line the tops and sides of the vehicle, proving that it's not just a prop Towelhead has borrowed from some theatrical supply store to conceal his true identity—whatever that is. Also, in a spotlight of clarity, I see that Towelhead's left hand, pushing the truck door open, holds no sign of a wedding ring, not even a white line on the skin's deep tan. Night before last, when I watched from behind the patio divider, I was so absorbed in Catherine, the ring on her hand saying marriage, that I just assumed that Towelhead was the lucky husband, even to the point of some half thought-out observation that couples are often mismatched: an attractive woman with a burly ordinary man or vice versa a plain woman with a handsome husband.

Towelhead leans to insert the ignition key, guns the worn motor like a teenaged rebel making his getaway, jerks the truck into reverse. The white gravel in the parking lot sprays up. He drives off in the opposite direction from Sandhills. Mirrored in the diner's front window, I see my mouth slightly agape in amazement. I shut it. There's nothing left to do but order breakfast and commiserate with the waitress over Towelhead's payment on the counter.

"Last of the big tippers," I say, and nod toward the wrinkled green bill beside his abandoned plate.

"A regular Rockefeller," she replies. A short buxom woman of around sixty, her pasty cheeks and spent hazel eyes register exhaustion and it's only nine o'clock in the morning.

"What do you mean?" I question, give her my "want to talk?" look.

"Oh, you know, beach bums, they come down here loving the sand and sun, thinking that's all there is to life, improving their tans. But then, wake-up call, they have to do a day's work like everybody else. I was married to one of those fools."

Pitiful, plain, aging woman, like so many, like my mother, pinning all their hopes on a worthless man. My father disappeared before I was born, leaving my mother and me to Grandpa Emile.

"Got to get my paper," I explain and ease away from the table.

Seems like she wants to go on with her story, get into, God forbid, the details. I head outside to buy *The Tribune,* knowing that my concentration on the crossword while I'm eating will keep her at bay.

When I leave, I place a five-dollar tip by my coffee cup to make up for Towelhead's cheapness and my lack of interest. "Here's nothing for all the women in the world," I silently say to the waitress, whose back is to me now. "All the women who didn't luck out with a daddy or a husband."

I return from my run, presentably sweaty, and spend a half hour under the hot water of a shower.

"Can Nursey make you some breakfast, Phillip?" Susan calls into the bathroom, but I holler back, "No," not revealing that I've already eaten that required meal. God forbid that we skip any food in a day. My in-laws, thank goodness, have gone to the Marriott to rest up from their long ride. The plan is that we will meet up for dinner.

"All's quiet on the Gulf front," I want to say that evening, again another buffet. No mention is made of my new "partner" status, but still, I'm being treated like visiting royalty by Miz Mildred. May leans against my arm, whispering every now and then, "You saved Moma." As if could I forget.

"Did you find my gadget?" I question Harry in my low-voiced rendition of master-spy working undercover. It's early Tuesday morning and under the pretext of another run, this time on the track of the local high school, I've driven off from the condo, before eight. I did give the reddish-brown oval two slow laps, and now I lean eagerly against Harry's glass cabinet, full of burnished guns on gray velvet trays. The seaside morning sun blazes outside, and no one else is in the dim tunnel-like pawn shop. I've out waited a young stringy couple who were here earlier, picking out a wedding ring. Poor saps, I gave that union six weeks at the most.

"Sure, Mr. Craine, I told you I'd find one." Harry's emphasis on the word "find" suggests that, as luck would have it, he was walking along a deserted street and came upon an eavesdropping device lying on the pavement. He rises, his rolling gait carrying him into a back room and in a minute emerges with a bulky camouflage-green case held together with black plastic latches. It's almost exactly as I'd imagined. No gift-box wrapping for this sort of equipment, basic army olive says, "We mean business."

Harry rubs his sooty nail tips together, a safe cracker ready to feel out the combination to the vault. Chuckling, he deftly unsnaps the fastenings. "Top of the line, Wolf Ears, parabolic head-set microphones. You press the super-sensor against any surface with this special box next to it; the power pack goes into your pocket or clips on your belt, and you're in business. Like I said before, a 'Catch um with their pants down' baby. You're right in the room, Mr. Craine, right in their bed."

Okay. I let his indictment that I'm a voyeur pass without comment. Why not? It's true. Why else would a person want this kind of equipment? Not like a telescope where one can pretend to his mother and grandfather that he's looking at the stars instead of at the neighbors. I pull the different black pieces of apparatus out of their foam-lined beds, marveling at each plug, each wire. Apparently there's a demand for this type of gear, a factory somewhere that turns out private-eye stuff. Setting it all back into its compartments, I ask, "How much?"

"For you, Mr. Craine," Harry sighs, "only a thousand and," another sigh, "five hundred."

In an effort to appear an honest business man, appreciative of my patronage, Harry tries to meet my eyes, hold me stare for stare, but then his heavy-lidded pupils shift to the side and downwards. He pulls his full-blooded lips in over his teeth to keep from speaking, perhaps controlling an impulse to give me a lower price.

"Fifteen hundred?" I question.

"It's like new, Mr. Craine. Man said he'd never even taken it out of the case."

"Yes, I can see. No fingerprints—but mine. He must not have looked at it, either."

It's the same haggling routine that we go though about guns, but this time with an extra edge because I know Harry's about $500 over the retail price. I always enjoy saying audacious things to him, like, "How far away can you be and still kill a man with this gun?"

It adds spice to my purchases, leading him to believe that I might really be a dangerous person, capable of mayhem. But now there is a certainty between us. The bastard is trying to rob me, and like a small piece of invisible road kill, the deed lies alongside of the Wolf Ears case on the glass surface of his counter. He knows it; I know it.

"What's the allowable legal mark-up on pawned goods, these days, Harry? What does the law say?" I ask, and turn and lean back on my elbows on the counter. I gaze out the shop's front window. Worn gilt letters on the glass spell out RIGGER'S PAWN & EX-CHANGE. The street and buildings on the other side are bleached out white by the late morning sun. Impossible to paint that scene, even with several washes; it always turns out too monochromatic. People want bright colors: O'Keefe flowers, bigger and better than life, and the sexual implications thrown in for free.

The question and my disinterested posture catches the old trader off guard. His voice falls away from our normal bantering, bargaining rhythm.

"Now Mr. Craine, this was a special purchase, you know. You ordered it . . . I'd never have paid top dollar if I didn't know I already had a buyer."

"Seven fifty," I say, as if in amends for mentioning the law, rules that we both ought to obey. Still I do not turn back, and since it is my custom to always start out offering an absurdly low sum, I know Harry feels that we have returned to familiar ground.

"Ahh, Mr. Craine."

But then I ask, "Can I order this kind of equipment out of a magazine?" He takes an almost inaudible breath behind me. What does this character take me for, some rich fool who doesn't know that this type of apparatus in this standard camouflage box can be bought anywhere.

"Seven, fifty, my last offer," I say, knowing I have Harry at a disadvantage. Perhaps I should have ordered this device from a specialty gun shop in New York or out of the back of a *Soldiers of Fortune* magazine. But, now, even I can hear the bluffing inflection in my words. Seeing Towelhead in Emily's Diner this morning has revved up my curiosity about Catherine and her situation, and I can't see waiting the week it would take for that purchase to come in the mail.

Baptizing the Cat

So, on Tuesday evening, well after dark, I press the small transparent disk and the tiny black box from Harry's $1,000 Wolf Ears set against Catherine's sliding glass door and just to the side of the drapes, where it can't be seen. To make sure the rooms are empty, I've waited a good fifteen minutes, staring from my hiding place into the living room, taking in that dead awareness that exists in every space when its occupants are away. Then I rushed, put the pieces in place, and hurried to position myself back behind the wall. But I needn't have bothered. It's ten-thirty before a key turns in the lock and a figure walks out from the short hallway. A light comes on.

Catherine's bottom lip is thin and yet has a distinct line in the middle separating its softness. I see this indentation, which wouldn't be noticeable except for the full flash of light that blazes up out of the top of a lamp on a table. The glare also illuminates the feathery tips of her eyelashes, tops and bottoms, the edges of pale brown eyebrows, two shallow lines across her forehead, and wisps of sandy hair, which she brushes away with her fingers. The strands slip back over her brow. She blinks, her eyes adjusting to the light. Then in an action I've seen others do—Susan, just the other morning—Catherine raises her head and scans the room, eyes questioning, shoulders slightly hunched.

She takes a breath, almost a sigh. The thin gold chain at her neck trembles, and her small breasts in a dark brassiere rise under an almost-sheer navy top scattered with small abstract white flowers. She could be an advertisement in a *Vogue* magazine of the privileged woman with golden legs and arms and tousled gilded hair. White walking shorts and leather sandals give her entire appearance an easy, dressy, beachy look. What was this elegant lady doing with a jock like Towelhead? And I'd bet money her ensemble wasn't put together by one of those aggressive sales people at the boutiques, who set themselves up as experts on what to wear to the shore. It's those people who dress Susan in those horrific green and orange muumuus and matching hats and carry-alls. But then again, what can you do with a fireplug figure?

Catherine turns on two other lamps beside the white leather couch, turns, scans the room again, and whispers to herself, "Hello?"

I flinch.

Her low, knowing voice, so urgent and close through the little foam pieces in my ears, rattles me, sends goose flesh up my arms and across my shoulders. She walks back to the kitchen out of my line of vision but still within hearing range of the super-sensor. Through the ear pads, I hear the preparation sounds of something to eat and drink, the rending of a pull-off tab from a metal can. Also, after a minute, along with these loud, ordinary rackets—I adjust the volume down—there is a slight shushing undertone that at first I take to be mild static in the transmitter. Maybe the plugs aren't securely turned in their slots? Then I realize what the fuzzy noise is. Catherine is half-way whistling, an odd contemplative piping between teeth and tongue. Grandpa Emile did the same in his shed, going about some chore he'd set for himself. Identifying the sound, I imagine Catherine's finely-drawn lips pursing, pulling back from her teeth. Her range of tones varies from a soft trill to a back-of-the-throat sibilant throb, and then converts back to hissing. I heard that sound often enough in my growing-up years so that now I do it myself, whenever I'm painting, when I'm really into the colors. Background music to real work.

Since I can't see, only hear the woman, I focus instead on the small transparent disk sticking like a leach to the glass. I've been waiting in the October damp for over an hour, alternately feeling excited and foolish. I grew so cramped and sleepy and also afraid that the guard from the front gate, an overpaid boob, would round the building in one of his sporadic checks that I was almost ready to give up on tonight's reconnoitering. And now, damn it, even though she's returned, I can't see her.

Then, still barely whistling, she's back in the visible room, carrying a white carton in one hand and a wine glass of colorless liquid in the other. The whistling stops, and again she scans the walls and the double-glassed patio doors as though reading the air for signs. She mutters, "Get a grip, girl." Tonight, her tone falls within a medium register, not the low, languorous tone of that evening with Towelhead. And her voice holds an easy note of command. Firm, confident, she definitely wouldn't employ that self-deprecating southern whine that Susan uses whenever she has to deal with a man. "Would it be possible to come fix the air-conditioner sometime this week?"

Baptizing the Cat

Always an imploring up-note at the end of the sentence. "Why did your run take so long this morning, Phillip?" Susan questions me in fake humbleness, a gentle twitch to my extended leash. One would think that my wife had no education, no strength of purpose, none of daddy's millions behind her. Yet I know that lying just beneath her surface is a great passive assurance, a resistance like an iceberg, large enough to sink a battleship—large enough to sink a husband.

Catherine turns on the television to the sound of a stock market report, some commentator declaring it's been a good day because the Dow is up 120 points. "A positive feeling, with a qualified victory in Iraq; one that will keep Saddam Hussein in check," the man says in one of those cultured voices that carry no identifying regional inflection. Tomorrow, if the market is down, he'll say the exact opposite. She switches from the news to a music channel, Mozart or Chopin, I think, much softer.

Catherine eats small bites out of the white box that looks like leftover Chinese and takes long swallows of what I realize is ginger ale or Seven-up since small bubbles show on the insides of the glass. But she's not paying any attention to the television; the music is just something to fill the air with noise. Instead, every few minutes, like a tense animal, a doe that senses danger, she raises her head and slowly, with darting eyes, surveys the room. At each inspection, I stop breathing and avert my own eyes down to the grass beneath my cramped crossed legs in the dark. Can she be so attune to her surroundings that she suspects she's being watched? Shit, can she see me? Hear me? Catherine rises and walks directly toward the sliding glass doors. My heart thuds in my chest; its pounding reaches my ears just as her hand touches the handle and flicks the lock up. With a practiced, energetic pull, she slides the heavy glass panel open.

Instinctively, I bend my head and scrunch my shoulders against the uneven surface of the wall, even though I reason that Catherine can't possibly see me through the cross-cut slot in the stucco—the lamp light is on her side and dark is on mine. I also wonder—funny what pops into your mind in a crises—if, in my attempt to flatten against the wall, I might be squeezing a spider, a black widow or a brown recluse? I'll come away bitten ten times, unable to explain where the bites came from. But I wasn't stung the other night when

I kept vigil in the same location. And where in the hell is Towel-head? At least he kept Catherine's attention inside the condo where it belonged.

I hold my breath. Catherine stands at the door. I can hear her breathe through the ear pads, short spasms with total quiet in between, and, except for the roar from the ocean below and the fluctuating currents of air that eddy around the building, there's no other sound. I try to pull in whatever energy I might be transmitting, for I feel the woman's entire attention is focused on the patio and the wall, scanning the grass out to the line of heavy weeds that's too close to the drop-off to be mowed. Is she holding her breath, too? Will she see the disk and the little box that I thought were so well concealed just by being set off to the side beyond the drapes? You damn fool, I curse. Just stay squatting here for another three seconds, and she'll find the box, and then she'll walk out on the grass and spot your stupid-ass carcass crouched up against the wall. She'll scream. And if you stand to run, she'll see your stupid-ass face and be able to identify you to the police.

These thoughts flash. I tense my calf muscles, ready to spring up and away. Better to be seen from the back, I calculate, fleeing down the dim passageway, than be confronted face to face, hunkered like a toadstool against the wall.

At that very moment, the telephone rings, horrendously loud in the ear pads. I falter, sag down with the sound. It rings again, and the reverberations cause my flanks to quiver, caught somewhere between rooted to the spot and full-out adrenaline flight. I hear Catherine's steps turn, not sliding the door closed, to go back into the condo. She stops the nerve-jangling trill coming through the ear pads by lifting the receiver. Now, I hear her every word, doubled, coming faintly through the doorway and then amplified coming through the receivers.

"Hello . . . . Oh, Claire, it's you. Thank god. I'm so antsy this evening. I'm ready to jump out of my skin."

I risk a glance upward through my odd-shaped spying porthole but just as quickly lower my head, and again I hug the wall. For although Catherine, phone up to her ear, is seated back behind the coffee table, her clear face and strangely dark eyes are still fixed in the direction of the open glass door, riveted to my position, just where the patio wall juts out.

"I've got to learn to be by myself, Claire. At least for a night or two."

My overwhelming desire is to sit tight and hear whatever else Catherine might say to this anonymous Claire, but sanity urges me, still close to the wall, to crawl as quietly and as quickly away as possible. "Escape, escape!" something screams inside my head. "Man, you've been granted a reprieve; leave while you've still got a chance." That woman in there will talk a few minutes, and the next thing you know she'll be out those doors and right on top of your ass again. She's the one in the horror movie who, against all common sense, with a single guttering candle, climbs the stairs of the haunted house to find out what's making the scary sounds.

Once more, I rise on straining legs, halfway between kneeling and crouching, just enough to catch another glimpse of Catherine's stare, still directed squarely toward the wall I'm hiding behind. I duck. She's speaking, but watching. Her calm voice and position behind the coffee table imply that she's taking a break and in a few minutes will be back outside.

Okay, I'm out of here. Fuck the equipment, fuck the long hours I was going to spend finding out about this woman. Fuck everything! Let her discover the box and the disk and freak out, call the police. God, my fingerprints are all over the black plastic! But who cares; they can't ink-pad every condo owner on the premises for a comparison. Or can they?

I ease up first onto one foot and then the other, and slowly, and then a little faster I inch along the wall. The surface scratches a bit, but the grass makes no sound and gives under each shift of my weight. Through the ear pads, I hear Catherine's voice, now a shade more relaxed, launch into a description of her inability to be alone.

"It's really all right during the day, you know. I go to the gym and the school in the morning, do my stint at the museum after lunch. It's a great place to read, right beside that winter scene of Monet's." Pause. "No, hardly anyone ever comes in. No. Remember I'm still married; very few men try to pick me up. And I'm still wearing my rings . . . ." Her words trail off as if these complaints have been said a thousand times before and Claire on the other end of the line understands all the history. "At least you still have Penny at home." Another pause. "Oh yes, I remember, teenagers are lousy company. My boys and I had great times together until Rand Jr. turned thirteen. Now, all I have to look forward to in the evenings are a couple of drinks."

Teenagers! She's my age, I reflect with each footstep taking me farther away from Catherine's wall and the view I so wanted to see. Her voice through the foam ear pads now sounds even more relaxed, but the reception dwindles. Apparently to have any clear reception, one must be within sighting range of the box or at least not have any walls between you and the prospect. By the time I'm at the corner of the building, where the hallways and stairs intersect and funnel the wind, I can barely hear Catherine's voice and am only able to catch a word or two . . . "not be afraid . . . not going to . . . outside"

At the word "outside," I stop and shudder, hold onto the metal railing to keep from collapsing down on my knees. Static rattles through the pads, and I jerk them off to hang around my neck. How am I going to get that damn disk and box back before Catherine finishes talking and again checks outside and finds them? If this peeping-tom stuff—peeping and listening—comes to light, I won't just be disgraced and divorced, I'll land in jail. The headlines blaze across my mind: "Phillip Craine, son-in-law of magnate, Ed Bowers, founder of the Bower's candy and restaurant chains throughout the U.S. found guilty of . . . ."

Chapter 8

Unable to think of the exact crime I'll be charged with: "Stalking," "Peeping Tom," whatever, still the vision of the newspaper headline stays with me. My father-in-law, who thinks a wild night on the town is a round of beers and a few racks of pool "away from the womenfolk," would have no understanding of this escapade. The very idea of hanging around a woman's apartment with listening equipment would boggle his single-hearted mind.

"So why the hell are you doing it?" I whisper, and rap my temple with the knuckles of a clenched fist. The surprisingly painful blow causes my eyes to water and my ear to ring, but despair urges me to move even farther away from Catherine's condo. "Get the lead out!" I order and climb the stairs. I trot a couple of steps down another hallway, turn left, pass the apartment directly over Catherine's, turn right, and come out on a balcony that overlooks the squares of backyards on this side of the complex. A single rectangle of light streams from Catherine's patio. Its uneven gleam on the grass shows clearly the part of the sliding glass door that is covered by blinds and the part that's open. I can even see the small dark shadow of my listening box set off to the side. Now that I'm beyond detection, I stop. Apparently Catherine is still on the phone, for between the gusts of wind and under the ocean's steady background noise, I hear a vague murmuring through the headphones around my neck. I put them back on my ears, and the reception is distinct again, like Catherine's right beside me.

"Oh, he saw me reading *The New Yorker* and came on like some intellectual—not that he's dumb—asked if I was attending the lecture the Art Center had on metaphysics. Really a good guy and smart, too. Took a few philosophy courses at some junior college up in Georgia. Works here for an electrical company. I liked him well enough, good looking and kind, something you don't often find. But God, way too young. When he told me he was only twenty-seven, I had to lie, say I was thirty-four. Which was fun, too, for about a minute. Help me here, Claire, I'm floundering."

Towelhead! I know immediately and stand immobile in the windy tunnel of the concrete passageway. The sound in the ear pads is clear now, much better on this second floor where I can see anyone coming from two different directions. But Harry must have used salesman's exaggeration when he said this gear would pick up anything within three city blocks. Three blocks with no buildings, maybe, but this single test run has proven that one solid stucco wall cancels out most sounds. Still, the reception from the balcony is remarkably bright and now underneath the sound of Catherine's talking, I hear another voice—male. I catch phrases in between her sentences, "Three kilos, and he'll make a delivery every three months. We'll make the drop on Thursday and pick up the cash the next day."

"Men," Catherine says. "I wish I were a lesbian." She laughs, a quick hiccuppy chuckle that recalls her tone on the night she was with Towelhead. "I came within a hair of going to bed with that kid. Can you believe it? Out of pure frustration and loneliness. I even had my bra off. But when I backed out, he wasn't pushy or mad or anything, just disappointed. He has a couple of girlfriends, one in Tampa and one here in St. Pete. You know how these young people are today; sex is no big deal like it was when we were growing up. I'll bet I was the last virgin in Tampa when I married Rand."

Whoa, so she didn't go through with it, didn't have sex with Towelhead after all. My thoughts are as muddled as the two conversations coming through the device, much like tuning into two radio stations at once, except I hear a man's words more clearly when Catherine isn't talking. I decide I've picked up a television show or a cell phone and lean far out over the balcony railing to see down the length of the building. At the very end of the row, a narrow sliver of muted light lies across the grass. The call or show must be coming from that apartment.

Catherine's voice takes over, "An affair wouldn't make things easier. Rand already thinks I'm sleeping around, guilty of what he's always done. Not that I ever gave him any reason—before now. The years pass, I loved him for the life we'd had together, for the children. I obeyed the rules, even if he didn't. Besides, divorce would have killed Dad, all that old-timey Catholic stuff. But he's gone, and I want to find out what I've been missing." She pauses, and I can her taking deep breaths. "All I really want is to find someone to love. Is that so terrible?" Again pause. "I'd be fair in a divorce, give Rand half the business, half of everything."

Now, unlike before when I could feel Catherine picking up on my presence, now all the intonations in her words are completely at ease and factual. Could it be that since I can't see her, her sense of being observed is deflected?

The interfering male voice comes through again, "We can do this operation from now on; it's perfect. I'll be back in touch Thursday." There's a click in my ear.

I stay, hanging out over the railing for another full minute, but there's no change in the light from the end apartment and no more male voice coming through the ear pads. I pull back in, bend stiff knees to sit, and adjust my bony rear against the cold, grainy floor. This corner of wrought iron railing and stucco wall makes a damn uncomfortable place to sit. I jot a mental note: bring a mat next time and a big beach towel to hang over the railing, too. Will I come back? Of course. Although the fall wind on this second floor balcony carries a definite chill.

The conversation from the apartment below continues, with Claire apparently holding down her side, for all I can hear now from Catherine's side are agreements, "Yes, he's upset, because he's afraid he'll lose the business. And he's completely obsessed with that house."

In almost total darkness—there's no moon tonight, and the light from the condo's windows doesn't extend to the beach—I watch through the railing the barely visible white lines of waves as they succeed one another, endlessly different, endlessly the same. I keep check on the square of illumination on the grass, making sure that Catherine doesn't decide, even while on the phone, to come out and take a quick look 'round over the patio again. At least from up here,

I'll be able to tell if she does and if she spots the box. Will she grab it up? Will she shriek? Serve her right, gutsy bitch, just to open her door that way, not even check to see if a burglar or rapist is outside.

What is she up to all day? At what Museum does she read and pick up men? What kind of life is that? I remember the Monet at the Tampa Museum. And who in the hell was that other voice on a cell phone? The man talking trash about kilos, a drop off, and cash. Son of a bitch! I should have gotten this equipment before now. There's more going on in Sandhills than I ever suspected. How much would three kilos of coke bring today? I never dealt with anything like that back in college. A few ounces of weed I shared with friends, usually winding up in the red instead of making any money.

Totally wiped out, I rest my face against the rail and feel my eyelids, heavy, start to descend like the roll window shades in my grandfather's house. I used to jerk those thick waxy things all the way down, by a string, and let them fly up with a snap, flip over fast at the top. A couple of times the little mechanism inside the roller broke, and then I couldn't get the shades to hold their original position, all the same width from the bottom sill, the way Grandpa Emile demanded, the way he liked things, neat.

Neat and orderly, the way he kept my father's things, the other Philip—the one with only one "l" in his name—in a locked, strapped trunk in the attic. Picking the lock, I found my mysterious father's birth certificate, his high-school diploma, a raft of school papers, essays, and report cards, A's and B's; and under those documents, old school-letter jackets and sweaters, even dress trousers and faded blue jeans. I unfolded and punched out a creased, moldy leather football helmet and pulled it onto my head, only to feel entrapped, to see my pale face reflected in the single dormer window, my forehead pressed down into wavy wrinkles. In a square fake-leather album, most of the pictures not glued in, I saw the grandmother I never knew and a young Emile, sinewy and dark-haired. They are posed with an almost replica of myself as a fat baby, a youngster, a teenager wearing the sweaters, the trousers, the jeans. My father.

I keep my eyes closed, deciding that I'll rest them for a second. I can listen to Catherine's feminine chit chat, catch a faint trace of that sexuality she employed but did not use completely with Towelhead the other night. And I'm barely aware of the flip of the switch as sleep shuts off the world. I'm suddenly behind the window shades, pulled down low, in my grandfather's house, all neat, tidy, and dark.

I rouse to a low clouded moon, barely up at the ocean's edge, and everything seems to have jumped out of a picture frame, an enlarged dreamscape, a nightmare. I'm not sure if I've been out for five minutes or five hours. Where in the hell am I? There is nothing but the physical hardness of the floor, the railing's shadows stretched across my legs, and the sharp, painful line I feel from the wrought iron bar imprinted onto the flesh of my cheek. Then my brain grabs the reins of recall and pulls me back in. My nefarious adventure of the evening returns in a single spasm: Catherine in her apartment, my listening through the ear pads, running up the stairs, and falling asleep here on the balcony.

A glance through the railing shows me that Catherine's square of grass is no longer lit, that she's gone off to bed. My Rolex, a wedding gift from Susan's family—I never wore one before and have not been without this one since—shows that it's two a.m. Jesus Christ, I've been asleep for almost four hours.

Getting up is not easy. I'm damp and every muscle fiber in my legs and back feels frozen. Still, I'm not hung over, having foregone my customary shaker of Rob Roys earlier. I wanted to stay absolutely clear for my first real foray into spying. I pull myself up, grasp the rail, and slowly stretch, un-kink cramped calves and the backs of my thighs. I imagine the story I would have told the night watchman, if he'd come upon me in the dark. "I was out running, listening to my Walkman"—here I would pull the ear pads down around my neck—"and leaned up against the wall to watch the moon rise and fell asleep." Since there's no door or even a window in this short span of hallway, nothing but the rail-enclosed, dead-end balcony facing out toward the ocean, it's a perfectly plausible story.

And yes sirree, I plan to spy again. This balcony perch is so much better to listen in on Catherine's life, although it's not going to be as satisfying as watching her slender figure from behind the patio wall. Still it's definitely safer. And maybe I'll hear more about kilos and drop-offs, too. I'll definitely have to find a better place to put the box and the disk, and from up here I'd be able to make a quick get-away along the second-storied corridor with no one seeing me.

Now, intent upon retrieving the pieces of equipment, I retrace my steps down the hallway and stairs and snort at my remembered panic. Why had I been so afraid? I repeat my previous actions, and edge my way along the wall and stand silently. I stay behind the wall for a good ten minutes, listening. It was the first and best thing I learned in my short time of Ranger training: "Never test the water with both feet." Hesitation, more than once, kept me from making an ass of myself, of jumping in, saying or doing something stupid. I peek through the top cross-cut hole in the stucco, squeeze my eyes tightly shut, and open them again. The lackluster moon is hardly a light source, but still it's brighter here, outside the apartment than inside. I'm sure Catherine finished her talk long ago and trundled off to bed since the television set is silent and the lamps that were on earlier are turned off. No glimmer comes from any of the bedroom windows, although I expected at least one small light. Does a lone woman feel comfortable, asleep in total darkness? Apparently Catherine does. Susan and Nursey are fanatical about "nightlights," little white plug-ins in the wall sockets, which cause a dull halo to constantly glow in every space of our condo and also in the Spartanburg house.

I scan the living room once, twice. Deserted, and yet I hesitate. Go home, I tell myself, collect your shit, and then you won't have to sweat Catherine's finding the box and the disk in the morning. I lower my eyelids and open them to look again. Some unseen movement or energy sounds a warning: a whiff of cigarette smoke. Then, like a shifting mirage, a dark image filters out, outlines itself from the even-darker background at the very edge of the open glass door. My God! What a mistake! I've looked through, past the door frame, past what I assumed was closed plate glass into the living room, rather than looking at what was within four feet of my nose. Holy shit! Right there, right at the edge of the threshold: Catherine, smoking. The glowing ash of a cigarette casts a barely discernable radiance across her face. She half reclines in a sling-backed chair ten inches inside the condo and ten inches out on the concrete. Had she moved over the metal runners, she would have been completely outside, and a foot closer to the slots in the stucco wall. She could easily have heard me creeping along and also easily seen the box and disk.

For the second time in one blasted night, I'm back in the same ridiculous position of being scared spitless. I hold my breath and pray that the loud surf below and the wind whipping through the corridors has muffled the sounds of my approach. Catherine lifts her hand and draws on the cigarette; it glows a shade brighter. Two in the morning and with all the lights out, why isn't this broad back in the bedroom? Why is she sitting in the doorway, a solitary phantom in total darkness? A concealing robe wraps her body and her bare feet are propped up on one of the ice cream parlor chairs.

What is the old saying about "assuming" making an ass out of someone? "You ass" I curse silently, not daring to inhale or exhale. But at least I'm standing, not squatting as I was before, I console myself and take giant steps backwards, long, slow, and, I hope, silent strides to return to the hallway.

This time there are no detours, no climbing of stairs to accidentally find a better listening post, no out-waiting Catherine so I can retrieve the equipment. This time, like a hound, I head straight for my own apartment and, upon reaching it, press the buttons in the lock, hear the hiss and the click, and let myself in. Christ, that was close! So what if Catherine finds the box in the morning? To hell with her and the equipment, too! To hell with the $1,000 I paid. Gratefully, in the dim glow of Susan's and Nursey's night lights, I slide down onto the cushions of the couch, pull one of Nursey's absurd orange and black crocheted afghans up over my chilled legs and shoulders, and pray to stop shaking, pray for oblivion. Forget it, I tell myself. Think about it tomorrow.

Of course, this escapist ploy never works. Now that I am entirely safe within my own boundaries, all I can do is return again and again to the turbid picture of Catherine sitting just inside her glass doors in chilly obscurity. Catherine totally without light or entertainment, Catherine practically immobile, smoking a cigarette. Why had she stayed awake so long? After she finished talking to her friend, did she deliberately set a chair in the doorway so she could find out what made her so jittery earlier in the evening? Could she be that brave? Was there a gun in her lap? Perhaps she'd gone to bed—some time during my unconscious period on the balcony—and then, unable to sleep, got up again. None of these explanations, the list of possibilities, seems exactly right. My overall impression of the evening, of this woman in the shadows, is one of resolve and melancholy, a photographic negative superimposed on a somber canvas.

I turn and try to find a satisfactory position by pressing against the cushions at the back of the sofa, raise one knee up over their edges. The couch always seems like a great idea, comfortable, when I first lie down, but in thirty minutes or so it turns into a thoroughly unsuitable bed. I regret my missed Rob Roys, regret not being able to sneak back into Susan's and my bedroom and slide under the covers, and especially I regret this entire foolish enterprise.

I have to stop thinking or I'll never get to sleep. I fumble across the end table, turn on the radio, find Public Broadcasting—Susan doesn't like all their "unhappy" reports—and listen to the BBC, to the Brits, as they say, "read" the news. Tonight, the program is all about the differences between American and Russian engineers—who cares?—and the Mir space station. The American engineers plan meticulously, while the Russians, with hardly any forethought, just throw their satellites up into the sky. Something about the Russians being able to take advantage of improvisation, the chance thing that makes things go right. What we called in art school "the happy accident," like the coincidence of seeing Towelhead in the diner and realizing that he and Catherine were not married. The happy accident, I think.

Then, as on the balcony, without warning, I fall into that dark chasm of reprieve, into sleep.

The next day is all anti-climax. Although that's not exactly true since nothing climactic happened the previous night, except in my head. I wake around ten to the girls sitting on the floor in front of the TV set, watching Saturday morning cartoons. Susan allows this two-hour morning slot so she can sleep late on the weekends; but what does she do on week days that's so different?

"We kept the sound turned down, Daddy," May twists and whispers. She's still in nappy pink pajamas, her incredibly tiny wrists

116

and ankles sticking out beyond cuffs and pant legs because she grew three inches this past summer. Long strands of blonde hair hang in uncombed tongues over her shoulders, and she has that sleepy look of funk and innocence. "If we just had a TV in our room like Nursey." This is an on-going argument between Susan and the girls, but here I agree with my wife. Television turns, too easily, into a drug, a constant drone of sound and pictures. Still, I don't come out openly on my wife's side because—well, because. I mumble, "We'll see" and rise to go into the kitchen. April, barely visible, hooded in a blanket she's dragged from her bed, doesn't acknowledge my existence. She's too engrossed in the flat, luridly colored characters on the screen.

I don't feel too bad this morning, and again I congratulate myself on abstaining from my beloved Rob Roys. After saying, "Morning" to Nursey, I ignore her question, "You slept on the sofa last night, Mr. Phillip—in your clothes?" I guzzle a cup of coffee and head out for a morning run around the condo. She's right; I'm still in my jogging jacket and pants from yesterday.

With no real plan, I leave from our salmon-colored door—incongruous against the pink stucco—and set out at a brisk walk along the concrete corridors throughout Sandhills. The complex is three stories high. Actually, if I ran every floor, up and down the stairs, it would be a pretty good workout of about three miles. The air is cool, and I'm glad for long pants, instead of the shorts I usually wear. I jog without thinking, round the back of Catherine's building, and within five minutes come to her section of grass. The sliding glass doors, that so totally fooled me last night by being open, are now tightly closed. The heavy ecru horizontal blinds and the same color curtains behind them are drawn, and the black-gray box and transparent disk, which last night loomed so large and caused so much agony, now seems absurdly small and of no consequence. The bright October sun slants sideways, dwarfs it, makes a small shadow of two black brush strokes against the glass.

I dart across the patio, swoop with my left hand—not often am I this dexterous—and with one deft motion pry the disk off with a forefinger and grab the box. Then I sprint, as if all the furies of hell are behind me, past the last pink-stucco wall, past the last line of manicured sod, past the last apartment where the conversation last night sounded like a drug deal in the making. Or did the ear pads pick up a television broadcast?

I stop short of the drop-off that towers over the discolored lines of eroded beach before I fully comprehend that this unplanned, improvised morning foray has been a success. The crappy little accessories are in my hands! After last night's two nearly disastrous episodes behind Catherine's patio wall, it's all so surprisingly simple that I want to click my heels together, do one of those spraddle-legged victory dances that football players perform in end zones. Perhaps this is the way all ideas should be executed: have a vague concept and then, not thinking too much about the details, the hows or whys, just go all out, full tilt—like the Russians, as the BBC reported on last night's program.

The wind whips my face and clothes, and the lines of waves make white squiggles, like from a fan tail brush, out to the horizon. I'm exhilarated, inspired. I've been too much like those American engineers, who spend months, even years, charting and calculating, just to see their projects end in disaster. I must take the Russian engineers as my models, who, with little pre-planning, use the "slap-dash method" and start building. This is what I want, exactly: a chance to get rid of Susan, a chance with this strange, alluring woman in apartment 3D. Somehow I feel linked to her already, drawn, compelled to find a new life, and somehow the key to that life is Catherine. As for Susan . . . here I hesitate, not wanting to use the word "dead." I settle for . . . well Susan—well—Susan out of the way. Because who knows what circumstances will dictate? I'll just head in that direction and take advantage of whatever opportunity comes along.

As I walk slowly back to our apartment, I admit I've already missed one fantastic chance that fate offered, as if on a platter, because I wasn't aware that opportunities present themselves in that fashion. If I'd just been the least bit alert, I'd have given Susan that extra nudge that would have sent her over the edge of the landing. Could I have done it? Perhaps it wouldn't have worked out to my advantage, but who knows? Now I'm ready, prepared to take what fate offers. I'm, for once, totally convinced that providence will hand me something I can use.

Baptizing the Cat

"They had you out all night?" Susan calls from the dining table as I come in the door to the condo. I hide the disk and box in my jacket pockets. My wife's voice is full of a long morning's sleep, flat and non-committal.

I delay answering her question—"they," my wonderfully convenient CIA bosses—and gather my late breakfast up from what Nursey has left on the stove: tepid scrambled eggs, limp bacon, dried-out toast. I'm far too excited to care, convinced that something fortuitous will emerge to help with my plans. At least the coffee's still hot. Then, I answer, "No, I came in at two. Bedded down on the couch. Didn't want to wake you, love." As always a good lie carries some elements of truth.

I eat at the counter, able to see Susan at the table in her thick orange terry-cloth robe, but still able to keep her at a distance. It's not easy to manipulate the newspaper and raise my fork from that low level. I just don't want to be close enough to take in my wife's sleep-encrusted eyes, her rheumy nose—all of which are understandable, but how much can a man take while he's eating? Last night's scene rises up, full of the minutiae of Catherine's apartment, of her person, the slender, immaculate woman, the vague impression of a dark bra under the nearly opaque navy blouse, the small pale flowers and buttons riding soft folds, the white shorts ending just above bare golden knees. The delicate movement of her hair and hands. Around her, all the clean shining surfaces of tables and counters, the uncluttered airy space that I imagine must smell of citrus. Overriding all my other impressions, already framed in my painter's view-finder eye, is that initial one, the moment Catherine first turned on the lamp and the light flared up from the open circle of the shade beneath her chin. The feathery edges of eyelashes etching faint dark lines over the barely-perceptible down of her cheeks. That is what I want to paint.

Without a word to Susan, I head to the bathroom for a quick shower, and then I'm off to my Tampa studio. I hear a dull whisper from my wife behind me. What's she asking? I pretend not to hear.

It's chilly inside my Tampa refuge, and again I congratulate myself on this one good use of the Bower Bankroll. I pull back the blinds and let the splendid October morning light fall through the store's front window. The bright rays pour in with an almost audible crash throughout the cavernous room and spread across the white canvases stacked against the wall and the blank sketch sheets I've tacked up on easels. With my widest brush, I quickly spread a watery white gesso over a standard-sized sheet of water-color paper, giving it a smooth hard surface, which will prevent any of the acrylic paint from soaking in. This process is probably normal for anyone painting with acrylics, but it's a new path for me. In watercolors, my regular medium, the whole point is that the thin paint sinks into the paper fast. It fans out, permanent, never to be redone. Fast and sure, get in, get out; it's what I like about watercolors—the oldest type of painting in the world. No going back, no second guessing. However, with Catherine's portrait, I want a new viewpoint, a new category of paint, which happily I have: tubes and tubes of acrylics, a Christmas gift from Susan, waiting on the corner of my work table for almost a year.

At the time, I viewed her present as a vague criticism. Did she think my painting would improve if done in a different medium? What does it say when one gives a violinist an oboe for Christmas? As often with our silent disagreements, I raised my eyebrows, and she responded with that blank wide-eyed expression that told me nothing. Did she really like the book on Degas and the diamond tennis bracelet I gave her?

I blow the paper with a hair dryer, waiting for the gesso to dry, which doesn't take long. Later, I tell myself, I can turn on the heat, put on coffee, and remove my jacket. Now, with every brain cell, I'm trying to hang on to the image of Catherine's face with the lamplight, a circle, ablaze beneath it. The mood's all there if I can just get it down on paper: the fear in the dark around her head will be like a black halo, the streams of electrified luminosity flooding upwards will capture her vulnerability but also her alertness. Her torso, arms, and hands will be in shadow, depicting what? Aloneness or loneliness? There is a difference.

Even as I trace very lightly with a charcoal pencil the downward slope of eyelids—Leonardo's best trick—the first tentative curved lines that will form the indentation in her bottom lip, another picture rises up on the back of my retina. I decide my next painting will be one of that animal alertness that possessed Catherine just before the telephone call, her neck elongated, her head raised in apprehension. It will capture the fear and also the courage that caused her to walk so quickly across the living room, the nerve it took to pull the sliding glass door open. For that project, I'll use those odd-shaped masonite boards I picked out of the rubbish pile in front of the condo over three months ago. The bottoms of cheap dresser drawers, I pulled them apart and carted them here. The wood will need sanding to dull the oil-based finish, and most likely I'll have to gesso them two or three times, and sand in between, to keep the resin from bleeding through, but the work will be different from anything I've ever done. The panels have been sitting for months at the back of my studio, slanted against the wall, like so many abandoned lean-tos. Why had I picked them up? Until now they've just been an aggravation, a reminder of my mother's habit of collecting junk. Of all things, I warn myself, don't start heaping up stuff just in case you might possibly use it someday in the future.

I see the vapor of my breath between me and the pebbly surface of the paper. My fingers tremble. I've not felt this excitement about a painting since those beginning months in college—a hundred years ago—when I first discovered I could draw as well as run the 100 meter in record time. That wonderful emotion stayed, bulldozed me through every tedious course I had to take to get my degree. All four years it was great fun seeing every face, every tree, every bar scene as a painting or drawing of some sort. Always looking for the negative space where I could put a pencil point to paper. Later, that feeling would return for a few hours when I was in Taos, doing Indian abstracts, as if the old pottery and rug designs were talking, leading me into a new reality. But it's been eons since I've had this wild anxious need to take a vision and execute it.

The morning passes. The quality of light shifts from spotlight intensity into one of diffused shadows. The sun has passed overhead and now it must be well past noon. Still, I refuse to look at my watch and confirm the time. I also reject turning on the fluorescent lights overhead, two long etched-glass pipes, leftovers from the time this shop sold greeting cards and party trash. The ugly fluorescents would distort the hues, give the colors below a ghastly, unearthly glow. In this observation, I agree with Susan, "I brought all these clothes home to try on because those lights in the dressing rooms

121

make me look sick—fat and sick. How is it possible to look both ways?"

I don't even turn on the track lighting I had installed either, although those globes, specifically bought for their blue tint, cast a more natural radiance and don't distort colors. I can't force myself to put down my brush. Diligently I apply the thin water-based paint in airy strokes. The pigment dries almost on contact with the paper and only a slight Play-Dough odor rises up, an invisible, pleasant haze in my nostrils; not like oils, which stink of turpentine, and require a lot of ventilation, and take forever to dry, but more than watercolors, which have no smell at all. Lightly, lightly, I caution. Women and children's faces require an almost invisible touch, no strong lines. And I have no need to put a Veronica underneath the paint. Here she is, on the surface: my perfect woman. Some outside sense informs me that I've been at it for hours, but I refuse to stop until every element of Catherine's face, the lamp, the bright circle flash under her chin, the larger, more scattered glowing below, and the background is at least minimally drafted in.

The telephone rings, once, twice and then on and on, but I ignore its metallic trilling, admonishing myself that I should have unplugged it when I first came in. More and more, the grating sound commands, demands a reply. "Go away," I mutter. It has to be Susan. I'd called out, "Going to the studio" as I closed the door of the condo. She knows I'm here, and she's not going to hang up until I give in. "Go to hell," I grumble, caught in this sphere of energy that I've created. Under my hands, Catherine's face glows on the paper.

Somewhere deep in my brain, I know I'm in that place all artists search and long for, a state that can ignore every distraction. I've heard this condition called a hundred different things. The author, Stephen King, on some talk show, described it as "the hole in the paper," and said he fell into it. I think of it as 'flow" when I'm not aware of time or place. It's been too long since I've had that sensation, and I refuse to relinquish it now.

How predictable, Susan the main grievance in my life, inserting her presence everywhere, now butting into my studio time, which she knows I consider sacred. The irritating tone of the telephone's clanging carries a curious similarity to my wife's own vocal quality: an organ piping away in an unpleasant minor cord.

122

Baptizing the Cat

At last, after more rings than I think Susan could possibly endure, I lay my paintbrush aside and go to the wall where the clear wire is hooked into the plastic jack. It's as though I'm watching from above, but the better part of me, the artist, is still back at the easel devising a strategy of how to tilt Catherine's head slightly downward and yet keep it at such an angle that all the planes of her face are visible. The other part is a furious man in a rumpled navy-blue jogging suit jerking out the telephone line with a snap that strips the wires from the plug.

"There, that'll learn you,"—Grandpa Emile's phrase—I tell the little tan plate. The tiny horns of the jack stick out beyond the plastic, an almost invisible insect's antennae. "No in-coming calls allowed," I say, remembering one of my grandfather's long-ago peccadilloes, a block on his own telephone. "No more long-distance calls allowed," he'd announced one afternoon, jutting out his chin and scraggly gray beard.

The ban effectively kept my mother from the hour-long conversations with her numerous and scattered family. On especially unhappy days, she'd walk to the nearest grocery store on Webber Road, and with a roll of quarters she'd scrounged up from God knows where, call her sister, Amelia, and spend an hour and four dollars listing her father-in-law's many shortcomings. Until I was about twelve and resisted, I was taken along on these forays, away from what my mother referred to as her "two-acre prison." I'd spend the hour wandering down one aisle of dusty canned goods after another, eating the lone pack of crackers and one soda my mother allowed, trying to tune out the interminable, repetitious analysis of my grandfather's behavior and personality. Back then, I agreed with most of my mother's complaints. Later, I saw things more from his side.

Yet, he'd admitted, as together we cleaned the stall of our only cow, that the telephone block was an inconvenience. "Try not to be spiteful in this life, Phillip. It always comes back to haunt you. Ever since that hindrance has been on the phone, I've had a great hankering to call your Uncle Dewey, to call someone, anyone, long-distance."

The brush is back in my hand, and the streaks in Catherine's dark blonde hair drape across the paper.

After that incessant ringing, the silence, like cool water, floods throughout the shop, rises up from the floor and settles down from the ceiling. A tangible quiet eases over me, a bubble of protection from distractions, from interruptions, especially from my wife. It occurs to me, in that part of my brain that flits from one subject to another, now that my hands are busy laying down the first washes, that distance is a protection for Susan as well. If I'm kept busy painting, I won't be around to take advantage of the "happy accident." Careful, woman, I warn her, don't pull me too close. If I'm on the scene, I'll be able to give you that extra push or slip you that extra pill, or do whatever.

Funny how the mind works. With the silence and my paint brush stroking on the darkness of background, I can go back over the medications Susan ingests, what I see and what she tells me about her new drug of choice, Theophylline. I wasn't interested before, but Dr. Youngblood planted a seed. "Theophylline, have to watch that drug" is what he said. Why? I determine to observe every aspect of my wife's illness: the coughing and hacking during the evening and early morning hours when her allergies kick in, what I see on her night stand, numerous small, yellow-brown prescription vials with white tops, taller clear bottles filled with red and yellow liquids, stained and sticky spoons. There must be a lethal combination lurking somewhere in that jumble of ordinary, innocent containers. I recall the oft-repeated film shot of a bedside table with a cut-glass decanter, tumblers half full of ominous dark fluids. The scene is always a foreshadowing that the victim will be poisoned from this source. Of course, I tell myself, the police would investigate Susan's medications first.

In this trance-like, spontaneous way of painting, I lose the thread, the thought of Susan's treatments, and again slide mid-stream into focusing on Catherine. No wonder. Her face, flushed from the bottom with the oval of lamplight, is under my hands, the narrow square of her shoulders taking form with each stroke of the brush. The spangles of brilliance from the top of the lamp are hard to come by. Except for white gesso, I've left the paper almost bare in that area, but the straight-up flood of luminance—always difficult to paint—a mixture of yellow, gray and white, brought down a bit, dulled on the palette, seems to be turning into a series of swirls, with sequins, like miniature lanterns glowing in a night sky. This peculiar light is far too difficult to accomplish on a first try. I go back to Catherine's face, the way her hair is pulled behind her sea-shell ears.

Why do I feel I know this woman? How will I find a way to see her other than from behind a breach in her patio wall, and then through open sliding glass doors?

A chill passes over my skin as the details of the previous evening roar back chronologically, first, all the reckless positioning of equipment, the running away and returning, the startle that jolted through me as Catherine's form took shape just on the threshold of her condo—so astoundingly close—and then the unthinking daring of this morning to reclaim the box and the disk. Whoah, back up. With all the excitement and jockeying back and forth, I've not digested the whole evening, made sense of everything I heard. From her conversation with Claire, obviously the scene I'd witnessed on the beach with Catherine and Towelhead was misleading. Yet they had looked so in tune. Was I so needy that I couldn't see a couple take an ordinary walk on the shore, two people talking, without turning the sight into a great romance—something that I know now didn't exist? Well, whatever, anything is better than what I have with Susan.

This time I do look at my watch: 3:15. All morning and well into the afternoon gone by in what seems like minutes. So what now? A return to the condo is out of the question. I'd have to face Susan's sideways questions of why I didn't pick up the phone when she'd let it ring over twenty times. Next, I'd probably be expected to entertain my in-laws until dark. They always stay at the Marriott and come over around noon when we're using the condo. I'll have to go along with whatever plans they've cooked up for the evening. Laughable, how my wife, who never calls when I'm whipping out a mundane seascape with required rowboat pulled up on dunes, took this morning to try and summon me home. Or worse yet just to ask a tedious question. Before today, I'd have welcomed any excuse to take a break, to quit painting altogether. Usually, I splash on color in a formulaic way for fifteen minutes and then get a cup of coffee; another fifteen and I'm staring out the store-front window, wondering if it's too early to go to lunch or stop in at Belle's. This day of all days, the first time I've felt inspired in years, this morning she picks to call, and I'd only just left the apartment.

My hands are truly on automatic, washing brushes thoroughly— so they'll be fresh and pliable tomorrow—spritzing the paint globs on the palette with water, covering them with clear plastic wrap, and sliding the whole business into the apartment-sized refrigerator that sits at the back of the studio. If the palette is left out, the acrylics will sour overnight, and no way do I want to lose that particular, slightly-rose flesh tone I've managed to blend into being. And I sure don't want to put up with a pungent odor, like curdled milk, when I start in tomorrow. Back in art class days, the fermented acrylic paint would conjure up Grandpa Emile's slanting back porch, the pails of milk and my mother's dripping, unsuccessful efforts to make cheese. Proust was right; memory lives in the nose.

Chapter 9

I leave the studio as if it were high noon, instead of 3:15. Gone is the option of going to lunch at Bayside and then on to Belle's to patch up that odd little talk we had of death and husbands. And I don't want to drive out to Archie's at Island's End again and screw around until dark. I'm full of that satisfied feeling of having met a quota of hours at the easel, something I've not done in years, and even better yet it's been worthwhile work. I sit in the car—still in my painting trance—and breathe in the warm leather of the seats and stare at the lavender wall of Violet's, the clothes boutique that is next to my studio and the last part of this little plaza mall. The concrete blocks have a few coats of lilac paint, but the edges of the rectangles show plainly through the rough texture. The surface is like the coarse gessoed paper I've been working on all morning, except for those indented lines. My imagination flares. I could paint a mural for Violet, the half-crazy woman who owns the store. At least she seems a bit off, often pecking on my paneled door, even when I have the blinds drawn, and not waiting for an answer, poking her head in, and calling out, "Has the muse taken up residence here?" She wears droopy old-fashioned garments, more like costumes in a 19th century play than everyday dress for the warm weather of St. Pete. I imagine painting Violet in her favorite purple and lavender get-up and putting in the diminutive black Singer sewing machines she has lining the counters of her shop. On her head I'd position a huge ornate hat, decorated with cabbage roses, turn her into a Victorian dress-maker for dolls, with some partly-clothed small porcelain figures sitting in a half circle around her. The concrete blocks showing through the paint would give it a mosaic quality, make the mural more interesting.

Even as I take a pencil out of the console between the Lexus's two front seats and start sketching Violet's garden-party hat on the back of an envelope, I recognize what's happening: creative overload. One half-way decent idea and one good morning's work, and my brain perks, offers more ideas, more projects than I could handle in a lifetime.

To escape the allure of Violet's blank wall, I drop the pencil and paper onto the passenger's seat, turn the key, and pull out of the parking lot with a screech of tires. Instead of cooking up more artistic undertakings, my true goal is the Tampa Museum of Art, to see if Catherine's there, sitting beside Monet's snow scene as she claimed to her friend, Claire.

The Museum is a low, plain white building with vertical windows behind columns. Surrounding it are the twisted dark-gray trunks and branches of sea grape trees, which makes up for the blandness of the architecture. Planted at intervals beside the flat, boxy structure are twenty or more of those snaky plants, which give the site an abstract dimension. A little imagination turns the veined, leathery pancake leaves atop the trees into cowled Druid nuns. They hold up their contorted arms, dancing in tandem, worshipfully, around the white building, like it was an ancient marble altar. These are the very same trees that intersect throughout the small cabins at Island's End and give the place so much atmosphere.

Coming from Ohio, a state that celebrates its trees, ten national Champion Big Trees on the Big Tree Registry, I'm tree conscious. Every fall, cars and buses and driving tours crowd the roads to see the fall foliage of Ash, Birch, Beech, Cedars, and Sugar Maples. So I'm always amazed that everyone in south Florida takes the sea grapes, these oddly coiled and tangled forms of greenery, for granted. Young sea grape plants account for most of the hedges and shrub landscaping in Tampa and St. Pete, and the older, scaly-armed versions are truly full-blown trees. I want to jump out of the car, sit on the hood, and sketch a black and white rendering of these weird shapes.

But again, I call a halt to my over-active fancy and redirect my energies to getting out of the car and walking on the dun fieldstones up to the white building. "Stay on task" I order. It's some of that education jargon Susan's picked up from the other home-schooling moms she meets with once a month in the library at St. Pete. Susan says, "Stay on task" at least ten times an hour when our daughters are working on math problems. It would be different if we were up in Spartanburg where my side of the house is out of hearing range of those ridiculously ineffective lessons and warnings. But in the all-purpose room of the condo, the school periods take on a two-edged aspect. The girls know what they're doing and pit me against their mother.

"I don't need to learn algebra," May says. "I'm going to be an artist like Daddy; then I won't need to know what x means."

I long to tell her, "You've got a rich grandfather, honey; you don't need to learn anything." But in case that fails, be sure to find a rich husband."

Inside the museum and out of the bright sun light, I let my eyes adjust to the dimness of the wall-papered vestibule, a surprising print of purple and green peacock feathers. Beyond this oddly-decorated entrance is an arch, from which the large museum room spreads out, cool and somber and apparently deserted. Not a soul under the high embossed ceilings, and each white wall displays one large painting by an old master or a minor American painter, a forgotten somebody. Sculptures of women in marble and busts of men in bronze sit on pedestals and are spaced across the floor and stand in the corners. The typical vacant feel of all public buildings slides throughout the uninhabited room. Two long wide hallways branch off to the sides and are also empty, except for a single blue-clad guard—hands folded behind his back—who suddenly appears and then disappears in the maze of columns. The staff in these places is always hidden away in other buildings or inaccessible offices, safe from demanding patrons. A visitor is lucky to find a tour guide or "docent" as the art world calls volunteers, those people who have nothing better to do than to hand out brochures or give simple directions. Today, it seems that no one in the Tampa Museum wants to be bothered with an off-the-street visitor.

I stroll through the large main gallery with two thoughts. First, Catherine is one of those docents who has nothing better to do with her days. And second, no matter how hard I labor or how much talent I'm able to put down on paper or canvas, the most I can hope for is that my work will hang like these forgotten pieces in some deserted gallery. Bummer. Although I can't really picture my seascapes with dunes, mountain scenes with deer, interiors with indistinct people—commercial crap, all of it—hanging next to that unbelievably large oil of cows that hangs on this side of the gallery.

It's one of those bucolic scenes with a background of gray buttes. The foreground is the surface of a pond reflecting a low limb of an oak tree—an elongated arm—and cattle standing in water up to their bellies, their large vacant faces staring out forever into a warm nineteenth-century afternoon. One animal has raised its head from drinking, and the water pours down from its mouth in flecks of white. A surge of pleasure rises in my chest that an artist can achieve this kind of perfection. It's miraculous, even if there's no one to see, except me.

Down this large gallery, hanging on a far wall, I spot Monet's gilt-framed winter scene that Catherine talked about. A low dark-wood credenza—surely an antique—is under the almost all-white painting, transforming it into an altar. And why not? A shrine is appropriate for a piece of art worth millions. And yet, after all, isn't it only paint and canvas? And there's no one sitting in either of the two padded gilt chairs on the altar's sides.

Of course, I really don't expect to see Catherine in one of those chairs—too much to ask for—so I can't say I'm disappointed. Yet it's as though she should be where she claims to spend most of her afternoons. But she isn't. Hell, hell, hell, a wasted trip. Well, since there's nothing better to do, I'll inspect the two other canvases on the side walls, leading up to the Monet.

The long Oriental runners on the polished floor dampen all sound, so I don't hear the guard, only see him after he moves by a far, arched doorway. A pallid, wrinkled man with dyed black hair, he stands, looking for a few minutes, unsmiling. Now his hands are clasped under his uniformed belly. Apparently deciding I'm harmless, that I don't have a knife to rip the paintings from their frames, or worse yet deface them, he slips away as silently as he came. The sun flares from the sky light down on the vacant space he's left on the carpet.

Suddenly, I long for seasons. I wish it were cold and raining outside, like Cleveland in early November, with low dank clouds pressing down on all the dreary buildings. The people outside would

130

be under black, rain-slick umbrellas, climbing the dirty steps of the city buildings. Here in St. Pete and Tampa, in every season, the sun flames away like a furnace, and when I leave this cool, solemn place, I will be assaulted by blue skies and fluffy white clouds and later by the good spirits of my wife and in-laws. I recall the little tonsured priest, Father O'Keefe, last Sunday at St. Vincent's, saying that November first and second were the days to celebrate the dead, that November is the month for the departed. It's a shame the weather here in the sub tropics doesn't cooperate with the church calendar. November should be gloomy, I grouse, all the good feeling of this morning's accomplishment drained away . . . by what? By Catherine's empty seat beside the Monet.

"Dimwit," I whisper under my breath and move to concentrate on another painting, the huge and truly wonderful still life in front of me. This painter has given his art over to a painstaking veneration of objects. It's splendid, and I can actually get in as close as I want to the canvas since there are no stanchions draped with silken cords to keep me four or five feet away. Evidently this is one of the few museums left in the world that doesn't have every picture set back out of arm's reach and wired with an alarm. The powers that be must feel that a single grim-faced guard is enough protection. I bring my face to within inches of the rim of a crystal goblet, inspect the flicker of candlelight on a silver vase, and study the brush strokes used to convey the velvet cloth of a book. I don't recognize the name in the bottom right-hand corner, and I don't want to return to the vestibule for a brochure. What I really want to do is to pull a jeweler's loop—that I don't have—out of a pocket and press it and my eye to the canvas, to run my finger tips across the faintly-crackled surface in order to feel which way the strokes of paint are angled, but I refrain. It drives me crazy when onlookers touch my work. "Buy the damn painting," I want to holler, "and then pick it to pieces if you want."

I move slowly, delay my progress as one who eats a good meal of steak and potatoes and lingers over coffee in anticipation of dessert. Finally, I come to the Monet, a blizzard of cold and snow in the heart of a south Florida museum. A few indistinct black lines in an enormous field of white designates a group of buildings—one with a rusty orange roof—possibly a French village, lost in a swirling storm of white. A faint winter sun hovers in the upper right corner of the composition, but mostly the painting is rendered in a murky, nebulous cotton-ball style. Why do the artist gods, whoever they are, think that this massive canvas of blobby, splotchy, snowy paint is better than the one I just left in the hall, which showed exactly the curve of a polished violin, the russet feather of a grouse, and a faded, curling page of music? I answer my own question: because the concept and difficulties of painting a snow storm are so unique, harder to put down and make believable, and partly, too, because this canvas is so large, 90 by 120 inches at least. And small still-lifes of musical instruments and feathers and books have been done unto death.

I bend closer to the Monet, try to decipher the technique that makes this painting of snow so improbable and yet so believable. My nose is within inches of the surface, and I can imagine the artist, Claude Monet, the rank smell of oil pigment and turpentine stinging up into his nasal passages. No wonder those old guys went insane or died early; they inhaled too many fumes.

"You're allowed to look but not take a bite."

The voice behind me is low, insinuating, female. Like the guard coming into the room earlier, I failed to hear footsteps. I straighten, not daring to turn, and say inanely, the first thing that comes into my head. "I wish I could scrape off a flake of paint, a taste, to see how he did it."

"What you need is a jeweler's loop."

I shiver inwardly at her nearness and the surprise of her voicing my previous thought. I halfway turn. Catherine stands three feet away.

"What?" I feel like a glass of cold water has been thrown in my face.

"You need a loop, you know, what jeweler's use, so you can examine the painting more closely. A lot of artists come in here with magnifying glasses or that thing I call a loop. Of course, they can't touch the paintings. That's what I'm here for . . . and the guard out there if you don't obey." She laughs then, a soft self-effacing sound that belies the stern warning.

I pivot to bring her into full view. *Catherine*, her name pops onto my tongue, a peppermint of sound, but thankfully it stays where it

132

belongs, inside my mouth. She's wearing a dark emerald green and gold hounds-tooth suit, a short jacket with loose fitting trousers, and a lighter shade of burnished gold underneath, some sort of blouse. Her hair, variegated in shades as a lion's mane, is unbound today, no clips or barrettes. The ceiling's skylight causes a soft sheen to fall directly across her forehead, eyes, and cheeks, and her skin and pupils shift in tints from green to gold and back again. I know it's make-up, deliberate magic, but I appreciate the subtlety, the faint olive on the eyelids, the pink smudge across the cheekbones, and this exact assemblage of clothes to match her coloring. She holds a thin green book in her left hand, diamonds on a wide gold wedding band glint, and her nails are short and unpolished.

"Just one little taste . . . to see how he did it," I repeat in my best joking manner.

"That's a new one on me; someone who wants to eat our Monet."

"It's absolutely wonderful," I say, and gesture to the swirls of white and gray, already critiquing my words as they issue forth. Come up with something original, you lamebrain, the voice-over in my head demands. "I was trying to figure out why this piece is considered so much better than those." I point back to the realistic canvases hanging behind us. "And why this one is worth so much more."

"The eye of the beholder, I guess" Catherine says. "But Monet really grows on you. When I sit here in the afternoon, I actually become chilly, as if the snow were real, and cool air is flowing off it and drifting down over me."

She stares at the Monet, and for a second I take her in, the whole picture: the white oval of her face, the mussed blonde hair, and a hint of some tangy cologne.

I chuckle, a hesitant sound out into the stillness of the museum that rings feeble to my own ears. How am I coming across? "I'm a painter," I say. "I'm overwhelmed by his technique."

"Oh, that explains it." Catherine takes two easy steps forward, positions herself by my side, which forces me to stop staring and return to my inspection of the masterpiece. "You probably know all about Monet and his history, but the museum has a little prepared speech if you care to hear it."

"Sure," I parrot. What else can I say with the sight and sound of her ringing in my head. And now with her slight body within a foot of mine, the smell of the acidic perfume drifts in citrus fingers through the air.

"Claude Monet," Catherine intones, like a proper school girl. "Born in France in 1840, died in 1926. He came from Le Havre to Paris to study at the Academie Suisse and in the studio of the academic painter, Bleyre, where he met Renoir and several other young painters, who would later participate in the Impressionist Movement."

She takes a little breath after every sentence as a good docent should, probably as she was taught by the museum's head curator. It's standard expository instruction in order to give the hearer time to take in and make sense of the facts. I can tell by her stilted inflections that she is copying someone else's presentation and has learned this Monet chronology by heart. She pulls it out of memory, bit by bit. Her little narration refreshes my own recall of Monet's struggles to be recognized, his change from a traditional turn-of-the-century painter into one who wants to catch the moment, the movement, the light, the feeling—the impression.

My quick sidelong peeks catch the line in her bottom lip, shiny, accentuated with what seems a fresh coat of coral lipstick. The pale illumination from the ceiling gilds the fine drift of hairs on the side of her cheek and the tiny, almost invisible, lines that fan from the corners of her eyes. She's not beautiful, nor young, but something in her face is interesting, disturbing, arresting.

Before I'm ready, Catherine turns and faces me full on, nods her head to indicate that she's finished her recitation. I wouldn't have been the least surprised if she'd taken a bow, expecting me to applaud. And I want to clap, for again I'm struck by her artful coloring, everything soft, blended, loose, and smudged; all the more attractive because they seem to be the result of no calculation whatsoever. She's done with her garments, her hair, and make up, exactly what Monet has done here with his snow scene, what I want to do in my lamp-lit painting, give the viewer one complete spontaneous sensation of a subject.

"Well," I pause, longing to respond with a comment of brilliant insight, one that will keep us talking for hours. "That reminds me of all my old art courses in college. The dates and events, but not"— here I delay again, for I suddenly feel I might be on to something that might sound reasonably intelligent. "What gave him the inspiration to change in the first place? When was the moment that said, 'Monet, don't keep applying paint onto canvas in the same old realistic way.' What gave him the idea that these splashes and dabs, and blobs—like we see in this snow scene here—could be used to convey fleeting impressions of landscapes that you see, over and over, and yet never again?"

I want to add "as he did with his hay stacks and London bridge paintings, at different times of the day and different seasons." But I realize in trying to sound knowledgeable and sophisticated, all I might be doing is presenting myself as a pompous ass; someone who, by listing a bunch of facts, only wants to impress. I don't even have the ease Towelhead had when I first listened in on his and Catherine's conversation, all those nights ago.

I stop speaking and turn back to the Monet, trusting that it's a good place to stop or it might seem to Catherine just another lecture from somebody who's had a few art classes. Wasn't that how she'd described Towelhead, "had a few philosophy courses"?

"I wouldn't know," Catherine says, and there's nothing put-on or considered in her voice, just an honest admitting, "I'm not an artist myself. I love the genius of them—the paintings I mean"—she motions to the others on the walls behind us—"and I guess everything that has to do with art. I majored in art education, thought I'd be teaching children the rest of my life." The faint chuckle that runs under this statement sounds slightly rueful, but I can't be sure.

"But isn't the one who knows and appreciates just as important as the one who paints or composes or does anything artistic, isn't he—or she?" I ask. "If we artists don't have an audience, what would be the purpose?" To my own ears, I sound overly ardent, but suddenly the idea of artist and loving devotees seems fresh and inspired. Haven't I hung on to my little coterie of buyers, dubbed them "*Las Patronas*"— they're always women—at times calling one of them, saying, "I have something that will knock your panties off." The old girls appreciate a hint of the risqué in our transactions.

One ancient bird, who comes to the studio in Spartanburg at least once a month, teases Susan, "You'd better watch this husband of yours; he's almost too sweet to resist." She's well past eighty and has a Halloween-orange fright wig on top of a million wrinkles. Susan's response to the joke is always a weak "Ha, ha" and a glance to me, the same baleful stare that our cow, Daisy, gave to my grandfather whenever he sat down to milk her.

Catherine and I shift in front of the painting, turn our heads toward each other as we talk, look, and then switch back to appraising the Monet. I am intensely aware that we are almost completely alone, and yet together, in this large echoing room. But what she is not aware of—and, of course, never could be—is the alert, feral scrutiny that she directs toward the Monet and then up towards my face. An arched-browed feline concentration that suddenly makes me think of the *National Geographic* television shows Susan allows the girls to watch. Catherine is one with the tawny pumas in Colorado, one who sits in the sun on top of a rocky outcropping and waits for an innocent deer to come by. I am that deer, ready to be devoured by those white sharp-looking teeth.

"Don't I know you from somewhere?" Catherine asks, squinting her amber-green eyes, trying to remember. Then she chuckles, realizing that under different circumstances this would be an obvious pick-up line.

I can't help but respond, "And what's your sign?" and we both smile widely. The exchange is corny and I can feel the grin on my face but am relieved to have yet another mutual thing, beside the Monet, to enjoy.

"No, really, I do know you . . . I just can't think of where. Tell me?"

I mock, "Is this what you do? Hang around art galleries all day, and tease poor, defenseless artists?" I almost say "hit on strangers" but change the words as they come out. "Hitting on strangers" is too crude.

"No, I know you, I promise. Don't I?" Now her tone is unsure. She turns her face away, her eyes hidden under the slanting gold-green lids, and tilts her head downward as if the answer to her question is written in the blue pattern of the Oriental carpet. The pale nape of her neck is exposed, a vee pattern of light tresses rising up into her hairline. I want to grasp her gently at that exact point, encompass the narrow column with my fingers, and without words guide her out of the museum. Now, it doesn't bother me in the least that we would walk out into bright Tampa sunshine. To hell with the weather in Cleveland. I'd be able to comment, "What a beautiful day."

I catch a glimpse of the guard; he stands at the far end of the gallery under an arch, his hands again folded behind his back. Has he been witness to this scene before: Catherine and a male visitor to the museum going through the first hesitant steps of meeting, the first steps perhaps of the ritual courtship dance? Of course, courtship, I assure myself, implies something more elevated than what Catherine had with Towelhead. He picked her up, she was wearing her wedding ring, a double carat diamond in a thick gold setting, just as she is now. Just as I am wearing my ring. Does a wedding ring mean anything? And how is this meeting between us, this little exchange any different from her encounter with Towelhead? I silently question.

Catherine raises her head, again gives me that direct appraisal, and asserts, "I do know you!"

"Yes, of course," I relinquish. No need to stretch out this pleasant game into some high-school charade. "I'm Phillip Craine. I live in the same condominium complex as you do . . . in Sandhills over in St. Pete."

"Oh, sure, that's where I must have seen you." Catherine's gaze returns to the carpet, her shoulders sag ever so slightly under the padding of the checkered jacket. "You're the artist who's . . . ." Her words drift to a standstill, and I can tell she's trying to remember precisely what she's heard.

Am I known as the artist who badgers the condo manager? As the one who saved his wife from a fall? As the artist who, what? "The artist who's . . .?" I encourage. I don't care how Catherine answers as long as we can keep talking.

Something shifts behind her eyes. A tangible link that was developing between us is broken. She's heard some gossip so distasteful that she can't repeat it, or won't.

"No fair, you can't start to say something and then stop," I protest.

"Yes, I can." Catherine smiles and lifts her narrow eyebrows. There's dismissal in her tone. A step backwards and a glance to the book in her hand indicates she's about to leave, or about to return to her chair beside the Monet, or maybe even about to depart from the Museum altogether.

"My wife said you were very kind to her and to our daughter last week—by the pool," I blurt, grasp at any thought that might lead us back into that pleasant, lightly teasing environment that we possessed just a few moments earlier. Although mention of Susan and the girls is not exactly the subject that I want to bring into the moment. Still any topic to forestall Catherine's retreat is better than none.

"Do I know her?" She frowns, a soft, puckered line on her forehead.

"Not really. They were at the pool; you smiled, spoke, and commended May on her swimming. My wife doesn't find it easy to make friends."

I wholeheartedly regret this last comment, but it's said in honesty, which I hope holds some weight.

"Neither do I . . . but still I can't place her."

"And yet you seem to know something about me that you won't admit." I sense that I've scored a fraction of a point with this argument.

"It's nothing really. You know how people are . . . ." She smiles wryly, her thin lips barely lifting at the corners.

I feel we've moved back toward that comfort zone of at least exchanging words, even if they hold no sense of direction.

Catherine shakes her head, raises the book, a print of black grill over olive green, to hide her mouth and says barely loud enough to be heard. "They say you don't exist."

"What! Who's they?"

"Please forgive me. It's really just one old woman gossiping an afternoon away. When I moved back in, she gave me the run-down on practically everyone who lives in our complex . . . at least from her viewpoint."

"And she says I don't exist?" I'm genuinely intrigued. How often does one get to hear an honest assessment of how he appears to the outside world.

"Well, something like that. She's my eighty-year-old neighbor and since I've just moved into Sandhills, living in my folks's condo, she started with the different buildings, describing each family, very exactly. She said your wife, a nanny, and two little girls live on the bottom floor in C behind us, but . . . . " Again Catherine pauses, pulling her lower lip under those white sharp-looking teeth.

"Go on, Catherine?"

Her head jerks and her eyes widen, "You know my name?"

Shit, now it's my turn to stammer, to explain, "Um, well, yes, I think Susan used it when she said you two spoke." Even as the lie's invented, I come up with a better explanation. "And it's like you said about your neighbor, everyone's keeping tabs on everyone else in Sandhills. My wife must have found out your name. She's down at the pool or on the beach practically every afternoon." I know I'm going on too long with this explanation. "But please, just tell me what your neighbor said."

Catherine's final response is a disappointment, told with side-ways glances and a sense of distance. "Well, she speculated that your wife was inventing a partner, that the artist husband she de-scribed was too perfect to really exist. And she said she never saw you around. My neighbor felt your wife had to make someone up to . . . to explain the two little girls." Catherine rushes to add, "And please don't think I believed her for one minute. Poor old soul has nothing better to do than invent stories about the people she sees coming and going past her front window."

I nod my head to encourage these comments.

"Thank god, the old dear takes long naps every afternoon and goes to sleep early or the whole place would have a twenty-four hour watchdog with an imagination. God only knows what she says about me to her friends." Catherine fans her hand toward her cheek in apology.

It's a lot of information, but like most wrangled-out secrets, I feel this disclosure has been tamped down, made more civilized than what the gossip actually said. Did the old bitch think Susan too un-attractive to have a husband? And if the old girl watches so intently, she must have seen me and just not come up with my connection to Susan. But I let any more exploration of my non-existence slide. The discussion would bring my wife and daughters back into focus, and for these few moments, I want to pretend that it's my family that doesn't exist. Bless the gods of coincidence for old-lady naps and early bedtimes, for if the antique biddy did peer out her window as much as Catherine says, she might have seen my nightly trips up and down the condo halls and my forays onto Catherine's back patio. This possibility rattles my barely-there poise of confidence.

"So you're *not* an artist," I say inanely. I want to edge the conversation away from Sandhills and all its citizens, want to put that place behind me with the same sense of relief I have when driving away in the evening on one of my make-believe CIA excursions.

"No, like I said before, only an admirer of art." She pauses. "I'm sorry about that bit of gossip; it just came out before I thought." She extends her unpolished nails, just the tips, for me to shake. "Nice to have met you, Phillip . . . ."

With the ends of my own fingers, I grasp her cool ones gently, curb an impulse to clutch, but hold on to them all the same. I ask, "Isn't it your job to show me the rest of the gallery, not just the Monet?" The small pads of each of her fingertips pulse with life, and I let her be the one to pull her hand free, leaving only a trace of my holding on. She glances back in the direction of the guard. Does she feel a need for his presence?

"Of course, but you probably know more about paintings and their history than I do. I'd be embarrassed to give a tour to a working artist."

"Then let me give you one." I laugh an uncomfortable "ha ha" after this suggestion, which to me sounds vaguely like the villain's chuckle after tying the maiden to the railroad tracks. Am I coming off as a pushy snowbird, someone who won't accept no for an answer? But then she surprises me.

"Sure, show me around. Maybe I'll learn a few new descriptions to say to visitors, not that we have all that many."

Who knows what I said to Catherine that afternoon? Even as we walked from painting to painting, from the Victorian marbles to the metal sculptures out in the courtyard, none of my words came through that part of my brain where coherent thoughts are registered and retained. My mouth was set on automatic, saying what I'd say to anyone walking through a museum. In some ways I knew I was making a fair impression. Didn't I have a thousand opinions on art and artists; hadn't I taken classes and poured over magazine articles, gone to art shows and galleries for what seemed like centuries? In my mind, at least, I'd painted and re-painted a thousand different images that never made it to paper or canvas. And isn't it always easier to talk about technique and talent than it is to actually create?

The last section of the gallery ended, and we moved through French doors out into a courtyard to stand and then finally to sit on uncomfortable wrought iron benches, the kind meant only for decoration. The sun moved down in the West, and its angled light reached that sanctum only by indirection. The fancy seats and thick clusters of broad-leafed plants circled a large sandstone fountain, shaped like a huge wedding cake encrusted with sea shells. Water splashed down the three glazed tiers of this centerpiece, and sometimes a breeze sent a fine spray of dampness across our faces. Again and again, I registered all the physical aspects of Catherine's hands, her features, the way her body tilted forward and then away, the evocative smell of her perfume.

What else is there to remember? I try that evening, slouched down in the one big armchair in the living room, with my eyes half shut, to conjure the scene up in my mind, pull every word we exchanged back into memory. The television set drones. Ed, violating all of Susan's rules, controls the remote, and the whole family—all but Nursey—have already sat through two sit-coms. Now we're watching some kind of detective series that doesn't contain one idea that could hold my interest. For the first time in my life, I wish I were a writer instead of a painter. As an author I would keep a detailed record of my life, a journal. Isn't that what they do? Write down who said what to whom. As a painter, I can describe the long afternoon shadows that stretched in melancholy lines from the white columns in front of the recessed windows and the stripes of dark and light made by the overhanging plants down the brick pathways—no problem. But as I try to recall our conversation, all I can drag out of my artist's brain are mental pictures. The scene, the walls and plants in the middle of the Museum would definitely have to be a watercolor. Only the quickness and transparency of that medium could capture the afternoon light and the green haze that hung over our first time together.

The Rob Roys I drank before and during dinner work on me and give everything a high polish. The room, seen through slitted eyelids, is encased in a halo. Ed sits on the couch between April and May, all three pairs of eyes fixed on the television screen. The girls are wearing Sunday clothes—frilly pale pink and blue outfits—although it's only Saturday, but my father-in-law likes them in dresses.

"He's so old fashioned," Susan gushes and hurries to put our daughters into suitable girly get-ups. The king of the family is acknowledged in a thousand small ways that would not be apparent to someone looking on from the outside.

My mother-in-law and wife lean on their plump arms at the glass table like two over-indulged ladies out of a Renoir print, the pale blue-greens of the room surround the opulent flesh tones of their faces and limbs. Only the crazy quilt orange and yellow geometric designs of their tent-like robes seem to belong to Picasso. At first glance I think the setting would make a good painting, juxtaposing the two different styles and palettes of two famous masters, but then I recall that mixing methods seldom works. I'm unable to recall a single instance of a successful painting done in that manner.

Catherine's dark gold and green suit flashes back to me like a message of sanity, of taste and decorum. With effort, I pull back our talk, mostly about art, something of my history in Cleveland, of my mother's and grandfather's house, of the odd coincidence that we were both living in the Sandhills' condos. She described growing up in Tampa and St. Pete, high school and college, sailing, horse-back riding, and the art classes she took at Tampa University. Yet, I cannot recollect a single utterance clearly, only Catherine's expression of total interest registered—what I first saw when she was walking with Towelhead—and that every few minutes, our eyes held a secret conversation that contained no words.

Then the guard came and told us it was after six and the museum was closing.

Catherine, a faint tinge of pink rising at the collar of the silk blouse said, "I should have remembered. Some days when no one comes in, I don't wait until six. I leave early. Docents can come and go as they please."

Baptizing the Cat

On the flagstones outside, in the diminishing light, I resisted the urge to ask her to go somewhere for a cup of coffee, for a drink, for a cold Rob Roy. The sour scotch taste on my tongue would have been doubly delicious if I were sitting across from this attractive woman in some dim corner of a bar. But before I could give into temptation, Catherine turned and looked back at the Museum. "It's quite a beautiful building, don't you think, with all those twisted trees in front?"

Above the squareness of the white structure and the branches of sea grapes, the clouds were purple, streaked with rose, against an amazingly flat blue sky. Only nature could get away with those combinations. "Yes, it is," I agreed, glad she saw the place as handsome as I first did when driving into the parking lot. "And it's good architecture, too, the windows set back behind those big columns keeps the bright light from damaging the paintings."

My attempt to sound intelligent must have distracted me, for before I knew, Catherine patted the cuff of my warm-up jacket and murmured, "It's been good to meet you, Phillip." Then she set off at a swift walk, going across the flaxen stubble of lawn toward the parking lot. Her car, a bizarre choice for a woman, was an early 90s, white Wrangler Jeep with a bikini top, a vehicle that one expects of a bare-chested surfer guy. Alongside my Lexus parked directly in front, they were the only two cars left in the lot. The guard's car must have been hidden on the other side of the Museum. Glad, in my male mind that I had an up-to-date expensive car, and wondering what Catherine thought of it, I trot after her, catching up, and grasping the back of her jacket sleeve, just above the elbow.

Now, I try to imagine how it must have felt, my grabbing her arm that way. And how did I appear when she turned? A middle-aged, tousled-haired, pale old fool, I know. Desperate, I hope not. But at that moment I felt despair as if I might never see her again. "Are you coming back tomorrow?" I asked, yet not wanting to put the question in that particular way. But what else could I say? I had my fingers on the sleeve of her coat, and underneath I could feel the heat and heft of her arm, round and firm.

She looked down quizzically at my hand on the soft weave of the jacket as if she might respond, "What business is it of yours?" But instead, she answered, "Tomorrow's Sunday. The museum's closed."

"Oh," I said, drawing a complete blank on how to proceed from that time constraint, that obvious shut-down. Where else could we meet? Would she be open to another location? Also, my mind ran down Sunday's activities, with church and brunch and the obligatory afternoon with Susan's parents since they were in town. How could I escape?

Catherine gave me a glance, full of cool, level appraisal, and then said, "Maybe we could have lunch Monday, before I come here."

Thinking back, it seemed there was a challenge or was it a question, lurking behind those green eyes, but, now, here in this armchair, I can't be sure. Knowledge from the previous night's phone conversation had colored every exchange between us. I had to be careful not to let any more information leak out; knowing her name was bad enough. Anything more would have been impossible to cover.

"Where?" I whispered to her suggestion of lunch. The lateness of the hour had sneaked in a gray wind off the bay front, and my question was whisked away from my lips as though I hadn't spoken.

"I like those restaurants in the Circle below the wharf. The Embassy is nice." She sounded as matter of fact as if she were making arrangements with her friend, Claire.

I knew the hotel she spoke of, one of those fancy, remodeled buildings left over from the thirties. They always had dark-patterned carpets in enormous rooms and an overblown fresh flower arrangement on a table at the entrance. "That would be great," I said, trying to sound off-hand and feeling exactly like I did in high school, asking the most popular girl in the junior class to go to a movie and being turned down, except this time I wasn't rejected.

"Meet you Monday, at one, at the Embassy."

Catherine slid her arm from under my touch and motioned goodbye. She walked the rest of the way across the lawn, taking a delicate step over the concrete log in front of the Jeep and opening its door. I held my arm high, making sure that when she was behind the wheel she saw my salute, making sure she signaled back. Recalling my gesture, so juvenile, but in the moment so important to me that we made that last connection.

Now, all I have to do is live through tonight and endure Sunday's rituals. Monday morning, I'll run a few miles, then go to the

144

studio to work on Catherine's portrait, which will at least keep my hands busy. There's a way of getting through, I console myself, a way to live through the next 36 hours and not be so anxious that I develop a case of nerves. If I weren't so sloshed, I'd get up right now, go down, and plant the Wolf Ears on Catherine's sliding glass doors—again—and find out exactly what the woman thinks of me. What would she tell her friend Claire? I'm torn between that desire and also a strange compulsion to start, at this very moment to play it straight with Catherine, not repeat the insanity of last night and spy. I realize as I slouch, eyes half shut against the noise and closeness of the room, against all the bodies, that I've never been completely on the level with a single soul, never in my entire life. As far back as I can remember, all the intrigues and silent controversies of my grandfather and mother's struggles, and my part in them, is the baggage I've carried through grammar and high school and beyond. Lies and lying, always having to remember what I said. No talk allowed of my father, Emile's son, Philip, ever. And my mother? How had she kept her secrets so completely? Well, I'll never know; they're all gone now, dead and buried.

In an unpleasant swim of alcohol and inertia, curiously as productive as this morning's burst of energy, an insight comes. Catherine might be the one person on the face of the earth with whom I could be totally honest. We're not married to each other, no commitments, and she's no saint herself, a husband and Towelhead. Maybe she'd understand how it is with me.

I decide two things: first, not to drink the second half of the shaker of Rob Roys sitting in the freezer; and second, not to jump up as though my beeper has buzzed my leg. In large part, pure laziness contributes to this last decision. I'd have to put on my stiff official face and say, "Got to make a call," and leave Susan to explain to her parents. Surely they know of my CIA connection by now, fake as it is. How tiresome all that old pretense has become. Also the previous night's adventures, almost getting caught, the wild surge of painting this morning, and ultimately the sheer intensity of meeting Catherine and making a date for lunch has supplied all the excitement I can handle. Good god, the monotony of all the dull weeks this fall in St. Pete wiped away in a day and a half.

I promise myself not to drink tomorrow, in fact, to cut back on alcohol from now on. Maybe one Rob Roy before dinner and a glass of wine with the meal. And I'll run two miles every morning.

I rise from the arm chair and feel through the mist over my brain that I am delivering an oration. I hope I'm not swaying. "Dear friends," I say to the family group, "it's been a full evening. But now I must depart for the boudoir. I did a great deal of painting today, and then with Nursey's wonderful meal, I am forced to retire."

It's a slurred and pompous speech, an imitation of Ed when he wants to get away with me and hang out at the pool hall. "Ladies," he says, "the gentlemen must be off to do manly deeds." Miz Mildred is on to him and always counters with the truth, "Play pool and drink beer, you mean." But this evening in her newfound esteem for me, the savior of her daughter, she, along with Susan's and Ed's murmured approval, graciously grants permission.

"We're all tired, Phillip, and we haven't done anything creative. You go on to bed."

In the glow of all this good feeling, I move along the couch, kiss my daughters and shake my father-in-law's hand. Kiss my wife, a peck on the lips, and my mother-in-law, a peck on the forehead. They know I'm drunk but smile indulgently.

Strange, because of my closed-eyes routine, I now look forward to attending Mass this Sunday. The time passes much more quickly than one hour should. This morning, as my in-laws, and then Susan and the girls and I file into our regular pew, I wonder if church is a proper place to contemplate the conscious decision to have an affair. After all, isn't that exactly what I'm planning? The scenario unreels in my head, the blueprint for seduction that everyone knows. Catherine and I will meet for lunch a few times. She will sit across from me and her smooth face, its ideal pallor heightened by candlelight— those faded hotels are always lit by candles—will be like gazing on a Vermeer, will flow consolingly over my agitated mind. We'll have a glass or two of wine; then, as the meals become more frequent, I'll order a bottle every time, our wine, a Merlot or Shiraz, a special one that I'll introduce and describe to Catherine. I'll show off my respectable knowledge of vineyards and vintages. After all I've read about different wines for years in Susan's *Southern Living*; they're the only articles that really interest me. Once in a while I buy the suggested brands, some from France but most often from California. I even have wine racks in the basement of the Spartanburg house, which Susan grandiosely calls, "our wine cellar." I don't often get around to sampling them, preferring Rob Roys and their immediate effect instead.

The sound of kneelers being raised is the signal for all to stand for the gospel. In my meditative state, it's a bit of a shock, like being pulled from a sound sleep by an alarm clock-buzzer, but I get to my feet, a tardy second or two behind everyone else. I fumble and find November's Feast of all Saints in the small paper-backed book that's printed every month and then thrown away, a great waste.

When Susan and I were first married, I rather liked bringing my own thick gold-leafed missal to Mass on Sundays. It reminded me of what I saw as a child in Cleveland, the Baptists down the road, grown-ups and children, marching to church, Bibles tucked under their arms, the King James version. Grandpa Emile, a Lutheran in his childhood, allowed that the Reformation translation, the King James version was the best. "Full of poetry," he'd said. As a wedding gift, Susan gave me a missal in a three-volume set with *Church History* and *The Lives of the Saints*. The church year was ever changing, so eventually the Catholic missal ran out the calendar in the back and did not correspond to the liturgy. It was hard to comprehend. Why not just have a Bible, like the Protestants, that could be used over and over? Every time I take the newly-printed missal out of the wooden rack attached to the back of the pew—sometimes the booklet has two months instead of one—I have a vision of all those inch-thick volumes, thousands of churches in the US, millions of Catholics, all that paper obsolete, dumped somewhere.

Lay people read the two epistles before the gospel at the dais to the left of the altar. First, a whispering woman, whose head barely reaches high enough to see the book, and then a man in black, a wanna-be priest. He wears an ebony suit, a black shirt, and the slicked-back hair of an Italian gangster. I immediately dub him Black Knight, for he moves stiffly and with great dignity. All he lacks to complete his clerical impression is the white Roman collar. His bow to the huge cross behind the altar is deep and slow as if to remind everyone what a solemn occasion we're all in for. I glance over at Father O'Keefe to the right of the altar. He wears a green robe with a twisting blue and silver design embroidered into the edges and his usually taking-care-of-business face registers impatience. "Get on with it, man," his flickering eyes seem to say. Then, as if to hurry Black Knight along, the priest walks to the middle of the altar, preparing to read the gospel, even before Black Knight has finished his last paragraph. The man glances over at the priest with a face that asks, "Why are you in such a rush?" He reads the last words of the epistle even more slowly than before.

This five-minute mini-drama confirms my long-held conviction that no one truly gets along with the people they live or work with. Friendship is different, but even there it's tricky. Before you know it, someone's keeping score: who bought dinner last, who calls more often, and God forbid if friends go on a trip or get into business together. Maybe that's why Catherine and I will have a chance at some honesty. Our association will have no overt obligations, be somehow pure, a friendship, plus the excitement of sex. What a great combination!

I glance over the tops of my daughters' shiny blonde heads to Susan, who looks up from her reading and catches my stare. Her eyes are completely hidden by the glare of light on the small eyeglasses she wears, and it's as though she is focusing two bright spotlights on me, checking. Last week she nudged me—I had my eyes closed—and whispered, "Are you asleep?" And as we left church, she informed me that I should at least keep my eyes open during the readings or the lay readers and especially Father O'Keefe would think me rude. Now, she's inspecting to see if I remember her warning.

One of the many paradoxes of my marriage is that if I'm disagreeable, nasty and withdrawn, and don't go to church or don't go to the beach, then she's all humble and quietly sad. But if I'm good-natured and play along with her little game of perfect family, then she comes up with yet another rule or stipulation. It's not enough that I go to church, but now I'm supposed to actually pay attention. Next, I'll have to keep my eyes wide open during the whole service, or some such other condition. When I growled, "Maybe I'm praying," she turned all deferential. "It's just that I feel sorry for anyone up there reading, Phillip, looking down and thinking you're asleep." It didn't matter that I told her that with my eyes closed I might be paying closer attention, listening more intently. That information didn't register.

I turn my head back toward the podium where Father O'Keefe is reading and deliberately close my eyes.

Unfortunately, in this sightless state, my hearing is truly acute, and I absorb every last word of the gospel. For some reason, it fills me with a vague sense of unease. The priest reads the familiar words quickly, in a matter-of-fact voice: "Blessed are the poor in spirit, blessed are the meek," all that jazz. As he goes through the list: "Blessed are the merciful, the clean of heart, the peacemakers," I cannot find one category that I fit in. I do not pine after justice. God no. No justice for me, please, for then what would I deserve? Leave me out of that 'eye for an eye" equation, too—please.

At the Marriott's Sunday brunch buffet, Susan and Miz Mildred compare the various offerings here in St. Pete to the one in South Carolina, and the lunch at the Spartanburg Country Club up there to the Country Club down here, to another restaurant somewhere else, and on and on. I dare not raise my eyes from my plate for fear of showing the absolute revulsion these two women create in me. My God, is there nothing else in the world to discuss besides food? What we're eating now? What we will eat this afternoon and tonight? What we will eat tomorrow? And, it's a given that the family—except for Ed, he'll take a nap—will spend the afternoon at the beach with a big picnic lunch, and then this evening stand in line at a seafood restaurant, whose most defining feature is its "all the crab legs you can eat."

Chapter 10

At the Marriott, I glance sideways at Ed, who is doggedly scooping his meal into his mouth, assured, no doubt, of its supreme value by the lifelong concern shown to food by his wife and daughter. I wonder if something's lacking in my own upbringing, my own taste buds, that makes nourishment so unimportant to me. Didn't I starve enough as a youngster? The Catholic Church recommends fasting, at least during Lent, but then again, has Susan ever known a hungry minute in her life? Or is it just these particular women's obsession that turns me off? "Three hots a day" is the term I've adopted for my wife and mother-in-law, for their sanity seems to depend on three "real" meals every twenty-four hours. "Sandwiches don't count as a meal," Susan says.

On our honeymoon—we'd already lived together for six months—Susan knew the number of hours between the evening meal and next morning's breakfast. If we ate a bit early the night before, she would be ravenous. "It's been fourteen hours," she'd inform me. I see now that there might have been some bulimia in her routine; she ate prodigiously back then but didn't gain. After we married, there was no attempt to keep up appearances for my sake. Strange, I counted the hours between sex, the number of orgasms.

I focus away from Ed across the table towards my two daughters. In that first bit of adolescent independence that will blossom, I hope, into full-fledged rebellion, they have chosen to sit at a table for two, separated by several feet from their Bower and Craine relatives. April, her cheeks and arms rounder than they should be for a child of thirteen, and looking more like her mother every day, concentrates on her plate. It's so obvious that the scant ten or fifteen years she'll have of pleasing voluptuousness will lead to fifty years of obesity that I can hardly take any delight in her as a youngster. In fact, I find I can no longer look at any curvaceous young woman without projecting into the future exactly how fat she'll become.

May, on the other hand, is perhaps too thin, long boned, already too much like me. She eats intermittently from her nearly bare plate, talks to April, who pays no attention. Then her waifish dark-blue eyes dart around the crowded restaurant, as my own have been do-ing. She catches me staring. An exchange passes between us. She raises her nearly invisible eyebrows in a question and, then, rises from her chair and comes to where I sit and leans her spindly body against me. She circles her cool arms around my neck. "I wish you were happy, Daddy," she says in a whisper. Her thin lips, brush my ear, causing the hairs to prickle. Her words reach into my chest, like a smooth hand stroking a sore spot I didn't know existed. A pressure of tears starts up behind my eyelids. I'm appalled that this six-year-old girl child can so easily discern my feelings. Is my mental state so obvious?

"Oh baby," I say, "I'm not unhappy." I hug her tightly so she can't pull away and examine my face, for that might give me away entirely, start tears streaming. "Aren't I here with you girls and your grandparents? Isn't it a beautiful day outside and we're all going to the beach later?" In a dishonest stab at being truthful, I don't number Susan in my list of blessings, and my words to my daugh-ter clang inside my head. What I say is true, so why can't I just be grateful for what I have and not ask for something more, or differ-ent. I train my eyes on my wife, try to find one characteristic that is appealing. Small dainty hands and nails, but she's using them to push in more food.

Susan munches, rapid voracious bites, the way I imagine a mouse nibbles its crumbs. Her fat cheeks vibrate with the motion of her teeth. I close my eyes. The sight of mastication by any human is repulsive. Sects in India make it a point of manners to turn away while they eat; I read it somewhere. Americans would do well to adopt that policy.

Early Monday, still almost dark, I run at six o'clock, first along the sidewalk past Catherine's front door and then through her back yard. I glance at the sliding glass panels, hoping to catch a glimpse of her or something related to her, or at least an open drape or blind. But every window, every entrance is like the rest of the Sandhills' complex, shut up completely in shades of eggshell, ecru, and beige. Pleased that I'm the only one up at this hour and yet exasperated at not being able to spy into Catherine's living room, I jog down the rickety stairs and out onto the beach.

A worn-out moon and a few stars are still visible in the brightening morning sky, and a curve of light, sunrise, starts up at the edge of the ocean's horizon, a sliver of incredible golden-orange. No wonder pagans worshiped the sun. It still amazes me that this huge tangerine ball comes up every day and that all of humanity is not out here on the beach, paying homage. But I am.

My steady run along the foaming water's edge causes the long-legged dark and white sandpipers to race off, sidestep the waves, and then veer out of my way without ever leaving the ground. The short-legged birds, whatever they are, which have just appeared on the beach in the last week, can't keep ahead and so fly up in startled bursts of brown-gray feathers. The fresh air is full of oxygen, thick and heavy to take in, like a rich liquor, an aperitif. I wish I could give this atmospheric mixture of sea and dawn a name, label its flavor as bars do after-dinner drinks. Instead of raspberry punch or grasshopper mint, how would I describe it? "Pure, virginal, fresh, original," but none of these titles fit, like trying to mix up a new color on the palette board. A word that would adequately describe this stuff I'm pulling into my lungs doesn't have a tag, or an identity.

I run a few yards, dash a few more, and then slow to a walk. Even though I've been up jogging every morning this week, my wind is still far short of what I want it to be. Get some reality, I tell myself, there's no way at forty-five that you can have the same lung capacity as you did at twenty. After two miles down the beach, I stop in front of a landmark, a huge unfinished house that's been going up for over a year. I've noted it from the roadside and from the beach side. It's right in front of this edifice that I often give out of energy, feel the strain in my calves and spine.

The house has an enormous flair of roof, an "s" like a sail, above gray concrete towers, interspersed with blue and gold stained-glass windows. This monstrosity of at least 15,000 square feet is something of a puzzle. The builders have been working on it, off and on, for the last twelve months. I've checked out the structure from the shore and from the little perimeter road running up to it, observing that the house—if that's what it is—is exactly two miles from Sandhills. Who could be building such a behemoth as a residence? Ed doesn't have a clue to the owner and the builder's sign is unfamiliar, though a couple of times I've asked my father-in-law to check it out. Ed knows the local construction bosses, here in St. Pete and in South Carolina, too, since he always has projects going on in his rental properties and restaurants. But so far he's not been able to come up with an answer.

Already dreading another meal with Susan and my in-laws, I turn and walk doggedly back down the beach toward our condo. The sun is behind me and a few old snow birds in baggy shorts and flop-brimmed hats are up now, looking for shells that the night waves have tossed up on the shore. Instead of these bent-over antiques, I wish Catherine were walking toward me in that brown racing-style bathing suit I first saw her in. But then I remember that's what she wore when I first spied her with Towelhead. An ugly question pops up in my mind: Was she with him last night? Just because he didn't bed her the first time doesn't mean he won't try again. If I hadn't been so lazy, so drunk, I'd have checked to see if she were home. I wouldn't have used the Wolf Ears, just gone by the front and back of her condo to see if the lights were on.

Up the stairs and returning to the mown grass of Sandhills, I wrestle against my desire to check on Catherine again, like a teenager, who keeps driving past his new girlfriend's house. "Just head to your own condo," I direct, but the command doesn't work. I start into a jog, run in back of the apartments, and take another pass behind Catherine's patio. Now, the drapes are pulled open and the sliding glass panels are apart. A bucket and mop, some stacked chairs, and a couple of throw rugs sit crumpled on the concrete next to a small pile of debris. And there, incredibly, in the doorway are Catherine's slim golden legs and her spherical rump under wrinkled gray shorts. She is bending forward, backing out, gliding a flat-headed mop—one I've seen Nursey use to wax floors—moving in reverse between the opening in the doors, exactly where I saw her sitting just three nights earlier.

I step up on the lip of the patio and, in a low voice so as not to startle her, whisper, "Catherine." Her name, on the empty morning air, surprises her anyway.

She turns and says, "Oh, good grief." Her face is pale, no make-up, and her eyes look even tawnier than they did Saturday at the museum. A multicolored scarf—a vintage Vera? Susan has informed me of the name, their worth—is tied around her hair. "What on earth are you doing here?" she asks.

I gesture down at my vented shorts and dirty running shoes, glad to be able to say, although I only started last week, "I run every morning."

"You do? I've never seen you?" There's an edge in her words, a question. But before I can answer, maybe explain that I've just started running again, she returns to her chore, says, "Wait, let me finish." She mops a few last swipes just inside the door, reaches to catch some place she's missed, and then plunks the mop into a bucket next to other long-handled tools. She turns back.

"Of all mornings." She puts her hand to the bright scarf. "I look a mess." Then squeezing her arching eyebrows up into a question, she asks, "Why are you here?"

I can tell she's troubled at my seeing her in these work-a-day clothes, a grubby off-white t-shirt that says "Las Vegas" across the front above unpressed shorts. Also, she's not wearing a bra; the nubbins of her nipples and the downward slope of her breasts show plainly through the material.

"I'll go," I say. "Pretend I'm an apparition." I take a step back, away from the patio.

"No, no, don't be ridiculous. Here, let me un-stack these chairs. You can sit."

"No, I shouldn't have come back along this side." And then without thinking, I add: "I've already been past here once this morning—hoping to see you."

She ignores or pretends not to hear my confession, keeps her head down and tries unsuccessfully to separate the plastic chairs, but it's

154

not working. Very conscious of a brush against her straining arms, I take the chairs, grasp one by the seat, and easily pull them apart.

"Ahh, for upper-body strength," she murmurs and settles with a breathy sigh into the chair I just freed.

"What?" I question, and take the other plastic chair to sit across from Catherine, careful not to let the back leg slip off the edge of the concrete. This is not like I imagined our next meeting to be. Where are the drinks, the dim candles, the background music? Instead we are sitting in bright seven a.m. sunlight, the surf rasping below the cliffs and my family sleeping just beyond the pool area. Birds from a nearby birdhouse dip and parry and the smell of floor wax wafts out of the condo door.

"Upper-body strength," Catherine repeats, with an educational overtone to her words, almost like her Monet lecture on Saturday. "The average man has five times the upper-body strength of the average woman. A proven fact. That's why they've downgraded the physical requirements for women entering military service. Men have the advantage. It's why men don't find housework as hard as women, especially vacuuming and mopping." She tips her head toward the open patio door.

The ammonia smell of drying wax wafts around us, exactly the odor that Nursey fills our condo with every other Monday, the stench that drives me out even earlier than usual.

"You're cleaning your own apartment?" I can't help but ask.

The rusted trucks and ancient jalopies always in the side-parking places at Sandhills testify to the crews of blacks and Spanish laborers who arrive daily to keep the apartments spotless. Sandhills employs a regular staff and their salaries are paid by condo fees. But many of the owners, like Susan and me, pay only for yard service and employ our own domestics—like Nursey. It's an never-ending battle by the owners against the management to keep this option. Management wants everyone to pay the even larger condo expenses that include maids.

"I have a scam going," Catherine says, and rolls her amber eyes in a semi-circle of amusement. "I scrub out my apartment every week or so, and my husband pays a hundred and fifty a week for a non-existent cleaning woman. I've only been doing it for two

155

weeks, but I figure to have five hundred a month that he doesn't have control of." Her tone is slightly bitter, but then she seems contrite for this deception. "And I really clean better than any help I've ever had. A once-a-week of my scrubbing lasts longer than any hit-the-high points by someone who doesn't give a f—." She says the letter "f," but stops before she completes the obvious vulgarity. "Sorry."

"I shouldn't have asked," I rush to apologize. Somehow there's more information in this brief description of why she's doing housework than I'm prepared to take in. The unselfconscious mention of "my husband" and the revelation that she's fooling him in some manner to profit by $500 seems too paltry.

"I shouldn't have told you. I should have lied and said, 'I just love housework.'" This last phrase she articulates in a mock southern drawl. "Men adore women, who just love to cook and clean. Don't they?"

"Not necessarily," I answer back, feeling off balance by her need to dupe her husband out of pocket money and by her mocking criticism of all men in general and at the way this conversation is progressing. No romance at all. And yet there's a thread of something here that I want to pick up on. "Most men know housework's not easy, that there's more to it than just dusting a coffee table." A skill my mother never mastered. "And I'm glad you told me the truth."

Of course, she's not in on my idea of total honesty, to start—what should I call it—our total friendship? And suddenly, in this bright setting on her back patio, the talk of body strength and housework, the labels "affair" or "liaison" for what I've been planning, don't seem to fit. After all, why can't we just be friends? The beginning, a chance meeting at the Museum. Later, some innocent chit-chat in the backyard as one would have with any neighbor. Still later, lunch at one of the Tampa hotels. That thought grinds things to a full stop. No, a lunch-time meeting would not look guiltless to a bystander— or be guiltless.

"Well, anyway it's a beautiful day, even if I had to get this cleaning done. Rand's due to drop by for a quickie inspection." Catherine looks upwards and around as one does when trying to think of a way to change the conversation. Of course, she completely misses my immediate sexual interpretation of the word "quickie"

"A beautiful day and there's still plenty of bugs in the air for the birds."

Gratefully, I catch at this suggestion, "Yes, it was terrific earlier, running on the beach. Where have all these new birds come from? What are they?"

There's something disjointed about our discourse, long pauses, we're too busy reading each other's eyes, interpreting body language.

"Sanderlings, they come back every fall; although some last through the winter." She laughs, "like the people who stay here year round, like me." Her lighthearted voice says she's no longer surprised at finding her upcoming lunch date lurking in her backyard. Now, her glances are not scattered but directed like laser beams straight into my eyes. Her own pupils shine topaz in the light, and I feel that pleasing electrical connection all the way down into my groin, like the first sip of scotch, only stronger and better. Good, I think, and note the pleasant sexual shift against my boxers. It's good to know I'm still alive down there.

"So, how far do you run?"

"About four miles," I answer.

"On the beach? How can you be so sure? Unless you have one of those gadgets on your shoe that tracks distance." She looks down at my ankles, and I wish my legs weren't so pale. It's a dead giveaway that I've not been running long or that I'm totally lying and not even been out in the sun that much.

"No, I've a marker half way down, that monster roof and round-tower house they started building over a year ago and don't show any sign of completing. You know, the one that sticks out on the horizon. I've driven the beach road and found it's exactly two miles, one way."

At this information, Catherine snickers, then puts her fingers to her mouth to cover laughter, takes her hand away, and presses her lips into a thin line to hold back giggles.

"What's so funny," I ask, half-way chuckling myself, carried along by her private joke even in my ignorance.

"That monster house is my husband's."

"Well, hell," I stammer and slide my tongue over my front teeth. It's a habit that Susan despises but expresses only through an irritated mocking with her own tongue and lips. Realizing I've not been so unnerved in years, I stop my tongue's gliding and stupidly ask, "Do you live there?"

"No, of course not, silly. It's not finished, and I live here, now, as you well know." She points to the sliding glass door with a finger.

"You're kidding. It's your husband's house?" I ask, already seeing a pattern that I can't quite make out.

"It's his dream house" she continues; "what he's planned off and on for the last five years. Enough rooms to get lost in, absolutely no style at all, and 'a showcase for all of St. Pete to see' . . . ." A wry grimace of her lips pulls all the amusement away from her eyes. "It's the last battle in the long war we've called a marriage." She half-way laughs without humor and glances down at her efficient-looking hands, at the wedding ring, two square white stones in a wide masculine setting of gold.

She re-focuses her attention. "Oh, don't fret. It's a long story." And then, as though struck by some kind of insight, she says, "You're married. You probably know as much about these arrangements as I do."

I nod my head dumbly. What can I say? "Are we still on for the Embassy at one?"

"Sure." She tilts her porcelain chin upwards into the bright morning sunshine. "I wouldn't miss it for the world."

Suddenly, from out of that left field I call a brain, with no pre-meditation at all, a question forms, and yet as I say the words, they sound pre-planned. "Didn't I see you walking on the beach with some young guy last week? You were wearing a dark brown bathing suit, sort of a racing style, with gold trim."

Even as I speak, I know I'm adding the description of the suit to pull her attention away from the words "young guy." I couldn't really know he was younger than Catherine if I hadn't eavesdropped, overheard her say so to her friend, Claire. In that same instant, I see a coolness settle down behind Catherine's eyes. An icy stillness falls into the space between our two chairs, a huge slab of absolute cold, transparent glass.

Completely ignoring my question, Catherine says, "Maybe lunch isn't such a good idea, after all." Then coolly, without a quiver, she stretches out her arms, turns her hands palms up, closes her eyes, and directs her pale face up toward the full morning sun. Her fine narrow nose is like the prow of a ship, and her spiky eyelashes cast shadows across her cheeks. It's an attitude of appreciation, of adoration of the light that I've seen on the faces of a thousand sun worshipers. Even that old leathery character down by the pool raises his face and extends his arms, an aging condor about to take flight, his worn-out flesh hanging in drapey folds.

Purely on impulse, I rise from my chair and take a few cautious steps toward Catherine. I know she hears me, and any second I expect her to straighten her head, flash her eyes open, and furiously say, "Go away," or something on that order. But she remains immobile as if I had disappeared and no longer exist. Is this her way of canceling our date, putting me in my place for asking such an impertinent question? I step closer and lean forward, grasp her wrists in my hands, slender compositions of bone and flesh. There's nothing else to do. If she tried to resist—but she doesn't—I'd have no trouble holding her. I slowly bend closer. Still, she doesn't respond. I am within three inches from her face. I know she can feel my breath, and yet she's refusing to look at me. I move and place my lips softly against her unpainted, cream-rose ones. I can't say it's a kiss. There's no motion between us, no parting of lips either by her or by me. It's simply flesh against flesh. A few long seconds pass, and I'm aware of the sounds around us: the birds, the air-conditioning units, the waves down on the beach. I'm even aware of the gradations in temperature between the outer edges of her lips and the line where they meet, where it's warmer. Her eyeballs shift slightly under their translucent lids. I start to close my own eyes so that I can better feel these two slender petals against my mouth, but a flutter stirs in her arms, and she lifts her lids, slowly, like curtains rising. Motionless she stares up.

In the bright light, only partly dimmed by the shade I cast over her, the spokes of her irises sparkle. Citrine and ochre lines and golden flakes glitter around jet-black pupils. A fine border of dry-brush ink circles all, defining the hues and separating them from the blue-white of her eyeballs. It's like looking through a microscope, almost seeing the atoms that make up iris and cornea.

Catherine sits absolutely still under my grasp, her eyes staring fixedly up into mine, so that for an instant I wonder how long can this non-kiss go on? How long can I hold her here? How long can she hold me? Then she closes her eyes, and I am dismissed. I straighten my back, which has begun to cramp and gaze down. Nothing else to do but stand up completely and walk away. Her eyes remain closed, continuing to shut me out.

Half expecting and not expecting a word of goodbye, I step off the patio, but no sounds of farewell follow me. I refuse to look back. I want to grumble "bitch," grumble that I can be dismissive, too, just loud enough for her to hear, but I don't utter a sound. I walk, turn, and pass the jutting edge of stucco wall where just four days ago I encamped so bravely. Now, the hours of watching and listening, the placing and retrieval of spying equipment appear the activities of a madman, someone I do not know. Imagination or not, I step across a semi-circle of grass that still seems pressed down from where I last sat those many nights ago.

The short jaunt back to my own apartment occurs without comprehension. Awareness exists only on the surface of my lips, which transmits in beating waves back to my brain, the cool and heat of those twin mauve petals. Are a woman's lips comparable to her labia, as some say a man's fingers are to his penis?

Finally, I come to full consciousness inside my shower stall. Up until the hot spray of water hits my head, I've been traveling on auto-pilot. I ran back to my condo, I opened doors, I instinctively grunted a greeting to Nursey and Susan on my way in. They sat, two immobile monoliths, hovering over cups of coffee at the glass table, so engrossed in their daily ritual of trying to caffeinate themselves into motion that they didn't even bother to look up.

After the shower, naked, I stalk the bedroom like an undecided sleepwalker. I pull open dresser drawers and leave them half out, open closet doors and don't close them. In spite of neighbors, who might see my bare parts, I step out onto the small, supposedly private patio outside our sliding glass doors and retrieve my paint-stained clothes. I always drop them on the bedroom floor, but Susan or Nursey hang them up on a hook outside. I stand with the clothing in my hands, noting that after twenty-four hours, acrylics have no noticeable odor. I'm unable to make up my mind whether to dress for lunch at one or just put on these work clothes and go to the studio in Tampa and work until twelve. But then I'd have to come back to St. Pete and Sandhills to dress, and then drive back to Tampa. Susan would ask where I'm going? Yet the overriding question is whether Catherine will show up at the Embassy? One minute I think not, and in the next second I'm sure she will. She let me kiss her, didn't she? Was that a kiss?

And what of her husband, the owner of that leviathan house on the beach? One has to be a multi-millionaire to build a house of those dimensions. Where did he get his money? Probably from family, like Susan. And why isn't Catherine living with him? Money usually binds spouses together, especially when one person has it and the other one doesn't.

A wild need to leave the apartment gnaws at my insides, but for a few minutes I can't think of an excuse to wear my new lavender shirt and loose gray slacks without Susan asking, "Why so decked out?" But then, like a bubble in a martini glass, an excuse rises to the surface. "I'm taking a new painting over to Belle's," I'll say. I often clean up for a delivery to Belle, so it's not so improbable. As for the painting, too enthused to keep the new work to myself, I mentioned at dinner last night that I'd started on a fresh, inventive approach and that I was using the acrylics Susan gave me last Christmas.

At last, I've made one decision, to dress and leave the bedroom. And after all my lying preparations, there are no questions from my wife. She's back asleep on the couch, a morning nap, something she often does, with soft raspy snores pulsing her open lips. The girls are watching TV. Sleep on, old girl, I silently tell her. Sleep on. I wish you'd never wake up. I kissed an interesting woman this morning, one who does housework even when she doesn't have to. One who doesn't live with her millionaire husband.

I grab a cup of coffee in the kitchen, all the while feeling Nursey's eyes appraising my virgin shirt. In all fairness to the old black woman, even though her stares may register a thousand questions, she'll ask nothing and say nothing to Susan.

Now, at nine, I'm again outside Sandhills, again free, and again stuck for something to do until one o'clock. I can't paint in these clothes, but out of force of habit, I crank up the Lexus and drive along

St. Pete's semi-deserted streets—retired people seldom leave their air-conditioned cocoons—and cross the Causeway toward Tampa. The bright day, promised earlier on my run and during the time with Catherine on her patio, has disappeared. The sky is clouded over, a few drops of rain spatter on the windshield, and a northerly wind works the water in the Bay into a froth. The waves, brownish and surfaced with foam, splash in three and four foot arcs against the graveled edges that line the pavement.

I focus on the asphalt for a few seconds and then glance to catch sight of the waves as impossible paintings. Surely no one wants a canvas of brackish, churning water on their living room walls. Yet the white spray lashing up into the air is full of designs and possibilities. I wish I were one of those painters, who could start out with only an inkling of an idea and smear paint on canvas with no thought of coming up with a composition that makes sense. I would cover an entire surface with coffee-brown acrylic, lighten it with cream, and then splotch on lacings of white ice cream into curves and parabolas, the patterns I'm seeing now, flying up against the sides of the road.

Coming into Tampa, the skies clear, but maintain a gray overcast that promises bad weather. Of all the hundreds of sunny days I've endured with Susan, why is today of all days gloomy? With no intention of painting, I still go through the motions, leave the car, and enter my studio. And even though the sky doesn't offer good sunlight, I pull back the blinds covering the plate glass window. I turn and on the easel at the far back wall, Catherine's pale face glows, a moon on canvas. Somehow the translucence I've captured in paint is similar to her un-made-up face of this morning. Shiny, pure. And although it's only been one day since I've seen the picture, the composition and colors are better than I remember. Catherine's head is tilted down just enough to keep it to the left of the canvas's center. The oval that is the lamp's top is below and slightly to the right and full of yellow and white spackles of radiance. Surprisingly, the drying process has achieved more of the effect I was after. The downward strokes of paint, that I'd started, to make up the darker parts of the lamp shade, have taken on the appearance of curved arm-like

162

rays. Even in this unfinished state I can see that this picture has a possibility of working out. I wasn't so sure at the start.

In the seascapes and deer paintings I do all the time, even if I try variations, I always know the outcome: a predictable, sellable, $300 to $400 piece of work when I'm finished. After I sketch in a leg, a breast, or a buttocks, my favorite parts of the female anatomy, I paint water and trees over them. I could do it in my sleep. But the aqua and coral interiors—too lazy to get out of the condo—that I've painted in the last two years have not been good sellers. Belle says they're "too melancholy"; although I can't see how a room full of beach furniture, muted coral and turquoise, with a shaft of morning light cast over it can be called morose. Now, the only ones Belle will accept on consignment are the old reliable repeats of everything I've done a hundred times before. She will probably laugh at this one of Catherine.

With that thought, I drape the painting with a protective white cloth, take it off the easel, and hoist it into the backseat of the Lexus. I seldom walk across the four lanes that separate my studio from Belle's shop. And there's still some moisture in the air, and I don't want a drop to fall on Catherine's face. I figure I might as well get Belle's verdict before I go any farther; though, I'm sure of her reaction. First there'll be a big belly laugh at my sentimentality and then total rejection. She'll ask, "Phillip, when did you of all people start painting portraits?"

I know that portraits don't sell, unless they've been commissioned, and even then there are always complaints from the clients. No one's mental picture of himself or his family is ever reliable. Working from a posing person consumes too much time, and working from a photograph, a flat image, causes too many distortions. Quite a few artists combine the two, real life poses and photos, and master the technique of making their subjects look good. These geniuses are able to paint their customers to look like themselves, yet with no wrinkles, no discolorations, no off-center eyes. There's good money in portraiture, but no real chance of artistic recognition, unless you're a reincarnated Rembrandt. And that type of painting just isn't for me. Always having to advertise, to promote, to get along with people isn't my style. Usually portraiture jobs come from rich families wanting a perfect oil of a kid who won't sit still or an old lady who wants to be immortalized, looking terrific, better than she ever did in real life, even at twenty.

Chapter 10

Belle doesn't seem at all surprised when I open the door and its brass bells jangle. She looks up expectantly with those big, heavy-lidded eyes—dark-blue shadow—and then she smiles in a slow, knowing way. A week of my absence hasn't made a dent in her appreciation of me or any change in her appearance. She's like an old comfortable mistress one can return to at any time. Her purple-red hair is still a mass of spirals, and her make-up is still thick and startling here at nine-thirty in the morning. Someday I vow I'll tell her how incongruous drawn-on dark eyebrows are on a near-white forehead. She's probably been advised by some cosmetics consultant that the colors will bring out her eyes, the same ones who tell my wife to wear orange and red flowered tablecloths.

"What's up?" asks Belle, and slides off her stool. She saunters, arms open wide, all eagerness to give me a full body hug. But the painting in my grasp prevents any such contact until I set it down. At that, Belle collects me into a surprisingly pleasant embrace. What is it with perfume and fly-away hair, the cushiony aspect of a woman's body—any woman—that perks up the senses, adds zest to the moment? In boyhood, I pushed away my mother's puckered, smacking, half-way swipes at my cheek, but they still gave me comfort. Now, I stay with my arms around Belle a second longer than she's expecting. She's ready to let go, but I keep my arms tightly around her thick waist. I'm glad I'm at least five inches taller than this woman or I'd feel dwarfed.

"Why, hon," she whispers against my chest; "this is more than I hoped for."

I pull back then, place my hands in friendship on her shoulders, and chuckle an explanation. "It's been over a week since I've seen you. Or haven't you noticed?"

She flares her head up and instantly assumes that semi-flirtatious mode she's adopted from the beginning of our business connection. "Oh, you know artists. Now you see them, now you don't. They come, they go. Want some coffee?"

"Sure," I answer. "Isn't that our routine?"

I'm comfortable again. We've returned to our old bantering territory, keeping it light, no talk of dead spouses to set my imagination burning with ways to dispose of Susan.

Belle scurries toward the kitchen, her backless pumps clacking a tattoo on the tile floor. Thunder outside rumbles a muted reply. "Unwrap your painting, love," Belle calls amid sounds of preparing coffee.

I stand, search a moment, and then take a common-place water-color of sand and shells off an easel, set it on the floor, and put my canvas of Catherine in its place. The soft easel light casts exactly the right luminosity down onto the work. I remember that I didn't sketch any female anatomy under the surface of Catherine's piece before I started in with the acrylics. Didn't need that bit of magic, I guess. Still, the thing works. Catherine's face and hair are almost perfect, almost match what I had in mind when I began. I'm struck again at the quality I've managed to achieve, even though now I can see where a few touch-ups are needed and that the lamp shade and the light itself are far from complete. But God, who can't paint furniture, static objects, slanting lines at the edges and curving strokes to show the fullness of circular patterns. And the lamp's base is in almost total shadow, as it was when Catherine clicked it on. So no problem there. Light is always difficult, but a few washes over the entire surface to soften every edge, to smooth out those clotted bits of yellow and white that I left—trying for that perfect instant, that flash of radiance as it blazed up into her face—and it will be finished.

I sit on the stool in front of Belle's counter and lean back against the black marble surface that serves as her desk. Outside, lightning flashes in irregular patterns, the fluorescent lights flicker, and lashings of rain begin to pelt against the shop's windows. Catherine

166

won't meet me at the Embassy, I silently tell myself; this weather will be all the excuse she needs to cancel. Still, I can sit here till the rain slacks off and contemplate her face. At this distance, the painting looks even finer than I thought at first, more than I hoped for, more like those venerated pieces in European museums, the glowing figurehead of some ancient goddess. To hell with Belle in the kitchen, to hell with Belle's opinion. I won't care if this piece doesn't meet her standard of commercialism. Let her laugh. I'm not planning on selling it anyway. Saved, placed at the back of my studio, it will shine like a beacon, greet me every time I come into work. It's a way of having Catherine even if I can't have her. For what did that kiss mean? Was it a kiss? If only she'd been a little more receptive, parted her lips a bit, sighed or something. And that cold stare? What was that intense flat look while our lips were still touching? And who's the husband who's building that huge house on the beach? That roof like an elongated sail, the first hurricane will blow that wooden contrivance off at its base and into the ocean.

Belle comes back into the cluttered room, carrying her usual tray of fancy coffee mugs and tidbits to eat. "Part of selling art is to delay the customer long enough for him to feel he owes you, that he should buy something," she says, and sets the tray on the counter between us. "Feed people, and they can't get away."

I turn from the painting to pour cream into my coffee, appreciative of Belle's selection of little cakes and pieces of cheese on crackers. I haven't eaten anything this morning but a half slice of dried toast that I snatched on my way out of the condo. My eyes hidden, I concentrate on the swirling eddies in the cup, the same beige colors as the waves on the Causeway driving over. I don't want to be looking at Belle's face when she views the painting, the substitution I've put up on her easel. This is the hardest part about being an artist or about any creative labor, the business of showing people your efforts. One feels like a little kid, jumping up and down, yelling, "Look at me, look at me. Aren't I grand?" And, of course, you're not. Most of the time the audience, whoever it is, is more than willing to give you bland platitudes, "That's nice. I like those colors." To hell with them, what do they know? Most people never try a creative endeavor in their entire lives.

Belle chatters on, some other mindless inanity about customers, her on-going assertion that selling art is also an art, and then she stops. Mid-sentence she falls silent. I can feel her glance behind my back, two headlight beams directed toward Catherine's portrait.

"Well, what do we have here?" she drawls and rises from her stool to walk toward the easel. I stay focused on my cup and forbid myself to watch Belle's inspection of what I now feel is too precious to be scrutinized by this low-class broad, this Philistine. What was I thinking? I'm not going to sell the painting. Why did I bring it?

Belle says nothing, but I can hear her feet move on and off the fancy Oriental carpet placed diagonally on the gray-white tile floor. She prowls, steps forward and back for a better, as she always says, "look see." She hums under her breath. Then, she purrs, "Well, love, what have you been up to?"

Holding the coffee cup up to my lips, as a way to hide my expression, I pivot on the stool. Belle stands to the left of Catherine's shining image. The shopkeeper's freckled weathered arms, a sharp contrast to her Geisha-like make up, are crossed on top of her slightly protruding stomach, and a look of bemused wonder is directed my way. Belle rephrases her question, "Using a model now, are we, love?" There's a hint of accusation in her query.

"Trying something different is all, love." I echo Belle's word. "No model for this one," I lie. "Just an idea, a compilation of women."

Suddenly, explosively, Belle squeals, "I love it, love it!" and in a rush, the woman descends upon me, hugs me again, this time in a truly spontaneous embrace. I juggle my cup away to receive this energetic squeeze and endure several hard slaps to my shoulders and then stinging ones to both cheeks. The coffee slops out of the cup, burns my hand. "Good grief, Belle," I protest. "You're making a mess."

She beams, a proud-mother expression on her face that I've never witnessed before. "Darling man, you've done the impossible. You've changed your technique, your medium, you've gotten better, come up with something truly original. Do you realize how hard that is to do in this fucking business? And you've got this woman, this com-pi-lation to thank for it. Where on earth did you get that word? Not that I believe it for a minute."

168

I'm dumbstruck by Belle's outpouring of compliments, seemingly so genuine, and realize my shoulders are still hunched as though prepared for more blows. Here I was expecting criticism, steeling myself for derision, and now I must consciously relax. The storm outside, the coziness of the shop inside, and the praise coming from Belle—pleasant, unexpected contradictions—it all helps.

"How did you do it, Phillip?"

Belle clacks back to examine the canvas, bends down close to peer first at Catherine and then back at me. "This woman's face, a strange, invented Madonna". . . and then barely touching the top of the lamp shade, she says, ". . . and the fucking Milky Way galaxy all rolled into one."

I start to protest, that no it's only the top of a lamp shade with the light coming on, and then I catch myself. Yes. Yes, Belle's hit on something. She's right. The fanning oval of light under Catherine's benevolent gaze looks very much like the photographs I've seen in *National Geographic* of the Milky Way—a whirling disk and spiraling arms of smeared stars.

I'm speechless. Why didn't I see that before? Why couldn't I see it? I gulp what's left of the coffee, set the cup aside, and lick my finger and thumb, trying to soothe the sting where the hot liquid sloshed onto my hand.

"Oh, darling, I'm such a klutz; you've scalded yourself. Let me get . . . ." Belle stops and wrinkles her face, "I don't have a thing in the shop for a burn."

"It's all right, some ice, maybe . . . ." Although the skin along my thumb and index finger zings with pain, I want to ignore the pin pricks, discuss the painting, have Belle explain more of what she means by "strange and invented." But the woman has already scuttled to the back of the store, has opened the refrigerator. She returns with a piece of ice wrapped in a napkin.

"All I have in the way of first aid, dearest." She places the ice in my hand and then watches with concern as I slide the cooling cube up and down the faint pink burn starting between my fingers.

"What do you mean by 'strange Madonna,' Belle?" I question.

"Well, love, it's plain that you're painting from a real person here, not some idealized holy virgin. The tip of the nose, going down that way—very Semitic—and the two sad lines beside her mouth, the hint of darkness under the eyes. Maybe a model, but definitely not some group of women, like you made out with that fancy word. In fact . . . ," Belle pauses, puts her large hand, four fingers crusted with costume jewelry rings, up to her chin, then rises to go back and re-inspect Catherine's picture. "Now that I really look, I could swear she's been in my shop before. Or I've seen her somewhere."

Bingo! Of course. Catherine might very well have patronized Belle's gallery, browsed, bought an arrangement or a print. Good god, what was I thinking? There's no way I'll ever be able to exhibit this canvas in public. Someone will recognize Catherine, tell her there's a portrait that looks just like her, hanging in a boutique on Quarine Street, down near the beach in Tampa. Somehow I didn't think I'd captured that good a likeness, but now that I study the piece from a distance, it's absolutely the woman, Catherine, herself.

I remember Dr. Jeffers, my old teacher's admonition, "Go for the feeling that emanates from a person; you'll catch them truly then, and when drawing children and young women, omit, omit, omit."

He'd bellow out those instructions, grab a kneaded eraser, and rub out half of some poor student's work. "Erase, erase, erase," he'd roar, and scour the paper as if scrubbing a sink. At first you'd think he was destroying the drawing, but when finished, you'd see he'd only taken off the surface, left, over all, what was there and even more subtly an impression of what was gone. "Nothing is ever lost," he'd say, with a flourish of the eraser, often throwing it at the pupil. The class, after the first heart-attack days of his bluster, grew to love him. Without knowing it, I'd followed his instructions: hit the high points, caught the curve of cheek, given a notion of chin and forehead, what her face looked like in totality, rather than de-tails, line by line. The on-looker's eye filled in what was missing.

"Well, it still needs some finishing touches," I say to Belle's back, "as you can see."

With my luck, someone could come in at this very moment and recognize Catherine. But I know, even as I start with excuses to get the painting out of the shop, that Belle's not going to let me leave without an argument.

She halfway turns. "I know this woman, just give me a fucking minute to remember."

170

"No, dearest, you're wrong," I protest. "How many blonde females are there on the beach? Hundreds in the restaurants down here—even traipsing back and forth in front of my studio window. She's imaginary, Belle—made out of the fucking parade." I adopt her profanity to show how up-front and honest I am.

"All-righty, how much do you want?"

Belle straightens, takes some steps to come back to the bar and settles her rump on a stool. Back into "business" mode, she leans forward on her elbows, two silver bracelets on one arm, a gold watch and bracelet on the other, a mish-mash of stones and metal, ten bright red fingernails tepeed in front of her. Catherine's plain child-like hands and thin unadorned wrists and forearms come to me, slender as reeds. I had them under my grasp as I leaned forward to kiss her.

"You're leaving me, love," Belle spouts, "getting that hundred-yard stare. This babe's got to you."

I pull back into reality. "How much do you think the traffic will bear?" These are Belle's own words from years ago, when we first settled on the $300 to $400 price range that I could get for a seascape. "Not too high, not too low," Belle had said. She took a 40% commission back then, which was 10% higher than the other boutiques and small galleries in Tampa. But over the years, those other shops had gone on to 50 and 60% cuts, while Belle's commission remained the same. I couldn't complain. The old girl was a good peddler.

"It's not finished," I say again, although now, seeing the lamp's top as the Milky Way galaxy, I realize that there's very little left to add; a few touch ups and maybe one extremely thin coat of wash for protection, and I'll be finished. "I really don't want to sell it, Belle. I just wanted your opinion."

"Baby, I have customers, collectors, who'll pay top dollar for this painting right now. They're remodeling, building houses. It has just the right cosmic appeal. That old-world quality, with a modern subject. Leave the painting with me for a few days. I'll take it around. They won't be able to resist."

Yeah, exactly what I need. Belle carting Catherine's portrait into homes until someone recognizes her. Still, I can't help asking, "What do you think you could get for it?"

Belle considers, chews her full-bottomed lip for a second. I compare her over-lipsticked, inflated lips with Catherine's narrow unpainted ones.

"Three, maybe four thousand," Belle smacks in satisfaction.

"You've got to be kidding," I say.

Why does this figure impress me? Doesn't the Bower Bankroll put that very amount into my checking account each month? Doesn't it accumulate into ten-thousand dollar clumps that I invest in CDs every three months or so.

"Three thousand?" I repeat, knowing I'll never get anywhere near that price, won't even get an offer.

"Baby, you can't take this lady away from me now, now that I've seen her."

Half laughing but deadly serious underneath her nervous giggle, Belle hops off the stool and takes a wide step to place her body between me and the easel.

Good god, this woman's a case. Does she actually think her physical presence is going to keep me from sidling past her and taking my own painting back to my own car. But apparently this maneuver is precisely Belle's assumption. When I get up and try to sidestep a degree to the right, Belle counters with a movement of her own and seems to think that if she makes a semi-joke of this game of keep-away that I'll think it's amusing, too, and give in.

"Belle, I'm not teasing," I venture, still with an effort to keep our exchange light hearted. "Honey, I'm taking my painting home."

She puts both hands onto my arms, and the overflow of bosom above her brassiere jiggles under the thin material of her teal blue sweater. The woman's very bulk, her thickness registers; the thought comes, and not for the first time either, that if Belle were a man she could take me.

"Listen, Phillip, dear, and reconsider. Haven't I always been your very best advocate from the very beginning? Have I ever gone up on my commissions? From day one, I've steered you right; haven't I? When you started doing those dreary interiors these past months—all blue-greens and oranges—didn't I say, 'No way, baby.' And haven't I always squeezed out top dollar for you, lugging your work over every inch of the bay area if some rich bitch seemed halfway interested?"

With each of Belle's questions, I nod in agreement. I've argued these same points to myself, and to Susan, debated in Belle's favor when it seemed like I might make more of a name for myself if I set up my own gallery.

"Now, that you've come up with something really original, really hot, please don't take it away."

"But it's not finished, Belle; I told you."

The woman cocks her head to one side and slants a skeptical glance out from under those ridiculous aquamarine eye lids. Why didn't Belle like my interiors; they're the colors she herself chooses?

"Phillip, I can get $5,000 for this painting, this very afternoon. I promise." She claps both hands against my biceps, which I tense, wishing them younger, harder.

"Also . . . it'll be the start of a whole new career for you. . . like, like"—inspiration dawns—"like Wythe, with his Helga paintings."

God, this woman's a born salesman. "You're good, Belle; I'll grant you that," I say out loud. "Do you really have a customer, already?"

She tugs at my arm, maneuvers me back on to the stool I've just vacated. "What's your problem, sweety? Tell old Belle." The capricious she-devil actually lowers her head to my shoulder for a split second and strokes the side of my face, my ear. The soothing feels good; a cool touch in the midst of so much agitation.

It's all an act, but I can't help saying, "Well, I'd rather not have the thing out in public view right now. It's. . . ." I'm flattered that Belle thinks she can sell the piece so soon and for so much, but I'm also stymied. What if someone recognizes Catherine?

"Baby, tell me your stipulations. Just private showings, I can handle that. In fact," she draws her head away, and again I see the wheels of commerce churn behind her eyes, "a private back-room viewing, special lighting, a few select customers, very hush-hush, and strictly the best people. Maybe, say, make-me-an-offer kind of affair. Pit Sam Pierce against Arthur Blake—those two can't stand each other."

No, shit, I think. One of those men might very well be Catherine's husband—God, I don't even know her last name. And I can just see it. Belle all set up, lights low, Catherine's portrait center stage, and some bull-moose roaring, "Where in the hell did you get a picture of my wife?"

"Belle," I start in, "it's too complicated to explain."

"Well, try for Christ's sake." She spreads her fingers with their pointed lacquered nails. "Here I am, good ole Belle, selling all your stuff—seascapes and sand dunes, same old tried and true as everyone else—and now when you finally hit pay dirt, you're going to cut me out."

In spite of her overbearing tactics, there's accuracy in what the woman says. "Here's the truth," I start. "The woman on that paper doesn't know I painted her. It's done from memory. Someone I saw once, turning on a lamp." So much for veracity. "In fact, that's what the Milky Way is, an unfinished globby attempt at the light flashing up out of a lamp shade—if you can believe it. But I like your idea of the Milky Way better. So you see, I've got to get permission from her before I can start showing the thing anywhere."

Belle pats my shoulder and sits, all business, back on her stool. "Ooo-kay," she drawls out. "You know this gal, right?"

"Yes."

"Would she refuse?"

"I don't know. I'm meeting her . . . today. . .to find out," I ad-lib, half truths and whole truths mixed together.

"She hasn't seen the portrait?"

"No, not yet. I brought it by for you to see first, before showing it to her."

I realize as I speak that the idea is not so preposterous. The painting could be in my trunk, and depending on Catherine's turning up at the Embassy—there's still that question to be answered—and how our lunch goes, I might unveil the portrait. Of course, I'd explain right away that the image she's looking down into is the Milky Way and not a lamp top. The galaxy would be just esoteric enough, would erase any question of "And when did you see me turning on a lamp?" before it even enters her mind.

"There's another reason I don't want you showing it to a bunch of wealthy clients, Belle." Wonderful to lay the naked facts out, with no additions or subtractions. "Catherine's husband is the guy who's building that enormous curved-roof house down between Sandhills and the Village."

174

"Rand Spurlock?

"Is that his name?"

"Yeah, he's been around the bay area forever, real estate man—always on the fringes—that is, until lately. His father-in-law, Arthur Lawton, died last year, owned real estate and stuff, that's really taken off in the last five years. Must have left it all to the daughter. I don't know about her—some kind of volunteer type. But I know you've seen his signs, those huge billboards with columns underneath as big as tree trunks." Belle makes a large unfinished circle with her strong, fibrous arms. "The Village council is fighting to have them banned, but so far no luck."

Spurlock, Catherine's last name is Spurlock.

"So?" Belle questions. "What can we do so that I get to sell this picture?"

"See—one of those high rollers you're talking about probably knows Spurlock, and knows his wife, too, Catherine." It feels good to say her name out loud, even if it's only in passing and only to Belle. "I have to have her permission. And I promise you, I'll get it."

And it's only with the idea of permission and with the promise to return the painting at soon as I get it that allows me to drape Catherine's portrait back in its white cloth and to leave Belle's shop without being assaulted. Still, all in all, the old broad's estimation of the painting's worth and her enthusiasm about it is exhilarating, flattering. Belle is right, I could do an entire series of paintings of Catherine, like Wythe did of that German-looking gal, in all kinds of settings. I could use universal themes, the galaxy and the Hubble telescope pictures, and ordinary settings that I've been painting for years: outdoor seascapes and indoor arrangements. I could keep Catherine blonde or make her into a red-head. A picture rises in my mind, a composition of Catherine as a brunette. I'll give her striking black eyebrows, she'll be sitting across the table from a man—he would be in shadow—a cut-glass cyclone in a silver stand, its single candle casting jagged patterns of light across her shoulders and breasts. Anything is possible.

With this new painting cooking in my brain, I go back over how I'd half-way agreed with everything Belle proposed, gave her nods and "sure's" that I'm not even sure of. I told her I would obtain

Catherine's permission to show the picture to a few select buyers—Belle would determine that none of them were friends of the hitherto unknown Rand Spurlock—and I would bring the painting immediately back to Belle. I would not return to St. Pete, I would not pass Go, I would not collect $200.

The rain slacks off as it often does down here on the Gulf, going from almost hurricane conditions to bright and balmy in a matter of minutes. I've taken the canvas from Belle's shop—feeling somewhat like a thief making off with stolen property—deposited it in the trunk of the Lexus, and now rush to open my smallest sketch book on the front seat for a few rough lines to portray the basic framework of the next portrait I have in mind. After a minimum of strokes, I realize it's almost one o'clock and I have to be at the Embassy. I plan to take the sketchbook inside, since Catherine is surely not going to show, and it will give me something to do, or pretend to do, instead of being totally stood-up.

The maitre d' shows me into the Hunt Room, in the back of the oldest part of the Embassy Hotel. I, with what I hope is an indifferent scowl and with my sketch book held to my side as protection, ask him for a table, "somewhere not too bright or too crowded." He, a slightly-built man in an immaculately tailored suit with a long, sad face, receives my request as if it's the most normal thing in the world.

"That will be the Hunt Room, sir," he says.

It's one o'clock on a Monday afternoon, so there's no danger of crowding or meeting people. And who really knows me? I have a few nodding acquaintances in St. Pete, and none at all in Tampa, outside of the regulars at Bayside's Cafe, Belle in her boutique, Harry at the pawn shop, and Violet next to my studio. Counting, it's more people than I thought. But then, they won't be coming to the Embassy, or would they? Stop thinking I order myself and look around.

The walls of the dim octagonal room are covered in splotchy burgundy wallpaper, fuzzy like suede, so that I want to put my hand out and touch to make sure. Susan would comment that this type of wall paper is put up to hide cracks in the plaster, and that assessment

176

is probably true since the Embassy is surely over a hundred years old. Unlit sconces are on the walls beside painted dishes of dogs and birds. The windows are narrow paned and tall, letting little light in through the thick greenery outside. Empty tables—round ones in the middle and square ones against the walls—with white table cloths and napkins in peaks, sit as if waiting for party-goers to arrive. At first, I pick a four-place table in the corner, but, after resting for a few uneasy seconds under Sad-Face's gaze, I decide to move to a smaller three-place table against the wall next to a window; one that looks out through the vines onto a small unkempt courtyard. The cheerless man silently follows me through my choices, leaves, and returns with a tall padded wine list, and then goes off again. A bulky young waitress in black pants and a white man's shirt arrives and introduces herself as Deirdre, my server.

"I'll wait," I tell Deirdre. "I'm expecting another person, a—a blonde—woman." I stutter over the word "blonde."

Isn't that what all the movies and television shows are about, about having an affair with a blonde? Deirdre, I'm sure, instantly knows the entire scenario, that I'm a many-years married man and that I'm meeting this blonde at one o'clock on a Monday afternoon for one reason only, to have an illicit, adulterous, sordid affair. Why couldn't Catherine be a brunette? That's actually the coloring I prefer: pale skin and dark hair.

My mother was fair. "A faded, dish-water blonde" is how she described herself, fluffing the thin wisps that hung straggling over the edges of her collar whenever she looked into the small mirror that hung crookedly next to the kitchen door.

Still, I sit and scan the empty room with pleasure. Tables in the Embassy are just as I imagined, white linen clothes with squat diamond-cut globes in pewter containers in the middles. The lit globes send long diaphanous strands of light up through the air, glancing off the walls in shimmers.

I try to envision Catherine's face in this shifting luminous setting, hawk-eyed and clear-skinned, but framed with raven hair. It's the image I carried away from Belle's. Mentally, at least, the transformation works, and I open my sketch book and start with the Medusa strands that I envision her hair to be. Dark waves, curlicues, tendrils spiraling up and around. The charcoal pencil's lead is perfect for drawing these wavy lines, and I give her a middle-part instead of that un-parted, pulled-back arrangement she favors.

"My, aren't we busy." Catherine's low voice stops my hand and the energetic curves the pencil is making. Even as I look up into the fair face that I've been picturing under black strands, I can still feel a tug to my fingers, as if the instrument wants to continue making those curls. Knowing it will only call attention to the drawing, I halfway close the sketch book, but still Catherine bends over to look.

"Hair?" she questions, studying the sketchy lines.

"Sure," I answer, glad that I haven't yet put any features on the rough paper. A blank space looks out from under the ebony tresses as if from under a wig. Then I stand and close the sketch pad completely. "Hair's hard to draw; I have to practice all the time." So there, before two sentences are exchanged, I'm already lying.

"I guess no artistic process is easy," Catherine says and slips into the seat across from me.

I wish she'd chosen the chair nearest mine but cannot find the words or the guts to say so. Still some emotion must show on my face.

"What?" she asks.

"Would you mind sitting here? It's easier to talk." I point to where I want her to sit, on my right, as I've dreamed since we first made this date and I envisioned it in my imaginary drawing.

"Okay," she says, and hardly seeming to stand, she moves from her chair to the one beside me.

Her action, in bending forward, causes a slight eddy of air to drift from her body, and I catch an astringent whiff of perfume, the same fragrance I detected at the museum. Not a sweet fragrance at all but electrifying. God, what could that aroma be called? "Jump" for the surge of electricity that runs through my body.

"Is this better?" Catherine asks, and sends me a small closed-mouthed smile.

I glance away quickly, feel that if I look into those ocher eyes, she'll be able to read my every thought, my every emotion.

She wears a muted silver-green dress, girded at the waist with a dark-corded material covered in black beads. Over this clothing is a matching jacket with the same dark webbing worked in, an underlay. The beads flash as she moves and brings attention to the inward curve of her figure. Every inch of the dress is calculated to please and the word "expensive" covers it all. Also, accompanying that thought is a wonder at my wife's own dresses, that no matter how much Susan pays—outrageous prices on the tags that early on I paid attention to, but no more—look like they're bought in thrift shops or made out of some great-auntie's leftover garments.

I command myself: No thoughts of wife, please, nor of her family either, or of my daughters. This is a time out of time. After all, putting up with Susan, her parents, and that Spartanburg crowd all these years should have earned me some freedom, some time off for good behavior.

"Would you care for a cocktail before lunch?" Deirdre, the waitress, is back and patiently stands at the edge of the table.

I open the wine menu and try, like an expert, to scan the list of names and prices, but can make no sense of what is offered. Even the small wine knowledge I've gleaned from glancing through *Southern Living* has disappeared in a haze before my eyes, and all I can remember are the small pen and ink drawings above the articles about vineyards in France and California.

Feeling like a stiff, dried-out paint brush, I ask, "Would you care for a cocktail, Catherine?" Thank god, the waitress has given me a coherent sentence to copy.

"No, just wine, please." Catherine grasps my wrist with her fingertips to pull my hand and the wine list to a point where she can read it. "But you have whatever you want." She studies the plastic-covered paper in its burgundy holder but does not remove her fingers from my flesh. She could be a nurse taking my pulse. My wrist thrums, vibrates under her fingers.

"I know nothing about wines," Catherine says, "but I love to read the names. It's like traveling to far-off vineyards where they're made."

I gurgle up at the waitress, "We'll just have wine, thank-you."

Under Catherine's light touch, I dare not ask for a Rob Roy. My heart would hammer, and she'd feel it thumping through the long embarrassment of trying to explain exactly what a Rob Roy is and how to make it. No one ever knows. Also the explanation would put me akin to those snooty yuppies Susan and I overhear at Sunday brunch at the country club in Spartanburg. "I'd like my potatoes au gratin, not hash browned; my eggs poached, not fried, please."

"Portland's Landing," Catherine reads from the wine menu, "Australian Meridian. They're like geography names, aren't they?" She releases my wrist and turns her fathomed eyes up to mine for an instant, but this time she glances away first, back to the list. "Here's one, Black Opal Chardonnay. Isn't that a wonderful name? Let's have it, please. Sort of an oxymoron though. Aren't opals mostly white?"

"That wine only comes by the bottle, Miss," Deirdre says. Yet the waitress's words are neutral, not a put down, a just-the-facts tone.

"We'll have Black Opal then," I say, "a bottle, of course."

I'm overjoyed to speak with some authority, some sure place from which to utter a coherent sentence. Actually, now, looking down the list, I notice that a bottle of Black Opal is modestly priced, $35.95, next to the bottom one, the cheapest, $29.

"Of course, we could have this Pinot Noir," I say, expansively; it's next to the top of the list at $150 a bottle.

"No, no, please. I wouldn't be able to enjoy my lunch knowing every sip was so extravagant." Catherine openly smiles now, showing the even line of her small white teeth.

She's delighted, I can tell, with my gesture. Still, I hope she doesn't think I'm some sort of show-off, trying to impress her; although that's exactly what I would like to do, impress her—press her. Her stubby-nailed, no-polish fingers, wearing only the large thick wedding ring, have moved to rest on the table beside mine. Totally of its own volition, my hand moves and covers hers lightly. She doesn't pull free. I marvel at my courage, and say, "I'm glad you could make it. After this morning I wasn't sure."

"I wasn't either," Catherine says, simply, flatly. The tone warns me to proceed carefully.

"That kiss was a mistake, I admit." I want again to get everything out in the open, so that there are no misunderstandings between us. "Your eyes were closed, and your face. . . ." I can't go on with the rationalization that her face was so unguarded, turned up in the bright morning sunlight, so that there was nothing left for me to do but to bring my lips down on hers, like you do when a child lifts its mouth to be kissed. "It was an impulse I couldn't resist," I finish.

"Good," she says, and her thin, dark-blonde eyebrows lift mischievously. "I like to be irresistible, especially at eight in the morning, with no make-up on and the scent of cleaning ammonia all around me."

"Well, you were . . . are . . . irresistible, I mean." Though I falter, this exchange feels like more familiar territory—what one sees in movies—how to be with a woman: courtship, compliments paid over and over, and then the big pay-off. The blood pulses through my body as though I'd just slugged down three Rob Roys straight in a row. What I wouldn't give for just one, right now.

"In an odd way, I guess, I've become attractive in my old age. I was gruesome as a child, all elbows and knees, and an unpleasant disposition to match." She takes in a deep sighing breath with this fragment of disclosed history.

I'm deadly aware of her hand under mine, warm and soft and perfectly still. Also I feel with every cell of my body, her corresponding body across from me, her form under the shifting green dress, the barest swell of flesh above the neckline as she breathes, the faint shadowy hollows beneath the highlighted edges of her collarbones.

"So, now, here I am, making a fool of myself with a strange man," she half sighs again.

The statement, a bald-faced declaration of infidelity, floats between us, suspended like a wisp of fog above a swamp. I can hardly believe this assertion from this sleek good-looking woman. No one in a film ever says, "Come, now we will be foolish with strangers" or as Susan's Catholic training would announce, "Now, they will commit the sin of adultery." It's something she sometimes whispers to me when we're by ourselves at a movie.

At that precise moment—thank goodness—a procession, the waitress carrying the wine bucket and the sad-faced man carrying the bottle of wine, arrive. Catherine withdraws her hand from under mine. A slightly damp hollow remains beneath my palm.

The little opening-the-bottle ceremony—cooked up I imagine by some snooty wine connoisseur—is enacted. The cold bottle is wrapped in a white linen napkin, the cork removed and laid on the table, and a small amount of liquid poured into my glass. And I, well, I go along with the whole bit of theater, smelling the cork and tasting the pale yellow liquid like some continental expert. I slosh the wine round in the glass, sniff, as one is supposed to. The surface of the fluid slants, an almost colorless disk of reflection. A round discus, it presents itself as part of the refractions of light that I plan to paint into my dark-haired portrait of Catherine.

"Perfect," I utter, not sure whether the wine is okay or not, for a slight resinous aftertaste lingers at the back of my throat.

"Very good, sir," Sad-Face says, and pours the two small tulip-shaped glasses to the half-way mark. He sets the bottle in its ice pail and then departs with Deirdre trailing behind.

Now, the tablecloth is flecked with diamond shards of light from the wine in the glasses and from the globes. I lift my glass, and Catherine raises hers. "To Black Opal," I say, and touch her glass with mine. I draw the wine into my mouth, as much as possible in one long sip. I swallow. It's delicious. To Black Opal, I think. That's what I'll call the painting of Catherine with black hair: "The Black Opal."

"It is a strange name," I agree. "Opals are usually white, opal-escent really, very hard to paint. Hard to get that pearly sheen just right." I am talking, making conversation, getting us as far away as possible from the topic of "making a fool of myself with a strange man."

I'm gratified to see a faint easing of the line between Catherine's brown-blonde eyebrows, to see those two slanting wings, a shade darker than her hair, rise up in appreciation.

"Do you always think about everything in terms of a painting?" she asks.

"Almost always," I say. "It's an occupational hazard, I suppose." There's no way I can tell her that I've not thought of painting with this intensity in years, not since I was in college or since those first dazzling days in Taos, when everything seemed a fitting composition for canvas and paper.

"Well, at least you're interested in something, something besides. . . ." Her voice trails off.

"Besides?" I coax.

"Oh, besides, you know, what most men are interested in . . . making deals, making money, sports."

"I'm interested in those things, too," I concede. "But lately, I've come upon a new project that has me very excited." Even as I speak, I see that this discussion might, with luck, lead where I want it to go, into showing Catherine her portrait.

Just then the waitress is back, waiting patiently at the edge of the table, order pad in hand.

Go away, Deirdre, I want to say, go far, far away. But instead, I keep all irritation out of my voice and say, "Give us a few more minutes, please."

Catherine looks down at her menu, and the light from the hurricane globe makes her lashes into lengthy shadows on her cheeks, just as they were when she turned on the lamp in her apartment, when I saw her from behind the wall, just as they are in the picture I have in the trunk of my car.

"So tell me about your latest project," she says. Briefly her eyes move up to my face and then she looks away and then back again without blinking. "It's so good to find someone with a passion for anything, something they really want to do, and not just for money."

It's exactly the exchange we had in the museum, not the words, those were different, but the feelings that are running between us.

I want to answer, find my way into an explanation that will lead to Catherine's seeing the painting, but I cannot locate the thoughts that seemed perfectly clear just seconds before. And just visible, Deirdre hovers beyond the alcove doorway, watching like a cat at a mouse hole, impatient I'm sure to take this one couple's order, bring it to them, and call the afternoon shift over.

Often, from one of her sporadic forays into the commercial world of service, my mother would come home complaining that a pair of customers had kept her waiting all evening. "They did nothing but talk and left a dollar tip."

"Maybe we'd better order first," I tell Catherine. "Deirdre isn't going to stop checking until she turns in our order."

I signal the waitress over, and we choose our food. Catherine selects some kind of nut-encrusted fish, and I, with a total lack of imagination, ask for fried shrimp, although the menu describes all sorts of delicious-sounding concoctions: Lamb Chops Marseilles, Oysters Rockefeller, and New York strip. Catherine sips one glass of wine; I drink two. The off-white liquid slides down my throat like water, no acrid after-taste now. I must have imagined the bitterness before, or it takes drinking a few swallows to anesthetize the taste buds at the back of the palate. I start in again to tell Catherine about the new project, but here I find myself off-track, unable to discover the link between painting in general and the painting of her. "I've found a new model," I finally say, since I can't uncover a lead into saying, "I've been painting you."

"Is one person that important?" Catherine asks. Her lipstick is a fraction past her lower lip, giving her mouth a seductive, mussed appearance, as if she's already been kissed. "I always thought it was skill or the different style of the artist that mattered."

I pour more wine into her glass, although it's still almost full. Somehow self-conscious—I can tell—but still with a certain amount of grace, she slips off her jacket and hangs it over the back of the chair. The dress is sleeveless, showing her slight arms with a faint etching of blue veins at the wrists and inside the bends of the elbows. She is, in the shimmering green fabric and the candlelight—I search for a single word to take back to my studio—resplendent, fetching.

"Oh, a model matters;" I continue, "really, everything does in the artistic process." I pour another glass of wine for myself and for her and find that we're almost down to the last third in the yellow-green bottle. I look around for Deirdre or Sad-Face, but now that I want service, there's no one in sight.

"It's difficult to explain. . . ." I start, trying to think on more than one level. I want to come across to Catherine as coherent and still formulate a plan, a logical explanation for a painting of her to be in the trunk of my car. Why had I been so foolish as to creep around in the dark, to spy into her apartment? First, to spy and then to buy equipment to eavesdrop. Women never understand that kind of stuff. Must be something left over from boyhood, all those free hours I spent in the woods behind my grandfather's acres, sneaking through brambles, staying where I could barely hear my mother's complaining voice and Emile's disgruntled whoops when he'd had enough.

"Different artists find inspiration in different ways," I add. What a dumb statement. "Monet did haystacks as seen in all kinds of weather and light." There, that insight is better. "Then he changed to lily pads, and later to the London Bridge. Picasso entered a new period every time he replaced a . . . a girlfriend." I start to say "mistress" but manage to change the word.

"So, you have a new model?" Catherine's odd-colored eyes seem different now, more yellow than brown with black edges, and they gleam with intuition, almost as if she already knows that I am caught in a labyrinth of lying explanation. Women, without question, have a sixth sense in this area, the ability to see past what a man wants them to think into the truth. My mother could always tell when I was inventing a story.

"Where is that waitress?" I ask, and glance around to avoid Catherine's question. "We need another bottle of wine. You'd think this place was packed the way they haven't come back to our table."

But then, as if on cue, Deirdre arrives with a tray bearing bread in a wire basket.

"We need another Black Opal," I tell her, and she scurries off. I hope that in the flurry of the second bottle of wine and the food, Catherine and I can take up a new line of discourse.

She lifts her glass and at the same time smoothes a stray hair from her round, intelligent forehead with her other hand. Her slender, short-nailed fingers visibly tremble and then cover her eyes, which she closes.

I reach up and still them. "What's wrong? Whatever, I'll make it right," I say, not sure why I feel she needs reassuring. I'm glad in equal parts to be able to touch her, somewhere, and also able to head off a return to the ridiculous topic of a "model."

"Oh, nothing, it doesn't matter." She removes her hand and shakes her head as if to drive away some inner disturbance. "Let's pretend there's no other place this afternoon but this beautiful dining room, and no one in the world but us. At least for a while." She sighs again, and again lifts an agitated hand to conquer the escaped strands. A trance-like, unfocused look comes into her eyes. This gaze makes her seem, both bewitching and vulnerable—but also slightly off balance.

"Exactly," I say, to calm her, to calm myself, and as an example I settle back into my chair. The waitress is opening another bottle of wine, and I want nothing more than to be in the moment. "I couldn't have said it better myself."

With the meal, we drink almost all of the second Black Opal, which tasted more delectable with every sip. The glimmering light from the lamp and the glasses seems ingested with the food and produces a wonderful feathery feeling in my gut, slipping down into my groin and legs. Maybe I should switch from scotch to wine if this euphoria is the result.

What did we talk about through the two hours or more it took to finish lunch? I struggled later to recall every word of the conversation, to conjure up each fragment and transmute it into paint onto the masonite board in my studio. First, we discussed the Embassy Hotel itself, its crumbling beauty. How did such a large building with what seemed so few patrons stay in business? And then we talked of the Hunt Room, its velvety red wall paper with the burgundy embossed scroll work, the wideness of the hurricane lamps, and the china plates that hung on the walls in twos and fours, painted with hunt scenes of dogs and horses. From those topics, we proceeded to the neglected garden with an almost hidden wrought iron bench that sat outside the tall windows.

"Just like the little courtyard at the museum," Catherine said, and the comparison seemed, to me, the happiest of coincidences.

But later, in going over every detail, I could not rid myself of questions. Mainly I wondered why had I been so unsure, so miserably uncomfortable right at the beginning? Catherine and I had already met in the museum, set up a date. We both knew the other was married; we both wore our wedding rings. And I was equally sure we both felt the same electric attraction that flowed like an undertow between us. My god, I'd even kissed her on her very own patio that very morning. Granted it wasn't much of a kiss, no return from her side. Still, what came back as I rough sketched in white tablecloths and the nearly invisible cones of glass and peaked napkins, was the jittery longing, at least on my part, for this affair—wasn't that what we were embarking on—that it would turn into something deep and true.

186

In my other marriages, and even in my romance with Susan, there was a play-acting quality about the whole business. I was too young to know what I wanted with the high-school Emily, and the two years with Jenny were a complete drunken haze. Even my marriage to Susan now seemed like a slowly accelerating train wreck. I had wanted each woman in bed, and they had wanted to get married. With Susan, it was a quick flirtation and the usual pick-up lines in a Taos bar: first, "Want to dance?" and then later, when we were both drunk enough, "Let's go back to your apartment." More often than not that come-on earned me a dirty look and not much else, but Susan took me up on the offer and kept seeking me out afterwards. She was cute, blonde, voluptuous, and she was always dropping clues about her family's money. Perhaps that's why I pretended to be with the CIA—something to balance up my side of the equation. But with Catherine, from the very first moment I saw her, there was something more: an instant recognition, a spiritual element that zinged through my brain along with the sexual attraction.

Finished with lunch, we leave the Embassy. I insist on paying the bill and giving a larger than necessary tip. Catherine argued, "I invited you." But I prevailed.

It seems absolutely necessary to pay, to hold her jacket when she rose, to take her elbow as she stepped down the wide cracked front steps of the hotel. I wanted this beginning to be exactly right, "mannerly" as my poor un-courted mother would have said. I want it to be an occasion to remember.

As we stand outside, there is no question of driving either car. The Black Opal sings in my brain. "I'm too drunk to drive," I tell Catherine.

"Me, too," she says. "Let's walk for a few minutes."

We find our way to the side of the hotel and step up onto the overgrown bricks of a deserted patio. The decorative pear trees in a line are shedding their leaves: orange, red, and even a royal purple. The bench is too dirty to sit on, but we stand beside it, and then, as if by mutual consent, we turn toward each other.

"I'm very, very tipsy," Catherine half-way chortles up in my direction. She is trying to step forward or backwards—I'm not sure which—but she keeps her face turned in the exact right position for a kiss.

Is it only in the remembering, in the re-examination of all the details that one discovers all the feelings? Why is it that in the moment, in the exact experience, one can never be totally absorbed? Part of the brain is always on the outside, looking on, saying now she is close, now you have your hands on her shoulders, now you are kissing her. And I was, and I did, kiss her. At first, almost emotionless, wondering if the kiss would be a repeat of this morning's cool, compressed meeting of dry lips, I bend and find that today her mouth is satiny and warm, her lips part a fraction under mine. Catherine's moist mouth; she leans into me, and I feel the soft yet firm cushion of her breasts against my chest and forearms. She takes a deep breath even as she moves her feet on the uneven bricks to keep her balance, and these sensations migrate through me in waves of arousal.

"We are very, very tipsy," I repeat the word against her mouth. "Tipsy" seems the most admirable of conditions. Tipsy, a good over-the-top-kind of drunkenness with none of that dull, please-god-let-the-next-drink-put-me-to-sleep kind of intoxication that comes after five scotches.

Still, she pulls away first before I can start that wonderful tongue exploration that is so exciting in the first real kiss. She leans back, her green-shadowed eyes closed—as they had been with that other non-kiss—and then she places her head under my chin and leans against me, sighing. Again and again she breathes in deeply as if trying to control herself.

"Do you want to walk down to the pier?" I question and press my lips to the top of her golden hair. Her breaths and posture indicate that she was not going to turn her face back up to mine.

"Sure," she says, the words muffled into my chest. Then, with head down so I can't see her face—is she crying?—she turns away and totters over the mossy bricks, the heels of her little strapped shoes, dark green, clicking faintly.

We walk across the grass and the paving stones in front of the Embassy to the circled pavement that probably once served as a driveway for carriages. Here, the colored leaves are heaped by the wind against the curbs. Then, out from under the hotel's trees and on the sidewalk that borders the street toward the pier, I become aware

Baptizing the Cat

that we are over and under-dressed for a windy walk in the cool air of November—although now the sun is out, a spotlight that comes on and then hides behind the clouds. I compare our almost formal garb to that of the other strollers, all in wind-breakers and tennis shoes, tourists, who filter in groups of twos and fours around us. In the same instant, she must feel this discrepancy, since she takes her elbow from my arm and buttons her jacket. Then she tucks her arm back under mine, and I grasp her hand. The side of her breast, warm, presses through the layer of cloth, but her palm is cool with a fluttery pulse eddying out of the ends of her fingertips, again the shakiness I saw in the restaurant.

"We don't have to do this," I suggest, not quite sure what I mean by "this" or what preliminary venture I could substitute in place of a walk. It seems that we must do something between three o'clock in the afternoon and this evening when I could logically take her to a bar or better yet to a hotel. "We can do something else . . . go somewhere."

"No, I want to walk," Catherine says. "I just didn't think we'd be outside, like this. I guess I dressed for evening."

"We'll go half-way," I say, glad she's mentioned nightfall, that she is thinking in that direction. "And, of course, it's our usual great weather, a mixture of storm and sunshine," I add, feeling totally astute to make such an observation.

"'Another damn beautiful winter,' as someone once said." Catherine gives a hiccup of a laugh, skips once to match her steps to mine, and flicks a quick glance upward. Her slightly smeared mouth is set in a smile, but her eyes glitter, full of unshed tears.

Now, on looking back, I see clearly the alchemy that lies in the details, the small signs and nuances of behavior that throws one into the ditch.

Still I have to agree, "another damn beautiful winter" and laugh at the curse word that is so appropriate to the predictability of seasons in Tampa and St. Pete—change and no change at all.

Chapter 12

Arm in arm, we walk. The street ends, marked off by concrete pillars to make traffic turn and go back toward the city. We stroll past the barriers, and in spite of my promise of "half way," within minutes we come to the end of the pier, which is made up of wide slabs of concrete, supported by salt-stained wooden pillars. We lean against the railing and look out at the Bay. The water, as on the drive over, is a roiling broth of brown, topped by white breakers. The pelicans don't seem to notice. They sit motionless, dark-gray statues on the tops of the metal-banded pilings. Sea gulls spiral over the water, and two worn old men stand fishing off the other side of the pier. The weather isn't worsening, and in the sky off to the south over the Causeway, dark clouds gather into an ominous edging at the horizon.

"Looks like St. Pete's in for more rain," I say, and wrap my arm lightly under the jacket, around Catherine's waist. How can I get back to kissing her, here in this public place?

"It can wash that side of the beach out to sea, for all I care," Catherine says. Notes of sadness and anger thread her words.

"Yes," I agree. A similar rebellion rises up in me. I see the Sandhills' condo, Susan inside, alone, towed out to sea by an enormous tidal wave. As an afterthought, I add Catherine's husband's tower house to the waves, complete with her rotund husband—surely he's fat—screaming for help at one of the stained glass windows.

"If it really storms, we'll be stuck here in Tampa, at least for the night," I add, trying to sound matter of fact rather than hopeful.

"Would that be so terrible?" Catherine, for an instant, gives me a direct, challenging appraisal.

190

Baptizing the Cat

"Of course not," I say, determined to follow the afternoon through anyway she wants. I yearn not to come across as a lover-boy or a smart ass or any of those roles I've taken on with other women. I don't even want to be a smooth CIA agent or a suffering artist. It's as though a theoretical intellect might be watching from above, saying, "Play it straight for once in your life, Phillip."

The weather isn't on our side. No selective hurricane appears to pull my wife and Catherine's husband out to sea. It doesn't even turn into a hard rain storm that could block traffic between Tampa and St. Pete. The menacing clouds, so promising when we first walked out from the Embassy, move away slowly, turn into the humped backs of retreating gray elephants, seen from afar.

And I needn't have troubled myself, wondering how I could return to kissing Catherine. Her hand over mine at her waist still flutters with nerves, but she turns, and with no encouragement, raises her lips to mine. Women are lucky that way; they decide. And what man in his right mind ever declines the offer of a kiss?

The afternoon sky brightens and darkens; the gusty wind rises and falls around us. We spend an hour on the pier. The two weathered fishermen, lines draped over the rails, pointedly ignore our embraces. The time is sweeter, perhaps, than if we'd passed the afternoon in a hotel room. For who could have said the first words in that direction? Not I. These moments are better, although throughout our meandering, the idea of an Embassy bedroom, old-fashioned and lavish, an Embassy claw-footed bathtub, large enough for two people, an Embassy bed with flowered bedspread keeps rising up in my imagination.

When we see that a storm isn't in the making, I suggest the Dali Museum, next to Tampa University's campus.

"What a great idea," she agrees, as though glad of a destination. We've both visited the museum before, but at least it's some place to go. The Dali exhibit never changes, except for one minor gallery where new artists' works are shown, often ghastly cartoonish paintings.

We go back to the hotel for my car, and I drive us to the Tampa campus, and then we decide to walk the college grounds instead.

Only later, do I realize that a university campus is ideal for this type of amorous activity.

We sit on one of the concrete benches lining the commons next to palms and sea-grapes; trees so old they are fully grown, like the ones at Island's End and the Tampa Museum. The thick silvery trunks twist in the same snake-like fashion. The day has just enough clouds to keep it from being stiflingly hot as it is so often in the first part of November. Temporary slashes of sunlight falls through the clouds, and shadows race across the mowed grass. We are more private here than we could be anywhere else in Tampa—other than an Embassy bedroom. Arm in arm, we lean against each other; we kiss again and again. Kisses that she pulls away from whenever I try to move my tongue too aggressively between her lips. Is she a tease? I ask myself, remembering how she changed her mind with Towelhead, even after she'd taken off her blouse and bra.

When the students stream out of the brick buildings, we stop and watch them settle into groups around the benches, or mill about singly with that lonely, lost demeanor that only a young person can wear. There is no bell—that I can hear—but one sees a sudden glancing at watches, and then as if by mutual consent most of the students trot back indoors, leaving only a few stragglers to observe our presence. And after the classes reconvene, there is solitude, an other-world quality to the stillness.

Catherine and I walk the edges of the common and came across a campus shop that sells sandwiches and, also, sports a beer sign in a small high window. I go in, purchase two large beers in translucent plastic cups, and we sit at an outdoor table—white metal under a striped umbrella—and drink. It seems an unspoken agreement between us, to keep the alcohol level in our blood just at that right, "tipsy" level.

The slight drunkenness frees me to be as bold with Catherine as I want, to drape my arm around her waist, to push myself against her—her back against a tree—to almost lift her from the ground when she steps up or down a curb. She takes off her jacket, and I feel the fleshy underside of her arm above the elbow, the skin an amazingly gossamer texture, like ground dry pigments when you dip your fingers into them. At the same time, the gesture allows me to feel the slight pressure of the rounded side of her bosom against the back of my hand. Once or twice I flex my fingers out, pushing them farther into her breast than I intend. "Sorry," I whisper each time into her ear, drawing her closer. "I'm out of control here."

"We both are," she says. "Wonder what those kids think of us two old people, making out like this in public?"

"Jealous," I say, and know the statement to be absolutely true. I see, now, how the energy of my youth has been wasted. I've used my coarse good health on some poor girls, even on my wives, and obtained release, but have never, as they seemed to do, squeezed real joy from the experience. Now, in a single afternoon beside Catherine's delicate shape, and in the unexpected troubled way she inclines her head as if attending to voices I cannot hear, a devout repercussion sounds through me. This wonderful afternoon, this wonderful woman is . . . is a gift from God.

I shivered with revulsion. "A gift from God" is Susan's phrase, one she piously intones practically every hour on the hour: for a good meal in a restaurant, for a good grade by one of the girls on a home-school test—one she taught and administered—or for the paltry sale of one of my paintings.

When I started instructions to enter the Catholic Church—no justice of the peace or other minister quite met the Church's high standards for a legal marriage—Susan herself embarked on a pious religiosity. She took to making the sign of the cross on her chest at the mention of any tragedy and uttering at any good fortune, "A gift from God." I should have been warned, one of the first of many unpleasant sea changes in my wife's personality and appearance.

But I cannot take back the phrase, "a gift from God," for it is so totally appropriate, so apt a description of the afternoon, and one that I will carry in my thoughts forever afterwards. Years later, the scene will come back in flashes, as one finds a jewel in an abandoned box. The coincidental meeting of two people, male and female, a cosmic view of the species, but also a view of the individuals. What luck! What a gift . . . from God.

At six o'clock, the sun edges below the palm trees that form the perimeter of the college. The numbers of students coming in and out of the buildings thins so that, at last, no one emerges on the hour's changing. Catherine and I, brave with soft kisses and beer, enter a building. Nevins' Science Hall is painted on a small wooden sign out front, but all the rooms down the long polished corridor are locked. The air is cold and damp, like entering a refrigerator.

"No wonder, the kids all sit outside—to warm up," Catherine says and shivers.

She starts to put her jacket back on, but I stop her, guide her into one of the recessed doorways, and begin a deep sucking kiss that includes sliding my hands up over her breasts. I push my hardness against her pubic arch, whose slight bulge I feel through the thin material of her dress. She wears no hose, only panties whose vague outline showed through the back of the dress on the way out of the hotel. At the tops of her hip bones, I felt the narrow connecting side bands of the flimsy garment. It would be nothing to reach up under the hem of her dress and pull that bit of clothing down. Fluidly, she bends into the leaning of my body and seems perfectly willing to let me do whatever I want. So different from Susan, whose thick flesh, in recent years, manages to remain in opposition even when she is under me, even in the very last stages of love making.

"Catherine," I whisper against her lips, unable to stop the words, "Catherine, I love you."

She draws back. Her saffron eyes, the skin crinkled at the sides, glitter with amusement. "You've got to be kidding." A little snorting laugh comes out her nose.

"I do," I insist and squeeze her slender back under my hands. Her ribs, beneath the supple layer of skin, seemed frail, like bird bones, and I resist the impulse to compress them more, as if by force, I can make her believe what I'm saying. "I do, I do. I love you," I repeat.

"You don't even know me," she says, and leans her head and shoulders back against the wall of the small alcove. My arms at her waist keep her from falling. Her hips and pelvis are pressed tight against mine. "You're acting out of infatuation or . . . ," she pauses and laughs again, "or lust."

I laugh, too, thrilled, imitating her edgy tone. "Of course, lust," I say, "totally."

How nice it is to bend over a woman, to kiss her, and to admit that I haven't the slightest knowledge of her internal life, of her values, her merits or demerits.

Baptizing the Cat

So, what else is new? an ironical note sounds in my head. How well did I know any of my previous wives, especially in the beginning. I know that marriage alone reveals the inner workings of a woman's soul. Susan's untamed hippie image in Taos was all surface: dangling jewelry, blonde hair, ripe breasts and hips, the trappings slowly shed to reveal the consummate, domestic animal she was underneath. Still now something deeper and truer, something I've never heard before, something harder to put into words, says, "Phillip, you are claimed." In response I silently vow, Catherine I claim you; you will love me.

Later, the whole business seems muddled and incomplete, probably because we didn't do anything but sit and walk, and hug and kiss, and, then in the science building, press our bodies tightly together. A janitor, a crooked black man, pushing a wide dust mop, comes down the hall. Surprised that someone else is in the building, he darts a startled glance into the narrow doorway but keeps going. On his second pass with the mop, without raising his gray curls, he mutters, "We close at seven."

I don't reach up under the hem of Catherine's dress to pull her pants down, not there in the hall and not later in the car. I couldn't let her think I said those fatal words just to get her into bed before the night is over. Granted it is unsophisticated to say, "I love you" the first time we are together, but in spite of my substitution of the word "lust," I still mean "love."

We drive back to the Embassy as the beginning lights of the city shines over and through the trees. In the indistinct hum of the Lexus, Catherine lightly holds my wrist with two fingers, keeping them there, even as I shift gears into reverse and then into drive. We don't speak, we are exhausted, almost as if we had spent an afternoon in an Embassy bedroom. At the hotel, I walk with her back to her Jeep. I don't dare suggest that we spend the night together. The words would be too crude, would ruin, I know, the afternoon for her and for me. She sits in the driver's seat and gives me one last kiss, hardly more than a peck—exactly like Susan—and then closes the door with its scarred-plastic side window. The last I see is her palm spread out against that pane in good-bye.

On Tuesday, on my six a.m. run, I follow the long line just where the water vanishes into wet sand. The sun has peeked up over the farthest edge of Florida, and I can imagine the long journey it has had coming over the Atlantic Ocean and then the peninsula to get a look at the Gulf. Then, when I least expect it, Catherine is there, right in front of me, lying in the shallow water. The barely visible waves pull her out a few feet in one motion and return her to the same place in the next. I walk to where she lies, then stop and watch. Her eyes are closed, and I don't think she's heard my arrival over the sounds of the swells. Also, she floats with her ears submerged and only the moon of her face shows above the water line. She wears the same brown racing bathing suit, as when I first saw her, with the gold borders at neck and arms that match her hair. She is the embodiment of some sea goddess with her water-darkened tresses fanning out in all directions, her arms and legs slightly splayed, the crystalline waters of the Gulf washing around her. How would one paint those three elements, air, water, sand that encircle her form?

"Be careful," I whisper, not wanting to startle her. Catherine opens her eyes as one wave, slightly stronger than the rest, pushes her body higher up onto the sand, almost next to my feet.

She smiles up through my shadow, which has fallen across her face and shoulders. A dusting of sand granules spackle her forehead and cheeks. "Of what?" she asks.

"Of the undertow," I say, reminding her of that Gulf danger.

Susan keeps a square rectangle of instructions on the refrigerator. "Don't fight the undertow; give in," is the main precaution.

"Oh, yes, the undertow," Catherine says and smiles up at me, "Not a bad way to go, wouldn't you say?"

"I don't want you going anywhere."

"I'm not. I was just hoping you'd pass by here and I'd get a chance to see you."

"Do you want to get some breakfast?"

"No. You go on with your run."

I want to stay and convince her, but I obey, do as she says.

On my return run, she's no longer in the water or on the beach or at her back-patio door. I tap lightly against the glass, but there's no answer. Is she hiding? No, I'm sure she's not inside; a hollow, empty feeling exists behind the drapes. Where has she gone?

Back in the early morning silence of my condo, I walk down the hall, glimpse the entwined forms of my daughters on one twin bed, Susan's snoring mound in the next bedroom, and Nursey's closed door near the end of the hall. Even with my coming and going, April and May will sleep till nine, and Susan and Nursey will not be up until ten.

After a quick shower, I leave for the studio and have a productive four-hour stretch, blocking in the figures I see so clearly in my mind. "I meant I love you, every syllable," I say to the masonite board as I spread the white gesso paint, preparing for the painting I imagined at the Embassy: a dark-haired Catherine caught in the gleam of candle light, a man, mostly in shadow, sitting across from her. Still, the question, Where is she? gnaws at the back of my mind. But most of my thinking is taken up with positioning Catherine's arm and hand at the exact right angle, elbow on the table. I play with the idea of her smoking, though I've not seen a cigarette in her hand since that night just inside her patio door. I didn't smell nicotine at the Embassy and didn't dare bring smoking up. How could I explain that I saw her smoking that one time. Still, a gray-white curtain of cigarette smoke trailing up in wreaths above her head would be effective, though difficult to paint. I could make the curves part of the theme of the painting, along with the wavy black lines I plan for her hair. Also, in drawing this likeness, in having Catherine's face, shoulders, and arms under my hands, it somehow mitigates not knowing where she is. It's as though I have control of her while I draw. Unfortunately, the feeling drains away as soon as I put up my equipment, wash my brushes, and leave the studio.

Since Saturday and then Monday, twice with that beautiful woman, the world seems different, better, thicker, richer—strange. Of course, it started when I first saw her on the beach, but now the colors of the sky and ocean on the drive over to St. Pete are more intense, the shapes of the buildings and trees are defined by black lines. Everything calls, "Paint me, paint me. I am so beautiful, paint me." More subjects than a hundred painters could use in a hundred years. I remember a poem from one of those first literature classes in college. Some old monk, writing in praise of all the different hues in nature. The teacher, a Mrs. Luke, made us memorize the entire thing, which was hard because it had lots of odd, similar words. And now I can only remember one line, "All things counter, original, spare, strange." That's how it is now; the world is strange, original . . . and new. How is that possible?

I vow on the way back to Sandhills to find the poem, to refresh my memory. Surely it won't be hard to learn the second time around. I'll say it to Catherine when we meet the next time.

In the condo, finally at eleven, everyone's up. The girls are in front of the television set, Susan is eating breakfast at the glass table, and Nursey is in the kitchen. Yet, the whole living room seems minuscule and far away, as though seen through the wrong end of a telescope. Ed and Miz Mildred are still at the Marriott, so at least I don't have to deal with Susan's parents. I realize as I come in the door, and not for the first time, that this condo, these people hold no real importance for me. I could leave and not miss a single one. Of course, I'd drive away in the Lexus—with Catherine.

The television cartoon blares and Susan says something as I turn into the hall, but her nasally words are as faint as an echo and make no sense. Behind me, I can tell she stands up from her place and loudly calls out a question. I turn and look but cannot quite—still trying to imagine where Catherine might be—make out what my wife's asking.

Finally, the question comes clear. "Do you want to go home to Spartanburg?" She pronounces the words slowly as if addressing an idiot.

A coral-colored terry cloth robe, the size of a small car covering encases her body, and the vee front gaps to show weathered flesh, lines of flattened breasts, and the millions of freckles that cover them. An over-ripe persimmon, split down the middle, comes to mind.

"What for?" I manage to focus.

"To celebrate your partnership. After all it's not every day that Momma and Daddy bring someone into the firm. It's never happened before. Momma thought a party at Smithbrier would be nice. I think so, too." Susan adjusts the robe, sits, and resumes chewing her breakfast, lips held politely together.

In other words, that's that. Momma and Susan's votes are what count around here, and don't you forget it. And "nice" counts, too. What Susan expects me to be, "nice" about going back to South Carolina. "Be nice," Susan admonishes the girls when they argue. That adjective, bland and innocuous, sums Susan and the Bowers up—in toto. What they are, what our life is: nice.

To think of a reply, whether I'll return to Spartanburg, I go back into the kitchen, edge around Nursey, and pour a cup of coffee. There's no way I'm leaving St. Pete now. A legion of devils couldn't drag me away.

Nursey is frying a second shift of bacon. Susan's already eaten hers and my share. "Don't do any for me," I tell the old maid and gesture toward the sputtering grease-filled pan. Hesitant and shy, still there's a dogged will about this woman—you sense the bone under the fat—a trait no doubt learned from her mistress. Nursey forks the slices in the pan and turns a baleful gaze toward me. Her rubbed-looking eyes, the whites, yellow and bloodshot, hold no sign of recognition, although she responds, "Yes, Mr. Phillip."

"Fry up the rest, Nursey," Susan orders across the counter that separates the kitchen from the dining area. "If there's some left, we'll eat BLT sandwiches for lunch.

"We eat or plan what we'll eat next—our existence," I mutter to Nursey, but she pretends not to hear. And if I know my wife, there will be no bacon sandwiches for lunch or any other time. Susan will pick, pick, pick, a half a slice at a time, until there's none left on the grease-soaked paper towel. It will be pimento cheese or peanut butter and jelly sandwiches for the noon meal as usual. I stand in the space at the end of the counter, drink coffee and nibble on an almost-burned piece of toast. It's Nursey's; she likes her bread charred that way, but she can incinerate another batch when I get through.

"I can't leave now," I say to Susan, with utter sincerity and with what I hope is utter finality.

She raises her pale brows in sloping question marks, "Why not? I thought you hated it here."

"I hate it there, too," I say, forgetting my vow to never speak my mind.

"You do?" Susan's indistinct lips droop, slightly open. "I thought you loved our home."

I backtrack. Her incredulous expression reminds me of my strategy, remember: kind, loving father and husband. "I do—our house—you and the girls. But not all that Smithbrier crowd, nosing into our business." I must, I pledge, somehow, rid myself of this albatross woman, and soon. "I'm right in the middle of a breakthrough. I can't leave now."

Her expression adjusts. My status as virtuoso artist gives Susan more credibility among the Smithbrier crowd than even my status as a covert CIA agent would, which she can't talk about, outside the family. "Phillip has to have his winters at the seashore to paint," Susan trills to anyone who will listen. Although I'm not exactly sure which of Susan's friends, if any, know of my supposed secret missions, my ex-Ranger, CIA identity. I've forbidden my wife to tell anyone, not even Myra her best friend in Spartanburg, that I'm employed by the Government.

"Oh, Phillip, that's so exciting; you never let on about your paintings until they're done." Daintily, she drags her fork with one hand and a tail-end of toast with the other across the blue-green plate, trapping the last curdle of scrambled egg. "Pass me some of Nursey's bread," she instructs, waves at the platter where the last piece of the maid's toast sits. "Sometimes those burned ends are good with marmalade."

No question on the nature of my breakthrough. Don't you want to know what's up with my painting? I ask silently, but then cancel that thought. Years ago, I tried to explain to Susan why I first sketched in a woman's face or form under my landscapes, that if one were aware, knew what to look for, the viewer could identify an eye, a nipple, the bend of a knee.

"Why?" she'd asked, crinkling her freckled nose in misgiving and disgust. "Seems like just more work for yourself."

"Art doesn't mean escaping from work, dear wife; in spite of what most people believe." I tried to define my system for making the most mundane sand dunes with boat or an old house and forest watercolor into something more interesting. "It's like having a private joke between the artist and the patron. It's one reason my stuff sells as well as it does."

"Well, just don't let any of our friends know that you've got a naked woman under all that paint. We like what you're doing without having a joke in it."

She meant don't tell any of her friends, and so I didn't.

I wait, another heartbeat or two, for Susan to ask a question or put forth another thought, but she's totally taken up with heaping as much orange marmalade as possible on a half slice of burned bread.

I give up on the idea of a shower or more conversation about a return to Spartanburg, and take my coffee cup to the couch.

"Morning, daughters," I say to no response—none needed, none expected. May turns for a half-second to send a quick, two-front-teeth-missing grin my way. I sometimes think we are the only two people really alive in this apartment. Susan, Nursey, and April are programmed robots, going through the motions.

Cereal bowls and juice glasses sit, half empty, forgotten, making rings on the glass coffee table. The girls are on the floor amid a rumple of blankets, two feet from the television, soaking up whatever pap Susan is letting them watch this week. Of course, they've been up since eight or nine, changing channels, watching whatever is on, with no mother to police the programs.

I shake out the newspaper to read. One of the few real pleasures left me, I think for the millionth time. But I can't concentrate on the news. Two thoughts wash back and forth: Where had Catherine found to go so early this morning, and how can I use Susan's asthma medicine in some way? The emergency room doctor said Theophylline was a dangerous drug. How so?

I look over the edge of the paper at my wife, still at the table. The orange bathrobe has slipped even farther down on her shoulders; white flesh shows, not unattractive from this distance. "Your allergies and asthma seem better this morning," I say. She stuffs the last piece of Nursey's toast into her mouth. No wonder she eats so much; she hardly chews—no chance to really taste—just stuffs it down as fast as she can, as if there will never be another meal.

"It's that new medicine, you know, Theophylline. Opens me up—a gift from God—but makes me nervous as a cat, and so hungry." She half-way stands to reach out and swipe a strip of bacon from the new batch from the plate on the counter.

Nursey leans on the other side of the dividing Formica counter, sips at a cup of coffee herself and waits, I guess, for another four slices of toast to char since Susan and I ate hers. Better hurry, I want to call out to the old maid, if you want any bacon. But, of course, I don't.

Seen from an angle this way, the black woman's huge shoulders and breasts are enormous hills under the aquamarine robe. It's convenient, having a servant the same size as the mistress, to wear all the hand-me-downs. A picture forms in front of my eyes: Susan and Nursey naked, the contrast, one model dark brown with large warty growths on her face and neck. I'd include her emotionless blood-shot black eyes. And Susan, white as alabaster, with golden freckles and her self-absorbed glass-blue orbs. Could I capture the differences and the dullness of these two women? Wonderful! But there's no way I could get them to pose nude.

"What's so amusing?" Susan asks. She stops eating, lifts her head, and narrows her eyes in suspicion. A smile or chuckle on my part always draws a question from my wife. God forbid I find any humor—an explanation is required—even from the funny papers.

"I was just thinking of painting you two, you and Nursey. It would make a good study in textures, a great dissimilarity in your different colored robes."

"Oh, I don't know," Susan says. She tugs at the orange lapel. "I've gotten so fat lately." A glance to Nursey. I'm not sure for what, confirmation or denial? "It would have to be on the beach— it's almost time to go down—and I look so bad in my bathing suit."

God forbid that anything alters Susan's schedule, which calls for the caravan to the sand to start at eleven, so lunch can be at twelve-thirty, or one at the latest.

"And Nursey refuses to set foot on the beach. Don't you, dear?"

"It's too hot for me, Miss Susan, and you knows it," the old maid states, a hint of petulance in her voice. Nursey stays in a half-way snit whenever we're in St. Pete. Although she seldom leaves the apartment, she complains about the heat, the sand the girls track in, the glare from the sun. But I believe it's the close quarters, all five of us crammed into one little apartment, that truly irritates her.

"I can take your and Nursey's pictures right here in the condo," I say, and give the maid a quick wink of understanding. Still, her dead-pan countenance doesn't change. The woman really doesn't like me.

"But you must promise to make me thinner, Phillip. I can't stand my rolls showing, even if you do use all those different colors to make them."

Before Susan can find any more objections, I rise from the couch and head for the bedroom and my camera. Should keep the damn thing dangling round my neck. It's always like this: a good picture and an idea come together and where is my camera—back in the condo, hanging in its case on the bedroom doorknob. I ought to have had one this morning when I saw Catherine on the beach, in the surf. Her hair flowering out into a watery halo around her head, the small waves breaking against her legs and arms, and the foaming sand bubbling beneath her. I was so overwhelmed with the image that I didn't think of it as a painting until I was five paces beyond her. And where in the hell is she now, Miss Smart Mouth?

"Are you kidding?" That's what she said when I said, "I love you" in the science building in Tampa. What kind of response is that? Doesn't politeness demand an "I love you" in return, or at least a "Thank you," or maybe a nod and a smile?

I spend the next thirty minutes snapping photos of Nursey and Susan sitting at the table, standing, and bending over and behind the counter, and the best one: the two of them leaning against each other out on the patio where the light is strongest, bright and zingy shafts coming through the palm fronds.

As they stand together, two complete halves of the color chart of opposing orange and blue, Susan questions, "Has this something to do with your new approach?"

"Sure does," I say, without elaboration.

In spite of my resolution to play the good husband, I let the girls and Susan leave for the beach without me. "I've been up since six," I explain; "already put in four hours at the studio. A little nap and I might go back. If I don't, I'll follow you down."

Susan glances up from packing the picnic basket. "I'll talk to Momma about putting off the party and the announcement till spring; that is, if you're really serious about this . . . what did you call it . . . breakthrough? Is that why you didn't answer the other day when I rang the studio." Her hands hold the wrapped pimento cheese sandwiches motionless above the wicker hamper. My wife is listening intently, is watching my face as I answer, is trying to read my thoughts.

She's no dummy, I tell myself; she remembered the word "breakthrough." She pays attention even when she doesn't seem particularly interested.

"You know my rule, not to answer the phone. And yes, the change is—to portraits—I think." As I speak, I feel my thin-skinned face warm with deception. Why? It's the truth. In painting Catherine, I might have found an angle, a style, something different from the other blue million artists on the Gulf Coast. "I took one over to Belle's yesterday. She said it's pretty good."

"Oh, Phillip, and you didn't let me see it first," Susan whines. She's lost interest in the food for the picnic—not a good sign—and both of her hands rest on the edge of the basket. "Maybe we can ride over to Tampa this evening and Belle can give me a private showing."

God no! Of all things, what possessed me to mention Catherine's portrait?

"No, I brought it back to the studio. Not finished yet."

"Well, describe it for me," Susan commands. The words are spoken well below her normal birdie timbre, a muted volume, yet full of power. Her indirect way of giving a direct order. She resumes loading a week's worth of provisions, but I can feel her wifely radar still honing in.

I scratch around in my thoughts, try for an inexact but plausible explanation and an ethical expression on my face to go with it. A fleeting question comes, will it be harder to lie now that I'm trying to be honest with Catherine?

"It's really about the Milky Way," I start. "A rendering of the galaxy with a woman's face—in the background." A good recovery, that is if Susan never sees the portrait.

"Oh, Phillip, you and those women under the paint. Why don't you try something not linked up with females for a change?" She slides a last package of munchies—the kind that leave tongue, lips, and fingertips covered in orange powder—into the hamper. The lid sits aslant.

"Come on down with me and the girls?" she asks, her voice and expression lively again. But I know the invitation is merely standard issue, like her request to Nursey, just another verse in that "you're falling down on your father/husband job" refrain. Over all the years we've been coming to St. Pete, not once has the old black woman gone to the beach with Susan, but my wife never stops asking.

"I'll pass today," I say; "maybe tomorrow if I'm not so worn out."

"Remember, you're not as young as you used to be. I don't know why you insist on those long morning runs and then not expect to be dog tired the rest of the day."

I rise from the couch even as Susan speaks and head toward the bathroom. Talk to yourself, bitch, I want to call back over my shoulder, but, of course, I don't. It's only another of her continual laments and observations, and she doesn't expect an answer. I'll take a shower, stay under the hot water until she and the girls are out of the condo, and then take a nap. Sensible Nursey is probably already asleep behind her closed door near the end of the hallway.

The hot water beats on my head and shoulders and runs down my legs, eases the tightness of muscles over-used from my run and four straight hours standing at the easel. Thank God for enough hot water. I never turn on the shower that I don't think of Grandpa Emile always adjusting the water-heater temperature down and Mom adjusting it back up. I must use hundreds of gallons of clean, steaming water each day, since it's my way to escape—hydrotherapy—even though letters from the condo manager stress conservation. First, let the bastards build a new staircase and stop mowing the lawn every morning whether it needs it or not, and then I'll cut back on showers.

Still, behind all these irritating notions, every other thought is, Where's Catherine? What could she have found to do before eight in the morning? Did she go back to wherever her husband lives? Workmen and a crane are still at that curved-roof castle each day, and it doesn't seem occupied. Should I look up her condo phone number and call? Now that I know her last name, Spurlock, could I find it? My cell phone's in the Lexus; should I ring her from the condo? What if she doesn't answer? She'll come home, not recognize my number, and return the call. Susan or Nursey will answer; they compete for the privilege of saying, "Bower's residence; whom do you wish to speak to?" Our phone has a caller identification process—although no one ever rings us but Susan's parents and sales people—so even if Catherine hangs up, Susan could call back. "Who on earth?" Susan would say and start dialing. She does it whenever there's a wrong number.

What a lot of shitty trouble it is to keep a wife in the dark. Now, if Susan were out of the picture, I'd telephone Catherine, leave a message. I wouldn't care, no need to cover my tracks. And I'd be rid of all that stupid Army Ranger, CIA crap, that subterfuge I've had to carry like a heavy piece of luggage all these years. How have the Bowers and Susan swallowed such a pack of obvious falsehoods, such cornball lies? TV true-crime shows detail, all the time, husbands and boyfriends who pass themselves off as decorated war heroes and secret agents and then take the life savings of the witless boobs who believe them. But Susan and her parents don't make the connection. I grab my sketchbook during those programs and pretend not to notice.

Out of the shower, I dry off and decide to shave and go out. There's no point in lying down for a nap. I won't have any peace until I know where Catherine is.

Opening the drawers on my side of the sink, I look for my razor, but it's gone. Susan's used it again. Now I'll have to change the blade, wash off the coarse, dried hairs on the edges. That woman! I move vials and jars around on her side of the counter, tall yellow-brown plastic bottles with prescription labels on the sides. I plunder through her top drawer: squeezed half-empty tubes of whatever, white inhalers with green and orange caps. I pick up another pharmacy bottle, "Theophylline" printed on the label. Must be a hundred or more pills in this vial and also in the one on the counter. I shake it; why so many? Theophylline is the new drug she takes and needs a blood test every week or so. She complained about it just moments earlier: gives her headaches, makes her "antsy" but, at least, lets her breathe.

I open the lid, take out a squat white pill with an indented line down the middle, lick the edge. No taste. I gnaw the side, chew at the slightly-lifted border where it was pressed in a machine, grind off a few grainy flakes with my teeth. There's an overall bitter taste as the medicine spreads across my tongue; I swallow a small particle. What kind of food would it take to cover up this caustic flavor? Something spicy. I spit what's left in my mouth out into the sink, look at the white powdery glob next to the metal drain, and realize, here's the answer! Now, where is the folded paper of pharmaceutical information that comes with each prescription, which tells the effects of an overdose?

I find two bent fingers of paper, which has THEOPHYLLINE printed in large type on the tops, but the rest of the printing is so small I can't read it. A sheet of paper, a computer print-out apparently from the druggist, gives a few of the possible side effects: muscle twitching, seizures, fast breathing, irregular heart beat. Those words have the most promise. If I can find a magnifying glass, I'll read more later.

Chapter 13

The curved-roof mansion sits on a slight rise, an acre or so away from the other newly-built houses on the ocean side of the highway going toward Tampa. I decide to check it out and drive past the imitation Cape Cod clapboards on stilts, past the wire barriers around Spurlock's edifice, and up onto a wide, round driveway in front of three tall turrets, like an old fortress. A fancy italized S in bright gold shows under a wash of left-over mortar and sand. Two staircases lead up to the main floor, and the whole structure, its drab color and tons of cement, gives one the impression of an ocean liner, all the levels, and it's also like a castle with its rounded towers. All that's lacking is a brass plaque set into the wall between the banisters announcing some ancient heritage. Two battered old clunkers sit off to one side—workers' cars for sure—but the rear end of a black BMW 400 shows just inside the four-slot garage. For a second, I debate whether to get out. But what the hell! I'm here, and I don't know where Catherine is. If she's visiting this man or returned to him even for a minute, I'm going to find out.

Up the staircase, the large mullioned-paned doors are slightly open, and I push them even farther apart, only to see two people inside the domed foyer. A young woman, dark ponytail in a red bandanna, cut-off jeans, and tight knit shirt, holds cleaner and a cloth next to a glass chandelier that's been lowered from the ceiling. She's obviously polishing each tiny bead and will be at the task forever. She asks, "May I help you?" in that arch way of the subordinate standing in for the master. The other person, a heavy man in dirty white overalls kneels at the threshold of one of the three inside doors that lead away from this grand entrance. He's doing a repair of some sort for he's down on his knees with tools, metal strips, and slivers of wood scattered about.

"I'm here to see Mr. Spurlock," I say, with barely a breath of hesitation before the owner's name. "Is he around?"

The two exchange a glance, but only the young woman speaks. "He's in the back somewheres." Her tone, now that I've spoken the overlord's name, is entirely different, mollified. "Checking on the pool, prob'bly." She points to the farthest door at the back of this elegant circle, "You can go out that way."

Well, why not, I reason, and head in the direction of the woman's pointed finger. It's hard on these working stiffs to distinguish the cops from the robbers, and in a resort town where everyone wears sandals, shorts, and T-shirts, how are they to know who's in charge? I could be Spurlock's business partner or the guy down the road, who's planning an affair with his wife. I could even be a Mafia hit-man—gun and silencer at the ready—but then I realize the need for the loose-fitting dark suit; that in my beach comber's garb, there's nowhere to stash a firearm.

I walk down a long hallway to a set of French doors, opening one to the outside and I see the master of this house, standing beside an Olympic-sized swimming pool.

Spurlock is large, a thick man, taller than I am by an inch or two, and, damn it, not fat as I imagined. He stands with his back to the doors and doesn't seem to hear when I open one to walk out onto the wide, white tiles that start at the edge of the house and extend in a dramatic arc to a cabana that lies beyond the immense aqua-tinted pool. The back of his head is covered in dyed black hair, and from the stiff dead appearance of the few strands that stick out in odd spikes, I know it's a toupee. He wears long silken black pants—unusual in this hot weather—a maroon t-shirt, and is apparently studying the water in the enormous oval pool. He doesn't turn but bellows, "Whatcha gonna do about this bum water?"

I feel an urge to push the rude bastard into his own lagoon and hold him under with my feet, but instead answer, "Not very much."

My words pivot his head and upper body sharply in my direction. He has a wide, flat, forceful face, pale, set with extremely light- blue eyes—"a sure sign of insanity," my mother would have said. Yet, in a voice as petulant and dismayed as any child whose toy has been taken away, he asks, "You giving up?"

I fight an impulse to say yes, but chuckle instead, "No, not at all. I'm not your pool man."

"Oh, well," he manages a half smile, showing slightly yellow teeth. "Who the hell then?"

"I'm your neighbor, Phillip Craine, from down the beach."

I reach out my right hand, Spurlock delays an instant, and then mutters, "Rand Spurlock," and shakes my hand abstractedly, a fraction too loosely, almost as if he's forgotten this form of introduction. Still, his grasp is rough, the palm dry, the fingers stiff and abrasive as sandpaper over wood. These hands have held Catherine.

"I live a couple of miles up the road in Sandhills," I continue, and point to that location. "My father-in-law, Ed Bowers and I've been watching this"—I wave a hand to the immense structure behind us, no way to call it a house—"go up, and we've been wondering who's doing the building."

There's something unkempt about Spurlock, almost slovenly. His chin and jowls are grizzled with several days' growth of beard, a film of oily perspiration glazes his forehead, the maroon t-shirt is grimy at the neckline, and the shirt pocket sags with pens and folded papers.

Spurlock pulls his upper lip down, clamps large open-spaced teeth on it, gnaws at the lip and does not respond to my information. Usually people know Ed Bower's name, ask if my father-in-law belongs to the Bowers of Bower Enterprises fame, and it's a real ice-breaker when you tell them yes. But Spurlock seems to be thinking of something else entirely.

"You know anything about clearing up pool water?" he asks. His dull tone implies that he's asked this question too often of late and of too many people. "See, see, it's all cloudy." He presents the large, rippling body of water, gestures with both of his enormous hands— two pink hams at the ends of hairy arms—as though I could have overlooked a twenty by twenty foot expanse of blue swimming pool.

Yet to please him, I look at the water directly, and do note that there is a distinct if faint milky undertone to the water. "Yes," I say, "but it's not too bad. The bluecolor is all an ordinary person would see. I wouldn't have noticed a thing if you hadn't pointed out that it was cloudy."

"Yes, cloudy, that's exactly what I've been telling those sons-a-bitches. It's cloudy." Spurlock says the word as though he hasn't said it first, as though by some sort of special insight into the nature of pool water I've managed to coin the exact word, "cloudy," to describe his problem.

"You'd think for half a mil, these people could come up with decent water—not cloudy." He plants his hands on his hips, bends his chin to his chest, and goes back to looking at the offending liquid, as if by standing and staring he can force the water to clear.

"Well . . . ," I begin, not knowing what else to say to ease myself away from this man and his water obsession.

This utterance brings Spurlock out of his trance. "Oh, sure, well, come on inside and have a drink." He turns and, with the bouncy step of many bulky men, leads me back through the French doors, and down the hall, past the workers without comment. I feel the young woman's eyes follow us as we turn into a surprisingly long tunnel-like kitchen, everything white and sterile as an operating room. From an upper cupboard whose pulls are barely visible, all being the same hospital white, he extracts a liter bottle of Jim Beam, saying, "A little early in the day, but I'm going through a rough time, the water and all, you know. Want a coke or something else."

"No, bourbon's fine," I say, although it's not really my drink. I've laid off the hard stuff for the last day, ever since my time with Catherine.

Spurlock pours two generous shots of liquor into squat crystal glasses, almost full. He hands one to me and leans his straight-sided hip against the snowy counter. He'd make a good nude study; one of those tall, bulky guys that the art classes at Ohio State hired as models. They didn't look so great in clothes, but naked, their full chests and arms, their almost non-existent butts and long muscular legs made them seem the embodiment of masculinity.

"The hair of the dog," Spurlock says, and downs almost half of his drink with one swallow. I sip mine, feel the sour alcohol spread its fiery tendrils down my throat and into my stomach.

"I really could've done without a kitchen, you know. Take all my meals out. No wife to cook for me—now."

"You divorced?" I ask, and try to keep any interest out of my tone. Just making conversation here, I want to imply.

"No, not yet, anyway," Spurlock says, and takes another long swallow, emptying his glass. Not looking at mine or offering me more, he refills his, and says, "I don't know what she's going to do. Never have." He stares ahead as he did at the pool water and shakes his head slowly. The black toupee moves in a slightly different direction. "You married?" His extraordinary light eyes lock onto my face, and I feel in a spotlight of interest.

"No—yes—I mean, I'm married. Been married forever, if you know what that means." Hardly, but the words are factual. Marriage to Susan has been a life sentence.

Spurlock nods and, now, not seeming quite so desperate, takes another long draw on his whiskey. His full lips compress in satisfaction as he drains the last bit of dark liquid from the fancy glass. "Come on, I'll show you around."

We walk, again pass the workers in the foyer; this time neither one looks up.

The house is monumental, is meant to be monumental, massive, impressive. Every room is over sized, over decorated, over spent, from the scroll work friezes at the tops of the pale gray, almost white walls to the odd-shaped pewter fixtures in the bathrooms. I follow behind the owner of all this grandeur, over yards and yards of soft, silvery carpet, interspersed with equally large areas of ceramic tile in muted shades of dark to light gray. The only real contrasts are gleaming black counters and sinks in the bathrooms, and, in the bedrooms, pale grey bedspreads and draperies spattered with streaks of ebony and smaller flakes of crimson. Wide glass windows look out onto the pool, onto the ocean, and onto the much smaller houses off in the distance. Outside it's some architect's dream and inside some decorator's dream, I'm sure, sold to Spurlock as the latest and the best.

Every once in a while, Susan becomes entranced with an idea like the black and white of Spurlock's mansion, on re-doing a room in Spartanburg, making it into something she's seen in a magazine or a furniture store's show case. This year her latest brain storm was to "spruce up" our bedroom with the colors rose and ebony—which

212

meant red and black—before we left for the beach. I fended her off with a promise of "maybe" after we come back. Hopefully, she will forget all about that decorating nightmare and be on to something new if we—or she—ever goes back.

I have plenty of time for my own thoughts because Spurlock is always two steps ahead, describing every square foot of the house and its cost. "Been photographed for *Architectural Digest*," he repeats several times and then explains that the article will come out only when the entire house is finished. The exterior is taking much longer than expected. In addition to the poor quality of the pool water, the roof—depictions of a ship's sails unfurled—are all that's left to complete, which explains the crane and the workers Ed and I have seen from the Sandhills' patio. At first, I try to pay attention to the man's rapid-fire explanations, but it seems as if each room and every article in each room, contains a story of difficulties that Spurlock, the exacting builder of a dream, has encountered. There were numerous devilish contractors whose only goal was to frustrate plans of tile and carpet perfection, and evil companies who delivered window sills too narrow by an inch from what had been ordered and then the wrong shade of blue for the stained glass windows.

"Had to fire the jackass they first sent out to install this marble," Spurlock begins, standing at the doorway of what I would call an enormous den, but he pronounces it, "My Library." He doesn't add "tadah" but might as well. A black marble structure, with white streaks, is a monolithic fireplace that covers one entire twenty-foot wall. "Belonged to Dupont in Chicago. Had to have it shipped down in three separate railroad cars," Spurlock says, as if describing the moving of the Pieta from the Vatican. I listen in half attention, keeping an ear out for any word that might refer to Catherine or "my wife" or maybe "children" for that would lead back to "wife."

Funny how the importance in life shifts as one's circumstances change. At one time I would have been fascinated, green eyed with envy over all this black and white opulence. The expensive car, the enormous house, and the job with a recognizable title were my sign posts of accomplishment, things which once meant so much to my mother, and me, too, I guess. But I quickly learned from Susan's crowd in Spartanburg that three-fourths of that country club gang were just like my wife and me, all living off what Daddy or some other ancestor had worked to create. Those heirs, now too old to be called kids, made careers out of what they could buy or where they could travel. I soon understood Susan's pride in having a husband who practiced art, although commonplace as dirt—might as well be coating walls with latex—because at least it was an occupation. For after you have the house and the car, and as many trips and gewgaws as can be accumulated, what then? All that matters to Susan, now, is what she will eat at her next meal and comparing who bought what, and where.

All that matters to me, now, is finding Catherine. So why am I following behind this overgrown cretin, as equally taken up with his possessions as any Muffy or Fluffy of the Smithbrier crowd.

From what must be the master bedroom, Spurlock slides a glass door open on the far end of the swimming pool, and again we are outside in the bright sunlight, made even more blinding by the spread of white tiles. "Well," I start, a preamble to, "I'll be heading out; thanks for the tour," since never, after that first instance, has Spurlock's monologue included his missing wife.

"Don't leave," he says, with a flash of hopelessness in the pale eyes set deep in their fleshy sockets. "I'm at loose ends here. The house . . . ." His words trail off into wide-lipped mouthings that I can't make out. When he catches my look, he says, "I'm good at big projects, you know," and again he makes the gesture he's been employing for the last half hour, the sort of "tah-dah" movement, opening wide his long arms and stretching out his thick hands, the wrists and knuckles grimly massive, toward the edifice behind us. "Catherine always took care of the details. Could get more out of hired-help, with her sweet talk, than I ever could with overtime pay. And they're not going to run the damned article in *Architectural Digest* until they interview her, and she won't talk to them, or to me."

"You don't know when you're well off," I say, aiming for some kind of joke.

Spurlock takes a step sideways over the tiles, as if to distance himself from my offhand remark. "Yeah," he says; "You'd think so, wouldn't you?"

The profile view of the man's face makes it seem incredibly long jawed, or perhaps it's because the chin is trembling, and I realize that Spurlock's mouth is half open, and he's trying to control tears.

Baptizing the Cat

"Women, real ball breakers, uh?" Spurlock says, head down now, not bothering to keep the weeping out of his voice. His fingers tremble as thumb and forefinger slide across his eyes and squeeze the bridge of his nose. "Years, we've been married years, and just like that . . . ." He stops to gain control, then says, "I've always wanted this house, from the beginning. It was our dream, a big house with all the trimmings (it's as though he's describing a steak dinner), but Catherine changed her mind, moved back into Sandhills, that little condo we lived in when we were first married. Says this thing is a show-off place, not a home." Again he flings an arm behind him toward the house.

All I want are more details about Catherine, so I take on what I hope is the tone of sympathetic listener. "It's strange how things work out," I say. "You start marriage with so many hopes." Mental pictures flicker: Susan and I in front of the judge in Taos, in front of the Catholic priest in Spartanburg, 'for better or worse'; now there's a bad bargain if I've ever heard one. I trail the words "so many hopes," encouraging.

"Yeah," Spurlock agrees, but then visibly shakes himself away from revealing more. "No need crying over spilt milk, is there?"

I nod. This man's not going to reveal much. The big burly silent type is how he's presented himself to the world all his life, and he can't change now. Probably regrets even saying the little he's already given away.

How hard it is to go from generalities, pleasantries, from the mundane to specifics. "How long were you married?" I ask, optimistically placing their union in the past tense.

"Twenty-two years," Spurlock answers. "Married her when she was eighteen. The most amazing woman, but strange, a little too religious for my taste. Maybe that's why I had to have her." He says these last words in a barely audible whisper.

It's the truth, Catherine is unusual. I don't think it's religion, though; she's not said one thing to me in that direction. She's open, friendly, but something enigmatic hangs in the air around her. She seems to tell all, and yet you feel she withholds the most important element of her personality. Her amber eyes flickered with half-concealed amusement the entire afternoon we were together, as if I were some kind of entertainment but not much more.

"You always lived in St. Pete?" I ask Spurlock. I'll drag the facts out of the man if I have to. That day with Catherine seems a hundred years ago: her lips, the soft pressure of her breasts against my chest, her ocher eyes looking away.

"Yeah, we struggled those first years. They were the best, when the boys were little. I had to break into the market, break a few rules, you know what I mean."

I nod again and respond, "Rules were made to be broken." It's what Spurlock expects me to say. "Thou shalt not kill" is a big rule, I think without wanting to.

Spurlock straightens, visibly shakes himself, suggests, "Let's take it back into the house, out of the heat." He lumbers toward the doors that lead to the entryway where the two workers are probably still dragging their jobs out. Hourly wages assures an hourly pace, just like those nephews the manager hires to work around Sandhills.

Back inside the cool white kitchen, Spurlock pours himself another drink. I decline, decide that trailing behind this portentous prick, waiting for a few crumbs of insight into Catherine and their marriage is not worth the effort. By now she could be in her apartment, and I'll miss an opportunity to see her, to set up our next meeting.

I offer my hand to the man, start to say, "Well, it's been great meeting you. See you around." But he's not letting me get away that easy.

"Come on," he whines, like a little kid, in a surprisingly high voice. He grabs my wrist along with the hand shake and doesn't let go. "Let me show you what I bought first thing this morning." With his other hand, he sloshes my glass half-full of whiskey, pushes it into my free hand, and leads me back to the library. I comply. What else, with this huge ox practically dragging me? This ignoramus, this lout, who has everything in the world but doesn't know what to do with it.

Back inside the enormous library, Spurlock releases his hold. Odd, to be pulled along by someone so much stronger. He opens a narrow cabinet door on the side of a large glass case containing dishes and ceramic pieces, possibly European porcelain. If I had time, these items might be interesting. Some have that original look of genuine work, not manufactured things that one buys in a gift shop. But Spurlock calls me away from inspection.

"Look at this, buddy," he says, and from the bottom shelf of a slender side panel, he pulls out a pearl-handled, chrome-plated firearm in a brown leather holster.

"Jeeze, Louise," I say.

Spurlock takes the words as admiration, but the emotion I'm feeling is trepidation, mixed up with a good dose of fear. Here, my hoped-for-lover's spouse stands with a pistol in his large hands. The headline "Killed by Jealous Husband" is not exactly the end I'm hoping for— although like everyone else I'm hoping for no end at all.

"It's a beaut, isn't it?" Spurlock says, unsnaps the strip of leather from over the hammer, and takes the long-nosed gun from its sheath. "Only $700 from that pawn shop on the strip. Harry's, you know the one."

"Sure," I say. "I've bought guns from him, too." I describe my purchase of over three years ago—what now seems another lifetime—the nineteenth-century rife I was so proud to find, its carved mahogany stock, the exquisite scroll work of camellias and leaves, an *objet des arts* to hang on a wall rather than just a gun.

"Man, I'd like to see that." Spurlock's pale eyes glitter with friendship. We're pals, comparing purchases.

He stokes the long muzzle of the pistol, and I'm forced to recall pop-psychology's claim that men view the length of a weapon as a symbol of their size and virility. But who said, "Sometimes a cigar is just a cigar"?

"When can I come over?" Spurlock asks, all eagerness, a kid with a new-found friend, saying, "Let's play at your house."

"Well . . ." I hedge.

"How 'bout this afternoon, or maybe we could go back to Harry's right now and check out what he's got in stock. There's a nine-millimeter German Luger in a leather case, I'm dying for, perfect for this library. I'd like you to see it, see if it fits in with the 'decor'." He crooks his wrist in a limp way so I'll be sure and not attribute such a feminine word to him.

Suddenly, I'm exhausted, feel as if I've spent too much time with this man. "Well, I need to go back to my studio for a few hours . . . ."

"Oh, that'd be great! I've never seen a real working artist's studio before. Catherine's always the one interested in all that highbrow stuff."

Inspiration, a full-blown lie comes, "Well, I have to take my wife to the doctor first," I say. "So . . . maybe later."

"What's wrong with her?" Spurlock asks.

"Breathing problems, terrible asthma, had it all her life. I'm worried," I embellish, and rub at the line between my eyebrows with a concerned hand.

For . . . here might be a witness, someone who could meet Susan, hear her complaints, see all the tissues, the coughing and nose blowing, and later testify how desperate she was to find a cure, or just something to relieve her congestion. And also to testify to her husband's concern. I'll have to backtrack on that bit about marriage being a life sentence, but perhaps it didn't make an impression on Spurlock.

Another thought comes: What food could cover up the bitter taste of Theophylline, the after-flavor, metallic and cloying, which sat on the back of my tongue for minutes after I swallowed the few grains I'd chewed off.

"I can come over this evening, maybe take you and the misses out for dinner," Spurlock continues. "Okay? What's your condo number? Catherine's in 3D. Maybe talk her into going out with us."

Good God, no! Spurlock's planning is moving the afternoon in a direction I hadn't imagined. "Sorry, old scout, but Susan's far too sick for a dinner engagement right now—or to go anywhere but the doctor's." Might as well make her out at death's door—for she is. "I'm just killing time until her appointment." I glance at my watch, glad it's a $12,000 Rolex, sure that Spurlock has been aware of the expensive timepiece even when I wasn't. "Some other evening, okay?"

I'll have to run this possibility past Susan, past Catherine, too—that is if I ever see her again. God, how can I explain hooking up with her husband of all people? And I sure don't want us forming a cozy little foursome, eating dinner, making small talk. Although Susan would love meeting the owners of this immense new house on

Baptizing the Cat

the beach. But that plot line is so predictable; it's in all the detective stories. Husband, friend, wife of friend, Susan and Catherine, Spurlock and me, diagonal lines forming between all the participants, an announcer's over-voice saying, "Nine times out of ten the killer is within the immediate family or a circle of friends." I've watched too many of Susan's true crime TV shows not to know the basic rules. Never be friends with your lover's spouse and never a hint to anyone of your plans. Your most trusted confidant will be wired for sound and your fuzzy voice recorded to rerun forever on late-night television, saying, "Back over her with the car—two or three times."

Spurlock turns, shuffles a few steps away to an expanse of clear window, which looks out to the clapboard houses on stilts. The white, pale pink, pale yellow, and pale green structures lie in the distance, far from his own great building, both in perspective and cost. Most of those cookie-cutter dwellings are built blocks away from what everyone comes to St. Pete for, for the beach and the ocean.

With a shrug of his wide hunched shoulders, he downs the last of his drink and lets the glass fall to the carpet with a barely perceptible "thunk." The silver gun dangles by his side in his other hand. He mumbles words I don't catch and then in one movement raises the damn thing to his temple.

"Don't! God, don't!" I rush toward the man with, I guess, some intent of pulling the pistol away, but before I can reach him, he turns and presents me with a grimly smiling visage. His eyes are full of unshed tears, his creased lips compressed into a wide slit in his face. With the muzzle pressed against his temple, the wrinkled flesh at the edge of his eyelid bulges, and he asks, "Why not?"

I step closer and lightly place my hand on Spurlock's biceps. In spite of the strength I'd felt in his earlier grasp on my wrist, now it seems there is no muscle under his skin. Still I use only the slightest pressure, just in case a single gesture will push him over the edge, will cause him to pull the trigger. Yet my artist's mind sees all, projects into the future. In some weird juxtaposition with reality, I can already see streaked blood and brain matter spattered across the immaculately clear plate glass we're standing next to.

"Man, she's not worth it," I say. "I promise you. Look what you've got here, what you've built. You don't need a woman."

Up close to Spurlock, I'm suddenly aware, again, of the physicality of the man, his height over me, and I can see the dark, indented circles of fatigue around his eyes, even a few leftover teenage acne scars under what I calculate is a two-day growth of beard. His face gleams with moisture. I'm too close. The rank odor of human flesh and unwashed clothes reaches my nose, covered only slightly by some expensive cologne.

"You're right," Spurlock says. He lets the hand holding the gun drop back to his side.

I don't try to take the weapon, fear that any action on my part might cause some sort of struggle. Headlines, again, flash in my head: "Local artist shot by jealous husband." Not exactly accurate, but the guard at the Tampa Museum might remember me talking to Catherine, or Deidre and Sad Face at the Embassy, or the two fishermen on the wharf, or the students at the Tampa University—the list seems endless.

"I'll tell you what," I say, in my best-friend voice. "Why don't we get together this afternoon, after Susan's appointment. Just you and me. We'll take in Harry's, see if he's got anything new, and then I'll give you a tour of my studio."

Even as I speak, I calculate a dash back to Tampa to put Catherine's black-haired portrait into the Lexus' trunk with the galaxy one, and then another dash to meet Spurlock at the pawn shop and bring him back to the studio all in one wide loop of activity.

"You sure?" Spurlock asks. "Don't want you feeling like you have to, just because of this stupid . . . ." He holds the pistol up slightly, and now I have the nerve to take the weapon out of his hand. The gun is heavy, more weight than I expected, the weighty potential of death.

"I knew you didn't mean anything by it, old man," I say. "It's a great piece. And who hasn't thought about ending it all, at one time or another. I've been kind of desperate myself lately. What with Susan's asthma and all; her coughing's enough to put us both in the grave."

I regret the word "grave," and now the idea that Spurlock might have some witness value seems ludicrous. The depressed ex-husband of my future wife could hardly fill the bill in that department.

If Susan dies, I'll need witnesses who will swear I was the best husband in the world and never looked at another woman. "Here, let me put this motherfucker in its holster." I turn back to a narrow table behind a black suede couch where Spurlock has left the gun's leather case. I slip the revolver into its rawhide sheath. Spurlock leans a shoulder against the wooden sash of the window and covers his face with one hand. His fingers shake.

"Why don't you lie down for an hour or so," I say, returning to his side, touching his shoulder again. I feel a catch in my own throat, glad to suggest some positive action. I could be standing in this room with brains and blood blown out across all that pristine glass, blown out across my shirt, across my tennis shoes. I could be watching Spurlock's life draining away on that white carpet.

If Susan dies, it must be painless—I promise—I really did love her once. Her end can have nothing to do with guns or blood.

"You're right. I've been up since three this morning, calling over to Catherine's, but she's gone or turned the damned phone off. Not answering since she knows it's me."

"Where would she go?" I ask, and then try to make my question more general. "Does she have family around here?"

Spurlock straightens, pulls himself into a more upright posture, though he's still deadly pale under all that glistening sweat, but now the moisture seems more like slime coating his skin than water. "A friend, Claire. She has a house down past the Don CeSar, in Pass-A-Grille. One of those little huts. Bought a bunch when you could get an acre of land for a hundred bucks. Made a mint, wasted it on husbands and booze, but still owns a duplex. Never sticks her nose out, except for Catherine."

Surprise! Catherine's friend lives in that same half-mile area where Archie has Island's End. Catherine must have walked those beaches up to the point, sat in one of the two bars, the Hurricane or the Realto, breathed the same air I did, looked at the same sky. Maybe that's why I was so drawn to that place, always hoping to find someone like her.

Spurlock shuffles past me, his steps cannot be called walking. He passes the long line of glass panels in the north wall and heads toward the back wing of the house, says over his shoulder, "I'm going to rest now. God, I'm so tired. See you about . . . ?" He turns and raises a line of dark eyebrows.

I'm not escaping this man. "About five," I answer, "at Harry's."

Spurlock's steps move him on down the tiled floor in the hall and after a few seconds, I hear the click of the master bedroom door closing. Without any sound, I still can imagine him sitting on the huge black and gray quilted bed spread, lying back, letting the whirl of drink and exhaustion push him under into darkness. I've played that scene out enough times to know how it feels.

Then I wrench myself into motion. Some directing force toward normalcy causes me to put the holstered gun back into the cabinet, although there's another part of me that says maybe I should take the weapon, just in case Spurlock decides to finish the job after I leave. Still that's not my problem. Let someone else tend to the man, let the two workers in the foyer hear the shot, enter the library, see the mess and the blood. Just let me be away from him and out of this weird house.

Chapter 14

Still, there's an unreal quality to my departure. I find myself down the staircase and outside those curved concrete walls, sitting in my car before I can process how I arrived. I was a thoughtless ghost walking past beautiful empty rooms, past workers in an ornate rotunda. I did not speak and neither of them looked away from their jobs. I had turned into "just another" of Spurlock's associates—surely the man has no friends—and they had taken on the sightless demeanor of employees, knowing their place. Now, only the Lexus' hot steering wheel in my hands and my foot on the gas pedal makes me feel that the scene in the library was real. Should I tell Catherine? Will I ever see her again to tell her?

The sun shines in through the windshield, just as it shone through Spurlock's windows as I pass those ridiculous imitation Cape Cod houses stretching off into the distance. The tall boxy shapes etched in pale colors would have been almost beautiful if you didn't know what they were: overpriced, homogenized yuppie dwellings. And how would they have looked if I'd seen them through wide slanting streaks of blood, if Spurlock had pulled the trigger?

I slowly inhale and exhale, and feel as if I'd been holding my breath for the last half hour. Calm down, I direct; it's a noon-time adventure you don't have to repeat. Still I have to make a decision: do I honor my plans with Spurlock or not? I told him five o'clock. A blind thirst stirs in my throat and I long for another drink, something cold and tangible, completely different from the large over-warm whiskeys I had with that man.

Down the long corridor of daytime beach traffic, I see the flap-ping flags and floats of the Coral Reef Bar and pull the Lexus into its parking lot. I still have that unreal, being in a movie feeling as I make my way to the counter and order a beer. My hands are steady but there's a jittery tremor inside as I lift the icy drink to my lips— exactly what I need.

My thoughts clear. Now, those plans made with Spurlock after his almost-suicide don't seem so unrealistic. I can rush to my studio and hide Catherine's portrait—so her husband won't see—and then meet Spurlock at Harry's. But first I have to sketch out my idea for a painting, a huge endeavor that's been hanging in my mind from the minute I saw Spurlock place the revolver up to his temple.

How to explain what takes over in the throes of inspiration for a painting, or I guess for any kind of art. Good or bad—it doesn't matter. One is blessed and cursed all at the same time, but the over-all emotion is exhilaration. The concept, the notion, whatever it is at the time, seems the product of some divine perception, poured into your very soul from an unpredictable universe. It's the best intuition you've ever had in your life, and the only question is: will you— petty, untalented goof-up that you are—will you ever be able to fulfill its grand scheme? I know exactly how the painting should look, but will I ever be able to execute the image, first onto paper and then onto masonite board.

Inside, my storefront room, I move as fast as I can, only partially opening the blinds in the front. In the back, I pull them all the way apart for the best light and take my spare easel from the wall. No time to take down the sketch of a dark-haired Catherine, surround-ed by fractured candle rays, from my favorite and sturdier easel. I clamp a sheet of drawing paper onto the holders of the flimsier one. In the days when my subjects were boats and sand dunes or trees and deer, I would spend hours getting ready: washing brushes, sharpen-ing pencils, but not now. I can't afford that luxury. Hurry, hurry, I command, pushed by a fear that somehow my brain will fail and the recollection of the view from Spurlock's windows will dissolve.

I trace faintly with vine charcoal the extended lines of the tall houses, feathering them out into shrubs and carports: high peaked roofs, long narrow windows, fake widow-walk railings above the eaves. On white paper, they seem ghost houses in the mist. Later,

Baptizing the Cat

I will add color: pale yellows and blues, wintery greens and pinks, the foliage around the stilts at the bottoms, a darker green, the curving cross-hatched trunks of palm trees with their bushy heads, yet all will be slightly distorted, as seen through a thick pane of window glass. It comes to me that I can make three panels of these landscapes, the size of the masonite boards, set into flat dark wooden frames, a triptych, although in Spurlock's house there were six, four-foot panels of glass. And the *coup d'grace*, which for now will have to exist only in my artist's concept, the lashings of crimson blood across the glass.

The drawing emerges from the paper, almost as if the charcoal was pulling the faint lines out of its textured skin rather than the carbon flowing onto the surface. Rest easy, dear Susan, I have to chuckle: no female form hidden under the paint here either, just the uncaring copy-cat bungalows in the distance with a few arching lines to show palm trees. In thirty minutes all the necessary landmarks are sketched in, a few serpentine strokes to the left to show the Gulf's waves. Good thing that acrylic is so forgiving. Whatever I put down incorrectly can be covered over with paint and re-done. Probably should have given up watercolors years ago. Can never go back over a watercolor and correct without muddying it up. Belle always said oils were more prestigious, but now I realize it's better to work in acrylics.

I stand back from my efforts, trying to see how it compares with what I have in my head. Well, okay, a good start. Will Spurlock recognized the scene? And what about the sketched version of Catherine at the table with candles? I examine it. No, that won't register with him, at this point, the painting could be of any dark-haired woman. But Catherine's beatific face hovering over the Milky Way is different. I'm glad it's safely outside in the trunk of my car, although that's not a good place to store it. The heat and humidity have already had over 24 hours to damage the piece, and I can't afford that. I look at my watch and see that I still have time to take it back to Belle's. At least it can be in her safekeeping until I give her the okay for a private sell.

Luckily Belle is out, so I don't have to have a thirty-minute chit-chat before I explain that now I just want her to store the galaxy painting. Her assistant, another hefty broad of Belle's same vintage, is keeping the doors of the shop open for her boss's long lunch hour. For years I've suspected that Belle met up with someone, a married someone, for a daytime rendezvous. She always takes a three-hour lunch, sometimes longer. "I nap; it's the smart thing to do if you're hardworking," Belle always said, when I slyly suggested that there must be something else going on besides eating.

More power to you, Belle old girl, I think now as I leave her scented lair. More power to anyone who can find a lover in this world of unlovable people. I put Spurlock at the top of that list of abhorrents. How could Catherine stand to be around that drunken blowhard? How could she stand touching that perspiration-drenched flesh? His thick forearm had been both moist and clammy under its prickly hair.

I drive back across the four lanes to the studio, thinking I will add a few lines to the sketch of Spurlock's view, but the day's events have worn me out. My shoulders sting with exhaustion and nerves. Besides all the excitement of the new painting and the long hour with that pompous bastard, I've done my brain in with thinking. It's funny how a thousand different subjects come into my head while I draw, and yet I can still put the charcoal strokes of the houses at exact right angles and sketch a tree or a bush that I don't even re-member being in the real picture. Random images run through my mind and don't interfere in the least with what I put down on paper. In truth, I've found it best not to concentrate too hard, but to start off with a few vague "what if's" about a painting, and then about life in general, and then let my musings go everywhere. My thoughts dribble away, out into space, until I'm not focused on anything. Just a lovely blank inside my head, and every line I want coming out the end of the charcoal.

I work for an hour then look around the studio and realize it's three in the afternoon, but it might as well be midnight the way the muscles in the back of my neck have constricted into a tight rope of pain. I lie down on the floor in front of the easel, close my eyes, and press my sore shoulder blades against the cool tiles. I drift away.

Baptizing the Cat

After what feels like only a few minutes, I start awake to see that now it's four o'clock. I fell asleep—blessed relief—while the black hands of the timepiece on my south wall whirled around. I've lost the extra hour or so I thought I had to spare. I give myself two choices: drive all the way back to St. Pete and Sandhills and check Catherine's patio door or drive straight to Harry's and meet Spurlock. Of course, the vision of Catherine wins out.

On the way to the condo, a picture forms: Catherine's behind those heavy drawn curtains, stretched out on the couch waiting for me to tap against the glass. She wears a plain white knit top over her small soft breasts and those mid-length shorts she prefers. Her wheat-colored hair is flared out on a big pillow, sort of the way it fanned out in the water when I last saw her on the beach. The impression rises up, a complete reality: she sips a glass of chardonnay and listens to Chopin as she did that one night I tapped in on her apartment.

So, I'm totally puzzled when Catherine doesn't answer my first tentative raps on the glass of the patio door. And then I'm convinced that she's hiding behind the drapes, waiting, willing me to go away. I bang my knuckles against the metal casing, making as loud a racket as I can, just to be sure she hears me—if she's in there, if she wants to hear. No good. I have to leave before someone notices me, a love-sick school boy, pounding on the back door of her condo.

Though I've parked my car to the side of Sandhills, the full complex between it and our apartment, still there's always a chance that my wife and Nursey might drive by on the way to the grocery store or that the girls might walk to the tennis courts on the left. I'd have to invent some quick explanation for my car being there, a convincing lie, something I'm not good at on the spur of the moment.

Nothing to do now but go on to Harry's and waste what's left of the day with that man, Spurlock. Though it's only 5:30, time seems to have stretched out beyond a normal twenty-four hour span. The excitement of seeing Catherine first thing this morning and then meeting Spurlock and all that business with the gun, has pulled the minutes into long stretches with wide spaces in between. Looking back, it seemed that Spurlock and I must have stood at least an hour beside those long windows, before Spurlock let his hand with the pistol drop to his side. What would Einstein make of this idea: that confusion and tumult, instead of space travel, slows time down to a snail's pace? That one can age a hundred years in a day?

I stop and peer down each open walkway to be sure Susan and the girls aren't where they can see me, and then I move cautiously down the corridors of Sandhills. All safe, no one around. Through the curved stucco archways, I catch a glimpse of the old man, the waver, at his usual spot on the ceramic edge of the pool. His back is to me, so I'm safe from his greeting. Slathered in sun-tan oil, the bronze skin across his shoulders appears to be a heat-cured slab of bacon. Again it strikes me, as it always has, how few people, out of the 200 or so persons living in these apartments, take advantage of the pool or the beach. Growing up in the monotonous gray of Cleveland winters, fed on television ads, I longed for the sun of a Florida vacation. The tourist depictions of white sands and aqua waters in front of tall Miami hotels seemed an existence lived by another species. In my young imagination, the "they's" who had money to travel and to live in those warm places were superior beings. They must be better, I thought then, to have somehow earned the sleek cars and the clothes that fell in long, elegant folds. How disappointing to find that a full bank account and the ability to buy anything one wants takes away much of the desire.

Back in the car, I realize I'm at least thirty minutes late for the appointment with Spurlock, and it will take another thirty minutes to drive to Harry's. I can only hope that the bastard has shown up, waited a few minutes, then given up on me, and departed. After all, what can he expect? He held a gun to his head right in front of me.

No such luck. The big BMW, so like Spurlock in its bulk and dusty condition, that it might as well have his name stenciled on the side, is parked in the gravel lot in front of Harry's. I'm actually not surprised. Spurlock would probably have waited a couple of hours or longer, hoping I'd make it. What else is there for the man to do? Stay in that big empty concrete and tiered-roof castle, drink liquor out of crystal glasses, watch his workers going about their business as slowly as possible? Think of that holstered gun in the cabinet?

Baptizing the Cat

In an objective, not altogether welcome insight, I realize that my days with Susan, Nursey, and the girls are not so terrible in comparison. At least human life is around me, even if it's just something to despise. And at least I've never put a gun to my temple. Of course, a weapon to someone else's head is an entirely different idea.

I open the half-glass doors of the pawn shop, which sounds its pinging bell, and immediately see Spurlock and Harry turn toward me in expectation. For an instant, something like a line hangs in the air between the two men, as though in pulling back and looking toward me broke their connection. Harry returns to his high seat behind the glass case, a wooden assemblage he's constructed himself—most chairs not made to accommodate his weight—and Spurlock, wearing a satisfied smile, straightens up from the counter and leans against the back wall. His easy adjustment implies that my appearance is owed him. The man does look considerably better and fresher. Apparently, for our meeting, he's showered and shaved and put on clean clothes, another red knit shirt but this time darker slacks. Harry and I are the typical locals in our brightly patterned shirts and loose tan shorts. Why hasn't Spurlock, who's been selling real estate in this area for years, adopted the natives' way of dress?

"Yo, Phil," he calls, overly hearty. "I'd almost given you up, just about ready to leave."

"Yeah," I answer, sure that the man would have stayed at Harry's if I'd arrived at seven o'clock instead of six. "Sorry, I had to check on . . . ." Now, if I can just remember what I told Spurlock. "Well, what's going on?" I ask, adopting—against all inclination—Spurlock's artificial man-among-men tone. It's like Susan's baby talk to our daughters that I imitate in spite of not wanting to.

"Harry and me, we've just been debating the value of long-range surveillance equipment over the old way of just planting hidden microphones and cameras," Spurlock says. He smugly hunches his broad shoulders. Not only have I shown up, but it's evident that he and Harry have talked, and now Spurlock has a bit of information that he can use. What will he do with it is the question.

"Yes," I say, keeping my voice steady. "Harry's managed to sell me some good stuff over the years." What I try to suggest is that I'm a collector of manly things, guns and listening devices. So what!

"Look at this gun," Spurlock says, and takes up a large square metallic weapon from the counter. I recognize a Ruger P-Series pistol. The chrome-matte finish on the barrel is satin and fluid, an almost impossible gleam to render in water colors. Acrylics are different; you can keep at it till the shine is just right.

Spurlock lifts his right arm out to the side, straight, TV cop style—thankfully away from me—and pulls the trigger three times. The clicks of the mechanism in this small dim room are much louder than I expect. "Schilick, schilich, schilick," the sound echoes against the walls even as Spurlock asks, "How's the wife?"

My brain is so addled from the long day and the non-thinking state that painting always induces in me, plus the incomplete nap that I answer automatically, "Fine, fine."

"Thought she was sick, that you took her to the doctor?" Spurlock's eyes squint in distrust. His arm has come down and in the act of putting the gun back on the counter, the barrel points toward Harry.

"Man," the pawn shop owner protests. "Careful!" He comes out of his chair—quick for a fat man—takes the pistol from Spurlock's hand and returns it to the shelf under the glass.

"Yeah, yeah," I answer, the lie about Susan's appointment comes back. "I did, but it's just the asthma she has all the time. And this new drug makes a difference." I resist the urge to say "Theophylline," better not show too much knowledge. "She's sick so much, it all runs together. But"—I pause, my strategy materializing as I talk—"this new medication helps."

"That's always the way. But you gotta watch it. One thing does you some good, but it's the twenty side effects that kill you," Harry says, the new medical authority on the block.

Good old Harry, setting the stage for Susan's demise and doesn't even know it. It comes to me then, that I can mix some of those Theophylline pills in spaghetti sauce, my one dish—my one kitchen skill, cooking Italian.

"My wife really takes too many medicines, antihistamines, aspirin, sleepers, you name it. And now, there's this new one, Theophylline. Has to have blood work done every week. Must be serious stuff." Good information that these two simpletons probably won't even remember. "Also some green liquid from K-Mart, glugs down a couple of big swallows—like a heavy drinker—every night before she turns in."

Harry and Spurlock laugh, me too, at these details.

"Really shouldn't mix drugs," Harry says, his jowls pulled down solemnly. "They're all the time running commercials, showing how one guy's wife keeps him from taking a cold medicine that would make his blood pressure go up."

This is the scenario I want: Susan taking more pills than allowed.

"You should see the wife's bags and boxes of 'meds'—it's Dr. Youngblood's word from the emergency room—"she has in our medicine cabinet. Pulls them all out, looking for what she doesn't have, and then sends me to the drug store for a prescription that's months past the refill date."

We all chuckle again in male allegiance against women's weaknesses, women's ineptness. Years ago, Harry's wife took his kids— he never says their names or how many—and went back up north. And Spurlock is just now getting used to the idea that his wife doesn't want to live in that big ship-tower house with him. What do these two losers know about women or wives?

What can I say about Spurlock's and my meeting? For in all its particularities the hours we spend together have the awkward quality of a blind date. First, my late arrival without a decent explanation, and then a long meal at an almost defunct steak house, and finally the last two hours of the night spent in a bar, where we watch a stupid football game with a lopsided score.

When I come back to the condo at two in the morning, drunk in a keyed-up, wide-awake way, I go back over every step, wonder how I could have escaped that dumb bastard. He really didn't seem to want my company either, which was the strange atmosphere that hung over the entire evening. On reflection, I realize that both of us were bored stiff, and while I wasn't as inebriated as I pretended, Spurlock was dead-out soused.

It comes back: one straight scotch for me and two vodkas for Spurlock out of the apartment-sized refrigerator in my studio. I'd forgotten my promise to show him my place, but he reminded me, so we embarked in his BMW and drive the two blocks. Against my better judgment, I leave the Lexus in Harry's parking lot.

I tried to get the pawn shop owner to come along, but no dice. After years of that creep's offering to set up a gun case in our condo, and an hour of rejecting his attempts to bug the place— somehow he thought I was spying on my wife—then, when I really wanted the son of a bitch to tag along, he refuses. Spurlock doesn't encourage Harry either, only adds a half-hearted, "Yeah, sure, come on," to my entreaties for Harry to join us. The two men seemed so cozy when I first came into the pawn shop that I thought they were good buddies. But later there was hardly a word between them. The question, What's going on with these two? kept popping up in my mind.

At the studio, Spurlock doesn't seem too interested in my art. He plows around, only glances at the seascapes and interiors I have on the walls. He does stop for an odd interval before the easel with the sketch of Catherine. For an instant I think he might see a connection, even with her in black Medusa-like hair, for he stands immobile in front of the drawing, clasps his hands behind his back, and rocks on his heels.

God, I think, is he able to recognize his wife even in that lightly-sketched charcoal?

But no, he moves on and stops at the next easel, too, with its huge rectangle of masonite board and the sketch I started this afternoon. He lingers. "Big drawing," he states.

"Yeah," I answer, "much larger than I usually tackle."

"What are those lines there for?" He points to the parallel dashes—about twenty inches apart—that I've traced over the landscape to show where the blood might be.

"The window frames," I explain. "See, the viewer is looking out through a window pane onto those Cape Cod-like houses in the distance. The entire thing will be washed several times, so you can tell you're looking through glass."

The ass can't see he's staring out of his own high picture window, from his own viewpoint. And no way do I add that the final piece will have grim, discolored streaks of blood slashed across the entire landscape.

"Make much money from a painting like this?" he asks, gazing unseeing at the drawing.

Baptizing the Cat

"No," I answer truthfully. "Not with an abstract, what this one will be. It's too artsy, a new direction for me. There's a few bucks in those." I point to my old reliable stuff, the seascapes on the walls; don't say the interiors of the condo never sold, not the first one. "My wife's father really supports us—and the kids. I don't have to do anything." What the hell, I don't care if Spurlock respects me or not. Should have been painting what I wanted all along; I could have, if not for that stupid desire to make some cash on my own. Might have come up early on with something good, or "original," like Belle said about Catherine and the Milky Way.

"My wife's dad, Arthur, got me started in real estate, but I had to work—no getting out of it. Still he left Catherine plenty."

At last, talk about that beautiful woman. I silently beg Spurlock to continue. How much is Catherine actually worth? No harm in her having an inheritance, I think. I'm used to a wife with money. But the god-damn bore is intractable, settles back into a brooding silence. He focuses on a middle distance between himself and the masonite board, his thoughts unreadable.

"Want a drink?" I suggest, just to have something to say.

At nine, almost too late for most places to serve, we drive though Tampa, to a huge, practically deserted, old-timey steakhouse, Brandon's. Spurlock orders for both of us, explains he comes here all the time, and drinks four Scotches to my two. He leaves the table every thirty minutes or so to go to the restroom, which gives me plenty of time to gaze around. The restaurant makes me think of a mafia spot, kept open for a few select henchmen. The place is divided into two levels of about fifteen tables each. All the white linen cloths are topped with lit votive candles in smoky globes, even with no customers in the whole place but Spurlock and me. The reflections in the dark window glass on the ocean side of the building repeats the images of round white tables and flickering wicks. The mirroring makes the room look enormous, an unending succession of white circles and lighted spheres stretching out into the scary darkness of the sea. An exquisite painting leaps into my mind—a black and white take-off on Monet's green and pink lily pads, but instead it will be a night-time restaurant whose black window glass sits at bent angles and reflects a room full of floating linen circles. Those white arcs would be topped by a single torque of fire and barely discernable circles of glass. In a far dark corner: loneliness, two men sit, not speaking.

Spurlock is back and again to break the silence, I ask, "You hear anything from your wife?" The man startles as though I've read his thoughts.

"No," he says, "no," and shakes his head. A visible shiver runs across his shoulders. "Should I?" he asks in a countering way, as though he's not revealed his marital difficulties to me just this morning.

"Well," I pause. At least it's conversation. Still, I don't want to bring up the pain of his earlier suicide mode. Was it just eight hours ago? "Women change their minds, you know. And Sandhills is a dump compared to that place of yours. She's had a little time to think, mull things over, maybe she's calling you right this minute to patch it up."

This last phrase of mine coincides with a wild hope that Spurlock will jump up, end this interminable evening, and speed home to sit by the telephone in the mistaken belief that Catherine might call. And she might; women are unpredictable. She sure the hell has not called me, not that she could, or should.

But Spurlock shakes his head in disagreement. "No, no she won't get in touch with me. I've given up on any reconciliation."

"You never know; women fool you all the time."

Spurlock leans back in his chair, peers out toward the windows. At first I think he's seeing the same scene I do, the unending images in the blackened slabs of glass, but then I realize he's staring into that in-between distance again, blank as he was in my studio. "I've fooled her this time," he says, almost to himself. A grim satisfaction settles into the folds around his thick-lipped mouth.

"How?" I ask.

Spurlock doesn't look towards me, doesn't answer my question, gives me time to speculate. Could he have recovered his business sense right after I left? Called his lawyer and started divorce proceedings? Maybe his desperation turned to anger? Maybe he'd figured out a way to transfer all their assets and keep Catherine from getting a cent. Okay. I'll take her with nothing. Then she'll be grateful. Really a woman with money is way too independent.

"How?" I repeat.

Spurlock twists his head to the side, makes his neck crack with an odd violent sound. I can tell he's mentally pulling himself back to my presence and my question. He begins, "That's for me to know. . ."; then he stops and draws his dark brows down into an even straighter black line across his forehead.

I think he's going to utter that childish line ". . .and you to find out." May often uses it to torture her older sister. "What?" I repeat.

"Oh, never mind," Spurlock says. "I'm wasted."

In an attempt to end the evening once and for all, I offer to pay the bill, which I imagine is enormous. Places like these don't even try to compete with the new steak houses out in the malls. But Spurlock waves me off. "They know me here; I settle up every couple of months. God, I'm so drunk."

His assessment is accurate, but that condition doesn't keep him from telling the waiter, "Give yourself a big tip." Clumsily he rises from his chair, motions for me to follow, and without a word moves to a side door, which leads to a bar, which apparently no one but insiders know exists. I trail behind, speculate how far the trek would be from this ocean-front bistro back over to Harry's. From now on, I vow to take my own car no matter where I'm bound. And one more drink with Spurlock and then I'm out of here, even if I have to walk.

We sit by ourselves at the bar, a gleaming curved wooden structure, so large that it resembles a runway more than a counter. We watch a ridiculous, lopsided football game with a score of 30-14. I writhe inwardly at this man's rudeness and waste of my time. Plus, I want to check on Catherine's apartment once more tonight. Surely at this ungodly hour, she'll have to be home.

"Really, Spurlock," I say. "It's late. You need to take me back to Harry's so I can pick up my car and head home."

"Get back to the little woman, uh?" he grunts but doesn't look away from the television screen perched above the shining bottles of liquor.

"She's hardly little—must weigh two hundred pounds," I say, my mood descending another notch of despair. Somehow this night, stuck with Spurlock, feels parallel to all the nights I've been imprisoned in the apartment with Susan, the girls, and my in-laws. Tomorrow, tomorrow, I swear, I'll grind up those Theophylline tablets, add a bit of water, and mix them into Susan's portion of spaghetti. Thank goodness, Nursey abdicates the kitchen whenever I cook, visits her relatives, spends the night away. A perfect opportunity.

"Well, I'll give Catherine her due. She kept her figure," Spurlock mumbles and raises his drink in a toast. "Always looked hot; I'll say that for her." He slumps lower on the stool, closer to the rim of the counter, murmurs something else I can't hear. He's on the verge of passing out, and I see my chance to escape.

I pay the bartender, take the keys from Spurlock's shirt pocket—where all evening they've been straining the fabric—and lead him by the elbow, unresisting, outside to his car. After some minutes of fumbling to find the right key, I open the passenger door, push Spurlock down into the seat, and lift his legs in. I get into the driver's side and maneuver the BMW out of the almost empty parking lot, out into the sparse traffic, and feel as though I'm steering a yacht out into open sea rather than driving an automobile.

Spurlock sighs, over and over: "I need you, man; I need you," supposedly, I guess, to keep from offing himself with that silver pistol he has back at the mansion. Still, there's no way this cretin is going to force me to waste another minute of my life with him. I don't care if the bastard kills himself twenty times over as long as I don't have to see the deed.

But suddenly, as though the thought has just occurred, he yelps, spit flies from his uncooperative lips, "Jeez, what time is it anyway? Gotta keep track of the clock."

I don't answer, figure that this outburst is just another drunken idea whose cause has nothing to do with the actual hour or reality in any way.

Spurlock flails his arm sideways. "I gotta know the time, man; it's important; you unnerstand, important." He strikes my elbow, openhandedly, not hard.

Still, the clumsy gesture riles me, and all the frustrations of the evening make me swing back. With no conscious decision, my arm jerks and my fist crashes into the side of Spurlock's head, sends it smacking against his window with a glassy thud. I don't care. God, help me, but I want to beat the man to death. I'm so irritated with the aggravation of the evening that it's all I can do to keep from punching him again. My knuckles sting, but then the anger I felt vanishes, a mental pang I can't explain fills me with regret.

"I'm sorry," I say. "It's late, we're both drunk. This is how people get killed." I'm trying to explain the quickness of my anger, the striking out, not really knowing what I mean. He's not speaking back, not even a grunt. Have I hit him harder than I intended, maybe killed him?

Spurlock, silent, stays leaning against his side of the car, against the side window. I've read that deaths from side-window impact are common because the side glass doesn't yield, doesn't break up like windshield glass. For a split second all the ramifications of a Spurlock concussed, dead in his own car, rise up in my brain. Harry knows I left with the man; the waiter and the barkeeper saw us leaving the steakhouse, but then Spurlock groans, "Gotta know the time, man, can't be home before one."

My guilt for the sucker punch vanishes and my exasperation returns. "It's one-thirty in the fucking morning, you fucking idiot. What does it matter? No one's keeping tabs. You don't have to explain where you've been. I don't have to explain my whereabouts to Susan either, but . . . . Besides, wasting an evening with a friend, with dinner and a game is hardly something to confess."

"Never confess," Spurlock slobbers against the glass. Next thing you know he'll be crying and throwing up on himself. For the first time tonight, I'm glad we're in his car. And I hope Catherine divorces this man's sorry ass and leaves him without a cent. At the very least, her husband's drunken ramblings, with a few embellishments from me, should make her ready for divorce, not to just get along on some allowance like she's been doing. Somehow I'll find a way to tell her about this evening, and maybe she'll want to kill him herself. Maybe Susan's death will give her the idea, and I can help her kill her husband. My head full of liquor and angry adrenalin, I consider all the possibilities at once.

In a mixture of drink and disgust, I drive back to Harry's and leave Spurlock in his car in the pawn shop's deserted parking lot. If the man dies by his own hand, or gets robbed or killed in this parking lot, it's no concern of mine.

Early, Not knowing how I made it into my own bed, I wake up—6:30—partly hung over and yet in some area of my brain totally alert, even more determined to find Catherine this morning. Without jostling Susan, I roll off my side of the bed, go down onto my hands and knees, and crawl the six feet to the closet. I really don't need to be so cautious. My wife's completely out, dead to the world as usual—really dead, I wish—but that event will come soon enough, I promise.

Deep inside the walk-in closet, I take out clothes to wear after I shower. All the while I vow not to come back here, here to this room, until I've found Catherine and made it clear how much she means to me, that my time with Susan is limited. Of course, I won't reveal any of the details of my upcoming freedom—to her or to anyone.

Outside, the morning is cool and hazy with a mist that will burn off by nine. Few people are astir. The beachcombers, the ones looking for shells, are already out at the water line with nets and buckets. The rest, like Susan—and usually me—are still in bed. I trot along the second-storied walkways of Sandhills, glance over the railing, and get a bird's eye view of the triangular flower beds and the rounded tops of shrubs. Up high, I can avoid the manager's noisy nephews on the sidewalks and grounds below. They are hard at their over-zealous mowing and clipping. In places the hedges are stripped to bare branches, and the higher spots in the lawn are skinned to the dirt by the mowers' blades. When I get my life back, am sole owner of the condo, then I'll take on this over-active crew of workers, who make so much noise and don't make Sandhills look any better.

At seven, I arrive at Catherine's back patio door, sure that I'm just repeating yesterday's futile trips. I rap hard on the glass, expecting nothing. "You know she's not in there," I whisper and lean my forehead against the cool pane. But even as I'm assured of the emptiness of the place, the folds of the draperies—that have hung motionless so many times before—move. I flinch backwards. Catherine's white hands and face materialize, inches away from my own.

She laughs, shows the rosy tip of a tongue between rows of white teeth, then slides the door open. "You always catch me unawares," she says, and gives a little snort of a chuckle, and then adds, "but today you look a bit undone yourself."

Unawares, undone, what delightfully different words. "I didn't think you were here," I stammer. "I've knocked so many times." Then, I'm struck dumb. Now that this incredible woman stands in front of me, every sophisticated remark I've planned flies out of my head.

"*Entre*," Catherine says, in mock seriousness. She opens the door wider, reaches with both hands, grasps the front of my t-shirt, and pulls me into the condo. Her touch sends an electric shock wave across my chest and arms. My hands of their own volition come to rest on her shoulders and a steamy warmth rises out of the short terry cloth robe she's wearing, the one she wore the night of her vigil at the door's edge. She must have just stepped from the shower, for her hair hangs in dripping curlicues over her forehead and around her ears.

The condo is dim. No lights on, except a few slanting lines from between the blinds, which cut narrow black and white stripes across the floor. Barely visible, the pale mask of Catherine's face is raised towards mine. It's the dream scene I've imagined time and again, which, incomprehensibly, is here at seven o'clock in the morning, in this perfectly secret place. My head swims. Desire rises in my groin, and something even stronger in the pit of my stomach settles, a feeling of arrival, coming home; that yes, here in this strange condo with this strange hypnotic woman is where I'm meant to be. But where has she been for the last twenty-four hours?

"I've come by, a dozen times or more," I croak, and slide my hands around her slender neck. My fingers touch at the back of the tiny stem, no bigger than one of my own daughters'. I gently shake, and her head bobbles. "Where have you been? Where? I've been going crazy?"

She leans into me and hides her face against my chest. Her breath comes in flurries through the thin fabric of the t-shirt. "Where have you been?" I ask again, although now the question seems unimportant. She's here, her narrow shoulders under my hands, nothing else matters.

"My friend's, Claire's, over in Pass-A-Grille," she answers, her words soft and muffled against my chest.

"It's all right," I tell her and put my lips against the wet part in her hair. The heat of her skin comes through that narrow line and the tips of hair dribble water over the backs of my hands. I shiver involuntarily at the trickles and say, "It's all right."

A hiccup of a sob sounds through her warm body, so close, so sweetly small. "No, nothing will ever be right again; I've made such a botch of everything."

"Shusss, baby," I mummer, as I would to April or May. Females take things much too seriously.

She lifts her face again. "You don't have a clue," she states flatly. Her body stiffens and a grim line pulls her feathery eyebrows together.

"So tell me," I say, and press my mouth against her forehead, feel the tiny furrows of the frown and feel even more the smooth skin. Then, I move my lips down to kiss her eyelids, force her to shut her eyes. I feel the flutter of lashes. Finally with a little struggle—she tries to step back but I hold her—I kiss her two cheeks and then her lips.

The warm slit of her mouth is a combination of cool on the sides and heat in the center, pink silk that fades down to red at the heart. I know, I've painted them a thousand times—roses and lips—placing madder rose and white on a palette and then in one brush stroke, carrying the two colors onto the canvas, to twist into petals. Just as I do with the brush, my lips and tongue graze down at slightly different angles on Catherine's lips, again and again. Even as I press harder and probe her mouth with my tongue, I wonder why this particular warm space between her two lips is so delicious, so exciting? Of all the mouths in the world, why do I want this one?

"Explain it to me." I say the words against her lips, then run my tongue across the narrow row of her teeth, feel their whiteness, test their sharpness. Her own tongue quivers at the touch of mine. She is so much smaller than I remember from our day at the college.

"I'm in such a muddle," she whispers. "I can't believe I'm doing this—can't believe what I've done. Complications without end, all my fault. All a disaster."

I smother her words with my mouth. Whatever she's talking about can wait, it's not a tragedy and not an accident. I'll make her understand. "Kiss me back," I urge, and glide my hands down to the lapels of the robe and then up and under, inside the robe, sliding it off. Tied in the middle, the garment doesn't fall off altogether but bunches and hangs from her elbows, like a pillowy growth from which Catherine's slim waist rises, a lily stalk of flesh.

And she does kiss me back, unexpectedly, hard and needful.

I want to tell Catherine that time and circumstances put the right people in the right places. We are those people and this is that place, but there is no space between us for speaking. Soft moans from Catherine and "yeses" from me are all the language we can manage now, a new vocabulary. The skin of her small buoyant breasts, just enough to fill my hands, turns to goose flesh as I stroke them upwards. She inhales deeply, and I mutter, "My God," as I bend to take a hard little nipple into my mouth.

I want this love making to be slower than slow; I want it to last forever, and to be something we'll always remember. I push her away slightly, maneuver us out of the shadows of the corner. In the bands of sunlight from between the blinds, I hold her waist and shift her back and forth, let the stripes of light fall first across her damp hair, then her white shoulders, and then her exposed breasts. Somehow the fates have delivered this woman to me, and I'm going to make the most of it. Take her in, study her as I would a still life— a bowl of fruit or an arrangement of flowers—I want every angle, every reflection. There is a enormous amount of visual material: the sheen of damp flesh, the softened bends of joints, and the faint aura of down that coats what otherwise would be the dark lines of shoulders, the course of a cheek, the slope that runs from armpit to the tip of a breast, the indentation of crooked elbows. The human form has no hard edges, only velvet margins that suck up every tint in a prism of colors.

When Catherine realizes what I'm doing, she relaxes, lets my hold on her waist act as a balance, and her head falls back. Her eyes are closed and a trance-like stillness lies under her eyelids. This complete surrender takes my strength away, dries my throat, and captures all the pent-up emotions of the last few days. I shudder, kiss down her bared expanse from throat to sternum, and still holding her waist, drop to my knees and press my face against the drapes of terry cloth. My goal, the center of her lies just beneath these few layers. I whisper, where she can't hear, push the words through the fabric, "I love you; I love you; I will always love you."

But it's as though she's heard, for she bends forward, a saint bestowing the blessing of her body. Her breasts sway downward, conical, on either side of my head. Together we pry open the belt of warm cloth at her waist. It drops in a cumulus around her ankles. Venus rising from billows of whiteness, I want to tell her. I want to hold this image in the back of my mind so that I can paint it later. But all I can do now is silently stroke her, raise my arms up—a worshiper—and slide my hands down, shoulders, waist, silken thighs. Her body is warm from the bath she must have just taken, but a more radiant heat comes from the small nest of hair that feels to me to be, even more than her lips, the central point of her body. I place my mouth at the start of the vee between abdomen and leg, a delicate, creamy ravine with indistinct blue veins spreading under the translucent skin. My lips feel the first few soft pubic hairs on the edge of the *mons veneris*.

Susan once had hers shaved down to a narrow reddish mustache, stiff and spiky as a wire brush. These days, she doesn't bother to shave anything but legs and armpits, and then not often enough.

But Catherine's pubic hair is a soft nest of ringlets. Lust, sharp and strong, flows over me; a rush I've not felt in years, like the first sex I had as a kid, that memory. It's as though all the women I've ever made love to have come together in this one. I want to say something to Catherine, something beyond this point, beyond passion. "This is forever," I tell her, which of course, doesn't come close to my true meaning. Our enormous good fortune at finding each other at this time in our lives. This woman, I know, is still not aware of how much I wish for. And she might not feel exactly as I do; she's behind in the time-line of experience. She's not watched me from the dark of a patio or listened to my conversation on a telephone or painted my portrait, almost twice. But I'll catch her up.

I feel we are encased in a glowing globe of light, that our emotion is an entity outside ourselves—felt mostly by me—but without Catherine it would be nothing. Without her, I would be nothing.

The idea comes: we'll have children. Another family to add to April and May. We'll have sons. Catherine already has two boys.

Baptizing the Cat

She's that type, the kind of woman who only has sons. We could have two sons together, or even a boy and a girl. It's all possible, now. Anything is possible. First, she'll say she doesn't want another family, but I'll convince her.

With that idea and on the strength of our full life together, I lift Catherine off her feet, and with the robe dangling, carry her down the hall. The door to the bathroom is open and the steamy air breathes out as we pass. I know precisely the layout of her condo and the location of the master bedroom on the left. I push open the door and place her on the king-sized bed, which sits in the exact same alignment as Susan's and mine in our apartment. The same and yet so utterly different as to be two separate worlds; the ones mathematicians describe in their diverging worlds' theories. This bedroom is sparsely furnished, with clean surfaces like the living room, Japanese in its simplicity. None of the knickknacks that Susan insists on buying even though there is obviously no room left for such. Consciously, I push Susan's habits out of my mind.

All of this bedroom is filled with good morning light, although a lamp also shines from the bedside table. Long rectangles of sunlight mix in with the lamplight and there are no shadows. It's perfect to make love in, perfect to paint in. Catherine's condo is better placed for light than Susan's and mine. We might live here in the beginning. Catherine will be the perfect mate. It's a shame that we couldn't have found each other earlier and unencumbered, but that's all right. All problems can and will be dealt with.

As I lay her down on the bed, she reaches past my head and tries to switch off the lamp, but I shoulder her arm away. She laughs, a full throated chuckle.

"What?" I ask. What on earth can be funny?

"Like a scene from a movie," she says. "You know, fully clothed man carries almost completely naked woman to bed—predictable erotic episode to follow—although I do hope you eventually plan to take your clothes off."

I manage a grumble of agreement, although the humor is not all that apparent to me. "What else could I do?" I ask.

"Take me on the floor," she says, matter of factly.

Some inkling comes, that Spurlock probably screwed her on this very bed, but thank god she turned Towelhead down. Still, an un-

243

expected irritation washes through me. "Okay," I say, and with one hand reach over Catherine's body and pull the robe's belt. It rolls her off the bed and onto the floor. She lands at my feet, face down, with a soft "plop" on the thick carpet. Her pale shoulders and hair are rimmed in the glow from the lamp, her arms tucked under her body, and the mass of terry cloth, pulled up, exposes one fleshy buttock and a narrow leg like a young girl's.

Her back and shoulders of unblemished flesh indented by her spine, quivers with what I think is crying. I lean down in concern, then immediately realize she's giggling. "That'll teach me," she says into the carpet, "to keep my mouth shut."

I try to roll her over, to see her breasts again, to take the robe off completely, but she's wedged against the bed in a tangle of white terry cloth against the printed squares—pale browns and yellow—of some kind of bed skirt. I try to pry her free, but she does not cooperate, and the bed is certainly not moving, and now Catherine laughs out loud and lets her head loll forward in an inert puppet-like fashion. I'm carried along, too; chuckles rise up in my throat in spite of feeling exasperated and horny as hell.

"Do you want to get fucked or not?" I ask, not the most romantic thing I could say.

"Of course," Catherine says. "I want to do it till our eyebrows fall off."

"What?" I ask, confused by the image, the idea of Catherine and me, too, sans eyebrows. But then I have to laugh at the absurd picture. Also, I'm totally exasperated, trying to move her away from the bed and out of the robe. I lie down, stretch my body against hers, the terry cloth uncomfortably bunched at crucial places between us. The bedside table, full of magazines and books, and the bed creates boundaries around us, a niche of shadow, where all else in the room is in light.

"What about eyebrows?" I ask again. Up on an elbow, I look down at the two fine arches of hair on her pale forehead. I can feel the vine charcoal between my fingers, shading the hollows on the sides of her temples, hatching the rise of the bones of her eye sockets, and individually drawing each hair, barely touching the paper.

"Yes, dear heart, she says; "fuck me till my eyebrows fall off, and I'll do the same to you."

Baptizing the Cat

In one adroit motion, she rises on a slender arm and pulls the robe from between us. Then she's up onto her knees and tosses the thick garment onto the bed. Her small breasts rise and fall with her movements. She bends and pulls at the hem of the T-shirt I put on this morning. For once, I wish for buttons, though I seldom wear a buttoned shirt. To help, I sit up and raise my arms. Catherine pulls at the shirt until it covers my head and holds my arms upright, tight, in place above my head. I'm helpless, encased in the dark blue cotton.

"Yes, think of it," she says through the fabric against my face. "We'll spend the whole morning doing whatever we're going to do, and then have to go out without any eyebrows left on our faces. Everyone will know what we've been up to." More laughter from Catherine. It's a cartoon image, but one I can appreciate.

With these words, she drops her hands from the shirt above my head and slides them down the tube of fabric that binds me in darkness, down to my arm pits. She gently tugs at the hair and then lets her nails glide down the sides of my body, barely grazing the skin. Tickled, I lash forward and bump my head, hard, against hers. "Conk," a slight pain and the sound comes through the shirt.

"Ouch," Catherine says, and then she pulls again, helping me out of the tight garment.

For the second time that morning, I ask, "Are you all right?"

"No," she says, again misunderstanding; "but it doesn't matter."

"It does," I say. "Everything about you matters to me."

I rise to my knees, in front of her kneeling form. We should pray, I think, ask for some blessing, ask for some luck. We're going to need it, but . . . but her hands are at my waist. She tugs at the draw string of the sweat pants. I wish again that I'd worn something more appropriate for these first moments of disrobing. I put my hand over hers, stop her motions.

Catherine raises the eyebrows that will soon go missing, a questioning smile showing her slightly asymmetrical teeth. "You know, we did a lot the other day at the college, everything but take our clothes off."

Her hands start to move again, and I clutch tighter. "We didn't do everything, and now's the moment of truth," I say.

"Listen, I have a pretty good idea of what you look like. You pressed it up against me hard enough." A rueful smile presses her lips together. "And, see, I need the company since I'm the only one who's stark naked."

I nod in agreement, for she is completely bare, a white statue on the carpet, somehow comfortable in her unblemished skin, somehow more seductive and more girlish than any other woman I've ever seen. Her thighs are rounded columns of purest flesh, her bush, thick like the hair on her head, but darker and curlier, so that individual circles shine in the light.

I think of all the times I've stepped out of my trousers without hesitation, or stepped out of them with a certain amount of pride, for though I'm not the biggest for sure, I know from locker rooms that I'm not the smallest. My equipment isn't as thick and dark as I imagined Towelhead's—why does that character keep coming to mind?—but my penis doesn't veer off to the side like some, still it's as I said, the moment of truth. I take her hands away, stand, and pull the sweat pants down. My dick—I'm happy to say—in spite of all the conversation and silly jokes, or maybe because of them—is still erect enough to snag for a second on the gathered waist band. I slide the legs off, along with socks and shoes, and push everything into a tangled heap behind me.

Catherine is still on her knees, her face directly in front. An unfortunate position for the moment, but maybe later. I step back.

Catherine takes the step as embarrassment. "No, no," she says, "You're fine—fine. Come here." I step closer than I intend, and unexpectedly Catherine cups me in her hands.

"Wait," I say, and pull away. God, don't let me come yet, even before we start. I turn my back and breathe.

"Oo-kee-dy," I hear her say, as she rises from her knees and comes up behind me. She reaches, presses her soft breasts and belly to my back and wraps her arms around me. The full length of her body, the warmth against my nakedness is almost as exciting as the squeezing of her hand had been.

I turn, hold Catherine at arm's length, and sit on the bed, but there is no escaping the pure delight she generates in me.

"Dear heart," she says, "You're too excited to wait." With no other preliminaries, she sits in my lap, and holding herself up, starts touching her bottom down, the way a butterfly might touch down on a flower. The heat of her. I gasp. It's enthralling but too much to resist. With one upward thrust, I drag her down, pushing myself completely inside. She moans, something between a laugh and a sob, and then with both hands, she levers me back onto the stiff brocade bed cover. Her hair is a shining areola around her face. I am the earth and she is the sun. With one upward motion, I raise my hips off the bed and burrow into her. My hands are at her narrow waist, at the beginning flare of her hips, and I force her down on me again and again. She rocks her pelvis back and forth. She whimpers. I hope I'm not hurting her, but I can't stop. I push harder. Keeping her inside, I roll us over. In the tumble, I feel all her small bones through the yielding flesh. And I come, come with an energy and release I haven't felt in years.

Later, I tell Catherine, "This is a morning in Eden."
"No, in Shangri-la," she says.
"A morning in the Elysian Fields," I throw back.
"That's good, let me think. A morning in Valhalla," she says.
I concede then, with the common old word "paradise." "This is a morning in paradise."

Then we hold each other until sleep slides between us. We wake and make love again, this time more slowly. I lie on top, inside her, and we kiss and talk: nonsense, gibberish, glossolalia. We make love a second time. Catherine whispers, "Please" and "Yes" and strangely, on the last go-round, she asks, "Why? Why? Why?" Her small frame writhes under me, the way I imagine a slender snake, impaled, would twist, trying to escape.

"Am I hurting you?" I ask, but do not stop the pace we've established, do not go any faster or slower. Somehow I know she'll answer, "No, no." She feels so slight, a narrow chamois bag with tiny bones lined up inside. I can't help comparing her lean flanks and ribbed torso to my wife's cushioned, inflated bulk.

In the last few years, I'm never really sure if Susan comes or not. "Oh," she moans slightly, and if I ask, says, "It was wonderful," and then turns over and falls asleep, no real passion. It's as though in our marriage I've had two completely different women. The first one, the beautiful, energetic Susan that I met in Taos, and for the last six years the Susan I'm married to now. Sex faded, became a memory that I wanted less and less and then desire disappeared altogether. Often, after stroking her inert arm a few times, receiving no response—not even an appreciative murmur—my erection deflates, and I'm glad, glad not to have to make the effort.

At eleven, Catherine and I eat. For someone so small, she keeps an amazing amount of food in her refrigerator. Eggs and cheese, bagels and muffins, oranges and grapefruit. "I love breakfast food," she explains; "the only meal I really, really enjoy." We eat scrambled eggs and cheese and muffins in the kitchen, and carry a tray back to the bedroom. She slices the blood oranges into quarters, eases the membrane off sections of red grapefruit, salts them, and pushes one into my mouth.

"A Salty Dog, without the vodka," I say, wishing for vodka. The juice of the ruby citrus runs down her hand to her elbow, and I lick it off.

"We're so lucky to have all this beautiful fruit growing right here. Can you believe it, in November?"

What's left on the grassy-green tray sits in front of us, a still life of pale yellow grapefruit rind and bright orange peels, the remaining reds of the pulp: cardinal, crimson, scarlet, scattered across a white plate—a Vermeer. I'm surprised when Catherine rises to turn the TV set on.

"We have to watch the noon news. Just so a comet won't hit or war break out, and we not know it.' Her back and hips are alabaster, marble, with blue tracings under the skin. She comes back to the bed, sits beside me with the sheet drawn up over her knees.

"Whatever makes you even consider a comet?" I ask.

"You never know," she answers, ducking her head down as though embarrassed.

"True . . . but a comet? Why a comet?"

"Think of it. Isn't that what people always say? They can't believe something cosmic has happened—whatever it is. They never imagined in their wildest dreams: the flood, the hurricane, the fire, *et cetera, et cetera.* See—what you can't possibly imagine is what happens."

Somehow I don't like this line of thought. I envision Spurlock running into the bedroom, silver gun in hand, or maybe Susan, her mouth forming a round "o" into a scream, but that's not so frightening. Still, I want a change of subject. If we can't possibly imagine what will happen, okay, but I can visualize a lot of other horrible things. I search the bedroom for some other topic to latch on to. Through the walk-in closet, I spy floor-to-ceiling bookshelves crammed with books and magazines, not many clothes or shoes, so I ask "You read a lot?"

"All the time," she says. "Keeps me from thinking."

Is that what Susan's doing, trying not to think? I draw away from that thought, go to a predictable line, "So tell me about yourself. I want to know everything."

"You already know most of it. We covered a lot of territory the other day. I have a degree in art ed. Went to school and worked with my dad in his real estate office after high school, even sold a little. When I married Rand, he took my place in the business. I had the boys right away and afterwards, kept house, raised children, taught art at St. Patrick's, did volunteer work for the library there and later at the Museum. They gave me a semi-official title because of my family's donations, but not any real work."

"You taught at St. Patrick's? So you're Catholic?" Spurlock had said she was too religious, but somehow it didn't register. It's only now that the information sinks in. Good God, another Catholic, just like Susan.

"I'm Catholic, too; I converted when I got married."

"Really" she says, and studies the tray in front of us.

"Yes," I say softly.

"Converts usually take the faith much too seriously."

I want to get away from this topic, too. She can't be like Susan, accepting all that other-world stuff. "So what else?"

"Well, I cooked a lot when the boys were at home, mostly Italian—spaghetti, lasagna, pizza, meatloaf. What they loved. Took them fishing with my Dad. My sons are my only real accomplishment, that is until the real estate went through the ceiling and Rand sent them off to boarding school. Rand, Jr's a senior now and Alex's a sophomore. They've changed so much since going away; they have their own lives. Maybe that's when Big Rand became so difficult. He changed, too." She stares out into the room as though she can see her husband standing at the end of the bed.

"It's all right, baby," I say, although I wish for some magic, one swipe of my hand across her forehead to erase "Big Rand." And she hasn't mentioned Towelhead. What about him? More so, I wish I could erase my own past—three wives, Jeez, that I haven't told her about—how can I present my history with women as anything but ridiculous?

Chapter 16

"Well, so what's your life's story, dear heart, in a nut shell?" she asks. "Mine took all of two minutes."

"I don't know," I say. "First off, I want to tell the truth, completely, but it's all so pathetic."

I'm on the verge of a litany that I've resisted telling Catherine before, starting with wife number one, when I realize that the past has no relation to the now, to Catherine, to me, and to this time. "Listen, let's just start fresh. Put all our old records into a drawer and slam it shut, never to be opened again."

"But . . . ," Catherine starts, and I can almost hear the cogs of her brain turning. "We're what the past made us, but maybe that's not always true. And, besides, a 'we' doesn't exist outside this room, does it?"

I can see where she's going. This morning is just a fling, two ships that pass, all that bullshit, in the same category as what she had with Towelhead. But I'm not going to agree. "Don't make predictions," I say. "We'll have a life outside this room, an entire history together. I promise."

She stretches slowly down into the bed, so as not to disturb the tray at the foot, and pulls the sheet up over her shoulder, up to her tousled hair. "Whatever you say, sweety," she says, "but I know better." She closes her eyes. The folds of the sheet drape under her chin and a tangle of dark-gold strands fall over her face. Somehow she's got the composure to put everything aside and go to sleep. It reminds me of her bravery that night, sitting in the dark, just outside the glass doors—scaring the shit out of me.

One part of my brain wants to let her sleep, to just relax beside her and watch. I wish I had my sketchbook and charcoal to draw a vignette of a woman sleeping. The drapery of the sheet and the twisted ends of hair would have a nice Michelangelo effect, all the curved lines complimenting each other.

Instead, I say, "No, no, listen. I love you, and I'm serious. I've loved you longer than you know. I've watched . . . ."

Here I'm on dangerous ground. I want to be honest but don't want to tell Catherine—not just yet—about the night I saw her with Towelhead or about the Wolf Ears outside the patio's glass door. Eventually, I promise, I will, when she believes in our future as much as I do. "I've seen you on the beach for weeks now." Here, I'm also taking a chance. All she knows about is that one morning when she was lying in the surf and maybe that other time when she walked with Towelhead. But she doesn't contradict me. For all I know, she could have been spending every daylight hour for months on the white sands down below Sandhills. Like Susan, dragging the girls to the water every morning and every afternoon. Of course, no one but a few young boys went out at night, looking for crabs with flashlights, on the beach when I was there. "Pay attention, I love you."

Catherine opens her eyes, the flecks of gold in the irises glitter. Her lips are pale and translucent. "It's okay; that's not a requirement to sleep with me. I gave up on that foolishness years ago."

So it's true, she thinks I'm just in it for the fun, for the moment, for the physical. "No listen," I say again, and inch closer, pull the sheet and blanket around us, draw her to me into a nest of pillows and bedclothes. I talk into her hair, which smells of shampoo, like my daughters', only theirs is strawberry and hers is lemon. "We have our chance now, maybe the last chance of our lives, for some real happiness."

"You go for it, Romeo," she rasps against my neck, and I can tell she's drifting away into slumber. She's worn out.

I don't answer, don't try to explain how we will fashion a life out of these twisted circumstances. I'm sure it would seem totally implausible. I'm married; she's married; we both have children. But isn't that what she just theorized: what happens is what you never expect.

Baptizing the Cat

I give up on explanations and lie motionless and silent beside her, doze, and in between watch the sun make shadow patterns on the carpet. The daylight shifts through the blinds, high noon comes with hardly any lines at all, and then the sun starts its downward path, marked by thickening configurations. Catherine lies still, her breath coming in slow even huffs against my neck. I don't completely lose consciousness but slip into that nowhere land between sleeping and waking. Outside, the lawn mowers are gone, the entire condo silent for a change, as if Catherine and I were in a bubble, the only ones in these apartments. But I know better. Only one building away are rooms that hold my other life, my wife and daughters, and down the road in the Marriott, my in-laws.

And what do I say to Susan about not returning for breakfast after my morning run, not following my routine? Susan's big on routine. Still, I'm almost always absent at lunch time, so no problem there, but what about the no-dinner with the family and her parents? And what about a long evening, an entire night in this bedroom? Is Catherine prepared to spend the whole day here, and an entire unbroken night? I know I am. Tomorrow I'll give Susan my stock answer, "I was called away, an emergency; they picked me up." The usual CIA crap I dish out whenever it's needed, my excuses sounding tinny and false even to myself.

About two in the afternoon, Catherine and I rise and eat again, this time lettuce, tomato, and cheese sandwiches and pale yellow wine, probably in the same goblets that she and Towelhead used. So what? We carry what's left in the green bottle back to the bathroom, pour and drink more, and set the glasses down on the cream-colored tiles of the counter. The two crystal stems and the bowls of the goblets barely reflect, but the tall yellow-green flagon is a smear of color. It's a remarkable still life, luckily one I can set up, again, any time. We shower together, a bath that turns into a lathery wrestling match. Catherine pushes me hard against the dripping wall, bumps the soft length of her body against my backside.

"Think you can take me, do you?" I say.

"I already have," she answers.

I turn, place her against the wall, and jostle against her glistening torso. Again, I'm moved by her smallness in comparison to my height and girth, that her wet head is under my chin, that there's hardly more than a hand-span of bones across her shoulders. Like May, the other day, when I carried her down the hall, her thin legs dangling against my kneecaps, she's delicate, fragile. When Catherine talks, that semi-tough act she puts on makes her seem larger, but here in the shower, I see she's not strong, hardly bigger than my daughter. The unbidden thought comes: someday soon May will have a boyfriend, a husband, a man with corruption in his heart.

"We can work this out some way," I tell Catherine, as we step out of the shower to dry off. I'm hoping to set up the next time we'll see each other, but the little vixen tries to trip me. "What are you doing?" I drop my towel, catch at the foot she's hooking behind my knee.

"Make you fall to the floor, but beat you to it," Catherine says.

At first, I don't understand.

"It's a joke," she says to my questioning face. "But never mind." She draws her towel into a bulky sarong of pale green, then picks up my towel and wraps it around me, keeps her arms about my middle. "Don't you like to play?" she says and jostles me back and forth.

"Play?"

"Sex is the closest thing adults can do to playing, that and games. Let's play hide and seek."

Before I can respond, Catherine takes off, her legs flailing out sideways from under her bulky cover-up. She turns the corner out of the bathroom and runs down the hall before I can figure out what she's up to.

She hollers, "You have to count to one hundred, and then come find me. Olly, olly, oxen free." The door of what would be Nursey's room slams shut.

I've imagined this encounter with Catherine so many times, but in my mind the meetings were always on the order of black and white images, a French noire film. There would be long lunches and dinners with plenty of liquor to set the mood, and later Catherine across from me in a black nightgown, maybe; languorous bed and bathtub scenes with candles, but never, never did a children's "hide and seek" come into those daydreams. Still, playing a game, being childish suddenly seems to have unique merit.

Baptizing the Cat

I walk down the hall, twist the towel tightly around me so it won't fall off, but I don't count to one hundred.

Later, in the rumpled bed, Catherine drifts off to sleep again. "Wake me when the sun goes down," she says.

Again, I'm left in a not-unhappy but not completely happy reverie, to analyze, to watch the peculiar shadows that can build and cling to furniture, to walls, to the inside of a closet. I've learned something about myself today, that there is more than just beautiful and female in this attraction concoction, the pheromone recipe of pleasure that stirs my reptile brain. And it's all in Catherine's small physique. Her pretend toughness, her wild response to being found in her game of hide and seek, are dimensions that I couldn't have envisioned but now only add to her appeal. Her wide-set breasts, her clear back, her dark blonde fringe are naked treasure, an answer in my blood. I'm drunk on her, drunk on the musty, crushed smell of the bedclothes around us, drunk on half a bottle of yellow wine. Odd to be so intoxicated, but as I said before in our word game, in "paradise."

We sleep and wake to watch TV again, just to be sure no natural disasters have carted the rest of the world away.

As the sky darkens, Catherine sits up and asks, "Don't you have to go home, sometime?"

"Not until I want to," I say. "How about you?"

"I've warned Rand not to come over without calling first. But he's so crazy lately. God only knows what he'll do."

"Are you afraid?" I ask, and remember Spurlock, his monster house, his gun—that weird night, the feel of his jaw against my knuckles, the thud his head made when it hit the side window of the car.

"In a way. When we first married, he was really great. We worked together, had the boys, but little by little the feelings changed. For him as well as for me, I guess. We quit talking, and he acquired a couple of girlfriends along the way. I forgave him twice, really, really forgave him. But then one morning I woke up and all the love I'd felt so strongly and for so long was completely gone. Is that possible? To be truly in love and then lose it? So afterwards, I didn't check up on him anymore, didn't try to find out what he was doing."

I slide my hand up and down her back. I want to console her, but still I wonder at the kinship of womanly flesh. Did Susan learn not to care?

"Then when the real-estate business took off, that's all he was interested in, the money, all he could talk about, think about, was how to spend it, show off how wealthy we were."

"Yeah, that house is unbelievable."

Catherine leans forward over her sheet-draped legs, elbows on knees. With both hands, she rubs her face and then inches her fingers into her hair to scratch her scalp. "The concrete nightmare, you mean." She says these words with a weary sigh.

"It's huge; I'll say that for it."

"Everything fell apart last year. My father died, Rand took over the business and the finances. At first I didn't care, but then he started building. It's supposed to look like a ship and a castle, but can you imagine three stories? All those rooms and bathrooms for just two people? Even if the boys came home now, it's not a house for teenagers. We already had a nice home on the Canal—he's trying to sell it—the yard and garden I'd worked on for years. We still had this condo, so why did we need another place, a palace?"

"We can have a house," I venture. I want to launch into my plans, start us on our new life.

"That's a problem; I'm past houses, yards, and children. When Dad died, I saw my life clearly for the first time, the changes you don't see until it's too late. I want to go on to something better or at least more stimulating, something that will fill up this longing. All I've managed to do so far is . . . is to sleep around . . . or try to."

"That's not what this is," I say. She didn't have sex with Towelhead. Were there others? I sit up, take Catherine by the shoulders, turn her partially toward me, "I'm going to prove it to you."

"How?" she asks, staring me directly in the eyes, a wry, wistful twist of unbelief settling around her mouth.

I see Catherine's not going to consider any plan I tell her right now, and, of course, I can't tell her everything. I'll just have to proceed: get rid of Susan, go through with all the gruesome details I've been dreading. It may take months, so no one will suspect, not even Catherine.

256

I change tactics. "So this is just an affair?" I say. "Just for fun?"

"Nothing wrong with that, is there, lover boy? Not enough pure frolicking in the world, I say." She snuggles down beside me, a hundred or so pounds that feels feathery and insubstantial under my arm.

At six the next morning, we wake and make love in a dreamy unintentional way, with slow, almost unconscious movements of our bodies. We shift together as if the bed were a boat, and we row in sync, in pleasure, out to sea. We sleep again, and at eight, I rise, put my clothes on for the first time in twenty-four hours. Catherine barely rouses as I smooth the rounded arc of her hip and kiss her cheek goodbye.

"Bye, dear heart," she says. I'm glad she doesn't call me "lover boy" again, although there's a thread of that generality in the "dear-heart" business. I keep remembering her calling her friend Claire "dear heart" on the phone that night I listened in on their conversation. Still, I take the words, thankful for everything, for the teasing tone, for the lovemaking that carries the seeds of a beginning, for the promise of an existence that Catherine doesn't expect.

As I leave the bedroom and walk down the hall, it comes to me: I'm exiting a dream, a paradise, and there's no way in hell I can ever duplicate this past day and night. Maybe I should turn around, sneak back to the bed, and kiss her once more. But I'm already three quarters of the way out of the apartment, and my reluctance to disconnect might reinforce her judgment of me as a Romeo, a Lover-boy, a Sweetie—a not very strong sort of guy. From now on, I'm going to show her, I can be all those names and still be more of a man than she's known before. I'll turn her opinion around, make a place for us that she's never even guessed at. After all, what has she had in her life but Spurlock and Towelhead? Not much to go by.

I ease open the glass doors and slide them shut, promising to return as soon as possible, maybe tonight.

Outside on the concrete slab, I hesitate again. Should I go back in, lock the patio doors, and exit by the front, or should I rouse Catherine to come lock up behind me? It's an old worry. I have all kinds of apprehensions about leaving places open, a leftover fear from my grandfather, who could never depart from the house without checking twice, driving my poor mother to distraction. "The world is a dangerous place," he would intone, after his second tour round his domain, only then convinced that a burglar would have a hard time stealing our valuables, whatever they were. The old Chevy truck we drove away in was the family's only real asset, other than the two acres of dirt. Even now I have to caution Susan and Nursey all the time about unsecured doors and windows. Yet, in this moment, I rationalize my concern; my future is in this apartment. But I put the worry aside. Next time, I'll explain to Catherine how important it is to keep doors locked.

Beyond the patio, the world is absolutely, precisely as I left it yesterday morning. The sprinklers hiss water, sending rainbows of color across the grass. The air is the same, heavy with brine from the sea, and the grass and bushes drip from the morning shower. The walkways are puddled in concentric pools, a nice monochromatic pattern that I step around to keep from getting my tennis shoes wet.

On the other side of the apartments, the supervisor's nephews are at it again, their clattering, whacking machinery breaking the early peace, clipping everything down into stubble.

Well, let them have their hourly pittance, I think, calm as never before in my newfound happiness, and for the first time I grant them a place in the order of the day. Besides, it's a shitty way to make a living, chopping plants that were skinned the day before and will not grow all that much by tomorrow. When I own Susan's and my condo completely, I'll insist at the owners' meeting that they only work after lunch time. Who owns Catherine's condo, I wonder; is it in Spurlock's name? In the future, I might have two condos to really give me some clout with the condo association.

At my door, I punch the buttons on the round dial and hear the whirring under my fingers, but there is no click at the end of the sequence, and the knob doesn't turn under my hand. I punch the numbers in again, but the same thing, no answering click. What's going on? I knock hard. What the hell? I can hear the faint shuffle of Nursey's feet on the tile, and she opens the door.

"Oh, Mr. Phillip, it's you," she says, her eyelids at half mast. She turns her chenilled shoulders and heads back toward the kitchen.

258

Baptizing the Cat

"What's wrong with the code?" I ask, but she doesn't answer, another annoying habit of hers, selective hearing. Her limping gait raises one huge hip and then the other under the blue-green of the ribbed-cotton robe. Why is it I have to endure my wife's bad taste in clothing, but I also have to view it, worn out and faded, hanging on my maid's back?

Inside the entrance way, the cluttered table against the wall, the throw rug on the floor, the inanimate objects declare: nothing has changed, all is as before. Breakfast is cooking and the fumes of bacon grease and half-burned toast hang in the refrigerated air. The television set bathes my daughters, still in their pajamas, in cartoon music and ghastly colors. Susan holds down her usual post, at the far end of the table, dismantled newspaper pages spread across the other three-fourths. No wonder I eat breakfast standing up in the kitchen, crowd Nursey, who doesn't want me in there either. The identical scene every morning, interchangeable with every other morning for the last twelve years. Predictable, predictable. Welcome back—husband returns from daybreak run—only a day and a night late—welcome back.

Susan glances up from the newspaper. "We missed you. Daddy kept saying to call you on your cell phone. "

Does she really expect an answer?

"Has the code been changed?" I ask, and stand just inside an angle of shadow cast by the arched frame of the breakfast nook.

"I reset it last night, when you didn't come home." She bends her head. The light from the chandelier shows the pink scalp through her sparse, reddish hair. She keeps one finger on a line of newsprint so as not to lose her place, then continues reading, or pretending to read.

"Why?" I ask, and don't bother to keep irritation out of my voice. We've not changed the code since Susan's parents gave us the keys and the stacks of manuals on policies and maintenance of the condo.

"I was nervous. You weren't here, and it seemed like a good idea," she says, and looks up with that flat confident stare of the completely entrenched. "Where were you?" Her voice has an overtone of concern, and, as always, a slice of suspicion.

"Change it back," I say.

"Of course, if that's what you want. Nursey, put the old code back in for Mr. Phillip." She lumbers up from the table, determined to make me tell my customary lie.

"Well, where were you?"

I turn and start down the hall; it's better to carry on deceit from a distance. Also, I must wash Catherine's scent off before Susan comes too close; in spite of her allergies my wife has a good nose for smells. "You know I can't discuss my work. They had some stupid check-out assignment and I was on for the night." Somewhere in the past I've come up with this secret-agent jargon. "There's always something afoot."

I close the bathroom door on whatever else Susan says.

"Always something afoot," I repeat, and turn the hot water on to splash down hard on the shower floor.

"Afoot," yes, something's afoot. Leaving the shower running, I open the bathroom closet. Like the cabinet behind the tall mirror on the wall behind me, it's crammed with bottles and tubes and small boxes containing all kinds of medicines, ointments, prescriptions—a miniature drug store. If Catherine's comet hit this afternoon, and we managed to make it through, Susan would still have enough antihistamines, pain killers, salves, muscle relaxers, sun-block lotions, and sleeping agents to keep her going for the next ten years.

Two tall, brown plastic bottles sit in a line. I take one out, labeled with all the necessary pharmaceutical information: Theophylline anhydr sr 300mg tab. God, she must have 100 of these pills stashed away here. Does she have more in the other medicine cabinet, and what about the cupboard in the kitchen? This is Susan's back-up supply. One, she bought with the prescription the emergency room doctor gave her, and one from her regular doctor, that she saw the following week, and one from the allergist she saw the day after that. Why three full prescriptions?" I questioned, when she had me pick up the third one from a different drugstore, away from the beach.

"I feel better, if I have extra on hand," she replied. "You never know when they're going to take a drug you like off the market. And Dr. Richards up in Spartanburg might not want to give me another prescription. These pills make me feel trembly inside, but they work. So I want to have plenty, just in case. You know, Phillip, people die of asthma every day. I don't want to take any chances."

Baptizing the Cat

Good, people die of asthma every day, good. And all this hoarding will be proof of her taking too much medication, proof she overdosed. I shake one of the stubby white pills, scored in the middle, out onto my palm, raise it, and lick its side exactly as I did two days ago. Bitter, yes, still bitter. Again the taste spreads through my mouth. I lay out my plan: I'll take twenty of these pills in my shorts' pocket, announce to Nursey and to Susan that I'm making spaghetti tonight so they can buy the ingredients. Then, Nursey will take the afternoon and the night off as she always does when I cook. At the studio, I'll grind the pills into a fine powder with the mortar and pestle I use for dried paint, put the powder in a baggie, scrub the tools, and grind some paint in afterwards, then come home and make spaghetti. It will be easy to put the ground-up powder in the bottom of a cup, stir in a ladle of hot tomato sauce, taste to see that it's not too bitter, and pour it over Susan's noodles. Rinse the cup, scrub it with a soap pad, and then run it through the dishwasher. An imperative: no trace of Theophylline on anything but Susan's lips.

My plan set, I step into the hot water that's steamed up the bathroom almost past seeing. Under the stinging spray, I try and relive the hours that Catherine and I spent together, yesterday and last night. The whole twenty-four hours seem as foggy and as hard to recall as a dream after waking.

"Phillip, what's keeping you?" Susan calls through the door. "You're going to miss your morning light."

It's the excuse I gave years ago for locking myself up in my studio in Spartanburg or leaving the condo here in St. Pete before eight o'clock. Along with the CIA scam, it gives me the solitary hours I need, sometimes just to take a nap. That's what I need now, to take the pills from the brown plastic jar and go down to the studio and nap before I put my plan into effect.

But the strategy I've sketched out in the bathroom doesn't gel. By the time I'm out of the shower and dressed, and with twenty-five Theophylline pills in my shorts pocket, Nursey has a roast in the oven—I can smell it—and she stands at the counter peeling potatoes.

"Why'd you start supper so early?" I ask. "I was going to make spaghetti tonight."

I'm halfway formulating a suggestion that Nursey turn off the stove and put her dinner back in the refrigerator for tomorrow. But I know that proposal won't fly, not with the old maid and not with Susan.

"You can cook tomorrow night, Phillip," Susan calls from the living room couch, having made her morning migration from one sedentary base to another. "Momma and Daddy are going home tomorrow. And you know how he loves pot roast. Besides, we've had that roast since Monday, and it has to be fixed." Susan and her southern cover-all word "fixed."

It enters my mind to suggest okay, cook the roast, but save it for sandwiches for the rest of the week, that I really, really have a taste for spaghetti tonight. But the words stay in my mouth where they belong. Besides, Daddy loves pot roast, and we all know who really comes first in this family. And how would it sound to the police, Nursey saying, "Mr. Phillip jest insisted on making sauce, made me put the roast back in the 'figerator'." Not good. And what's one day more or less, for the deed, for the dead? I can still grind the pills and have them ready to use tomorrow.

"Okay," I say. "It's pot roast today and spaghetti tomorrow night, Nursey; just make sure I have everything I need."

Shrugging at the delay, I head out for the studio. No need to sit around the apartment any longer than necessary. Being with Susan would just make me wonder exactly how the ground-up pills will react in her system. But still, on the drive over to Tampa, I speculate: Will the acid of the tomato sauce speed up or completely kill Theophylline's effectiveness? What if Susan doesn't die quickly? Will she become ill right away, or will it take hours before the toxic reaction sets in? How much time should elapse before I call an ambulance? If she moans or screams, the girls will hear, and I'll have to dial 911 right away to be convincing. I haven't sat through a hundred true-crime stories, heard those phony voices crying on the recorders for nothing. Everyone, from in-laws to complete strangers, expects a lot of emotion from the husband, and everyone suspects that he killed the wife from the git-go. Can I fool anyone with my act? Haven't I been fooling Susan all these years with the CIA stuff?

Questions swirl: Will they put me on television? No, not necessarily, since Susan won't be missing. Will Susan's father bring up my CIA background, maybe in an effort to vindicate me? How many times have I warned Susan that no one can know. In the last few years I've down played that whole stupid lie, kept saying that I'm only a consultant on some stuff from years ago. But then if the police check, they'll find out I've never been an agent, yet lying is not a crime. Still if you lie about one thing, they figure you'll lie about others. Doesn't the wife's family always start out believing the husband is innocent, and then later change their minds? I must convince Ed and Miz Mildred above everyone else. Won't have any of the good life unless they think it's all a tragic accident. And Miz Mildred's called Susan a hypochondriac more than once so that should carry some vindication.

God, it's the same rigmarole—questions, questions—that I went through when trying to decide. What if? What if? The pills in the baggie I took from the kitchen drawer weigh one side of my shorts down. Who would have thought a wad so small could be so heavy?

Yet in the studio, I do exactly as planned. I grind the pills, put the white powder in the baggie, and set it up on the counter. I wash the dark-gray granite pestle and mortar with a scrub brush and dish soap, grind paint again, and then decide that I haven't scoured the implements hard enough. What if there are some minute cracks in those smooth polished surfaces that I can't see? I re-scrub the speckled bowl and the rounded pestle a second and then a third time. I let steaming hot water pour over the two parts for more than five minutes. What if microscopic bits of Theophylline can still be found? What if there is no way to remove them, that somewhere between all the layers of paint that I've ground in the last years is a layer of Theophylline? There's no recourse; I'll just throw the damned thing away, even though it's been one of my favorite paint-ing tools, a gift from Jenny, my second wife, from the time when I ground paint all the time because it was cheaper than pre-mixed. Should have thrown that gadget out years ago. Now I'll toss it in with the trash, put it in a black plastic garbage bag out in the dump-ster, but not behind my studio, maybe behind some other group of businesses. Will someone see me?

I can't stand it. I'm driving myself crazy with what if's. I put the pestle and bowl in a garbage bag and go out to my car. What if Miss Violet, of Violet's lavender walls, sees me and tells the cops?

"I suspicioned something right away;" she'd say. "He left here with a black garbage bag with nothing in it." I try to look around without appearing to, but no one stands in a doorway or peeks out a window. Still, you never know.

I put the bag on the back floor of the Lexus, drive to Bayside, and instead of a single beer and sandwich, I order a tequila shot with a beer chaser. The owner, Paco, dark circles under his eyes and a fading bruise across the bridge of his nose, says, "A change once in a while is good, mon." He sets down the shot glass and icy mug, then returns with a long-necked Bud.

So, hell yes, here's another witness who's noted the variation in my pattern. "Never orders anything but a beer and a sandwich, but that day he wanted to get drunk," Paco will say from the witness stand. "Then *mañana* his wife turns up dead."

I order another boiler-maker. Okay, so I have to wait a day longer. Get rid of the pestle and mortar somewhere and return to Bayside for my beers and sandwich routine tomorrow.

I read the paper, have another boiler-maker with a sandwich this time, and feel a little numbness settle in at the base of my skull.

About twelve thirty, I give up on whatever it is I'm trying to do: get drunk? work up the courage to kill Susan? I drive back to Sandhills by side streets, avoid the main drags where the cops are always on the look-out for drunk college boys. After a couple of wrong turns, I realize I've made a habit for the last ten years to take only the main road, Hwy. I-275, from Tampa, across the Causeway, and back to St. Pete. I've transformed two big cities and its one bridge into my own small hamlet and waterway, just as my mother did in Cleveland, never going anywhere but to the grocery store and the cafe where she sometimes worked. My grandfather's world was even more circumscribed, the two acres he hardly ever left, patrolled like a separate state.

"Kept him out of trouble," I say out loud to the November sun hanging in the corner of my windshield.

Exhausted down to my toes, I finally navigate into familiar lanes, and an insight comes with the return to my habitual streets. Some lives are blessed with the grace of few choices. The idea makes me wish for some such modest territory, a simple life, which didn't offer so many possibilities.

Baptizing the Cat

Although it's only one o'clock in the afternoon, and I'm so drunk and tired I can barely breathe, I decide to check out Catherine's apartment, not go in, just make sure she's all right. That damned unlocked patio door has snagged in my mind and won't go away. I park the Lexus in the front of the condos—where Susan won't see— and, in what has become my practice, climb the stairs and slog along the second-floor walkways. I pass over our apartment, descend one staircase and ascend another, and then at Catherine's complex, I descend again, walk down a dank passage that doesn't get much daylight, and come to stand again on her concrete slab. The sun hammers down in relentless streams, and the hot-pink stucco walls of Sandhills seem white, bleached out. I don't tap on the glass; I'm too exhausted and too smashed to even talk. And I don't want Catherine to see me like this, so out of control. I pull on the chrome handle and it doesn't give. Good, she's locked up. I lean my forehead against the glass. "You're safe," I whisper, but at the same time feel that Catherine's not in the apartment. That's okay, she probably went to her friend, Claire's. Will they talk about me?

Jesus, women and their need to gab. Still, somehow the feeling behind the glass and the drapes is too vacant. What if Catherine runs away, doesn't give me time to get rid of Susan—that might take weeks—doesn't believe that I can pull it together for us. The liquor, the disgusting hamburger that I ordered and forced down with that last boilermaker—trying to show that all was normal—suddenly wants to come back up. I step to the edge of the patio just in case I vomit.

Nauseated, the saliva boils in my mouth. I stand very still, half on and half off the squares of concrete, and look back to Catherine's metal-framed glass patio doors. In the startlingly bright sunlight, the dark folds in the fabric have disappeared, and the entire surface behind the glass is whitened out to a complete blank. In a drunken split second, I understand Mogliani's totally white on white canvas that hangs in the MOMA. Perhaps this experience is what he was trying to express, the lack of response I see in those white curtains, the uninhabited void that exists on the other side. Vacant, abandoned, barren, the lack of color or shadow speaks. Gone. All gone.

Numb with fatigue and liquor, I trudge back to the car, but the thought of Catherine "gone" follows me. When I see her again, we'll set up some parameters, some system so she can let me know where she is. "When you leave, tell me where you're going," I'll say. She can call on my cell phone. It would be good to receive a few real calls for a change and not just pretend ones. I'll explain my cryptic responses, and it'll give me some peace. I'm not ready to go through another day like that last one; Catherine vanished and my not knowing where.

I drive slowly around to our parking places on the left side of Sandhills, but when I get to the door and punch in the numbers, again the code doesn't work. Didn't Susan tell Nursey to change it back? I heard her. I bang on the door, but here, too, no response. Of course, I remember, Susan and the girls have made their daily trek to the beach. Then, where is Nursey? Of course, she's gone to the grocery for the ingredients for spaghetti for tomorrow night. Jesus H. Christ, these females are killing me. I won't have to murder Susan; I'll be the one killed, done in by the gentler sex. Grandpa Emile's words: "Women, the weaker sex—no damn way."

I circle to the back of our apartment and stretch out on the chaise lounge. It's really too hot to be outside, but my only alternative is to go back to the car. I could keep the engine and the air conditioning running, but the seat doesn't recline all the way and that would be too uncomfortable. Besides I'm too wasted to walk anywhere. It's better to lie here, try to grab a nap, and wait for Nursey or Susan and the girls to get back. I drift, knowing it's better to sleep it off, so Susan can't smell the liquor. In the past, her constant comment on my night-time excursions was, "The CIA must have a big budget for scotch." My answer was always, "Sure. We have to establish friendly relationships with our contacts."

Of course, there was no way to explain that I was just passing time, drinking in a joint because there was nothing better to do. Still the feeling of futility as I lie down is pretty much the same as if I'd been out in a bar looking for a woman. Funny, the entire day and night I spent with Catherine in her apartment or that day we spent at the college left no such unpleasant aftertaste. The euphoria, holding and kissing that slender woman, carried over as though I'd been touched by a good fairy, received some sort of blessing. I'd been more tolerant of Susan and patient with the girls, kinder to Nursey.

Baptizing the Cat

The rest of the day is a blur. Nursey returns, and I help her haul groceries from Susan's van. I grouse about the code not being switched back in, about having to wait out in the heat.

"Musta put in the wrong numbers, Mr. Phillip," the old maid says, not one bit sorry.

This time I watch to make sure she punches in the right buttons; I call them out to her. Funny how Nursey can drive, use the ATM for cash, but anything relating to me or my wishes gets bungled.

I crash in our bedroom and refuse to come out. Still the evening family noises swirl into my hearing, even through the shut door. "Nothing to eat, must be coming down with the flu," I call out to Susan when she tries to get me up for the pot roast that put my plans on hold. And the lie seems partly true, whether it's the boilermakers, the hamburger, or the heat from an hour spent outside on the patio, I feel flushed and ill. But at last the girls are in bed, my in-laws are gone back to the Marriott, the TV set off—Susan never stays up past ten. She comes into the bedroom, and I move out to the couch.

"Don't want you catching this bug, not with your asthma," I explain, and drag a pillow with me.

In the living room, the fall moon shines through the glass doors, as it must be shining on Catherine's back entryway. I pull the heavy slide, stand on the threshold, look out in the direction of Catherine's apartment. The ocean's sounds are a constant background against the moon's silence. Should I go down and tell her I'm thinking of her, but not repeat "I love you" until I have a chance to explain. No, I'll do that tomorrow when I feel better. Right now, I truly need rest.

Somehow during the night, on one of my many trips back from the bathroom—my stomach is a mess—I, out of force of habit, take a wrong turn and go back to Susan's and my bedroom. I realize I should have made for the couch but don't want to alert my wife to my condition. She'll insist on dousing me with one of her remedies, so I ease onto my side of the large bed and turn as far away as possible.

"God, Phillip, what time is it?" she mutters, and hitches her thick body two or three times to slide closer and throw a heavy arm over my side.

"Almost five," I answer, knowing she'll go back to sleep immediately and stay that way at least until ten. The girls will rise earlier, for here at the beach Susan still enforces a nine o'clock curfew. Against my wife's protests, I've extended that hour by letting them keep a light on as long as they read. Odd, what brings back the past. I remember only too well my grandfather's early-to-bed edicts. For what seemed like eons, I'd watch an evening sky go from light blue to gray to dark with all the speed of a glacier. So I've adopted my mother's compromise—strangely Susan agrees—"You can keep a lamp on," she tells the girls, "and read as long as you want."

Yet it's full daylight when I hear the doorbell ring and Nursey's distant answer. One lifted eyelid tells me Susan is up, so I know it's past ten. Groggy, I turn, determined to pull another hour of sleep out of my semi-conscious state. That way I won't have to spend as much of the morning in the apartment. And I vow to see Catherine today, even if it kills me, no matter if I have to sit on her back patio or ride down to Island's End and search out where Claire lives.

My brain sends a single throb of pain down the back of my neck, reminding me of yesterday's booze, and the emotional ups and downs of the week. For a basically lazy painter, who sat in his condo or studio for the last ten years, I've made up for all that inactivity in just one week. Went to my lover's husband's house—might as will call her that, it's what she called me. The bare-faced nerve of that visit and the encounter with Spurlock still gives me a ripple of chill bumps down my arms. I met the man, walked all over his black and white territory, and finally took a gun out of his hands. Then a day later, I spent an entire twenty-four hours with his wife. How's that for balls?

Susan stands at the bedroom doorway and in a soft, mannerly voice, unusual for her, says, "You better get up, Phillip, there's a policeman and another man asking for you."

I grunt, "Uh?"

This time, Susan hisses, "Please Phillip, it's the police. They seem serious."

I roll from the bed and pull on the same pair of shorts I wore yesterday. All the possibilities of the previous night jams into my thoughts: Somehow when I was with Catherine, my car was stolen and returned after the thieves robbed a bank. Or a night earlier, after I left Spurlock, he was stopped by the police and claimed his drunk driving was the result of my knocking his head against the side window of his BMW. The question also looms, how did he drive home after I left him in Harry's parking lot? I hadn't waited to find out if he'd even moved from the passenger's side to the driver's seat. "Friends don't let friends drive drunk." Well, Spurlock was no friend, and I didn't care if he got in a car wreck. It would be one less spouse to get rid of. Maybe Catherine's apartment's was robbed—what with that open door—but then it was closed when I tested it later.

I stand inside our walk-in closet and put on my shirt. The unbelievable thought rises that somehow the police are on to my plans to dose Susan with her asthma medicine. I'm wearing the shorts with the baggie of ground-up Theophylline pills in the pocket, and it knocks softly against my leg. Is that possible? They have psychics who figure out where the body is after a killing, why not have someone on the payroll to figure out who's going to commit a murder? Head the killer off.

I'm dressed but far too muddled to find my slip-on shoes. Must have left them by the couch. Besides, Susan keeps murmuring, "Please hurry, Phillip. They're scary, using your middle initial like they read it off a rap sheet."

My wife uses her detective-show words, but I answer patiently, "I'm coming, I'm coming" and move carefully around her in the doorway and then down the hall, willing myself not to stagger. Exactly how many boiler-makers did I have yesterday, and can they arrest you—after the fact—for being drunk or for just being hung over?

Susan's right, the two men in the narrow entrance way are serious, intimidating with their dead-pan faces and we-mean-business postures. One is a hefty policeman in full navy uniform with badge and gun belt, and the other is an equally thick man in dark pants, pale plaid sports coat, white shirt, and black tie. Their haircuts are identical, short buzz on top and no hair at all on the sides, seemingly fresh razored that morning, just above the ears.

"Mr. Craine, Mr. Phillip E. Craine?" the man in the sports coat reads from a clipboard. His fleshy jaw is red from shaving, his light-blue eyes intense, and his tone holds more of an accusation than a question. His voice is too loud for this cramped foyer.

"Yes, it is I," I answer, using my mother-in-law's pompously correct English. Suddenly curiously calm, I suppress a desire to be flippant by adding, Who else would Mrs. Phillip E. Craine drag out of her bedroom?

Nursey stands to the left of the kitchen bar, right behind the pillar that supports the roof, just out of these two men's sight. Her dark face bears a resigned look as though she's been through this sort of encounter before. I remember some talk in years past of a nephew who went to jail. April and May, wide-eyed and disheveled, sit on the couch with their pale blankets up around their shoulders. The television set blares its usual colored cartoon along with its bright noise.

"I'm Detective Berstow, and this is Officer McGill," Sportscoat says, and opens his jacket to show a laminated picture identification hooked to his belt. McGill, olive skinned and bushy eyebrowed, barely nods.

"You want to step outside?" Sportscoat asks.

I nod and follow the two men out into the morning air, ablaze with early light. The inner door clicks shut and the slated outside door, on its poorly aligned hinges, bangs. McGill, on my left, pulls out silver sunglasses, the kind you can't see into, from his pocket and puts them on. We three—me in the middle—stand and face outward on the walkway that overlooks the trapezoid of grass next to our condo's front door. Small plantings of orange marigolds and one large sago palm complete the neat scene edged by the hot-pink walls. It occurs to me—for the millionth time—that any view from an odd angle, no matter how mundane, beautiful or trashy, makes for a good painting.

Sportscoat clears his throat, and here, beyond anyone's hearing, he lowers his tone. "Before we start, I have to inform you that the body of Mrs. Randolf Spurlock was found this morning, around three a.m."

"Who?" I ask. My brain reels and asks silently, Who is Mrs. Randolf Spurlock?

270

Baptizing the Cat

Sportscoat repeats the words, "The body of Mrs. Randolf Spurlock was found this morning, around three a.m."

The concrete walkway shifts under my feet. I step forward, reach out, and touch the terrace rail for support. The metal is hot from the morning sun, heats the tips of my fingers, but I press harder. A roar fills my ears so that I hear what the detective says behind me, as if I'm far away and under water.

"Will you tell us of your activities for the past week, and your whereabouts as of last night?"

"Well," I begin, and hesitate as though trying to remember, glad to have my back to the two men.

"Would you please turn around Mr. Craine?" Sportscoat asks, overly polite.

I wait while something inside splits me into two halves. The first half bends over the railing, vomits, wipes his mouth, and stands upright, silent. The second turns, leans back against the railing, calmly pauses, then says, "Well, that's hard to recall. Pretty much the same every day, mornings here and then painting at my studio in Tampa all afternoon, although I did drive over to Mr. Spurlock's house on Wednesday. He gave me a tour. I returned to my studio to paint, and then in the evening we met at Harry's Pawn Shop, went to supper, had a few drinks and watched a ball game. Tampa Bay, 30 to 14."

It's an easy recital. I've been over the entire day several times, marveling at the oddness of the circumstances. Of course, I omit the business with Spurlock and the gun, and my trips to knock on Catherine's back patio door, and the day and night I spent with her, just twenty-four hours ago. Did anyone see me?

"Was Wednesday the first time you met Randolf Spurlock?" Sportscoat asks. His tone has risen half an octave, and he blinks his light eyes in the sunlight as he looks down to the clipboard and then back up to me. Maybe he should wear sunglasses, too.

"Yes," I answer.

"And Mrs. Spurlock? Do you know her?" He swallows, his large adams apple pushes against the edge of his collar.

A watery film rises in my eyes. I glance sideways, down over the edge of the railing. "Yes," I answer, resisting the impulse to say no. What good would that do? "Tell the truth as long as possible," my grandfather advised whenever my mother would lead me into a maze of questions that finally revealed me for the liar I was—and still am.

"And how do you know Mrs. Spurlock?" The pitch of the words is softer, and Sportscoat's mouth sounds full of spit.

"She's our neighbor, lives one building over, in apartment 3D. I've talked to her on her back patio, when she was cleaning—after a run, several times." I hold my voice level, although bile rises in my throat, "Had coffee and a glass or two of wine," I add, knowing Susan can't hear, and besides my fingerprints are inside Catherine's condo, all over the place. Then I ask, "You found her? What happened?"

Sportscoat intones, "We're not allowed to give out that information."

"Where did you find her?"

"On the beach, just down past Bayside,."

He start checking off items on his clipboard. "Did Mrs. Spurlock mention her husband?"

Up before my eyes, like a black and white film between me and the two policeman, is an image of Catherine lying in the surf as I saw her, her hair fanned out in the waves. I pause, pretend an effort to remember. "Not that I can recall. But then Spurlock himself told me a lot about their separation when I was there."

"Why did you go to Mr. Spurlock's house?"

"Curiosity. My father-in-law, Ed Bowers and I've been watching that place go up for over a year. We wondered who owned it."

"And you've never talked to or met with Mr. Spurlock before?"

"No, never."

Incredulous at the composure of this other self, I match Sportscoat's manner, the clipped tone of his questions. The policeman beside me keeps his sunglasses aimed at my face, and I can't tell from sidelong glances if he's truly watching me or if his eyes wander. Maybe that's the opaque glasses' purpose, to allow scrutiny without seeming to. I lean back and slide my hand farther down the railing behind me, just enough to find more of a burn, a physical pain to match the paralyzed feeling inside.

"What exactly did you and Mr. Spurlock talk about when you were with him? Walk me through your conversation." Sportscoat anchors the clipboard against his belt buckle, his pen poised to write.

Baptizing the Cat

Instinct tells me that he is trying out his intuition, straining for that one small detail or word that will catch me in a discrepancy.

"Well," I say again. "There's not much to tell. He showed me around that huge house—very proud of it. Said his wife and he were separated. He seemed upset."

I immediately wish I hadn't given Sportscoat this last bit of extra information. Not that it amounted to much, but that's how police interrogation works. They weasel one thread of a fact out of you and soon they've undone the whole fabric of your story. But what am I lying about? It's all a big mistake; Catherine isn't dead.

My head swims. The sun's radiance shifts suddenly into my vision, and a bright band of yellow flashes in spasms behind my eyes. I hear my mother say, "I'm having a sinking spell;" hear myself mumble, "I've got to sit down. I've been in bed with the flu."

I feel Sportscoat on one side and the policeman on the other. They hold me up at my elbows. Against all logic, considering my calmness up until that moment, my knees give way, but the two men hook me up between them and with much jostling wedge me back through the doors and the foyer and plop me like a sackful of clothes onto the couch.

For an instant, Susan stays, stolidly at her place at the table, and Nursey at hers in the kitchen, but they're not eating or cooking. They haven't moved or altered since the officers and I left, even the television is still on, too loud. The whole room is frozen, all persons listening, waiting to find out what happened outside on the walkway.

Then, Susan shrieks, "Phillip!" and rises. I have an impression of Nursey in her blue robe, stepping back into the shadows of the kitchen, leaning against the refrigerator for support. My daughters scurry out of the way to stand silhouetted in front of the glass doors. In unison, they turn their heads, watching, from me to their mother and back.

"It's all right, Miss, all right," Sportscoat says, "just overheated out there in the sun." He bends and sits on the edge of the couch.

This close, I smell sweet aftershave, see streaks of perspiration lining the side of his ruddy face, realize that in dress shirt, tie, and jacket, he's speaking more for himself than for me. I haven't even broken a sweat. My t-shirt and shorts feel dry and feather light except for the weight of the ground pills in my pocket.

Susan comes from her site at the table to punch the television set off, and then she maneuvers around the coffee table and sits heavily onto the couch on my other side. She covers my hand with hers.

"What's wrong, Phillip? Why are these men here?" A layer of panic underlies every word. She's not asking about my physical condition but about what happened outside. The orange chenille robe she's worn the last three months, gapes in front, showing a large vee of freckled, lined flesh.

"Nothing to worry about, dear," I say, slide my hand out from under hers, put my hand on top, pat her fingers. "I'm just light-headed from the flu." I drop my head back against the cushions, away from these two large individuals hemming me in. Susan weighs the cushions down on her side as much as Sportscoat does on his. I stare up at the square acoustical tiles overhead.

"What's going on, Phillip?" she repeats. A history of misgivings lies behind her questions. I was absent an entire twenty-four hours just a day ago—something I haven't done in years—and she knows I probably don't have the flu, that I was drinking heavily yesterday.

"Mrs. Spurlock is . . . dead," I say to the ceiling. Not Catherine, not Catherine, just Mrs. Spurlock.

"What?"

"You know that woman we liked from the other section." I motion with my hand in the direction of Catherine's apartment. "The one who said May was a good swimmer." I hope Susan doesn't pick up on the "we."

"What does that have to do with us?" Susan turns her pale, spotted face toward Sportscoat. I observe from a sideways glimpse, resentment, my wife's most ready emotion. Indignation raises her pale eyebrows and draws the corners of her narrow lips down. Money and a place in the hierarchy turns mice into lions, even a mouse clad in an ugly orange bathrobe. Susan has never had any trouble dealing with "riffraff," her word for tradespeople, public servants, and the like. Unbeknownst to Sportscoat and the policeman, they occupy the same category of "riffraff" and are of no real account in Susan's great chain of being.

Apparently, without comprehension, Sportscoat responds to the imperious tone, to the well-appointed apartment, to the fearful maid in the kitchen. He, too, knows the order of things, is aware of rank, the clout that money bestows. He explains, something he didn't do outside on the walkway. "Mr. Craine spent an afternoon and apparently almost an entire night with Mr. Spurlock this past week. Randolf Spurlock is using your husband as part of his alibi."

"Oh, well," Susan says. Her face is impassive; she lifts her shoulders in a partial shrug of unconcern. "My husband has many associates and business acquaintances. He is part-owner of Bower Enterprises, plus being a full-time artist."

"Did you know Mrs. Spurlock?" Sportscoat asks across my body, with a differential dipping of his close-clipped head toward Susan.

"Not well, we spoke sometimes. I take my daughters down to the beach and to the pool every day, if weather permits. She walked a lot on the beach; she was a friendly person."

I have to hand it to the old girl. She says her lines perfectly, not the least bit discomforted by Sportscoat's questions or by the thick navy-blue presence standing with a gun on his hip in our vestibule. Although now that's Susan's stopped speaking, I feel a faint tremble in her fingers under my palm.

"Would you both be willing to come down to the station and make a statement?" Sportscoat asks, and moistens his lips with a surprisingly gray tongue. But he speaks in a polite, almost apologetic way that's appeared since coming back into the apartment.

"Of course," Susan says and stands, walks around the coffee table and pulls the belt of the orange robe a little tighter. Still she does nothing to adjust the almost off-the-shoulder effect of her décolleté. Her posture loudly proclaims: You and your cohort, there in my entryway, are dismissed.

And they are, more or less, evicted. It wouldn't have surprised me if Susan had started a shuffling walk towards Sportscoat and bodily edged him and the policeman out the door. Instead, Sportscoat matches Susan's movements. He rises and asks if we can make it to the police station by tomorrow. "That is if Mr. Craine feels well enough, or you both can come down in the next day or two." April and May, sneak from in front of the glass doors and take the places that Sportscoat and Susan have vacated. Sitting on either side, they lean against me, in consolation for what they can't understand. Nursey starts moving pans in the kitchen.

So.

So, Sportscoat and the policeman leave, the door closes behind them, and Susan looks at me in that flat-line, blue-eyed way she has when she doesn't quite understand a joke.

I say, "Please pull your robe together" and gesture to her chest, not meaning for the words to come out so sharply.

"Why should I?" she replies, and tilts her chin up, steps from beside the coffee table, and heads back to the dining area. The tight bronze corkscrew curls on her head bounce with irritation. "This is my house, I'm decent, and those people don't mean a thing to me. They're just doing their job, what they're paid to do."

"But Mrs. Spurlock is dead," I say. The sound of my voice echoes inside my head, inside my chest. I'm glad I'm not standing, glad that I'm sitting on the couch, glad for my girls' small bodies against me.

Susan turns and her face softens. Unthinking, almost as a courtesy, she pulls the front of the robe closed. "That is bad," she admits. "What do you think happened? Why didn't we ask? Did she drown?"

My head beats with a throb of pain from temple to temple. I move farther down on the cushions, stare up again at the white tiles, draw my daughters closer.

"Poor Philip, you really are sick." Susan backtracks to the couch and leans over our trio of bodies to place a cool hand on my hot forehead.

"I just need sleep," I say, barely a whisper. I want to say, I just need to be unconscious.

Perhaps the unspoken words register in Susan's mind, for she bustles down the hall and returns with an orange-brown bottle of pills. Shaking them like castanets toward me, she rumbles into the kitchen to run a glass of water. "See, I knew these would come in handy. My sleepers."

"Give me a double dose," I instruct, and my wife brings four pills back without argument. I take them. They are longer versions of the ground-up Theophylline, the ones I have in the baggie in my pocket. God let these pills kill me, I think and watch to see where Susan sets the bottle down on the counter. I'll take more in a few minutes if necessary.

Baptizing the Cat

The girls slip down to the floor, the television set comes back on. Susan tells them, "No, don't disturb, Daddy," but I say it's all right, just keep the sound down. I stretch out, turn my face to the back of the couch, cover the side of my head with one of its many odd pillows, and drift, drift between visions of Catherine in the water, Catherine in the shower, Catherine at the Museum, Catherine under me. Noiseless tears slide from my eyes down my nose onto the aqua green leaves woven into the cloth. Susan and Nursey leave the room for their morning dressing rituals. I get up, take four more pills and a shot of scotch, and return to the couch to finally pass out.

I wake with a blanket over me at four the next morning. The kitchen clock on the micro-wave blinks the time. Immediately I remember the police, the news they brought about Catherine. I sit up, and a heave of anguish twists me forward, but I don't whimper out loud. I go into the kitchen and find Susan's tall bottle of pills and go outside to stand on the walkway. Can it be that only this morning two policeman and I stood right here? Here, they told me she was dead. I take two of the pills without water, swallow hard, but they hang in my throat. Maybe I can die from strangulation. No—too easy. Just keep swallowing, feel the dry things stuck halfway down. I take the baggie from my pocket and shake out the ground-up Theophylline, watch the powder sift in a white mist across the triangle of grass beside our condo. Susan's death lost in Catherine's. No need for plans now, no need for ground-up pills, now. I go back into the apartment, gulp a straight shot of scotch out of the bottle, trot to the hall bathroom, and stand in the shower under the hot water until it runs cold. Then another two pills, wash them down with a second shot, and lie back onto the couch. Within seconds I fall over that dark edge into oblivion.

Actually, Susan's pills are a muscle relaxer and a mood elevator; I read this information on the label at noon. How's that for a crock, but whatever. They get me through the next few days and the interview at the police station. Surprisingly, Sportscoat and the cop who came with him are not the ones to take Susan's and my statements. My wife is confused, or seems to be, about actual days of the week and attributes my missing day and night with Catherine to the day and evening I spent with Spurlock. No wonder, her pills—I've almost reached the bottom of the bottle—make every-thing swim together. She says nothing about my CIA connections, but is loquacious about my business dealings as though I've been a full-time partner in Bower's Enterprises for years and not just for the last week.

I tell the truth about Spurlock and the tour of his house, that he was upset over his wife leaving but never mention the gun that he held to his head, never mention that I knocked him against the car window at the end of our evening together.

As the scenes play out, roll down from disaster to common place, Susan and I learn all there is to know, the information on "the case," as it's called, from television news shows and from the *Tampa Tribune*. My wife reads the articles aloud, and I lie on the couch, in a haze, reach the last of Susan's pills, but she assures me she has more.

Chapter 17

Within the week, the entire story comes out. Apparently, Rand Spurlock paid Harry of the Pawn Shop to find some people to get rid of Catherine—just like that, as easy as pie—as easy as coming up with a listening device for a customer. Right away, the bastard Harry confesses and names Spurlock and two other men—those who dragged her away, not from her apartment that morning I left, but from her Jeep that evening in a grocery store's parking lot. Took her from her jeep, the bagels and oranges scattered on the back seat. From a newspaper report, the coroner says, "She put up a fight."

How did they find Harry? Maybe my telling them I met Spurlock at Harry's Shop? He spilled his guts to the detectives, probably to Sportscoat and the Uniform. I can imagine the scene.

So they have a confession. So maybe there's no need to take fingerprints from Catherine's apartment, although I know nothing of real police procedure. Did Towelhead know, breathe a sigh of relief, as I do now, a sigh that starts moisture filling my eyes. At times, I halt Sarah's reading of the newspaper accounts; she's gone out and bought the *St. Petersburg Gazette*. I tell her my head's killing me, take another two pills and another drink of scotch and lie on the couch, and again turn my face to the aqua cushions. Still, after a few minutes, I ask her to continue the newspaper reports. Every morning there's a column or two on the murder in the first section of the *Tribune*.

Catherine was shot in the parking lot. God, how she must have resisted. The writhing of her slender body under mine had been surprisingly strong. Then she was taken out on Spurlock's boat at the marina. There were witnesses—people drinking on the dock—

although it was already two in the morning. She was dropped overboard with concrete blocks, wrapped in a tarpaulin that came loose and let her body wash up hardly a mile from Sandhills. A sickening account that one can read every few months in any newspaper. Wife and husband alienated, separated. Husband arranges to have wife slain. "Wealthy, beautiful mother of two teenaged sons, killed by estranged husband," the headlines read for two days, with a picture of a much younger Catherine, her eyes more round, her cheeks and brow exquisitely smooth.

The different articles and TV news repeat the tale over and over with hardly any variation; the reasons come out, bit by banal bit. Catherine, worth millions, owned all of Hornsby Real Estate Company, left to her by her father. Catherine, "a kind and lovely woman, with a wicked sense of humor," one of the real estate agents says in an interview, and adds again, "a lovely woman." Genuine sorrow alters his voice on the last syllable. Randolf Spurlock, from Los Angeles, California—wouldn't you know—started as a rookie salesman, married the boss' daughter, and little by little took over the agency. Catherine, it seemed, was comfortable with her mother-housewife role, had two sons, was an art teacher at their elementary school, St. Patrick's, contributed to and ran a campaign that added a library to the facilities, and later became an assistant curator at the Tampa Museum. How little we know of a person's history until all the details are listed in an obituary. Randolf Spurlock was, the papers say: "a competent salesman"—faint praise—and when the building boom hit south Florida, as it did every fifteen years or so, Hornsby Real Estate and the land Catherine's father owned developed into a bonanza, and it all was in Catherine's name.

Harry, that wretch, the picture of his mug shot, his bullet-shaped head, his greasy gray skin telegraphs his character. I can imagine his gummy lips regurgitating every word Spurlock said over the last month of their killing plan. "Rand said she didn't want to live in that big house he'd built on the beach, said it was too fancy. Said she wanted the boys to come home, didn't like that ta-ta school they was going to; said them fancy schools was mainly for delinquents. Said she wanted the boys to come home to the house on the canal—their real home. That the new house wasn't right for teenagers. Rand said she was seeing other men." This last accusation is belligerent,

Baptizing the Cat

a good enough reason to kill a wife. Harry's interview is repeated over and over, verbatim in the papers and on television newscasts. Pictures of the concrete towers and the three-layered tiers of Spurlock's house are shown from all angles along with the accounts.

Unfortunately, there are no other scandals that week, no hurricanes, no different homicides to take the reporters off the story. The murderers among us lie low, reconsider their options, tell confederates, "I wasn't really serious, you know; I joke about doing away with my old lady all the time." The local TV stations are stressed for more footage. A modest home is shown, actually a cool million is what it would take now to buy the Spanish-styled house on the canal, what once was Catherine's father's and mother's place. A wedding gift to Catherine and Spurlock, since by then the parents were living in Boca Raton. And then a wide shot of the beach side of the Sandhills' condo and a picture of Catherine's back patio door. "Where the murdered woman lived after the separation," Sarah reads in an over-emphasized manner.

On the hour, every hour, over and over. Sarah watches the news stations, can't seem to get enough of the particulars, which are repeated practically word for word in every program, and I can't find the strength to tell her to change the channel. Can't seem to give up the hope, that suddenly it will be announced, "a mistake, Catherine Spurlock is alive." Someone else was murdered.

When one reporter gleefully announces, "This story might make *20/20*," I leave the apartment, drive out of St. Pete and across the Causeway to my studio in Tampa. It's November windy, again, like the day I met Catherine and we went to the Tampa campus. The waves blow against the built-up road, not quite sending water across the middle line. In the parking lot, getting out of the car, I don't look either way. Where's Violet? Is Belle watching from across the highway? She has Catherine's Milky Way painting. What is she thinking? But who cares who sees me now. In the shadowy domain of easels and paint that once was my refuge, I don't open the blinds or turn on the lights. I lie on the cool tiles of the floor, under the huge clock that ticks off the minutes. I've never noticed that sound before, but now the mechanism sends a crick and then a crack of tinny metal against my eardrums.

Catherine's funeral is tomorrow at St. Elmo's in Tampa, the old church that her parents attended but that no one except tourists goes to anymore. I enumerate all the details; two weeks have passed, Randolf Spurlock and Harry Riggers are in jail "awaiting indictment," the two scum who killed her are nowhere to be found, and I'm lying on this floor in my studio, my life's blood sucked out of my veins.

Susan plans for all of our family to attend the funeral Mass, sends my best dark suit out to be pressed. "Maybe Mommy and Daddy will want to come." Susan's parents have stayed on. Why?

"Why do any of us have to go?" I ask.

"She was our neighbor, Phillip," Susan says. "We spoke often"— a lie—"and she was Catholic."

"But why the girls?" I question.

"Because they need to realize that death is a part of life." Susan issues this edict as though she were discussing a curriculum requirement with that other home-schooling mom she sometimes talks to on the phone.

However, Miz Mildred convinces Susan to let our daughters skip the ritual. Thank you, mother-in-law, for the first time in all of our acquaintance, a truly heartfelt thank-you from the bottom of my soul. From my vantage point on the couch, I'm privy to every word of Susan's conversations with her mother, sometimes as many as four times a day. The girls will stay with Miz Mildred and Ed, in their grandparent's suite at the Marriott. They were lucky not to have caught Phillip's flu. Nursey will take the girls there and remain to help out.

At Susan's direction, we arrive an hour early at St. Elmo's to find that no seats are left in the small, antiquated church, except the ones on the far side, down near the front, which, after my wife's "Who are all these people?" turns into "the best pews in the house." We have a direct view to the right, where the family will sit.

I kneel with my eyes closed, numb from three pills and two shots of scotch, somewhere between conscious and unconscious, and for once Susan doesn't nudge me, doesn't say, "Don't go to sleep." After what seems only minutes, she whispers, "Here they come," and we rise to see the casket, a bronze affair with dull gold trim—oddly reminiscent of that brown and gold bathing suit—pushed down the center aisle by two black-suited undertakers. Catherine's relatives and sandy-haired sons follow and sit directly across from us in the mahogany pews. The boys favor their mother in some indefinable way. Both are fair, in navy blue suits, the edges of white collars and cuffs show, the skinny look of youth still about their necks and shoulders. A woman, a few years older than Catherine with dun-colored hair in a bun—might be the friend Claire—and an older, larger, gray-headed male walks and sits with them. The youngest boy—exactly like my May would—leans against the large man. From a television interview, I recognize him, the cousin from Philadelphia, who seems choked up over Catherine's death but can still stand outside the Sandhills' patio and talk to reporters at least once a day.

God, why am I here? I question, and kneeling again, my hands cover my face. But I made no objection when Sarah sketched out the day to Nursey. "We'll be through by twelve and can meet Momma and Daddy at the Marriott buffet, even though it's not Sunday. No need to go to the grave-side service; is there, Phillip?" my wife asks.

I don't have to answer. For the entire week now, except for that one evening at the studio, I lay or sat on the couch, which became my station, just as the dining table was Susan's, the kitchen Nursey's, and the floor in front of the TV set belongs to my daughters, with their occasional forays to my borders. Without words they seem to know my need for consolation. May leans, weightless as a sprite, against my arm, and strokes the stubble on my jaw. Her eyes, so like her mother's in color, crystal blue, but so different in the light of intelligence that shines out, searches my face. She's not fooled as to my sorry state and not put off by her mother's admonishments, "Don't get too close to Daddy; he's been sick." April volunteers to read. "I can pronounce words I don't understand, if you want me to read an art book or the newspaper," she offers. Not as comfortable in her twelve-year-old personhood as May is in her six, still April has the good sense to copy her sister—the way a daughter should behave—and sits next to me. The physical warmth seeps out of their small bodies into mine, much like Susan's pills. Their gentle compassion edges me away from that concealed land of despair where I am headed.

I look up and am astonished. The priest for the funeral Mass is African—very black, unusual for a Catholic pastor—and very old, with that thin frazzled silver-hair that says he is in the last years of life. He wears a cream-colored vestment with a large purple and red geometric pattern, an African design, all angles and circles, embroidered from neck to floor. He seems too ancient to conduct a funeral, like the pope, all bent over and worn out. When will those old prelates give it up? He fumbles, opens a large red book, falters over his place, reads the first parts of the Mass in a thin, uncertain voice, and totters on unsteady legs back and forth from the altar to a high-backed gold chair. He has a useless cane, which never touches the floor, crooked over an arm, but when one of the altar boys, a sturdy thick-haired teenager, tries to help seat him, the old cleric swats the youngster away.

I pray to God that this ancient black man isn't going to preach the eulogy. What on earth could he possibly say about my vibrant golden-haired Catherine?

But as with all my recent prayers, this one, too, is denied. Halfway into the ceremony, after the white cloth has covered the casket, after the incense has been lit, after the aged priest has swung the golden censor, filling the air with that strange odor, and after he has circumnavigated the open space between casket and altar—which might as well have been the globe for all the speed he employed—he calls in a wobbling tremor on God to give Catherine peace. The Mass proceeds and then, this poor representative of 2,000 years of Christianity digs into a concealed pocket in his robes and brings out creased papers. He bumbles his way to the podium. Uncertainly, he sways, hangs his cane on the edge of the dais, smooths out the folded papers, fingers his glasses, peers at the disheveled sheets in front of him as if he's never seen them before, and clears his throat.

"My name is Father Christopher," he says in a weak, dispirited voice, and squints his wrinkled face up to look out at the congregation, which now has people, two deep, lined up against the side walls, towered over by statues. "Most of you don't know me." Again he fingers his glasses—so greasy with prints they'll be impossible to see through—and again, he looks up and squints. "I was pastor of St. Elmo's for fifteen years, twenty years ago, and I was not young then. I was a late convert to the Catholic faith, and a much later vocation."

Oh, my God. How on earth have they come up with this relic? He's going to talk about himself. And I am not wrong. The old cannibal, in a barely audible voice—they won't be able to hear him in the back—launches into his personal history.

"I've been a priest now for forty years and still don't know exactly how or why. My faith is a puzzle—a secret—an enigma—to me—and probably to everyone else, too." He stretches these phases out, with pauses in between. He chuckles faintly, peers over the edge of the podium, and pulls his wide, full-lipped mouth into a line, a grimace. Is he smiling? Are we getting the joke? Can I kill him? Is there a police man in the church who will shoot me afterwards and put an end to this suffering?

"What we have here, dear brothers and sisters, with this death, the death of Catherine, our friend and your mother,"—he motions to the front pews—"is another puzzle, another secret, another enigma."

The old, self-satisfied scoundrel barely whispers, and is that smirking? Still he shuffles his papers, as though he's revealed a great truth to the masses. Has he lost his written sermon and now is floundering, trying to come up with something to say?

An impulse to jump up and flee down the side aisle pulls at my insides. Do I have to sit through a funeral that's turning into a minstrel show? What good are funerals anyway? I didn't go back to Cleveland for my grandfather's, although my mother begged me. "The old man's dead," I said on the phone, but for her benefit didn't add "finally." Isn't that what she'd always wanted: to bury the secret of Emile's lost son and her lost husband in a grave? I went back for her funeral, but just long enough to see her into the ground beside her father-in-law, where she was condemned to be most of her life and now had to be in death. When every stick and paper out of that trash heap of a household was burned, I sold the place for half its worth; for by then the city had grown up around it. It's how I financed my year in Taos where I met Susan.

The old priest pushes the glasses up onto his shining pate, edged by the thick curls of his race. Has he given up on being able to read his sermon?

"I have known Catherine Hornsby for over forty years, from the start of her life, when she was born to older parents, a child born to a couple who had abandoned hope of having a child, much as Sarah and Abraham had abandoned hope."

At the word "Sarah" I feel a twitch in my wife's oversized thigh; it's her middle name. Often she loses focus, hums along in some fuzzy place inside her brain until she's startled into awareness. But just as quickly I feel her relax back into her comfort zone.

"I was a new priest then," he continues, "taking the miracle of my conversion and my late priesthood as my right, as ordinary, and I barely comprehended what the coming of the child Catherine meant to the Hornsbys. They were good people and had many wonderful years with their daughter and their grandchildren. And I am glad today that they are spared, are not here to suffer, as her sons and relatives are suffering . . . as we, too, my brothers and sisters, are suffering."

With these words he bows forward, touches his wrinkled fore-head, with the smeared glasses atop, onto the podium. Then he raises his head, his over-large black eyes full of tears, and in a much stron-ger voice says, "I salute your pain with my own pain . . . which is great." He shuffles his feet, shuffles the papers, and almost knocks the cane from its precarious perch on the edge of the podium. Is he trying to regain his composure; is he trying to remember what he meant to say?

"Pain and suffering brought on by natural circumstances is hard to bear. Pain and suffering brought on by evil is even harder, almost impossible, to bear. Evil would have you believe that it does not ex-ist and that all tragedy is the outcome of society's ills. But I'm sorry to inform you that evil truly does exist. That today you see the out-come of true evil, the evil that resides in us all, in greater and lesser degrees. Evil always brings pain and suffering with it, and great evil brings the most pain and the most suffering. And I'm equally sorry to inform you that pain and suffering are essential, a necessary part of existence. Pain and suffering brought on by natural circumstanc-es or by evil calls for us to change, to change our ways. It forces us to change. And a great evil forces us to change greatly." As his words pour forth, he becomes transformed in a slow but perceptible way. His bearing is more erect and the tremor of only a few minutes ago has disappeared.

"Today, unfortunately, we witness change brought on by a great evil, and we wonder why? A life stamped out by a great evil and we ask why? One good woman dead, two men incarcerated, and two men fleeing from the laws"—the old black man actually says 'laws'— "many lives transformed, and families and friends left to wonder and to suffer."

This ancient patriarch now speaks in a completely audible voice, and his posture, which before was so bent, is upright, straighter, stronger.

"Maridith and Authur Hornsby were changed forever by Catherine's birth; their lives were rendered more meaningful and full. I and many people, even those who did not know them or Catherine, were touched by their friendship and hers, over many years and in many other parishes. The Hornsbys' and Catherine's charities were great, world-wide and parochial. They gave to individuals and to organizations; they gave of their money and more importantly, they gave of their time and energy." He pauses and again squints out at the congregation as though by sheer force of his gaze he can compel us to see what charitable works Catherine and her family accomplished. And now the old chameleon does not shuffle papers or hesitate.

"Her sons, especially, were brought into this world and changed by her motherhood. They sit here before you in their youth, whole and complete, a tribute to a mother's care."

One of Catherine's boys lets out a muffled sob, but I can't bring myself to look.

"Her relatives and her friends here were changed by her concern and her presence. She had many kinfolk and many friends, as evidenced by these pews filled to overflowing before you." He stretches out both large sinewy hands; the sleeves of the creamy robe with its purples and reds drape down like wings. "She had many, many friends, people she loved and who loved her. People who knew her and did not know her. Catherine was not a pretend kind of woman. She wanted a simple existence, to be generous because the world had been generous to her. Catherine did not have to have the best or the most. Catherine was a noble woman, a real woman, a genuine woman with human failings, but with many, many more virtues."

Now, the old priest raises himself up to his full height, at least six feet, stretches the wings of his robe, full blown out on either side, and booms his words out over the congregation. "The life of a good person is sweet. The life of Catherine Hornsby was sweet, sweet like blended incense." His voice, even stronger, rises, and he turns his veined, heavy knuckled hands outward to indicate the last remnants of the heavy fragrance he'd released with such abandon from the censor. "Like blended incense made lasting by a skilled Perfumer." He pauses, and his voice is yet louder. "Beautiful is her name—Catherine—precious is her memory, like honey to the taste, like music at a banquet."

The old cleric hunches his shoulders as if preparing to levitate above the pulpit. His powerful voice rings out an incantation over our heads. "Go Catherine, go! Go now sweet woman, to your eternal home. Go now where no evil, great or small, can touch you. Go now and rest from your labors, rest now in the bosom of Abraham, rest now in the hand of God." He inhales deeply and in a slightly softer timbre, intones, "For whatever mission you were sent upon this earth to accomplish is accomplished. Whatever lives you were meant to bring into the world are brought forth. Whoever you were meant to sway are swayed, and whatever lives you were meant to change are forever changed—changed forever—forever changed."

"Forever changed—changed forever." The words reverberate in my head as we make our way down the aisle and out of the crowd at St. Elmo's. Some people from Sandhills speak in undertones to Susan, and she bubbles a whispered reply, "Yes, it's awful. Poor children, can you believe it?" I rush ahead, stare at the Terrazzo floor, feel that I might fall under the feet of these uncaring onlookers, feel that I might fall under the burden of their token words.

In the muddy morning light of the late November day, the parking lot is a sea of cars. Where did we leave Susan's van? I wait for my wife, and finally, her navy-blue bulk, along with the other so-called mourners, is swept out of St. Elmo's huge doors. With mincing footfalls, she navigates the three steps down toward me. Her large over-white teeth show a smile of complete aplomb.

Baptizing the Cat

We ride in Susan's van. "You drive," I tell her; "I'm still feeling shaky." We head back toward the Causeway, head toward the Marriott and the Sunday routine of lunch. "It was a nice funeral," Susan starts, guiding the car through the tangle of vehicles that wait to go to the cemetery and those trying, like us, to make our escape. "But that preacher; could you believe it? I can't believe he's a Catholic priest. Seemed more like a Baptist revival minister with all that calling out at the end, all that bosom of Abraham stuff."

The sky is overcast, stripped of all brightness, and on the Causeway the water has calmed somewhat from what it was earlier, and now just lashes of white caps flow against the stone gravel on the sides of the road. "Forever changed, changed forever" beats a cadence in my temples, seems to have taken up residence in syncopation with my heart's pulse.

I stare out the side window, realizing that it's beyond my power to pretend to be normal for another hour, that I cannot go with the family to the noon buffet, which starts, so conveniently, at ten-thirty. Cannot sit and watch people eat, cannot force down a bite of food.

"You have to take me home, Susan; I'm sick," I say.

The traffic has slowed, coming up on the toll gate, and Susan will have to make a U-turn and go back to Sandhills to avoid going through the gate. She swivels her head. The unusual addition of pink make-up, rouge, and lipstick has given her face a disguise-like quality and swipes of brown pencil form two unevenly-shaped crescent eyebrows—which she now raises—over irritated blue eyes. "You have to eat, Phillip, if you're ever going to get over this flu bug." Food, her answer to every crisis, every occasion.

"I can't. Let me out here. I'll walk back."

Something in my manner squelches the other arguments that I can see forming in her intractable face. "Okay, okay, but what can I tell Momma and Daddy? They're expecting us all to eat together." The edge of her stiff navy dress is smeared with makeup, and her underarm quivers as she guides the steering wheel into the circle that lets motorists, those who have changed their minds, avoid the toll.

"Say I'm sick, say I've been sick all week." Something inside me wants to say, "sick for years." I press my face against the cool side window, look out at the high-rise apartments gliding by, the glistening ocean off in the distance, the channels with yachts, the houses with the people who own those yachts. All those possessions, every house, every apartment, every room filled with fine things.

At Sandhills, Susan asks, "Do you want me to stay? You're pale as a ghost."

I've managed to step down from the high seat of the Range Rover and now steady myself with my hand on the door frame.

"No, no, go on," I push the words out, past a wail I feel rising in my throat. "Go . . . you have to pick up the girls and Nursey anyway. There's no need."

My legs feel weighted as I walk away from the car and down the sidewalk; I feel Susan's eyes following me. But I know she won't move from the driver's seat, her natural aversion to motion of any kind, and besides "Momma and Daddy" and the Marriott's buffet awaits. I open the slatted door and punch in the code. It works so at least now I can enter my own condo. I hear the car back out of the parking lot and drive away.

In the foyer, I lean my back against the door and then slump down onto my knees onto the floor. "God, oh God." The words echo against the walls, the sobs seem to come from outside myself.

At one, after three scotches and an hour of looking out at the dun-colored winter ocean and sky, I decide to drive over to Archie's at Island's End. I haven't seen him in weeks, and the thought of Susan, her parents, the girls, and Nursey filling up the condo with their bodies and chatter—the television news show, which will probably cover the funeral in detail—is more than I can bear. I'll take my portable case, set up on the point, paint or not paint, it doesn't matter. If Archie comes out of his two-storied fenced-off section, okay, if not, okay, too. What can he or anyone say; what can anyone say or do, now?

At Island's End, Archie is nowhere in sight. Tentatively, I walk past the high board fence and its hanging sea grapes and bougainvillea, step down the weathered wooden walkways, ashy with wear, and come to the little central enclave surrounded by the individual cottages. I've never been here in this kind of leaden daylight before; before only bright sun-filled days pulled me out to the picturesque

Baptizing the Cat

point of Archie's property. The sea-grape trees with their twisted trunks and leather leaves are droopy, tired looking, and like a spell, a chill silence blankets the entire complex. Did Archie close down for vacation? No, of course not, the winter months are his peak season. Are the occupants, the snowbirds, all departed just because of one cloudy day?

Looking for some life, even if it's just the cats that Archie keeps, the ones the signs say not to feed, but not seeing any, I sit in one of the outside chairs, like last time, next to the gazebo. The artificial stream that winds through the complex gives off a ripple of sound, barely audible under the clamor of the ocean, the waves just visible past the dock. Some slivers of sunlight are straining through the overcast clouds but not enough to change the mood of the weather.

I let my head fall back to catch a bit of that elusive shining, close my eyes and hear again: "changed forever; forever changed." Yes, the old codger was on the money there. We are changed forever; I am forever changed. It could have been Susan in the casket; it could have been April and May at the funeral. I could have come down the aisle with my daughters leaning against me, the whole business: rosary and wake before the funeral, funeral, grave-side service, casserole meal at the church hall. And what about the police investigation, the newspaper stories? Even if Susan's death was ruled an accidental overdose, there would still have been endless explanations to the authorities and endless discussions with Susan's parents. Ed might have passed out at the funeral, the way he did that day at the vets when they put down their old dog, Precious. He might even have died of a heart attack. And then I'd have had Miz Mildred on my hands. Well, it's all academic now; isn't it? It is Catherine, as the priest said, "that sweet woman" in the ground. In the ground because?

Somehow, in a way I can't discern or explain, I know I'm responsible, too. I'm guilty, too. I'm guilty and I deserve this punishment. In some way, I'm on the same evil side, along with those creeps, Spurlock and Harry, and those two men I don't know who shot Catherine. I was going to kill Susan. And somehow I've played a part in Catherine's death.

I hear Archie's limping steps behind me.

"Ho, partner," he says. "Where you been?" He drags a chair alongside mine, into a band of sunlight, a bit brighter and warmer now, but he remains standing. "How 'bout a beer?"

"Sure, why not."

I banish that line of thought that was leading me who knows where, before Archie's arrival. Better not to think, better to sit here in these beautiful—if somewhat wintery surroundings—and drink myself drunk, while talking to an old friend on subjects of no consequence.

"Here, we go." Archie is back with a small cooler, blue and white, the exact size for a six-pack, which rumbles with ice as he draws two cans out, wraps one in a paper towel and hands it to me and does the same for himself. He pops the top off and gulps his first swallow—half a can—as I do, the draft of icy-cold sour liquid stings my tongue and throat on the way down.

"Where you been in that suit?" Archie asks. His whiskers glisten beer-wet in the gloomy light, and he settles into the sway-backed canvas of the home-made lawn chair, stretching his crooked hairy legs out in front. He's wearing his uniform of faded khaki shorts and a white T-shirt.

"To a funeral," I say, realizing that I still have on my wrinkled gray suit and shiny black shoes, that I forgot to change clothes back at the condo.

"For that woman in the news, killed by her husband? She lived at your place, at . . . ?"

"Yeah, Sandhills," I say.

"Well, you never know, do you?"

"No, you never do." I agree with the clichéd, acid phrase, the words dripping from my lips, burning into my understanding. Yes, that was Catherine's conclusion, "You never know. What you don't expect is what happens."

"Do you think they'll find the two guys who actually shot her?" He chugs down what's left of his beer and turns his shaggy face toward me, expecting an answer.

God, I can't talk about Catherine or her death. I will Archie to be silent, as he usually is.

"Probably," I say, "eventually."

292

Baptizing the Cat

What does it matter? Spurlock had Catherine killed, two men murdered Catherine; I was going to kill Susan.

Then, without volition, tears rush into my eyes and a sob comes up into my throat. I have no control over the emotions or the sounds my body makes. Didn't I get my fill of these waterworks back at the apartment; didn't the scotches numb me down enough? I didn't think I would cry any more, but there it is, a dry whoop escapes my chest, heaves my upper body forward in a motion I can't control, tips me out of the chair onto my knees, onto the gray planks of the walkway, my hands on the little cooler.

"Oh, God!" I keep myself bent in half while moans torture their way up and out of my throat. I keep my back bent so I can't see Archie's dismayed response, but I know what it looks like.

Without thought, I pound the lid of the ice chest with my fists. The pain of the blows shoots up through my hands, up into my arms. I pound the damn thing again and again, feel the granules of Styrofoam crack and pulverize under the blows, feel the ice inside the chest fly and scatter, and finally feel the tops of the beer cans. Feel the skin come away from my knuckles on the unforgiving metal.

Archie grabs at my shoulders, grabs at my arms. "Stop it, Philip! What's got into you, man. You're breaking your hands." He jerks me away, sends the chair and my body sprawling back onto the wooden floor of the built-up platform. "Whatever it is, man, you can't change it by beating up on an ice chest."

He stands above me, large and bearish, and the concern on his face registers. I'm making an ass of myself. I am an ass. I sit up, rub my face, feel the blood on my hands smear it along with the water that was in my eyes, spread it out so he won't see.

"Archie," I say, blubbering, then struggle to find something else, "Where is everybody?"

He kicks the spilled ice and Styrofoam granules out of the way, and with one hand, rights my chair and pulls his closer. I rise on trembling legs and sit back where I was before.

He hands me a paper towel.

"There's a hurricane warning—not much—just one of those blow-hard maybes that the weather men hope will turn into the real thing. Didn't you know? The chicken-shit cowards here"—he flips his customers off with the back of a hand—"have all scooted back to the mainland, bag and baggage, to my motel in Tampa. I'm putting them up there."

He swipes at his beard and opens another can of beer. "Now, come clean; I've never seen you like this before. What's bugging you, man?"

I stare off into the space between me and Archie's dock. The wind ruffles the pelicans' feathers, two of them sitting on the high pilings.

Not looking at Archie, I ask, "You ever, almost do something really bad? Something you couldn't undo or take back?"

Now, he's silent. It's his turn to consider what he's going to say, but I don't add anything to my question, don't take my eyes off those statue-like birds. If Archie can't bring himself to answer, so be it. This sure the hell isn't confession, and I'm sure the hell not a priest for him or for myself. He doesn't have to admit to any transgressions. And I won't admit to any of mine. I retrieve another beer, see the blood ooze out of my skinned knuckles, and begin to wonder if Archie will answer at all.

"Almost?" he finally questions, and when I don't respond, asks again, "Almost? Almost don't count one god damned bit."

"Okay," I say. "Pretend I've really done something unforgivable, something permanent. That I can't undo or take back. What then?" Somehow in my brain, I've achieved a position high above the circumstances of this past week, an omniscient perspective. What if I'd murdered Susan with the Theophylline, gone through with my plan to put the ground-up pills in the spaghetti sauce? Susan would be dead and Catherine, too. It comes to me as it has a thousand times in the last week that timing and a god damned pot roast was all that stood between Catherine and Susan's deaths.

"You have something to do with that woman getting killed?" Archie asks under his breath. Unbelief comes through the whispered quality of the words.

"No, of course not, but I . . . ." I stop, don't add that word "almost" because he'd just said "almost" didn't count.

"Well," Archie sips at his can, and I can tell he's waiting, weighing what he's going to say next, still not willing to give away much of anything personal about his history. All that talk over the years about TCI, and I never knew what he was really in for, besides not ratting on his friends. Was it murder, drugs, money?

"Everyone makes mistakes, but I guess what you're asking is more serious?" The last syllable rises in a question.

"Yeah, I was planning something . . . and then it didn't work out." Archie doesn't have to be a genius to figure out my intentions. One fat, rich wife—twelve years married—do the math.

"Well, be glad it didn't work out. You were spared, at least this time."

We're talking all around the subject and not saying anything specific. "Spared?" This time the question is in my voice.

"Yeah, spared that you didn't go through with your plan. 'Cause it never works out like you think."

Catherine's words, "What you don't expect is what happens."

Archie continues, "When we were in the Marines on Paris Island, all that work, all that training. You think you're ready, that you're the man, that you can kill. Hell, you've even seen someone wounded when they used live ammo. But Vietnam was different." He stops talking abruptly, like he's already let too many defenses down, given too much away.

"So, what happened?" It's the first time I've ever asked Archie a direct question about his time in Vietnam.

"Well, at first you follow orders, and then you get off track like everyone else, do anything you want to, over there and then back over here, too, 'cause you're already fucked-up way past fixing." He pauses, takes another long swallow. "And then you land in jail with all the other fuck-ups, who were out there doing what they wanted."

I don't repeat, "So what happened?" I wait, sit silently, pull the beer in, hoping Archie will go on, point me in some direction. I don't care where the hell it might take me.

"Jail time was good for me. Might not be for everybody, but it worked for me. Spent a lot of time thinking, watching. I watched the guys and their wives, their kids, in the visiting yard. I watched the trees outside my cell window, watched the sky and the birds. Spent a lot of time on my knees."

"You learn anything?" I ask, a half sound escapes my mouth, a moan of sorts.

"I did some things over in Vietnam, things like you were talking about . . . things I couldn't undo or take back. Over here I did other things, too, but nobody died, and by then that was my only yardstick, that was all that mattered . . . that nobody died. I hope." He reaches for the last beer. "If you've got any brains at all, you learn something. You go the way you have to, whatever that is, and you hope you don't kill anybody else . . . not by accident or on purpose."

The afternoon brightens, a late sun comes out and starts burning the murky sky away. Archie rises, goes into his fenced-off section of Island's End, which takes some ten minutes since he moves so slowly, and brings back another six pack. We drink them, practically swallow for swallow, three cans apiece. I rise, shake Archie's hand, don't say goodbye. I walk out past the little cottages and the board fence, get into the Lexus, and turn the ignition.

The drive back is identical to coming over: up past the small bungalows, past the pink and white cupolas and turrets of the Don Ce-Sar, and through the toll gate, but everything seems in slow motion. It takes a hundred years to reach the curve of Sandhills' entrance way, the concrete wings that carry the name, the crisscrossed trunks of the palms. I pass by and look back over my shoulder and can just make out Susan's van and her parents' Lincoln parked in our spaces. I obey the speed limit, 35 miles an hour, past Spurlock's tower and ship building, barely visible across the yards of scrub bushes, the twisted pines, and spindly oaks. One crane still leans towards a rounded surface of gray concrete, but there's no movement of the pulleys, and the protective plastic webbing furls out in long gray strips on an ocean wind. I stop at the stop signs of the new development, more of those new Cape Cod imitations going up every day. Where will they find enough people to buy them? I drive across the Causeway, and come into Tampa, drive to Belle's shop.

She's inside, in her usual get-up of clothes and hair, in her usual place. Funny how so many things stay the same when the only thing that's changed is the only thing that matters. Yet Belle's not smiling, and thank God she doesn't come toward me with outstretched arms. She stays on the stool and says, "You've come for your painting."

Baptizing the Cat

I nod, turn to look out her front window at the same view I've seen for the last twelve years, but quickly close my eyes against it. Her shoes click-clack on the tiles as she goes to the back and returns.

"Here," she says, and sets the painting down beside me, leans it against my leg. I bend slightly to pick it up. The white cloth is gone, and the painting is wrapped, the brown paper edges neatly mitered off and glued down. It's how Belle custom wraps any painting for delivery.

"You're not going to sell it, now, are you?"

I don't answer her question but force myself to say, "Thanks," as I walk out the door.

Inside my studio, again I don't turn on the lights, like that first night after I heard about Catherine. I lay the brown paper package on the big table in the center of the room—will I ever open it?— and sit in the one cloth chair back by the wall, next to the masonite board I'd started on that afternoon with Spurlock.

Catherine's portrait, the one he didn't recognize, because there's hardly any face, sits on the rickety easel to my right. The cloth he pulled back shows her, barely sketched in. I never had a chance to add background or foreground, so it's an indistinct Catherine, almost smiling, with curling black hair and a cigarette in one hand, the spiraling smoke rising above her.

About the Cover Artist

Ann Johnston is a lifelong sculptor and painter. She has served as art director for downtown Valdosta's City Market and is past president of the Souther Artists League.

A six-year cancer survivor, she serves on the Board of Directors of the Lowndes County Partnership Cancer Fund. Ann currently keeps an art studio in downtown Valdosta and can be reached at sann511@att.net.

About the Author

Roberta George lives in Valdosta, Georgia, with her Lebanese husband. They had seven children, who are now grown and live all over the country. She's a yoga instructor and the founding editor of Snake Nation Press, which was named as one of the five Best Small Lit Presses in the nation by *Writers Digest* for over five years. She served as the Executive Director for the Lowndes/Valdosta Arts Center for 12 years and has had stories and poems published in small literary publications.

Baptizing the Cat is her third completed novel. She's won prizes for stories out of a collection of short stories called *Below the Gnat Line* in the Augusta Arts Festival, and Rosemary Daniels chose another one for the Women's Studies Conference at Berry College in Rome, Georgia. Also, a short Christmas memoir of her father's service in the Border Patrol in Arizona won a newspaper competition. She has another non-fiction book, *Ordinary Magic*, which is a combination of spells, recipes, and anecdotes that the Snake Handlers Writers' group thinks is funny and interesting.